A Whisper of Roses

TERESA MEDEIROS

BANTAM BOOKS

New York · Toronto · London · Sydney · Auckland

A WHISPER OF ROSES
A Bantam Book

PUBLISHING HISTORY
Bantam mass market edition published October 1993
Bantam mass market reissue/February 2007

Published by Bantam Dell
A Division of Random House, Inc.
New York, New York

This is a work of fiction. Names, characters, places, and incidents
either are the product of the author's imagination or are used
fictitiously. Any resemblance to actual persons, living or dead,
events, or locales is entirely coincidental.

Bantam Books and the rooster colophon
are registered trademarks of Random House, Inc.

ISBN 978-0-553-59030-2

Printed in the United States of America

www.bantamdell.com

OPM 10 9 8 7 6 5 4 3 2 1

"HELLO, BRAT," HE SAID.

She felt that old, familiar kick in the stomach and knew she was standing face-to-face in the moonlit tower with Morgan MacDonnell, his boyish promise of masculine beauty come to devastating fruition.

Mortified by her own boldness, she snatched her hand back.

A wry grin touched his lips. "I suppose if you'd have known it was me, you'd have let me bleed to death."

Terrified she was going to revert to a stammering six-year-old, she snapped, "I'd say not. You were dripping all over Mama's Flemish rug."

To hide her consternation, she lowered her gaze. "You've grown," she blurted out accusingly.

"So have you."

His low, amused tone warned her. She looked up to find his gaze taking a leisurely jaunt up her body, finally coming to rest with bold regard on her face. A splinter of anger twisted in her heart. For so long she had yearned for him to look at her with affection.

Why did he have to choose now, when she sensed his admiration might be even more lethal than his enmity?

I remember rainy days and countless games of Aggravation. You were the Kool-Aid mom and all my friends wished you were theirs. You were born to be a mother, Mama, and I'm so thankful God made you mine.

To Wendy and Nita, for their steadfast support and for being such joys to work with.

To Ada Hatcher, for always being there and for being a "mom" to all of us.

For Dan and Doris Medeiros, who gave me my house, their love, and the greatest gift of all—their wonderful son.

ACKNOWLEDGMENTS

I want to thank *all* the booksellers who have given me something even more precious than their support—their friendship. Roses to Vivian Witherow, Pam Young, Dee Clingman, and a special bouquet to Nancy Stratton and Sandra Porter, who have been with me since the beginning and have never had me arrested for loitering in their store.

To the memory of Gene Roddenberry, whose own creation has given me countless hours of pleasure and a swashbuckling hero to fuel all my fantasies.

A Whisper
of Roses

Prologue

Sabrina Cameron rubbed one of her mother's plump tea roses beneath her uptilted nose. Tiny feathers of pollen tickled her nostrils. She sneezed, then clapped a chubby hand over her mouth and burrowed deeper into the hedge.

The MacDonnells were coming, and one careless move might see her bones melted to Cameron stew before this day was done.

She shivered in horrified delight. The MacDonnells had haunted her nightmares for most of her short life. Fearsome giants they were, her brothers whispered by candlelight, half man and half beastie. Great shaggy creatures who walked on two legs and wore nothing but fresh animal skins. The children of Cameron Glen trembled in fear of them, and men full grown took care not to wander far from the village after dusk.

On moonless nights, when the hounds whimpered and howled around the manor walls, it was said a MacDonnell was stalking the shadowy forests, searching for a naughty boy or girl to carry back to his lair.

Sabrina parted the glossy leaves to peer out. Her mother knelt at the edge of the garden path, stabbing the earth around her rosebushes with a silver trowel. Low-hanging clouds that boded rain splintered the sun into dazzling spills of red in her upswept hair. A knot of pug-faced puppies nested on her abandoned mantle.

A grunt and a giggle sounded a warning as the iron gate came crashing open and Sabrina's brothers galloped into the garden. Brian rode on Alexander's shoulders, bellowing orders and whacking him with a rowan twig. Alex's whinnies rose to yelps. He arched his back, tumbling his younger brother into the slick grass. They rolled, locked in battle, straight into the folds of their mother's skirt.

Elizabeth Cameron separated the roiling mass of strawberry curls with a skill born of ten years' practice. The boys hung by their tunics, trapped into sheepish surrender.

She shook them gently, her English accent clipped with annoyance. "I ought to bang your stony little heads together. Do you want your baby sister to learn your roguish ways?"

She brushed at the grass stains scoured into the knees of their finest trews. Brian returned the favor by spitting on his palm and scrubbing a smudge of dirt from her cheek.

Alex clicked his heels together, his own Scots burr bristling with importance. "Papa sent us with a message. The MacDonnell is a-comin'."

Brian cast the quivering hedge a sly glance. "And they say he's hungry. With a taste for wee black-haired lassies."

Sabrina came scrambling out of her hiding place. "Did you see him? Is he truly covered with hair from head to toes?"

"Aye, and he's got sharp, pointed fangs fair

drippin' with blood." Alex curled his hands into claws and bared his teeth at her.

"Alex!" his mother said sharply. "Stop filling your sister's head with nonsense."

"Pay your mother heed, lad." The lilting burr snapped all their heads around. "My princess's wee ears are fairly bursting with nonsense now."

"Papa!" Sabrina hurtled toward the man at the gate.

The Cameron's presence seemed to fill the walled garden as he swept his only daughter up into his arms. She was such a tiny replica of him that he might have sculpted her with his own hands. Her dark blue eyes sparkled beneath smoky lashes. As Sabrina smacked his beard with kisses, he winked at his wife over her inky curls.

Sabrina tweaked the chest hair spilling over his doublet. "Is it true, Papa, that MacDonnells have great tufts of hair on the soles of their feet and all their spoons are carved of human ribs?"

Alex and Brian punched each other, choking back giggles.

"Perhaps you should ask our guest yourself when he arrives." The Cameron glowered at his sons. "Until then, do not heed the gossip of young idiots."

As he lowered Sabrina, she gazed up at him, a whisper away from confiding her deepest hope about the MacDonnell. But he was already striding toward his wife.

He pressed a kiss to her upturned lips. "I'm in your debt, Beth, for agreeing to let the lad come. If the MacDonnell can trust me to foster his son for the summer, perhaps he can learn to trust me in other ways as well."

Alex poked a worm with a stick. "Papa commands we be kind to the boy. He says we must make him welcome and never mention the fact that his papa is a treacherous bastard as likely to gut a man in his sleep and roast his entrails as—"

At his wife's shocked gaze, the Cameron clapped

a hand over Alex's mouth. "I never said that. He must have heard it from one of the other men."

Brian took advantage of Alex's captivity to deliver a pinch to his brother's thigh. Alex tackled him, fists flying. Sabrina took a step out of their path and fell over the sleeping puppies, who awoke with a cacophony of piercing yelps.

From where she sprawled in the grass, Sabrina was the first to see the boy. His stillness was absolute. She had no way of knowing how long he had stood there, watching them. Too long if the sullen set of his jaw was any indication.

Curiosity overcame her fear. She climbed to her feet. The MacDonnell did have a lot of hair, but most of it hung in a wild, sandy tangle past his shoulders. His furs weren't fresh or dripping blood, but ratted and worn bare in spots. Sweat and dirt streaked his face and grimed the bare feet poking out from beneath his leggings. A tattered pack hung over one shoulder. To Sabrina, this MacDonnell did not look particularly fierce.

But as she crept toward him, she realized she was wrong. A feral energy coiled in his stance. He reminded her of an animal, wild and far more dangerous for being cornered. Her nose twitched at his crisp scent. He smelled of freshly turned dirt and sunshine as if he'd spent more than one night sleeping under the pines. His skin was bronzed, his eyes the dusky green of a glade on a summer day. The undeniable light of intelligence glimmered in their depths.

She danced forward and made an awkward dip. "Hello, boy. Welcome to Cameron."

The blows between Alex and Brian ended in a soft thud. The puppies' yips died to whimpers. With a haughty flick of his eyelids that would have done a monarch proud, the young MacDonnell dismissed Sabrina as if she had been a slug that pushed its way out of the dirt at his feet. Her cheeks flamed.

The fire in them cooled as her father's hands fell on her shoulders. "My daughter phrased our welcome as well as I could have. Welcome to Cameron, lad."

"I ain't your lad," he barked. "My name is Morgan Thayer MacDonnell, son of Angus MacDonnell and heir to the chieftainship of MacDonnell."

Sabrina was impressed by the number of "MacDonnells" he'd managed to cram into one sentence. He stood so straight that it made her spine ache. She offered him a tentative smile. He looked away. Brian and Alex blinked at him, their gazes measuring but not unkind.

"We hope you'll do us the honor of considering Cameron your home until the end of the summer," her father said.

"Can't come too bloody soon for me," the boy murmured in a burr thick enough to cut with a blade.

The Cameron opened his mouth, but his wife waved him to silence. She was the only one who realized Morgan kept his jaw clenched to keep it from trembling.

Elizabeth came forward and gently laid her hand on his cheek. "I dare say you'll be missing your mother and father, won't you, son?"

He shoved her hand away. "Never had no mother and I won't be needin' one now. 'Specially not some bloody Sassenach." Sabrina did not understand the word, but her mother paled.

The lad did not flinch when the Cameron's shadow fell over him. He stood tall and straight, his eyes blazing a cold green fire. He had to crane his neck to look the Cameron in the eye, but he did it. Brian and Alex snickered. Sabrina covered her eyes and peeked through her fingers, bracing herself for the boxed ears that would surely result from such impudence.

But her father's thunderous brow slowly relaxed into crannies of amusement. He reached to ruffle Morgan's hair; the boy was too stunned to duck. "Spoken like a true MacDonnell, lad. A warrior born and bred just like your father. You'll serve Cameron well."

Morgan quivered with rage. "I serve only MacDonnell. I hate the Camerons."

Brian's and Alex's snickers broke into open laughter. Morgan swung toward them, fists clenched. "How dare you laugh at a MacDonnell, you wee freckled weasels? I ought to knock your teeth down your throats!"

The boys found this new threat even funnier. They doubled over, clutching their sides. Before their mother could reprimand them, Morgan bolted the garden, leaving the Cameron standing alone before the gate.

"Boy! Boy!" Sabrina called. If the MacDonnell disliked Brian and Alex, perhaps he would not disdain her simply for being a girl.

Without a word of explanation, she ducked through the hedge and scrambled over the wall after him.

"Sabrina!" Elizabeth cried out.

The Cameron caught his wife's arm. "Let her go. If anyone can charm a heathen MacDonnell, 'tis that one."

Finding a niche in the ivy that twined along the wall, the laird of Clan Cameron heaved himself up and watched the two small figures race across the meadow only a length ahead of the gray, scudding clouds.

"God go with you, princess," he whispered. "I fear you're going to need all his wiles and your own as well."

"Boy! Wait, please, boy! Wait for me!"

Sabrina's chubby legs pumped up and down. Her cries deepened to gasps. The sun had dipped behind a mass of roiling clouds and the boy was already a dark speck melting into the forest. She mentally added running well to his list of talents before falling flat, burning her knees on the stubby bracken. Spurred on by the scent of the approaching rain, she scrambled up and plunged after him into the murky gloom of the towering oaks. A root twisted around her ankle, sending her tumbling.

She landed on her rump and cheerfully deduced she was lying at the bottom of a ditch with her skirt over her head.

"Are all you Camerons cursed with both stupidity and stubbornness?"

Sabrina poked her head out from under her skirt. Morgan MacDonnell stood over her with arms crossed, staring down his nose at everything that was supposed to be tucked safely beneath her smock.

She pushed down her skirt and offered him a hand. "Hello, boy."

He pulled her up, then wiped his hand on his grubby tunic as if her touch had soiled it. "My name is not Boy. I am—"

"—Morgan Thayer MacDonnell," Sabrina intoned solemnly, "son of Angus MacDonnell and heir to the chieftainship. You serve only MacDonnell and hate all Camerons. And I am Sabrina, the daughter of Dougal Cameron."

"There's no denyin' that." Morgan's voice was choked with bitterness. "You're the devil's own image."

Sabrina frowned, searching her mind for some common ground where they might meet. "Do you like worms?"

"No."

"Beetles, perhaps?"

"Warriors have no time for such nonsense."

Her frown deepened. Brian and Alex had time for worms, beetles, and the spiders they delighted in putting in her bed. Perhaps she should ask him if he really did have tufts of hair growing on his feet. But the grim set of his jaw discouraged her. Thick, sandy lashes veiled his eyes.

"What do you like, then?"

"Fisticuffs. Swords. Guns." His sulky lips parted to reveal a row of straight white teeth, not a fang among them. "Winnin'."

Sabrina felt slightly dazzled, as if the sun had crept out from behind a stubborn cloud. Emboldened by his smile, she laid her hand on his arm. "There now. I do believe we shall be friends. I like you most fiercely already."

He stared down at the pudgy little fingers stroking his arm. Morgan had never known anyone in his life but clan and enemy. An array of emotions flickered through the lush green of his eyes. Shock. Fear. Uncertainty. Longing.

He wrenched his arm away from her. "I ain't your friend. And I don't like you."

Her smile flickered but did not fade. "Why, of course you like me! Everyone likes me. Papa says I could charm the whiskers off a wildcat."

Morgan's eyes darkened. Sabrina took a step backward. "Have you no understandin' of anythin', lass?" he asked. "I don't like you. I don't like your brothers. And I sure as hell don't like your Sassenach mother and your filthy-rich bastard of a da."

Sabrina's eyes welled with tears. The adoration she had received all her life had not prepared her for his rancor. His words held none of her brothers' good-natured teasing.

He flung out his arm in a gesture of contempt. "Go ahead and cry. I'd expect no better of a silly wee babe!"

"I am not a babe! I am six years old!"

He advanced on her. Sabrina held her ground until he reached out and gave her chest a slight push. She sat down abruptly in the leaves. Tears spilled from her eyes.

She scrambled to her feet, rubbing her eyes and sucking back sobs. She started up the slope, choking out each word. "Papa won't like it that you pushed me."

Morgan's mocking laugh rang out behind her. "I dare say he won't. Run to your papa, princess. Tattle on me. Tell him the rude boy pushed you down and bruised your precious pride. Perhaps he'll toss me in his dungeon to rot as his father did to me own grandfather. Or have me beheaded as old Eustace Cameron did to Lachlan MacDonnell."

Sabrina stopped. Her back straightened. Drawing every inch of dignity she could muster into her tiny frame, she faced him, sniffing furiously. "Oh, no, Morgan MacDonnell. I'm not a babe and I'll not tattle on you. There's nothing you could do to make me tattle. And I swear to you, you'll never make me cry again. Not if I live forever will I shed a tear for such a wicked boy. You—you—" Her limited trove of insults did not contain a word vile enough for him. "—MacDonnell!"

She marched the rest of the way up the slope, digging in her toes and grasping at exposed roots to keep from sliding back down at his feet. She scrambled over the rim of the ditch, chased by a flood of Gaelic curses she was better off not understanding.

The first fat raindrops pelted her as she broke into a run. A rumble of thunder drowned out the broken noises that rose from the ditch as Morgan MacDonnell, heir to the chieftain of MacDonnell, wrapped his thin arms around a tree and cried, his bitter tears mingling with the rain.

Dougal Cameron was toasting his toes in front of a crackling fire when his daughter burst into the drawing room. Dripping all over her mother's precious Oriental rugs, she flung herself into his lap.

"Caught in the storm, were you, lassie?"

She nodded, her head bumping his chin. He cradled the small, damp bundle to his chest and waited for her shivers to abate. At first he feared it was sobs that shook her, but when she lifted her eyes to him, they were dry and bright with anger.

"You should have boxed his ears, Papa. He's a very naughty boy."

"Aye, that he may be. But the MacDonnells are a rough and tumble lot, princess. I fear the lad needs a bit of love and understanding more than he needs his ears boxed."

Her little face screwed into a terrible frown. "I do not wish to displease you, but I shan't love him."

The Cameron chuckled. "'Tis just as well. I suspect that face of his will earn him love enough in the years to come."

She hooked her arms around his neck and

pressed a kiss to his beard. "I love you, Papa. I will always love you best."

Dougal buried his chin in her silky curls, torn by his desire to spare her the mortal pains of love and living. "'Tis not so, princess," he said softly. "But 'tis a pleasant thought. A pleasant thought indeed."

PART ONE

'Tis the last rose of summer
Left blooming alone;
All her lovely companions
Are faded and gone.

—Sir Thomas Moore

Chapter One

"The MacDonnells are a-comin'! The MacDonnells are a-comin'!"

The cry shot like cannonfire through the sleepy village of Cameron Glen. The villagers raced madly through the cobbled streets, not knowing whether to hide their livestock or their children. One cynical crofter tipped back his chair, took a long, slow draw off his pipe, and announced dourly that sheep or daughter would do just as well to a MacDonnell in an amorous bent of mind.

The few who could afford the luxury of curtains jerked them shut. Hammers tapped in frantic rhythm as boards flew up over windows and doors. The Camerons and the MacDonnells had been feuding for so long that no one could remember the cause. To the villagers their laird's foes were still more myth than men.

For decades they had done their thieving and ravishing in stealth. If a village lass returned from a mountain walk rumpled and dazed, knowing whispers would greet the subsequent swelling of her belly and the birth of her tawny-haired babe.

Kneeling in the road, a withered old man gathered a group of awestruck children around him. "I was but a wee lad meself, but I'll ne'er forget the last time the MacDonnells marched through Cameron Glen. Giants they were, o'er eight feet tall wi' thighs as wide 'round as tree trunks." A freckled little girl hid her trembling face against his leg. He lowered his voice to a whisper. "And 'round each o' their waists hung their turrible trophies—the severed heads o' the Camerons."

The children squealed in delicious horror. Caught up in his own lurid tale, the old man cast the manor house on the hill an ominous look. The stone tower of ancient Cameron Keep sprouted from its timber-framed wings like an embattled mushroom. He knew the MacDonnells had been invited to Cameron not to battle, but to banquet. But why would Dougal Cameron invite his enemies to his home when he knew they were more inclined to eat the family than the feast?

His palsied hand absently smoothed a boy's cowlick. "Daft," he muttered. "Our own laird's gone as daft as a rabid hare."

At that precise moment, the occupants of Cameron Manor might have agreed with him. The drawing room had been thrown into chaos by an army of servants and helpful Camerons. Caught up in the pervasive atmosphere of terror and glee, Sabrina rushed back from the old buttery, where she had hidden her mother's silver tea service. She tripped over the small, grizzled dog curled up in front of the hearth. He bared his one remaining tooth and snapped at her.

"Sorry, Pugsley," she murmured, pausing to straighten his jeweled collar.

"I won't have those ham-footed Highlanders

stomping my rugs to death," Elizabeth Cameron announced. Heedless of her silk skirts, she dropped to her knees on the bare stones and began to roll up a plush Persian carpet.

"No worry, Mama." Brian lounged on an over-turned Louis XIV gilded armchair, ignoring Alex's obvious grunts for help beneath the weight of an ornately carved Elizabethan chest. "The MacDonnells will never make it this far. We've been at peace for almost a month. Without our throats to cut, they'll be cutting their own by now. I predict extinction in"—he drew a gold pendant watch from a ruffled pocket—"three hours and seventeen minutes."

"I'm surprised they haven't extincted themselves already with all that inbreeding," Alex gasped, letting the chest drop dangerously near the polished toes of Brian's shoes. "I've heard they share women like other men share—"

"Alex!" Elizabeth cleared her throat, jerking her head toward Sabrina's avid face.

Her elder son lapsed into silence. He might tower over his mother by half a foot, but he knew when to curb his tongue. Beneath her willowy slenderness lay a spine of fine English steel. The coils of gray in her fiery hair had yet to soften the temper that accompanied it.

Sabrina affected a sophisticated shrug. "Don't scold on my account, Mama. Why, only this morning I learned a new song from one of the kitchen maids." She locked her hands at the small of her back as she'd been taught to do when serenading guests and primly sang:

> Ride hard the MacDonnells wi' their wild golden locks,
> Fierce their long claymores, but nary as fierce as their—

"Sabrina!" Her mother gasped a warning.

"—tempers?" she hastily warbled.

Alex choked back laughter and applauded. "Carry

down your clarsach, Mum! My baby sister can entertain our guests after we sup tonight."

"If I've my way, she'll be bolted safely in her chamber until those lascivious rogues are gone," her mother said grimly.

Sabrina knew that if her mother had her way, she'd be bolted safely in her chamber until her journey to London in the spring. It was her mother's fondest wish that Sabrina's jovial uncle Willie introduce her to some eligible country parson who couldn't find the Scottish Highlands on a well-marked map.

"It seems our MacDonnells are known for more than just their fighting prowess," Brian said dryly.

"As are you, dear brother," Sabrina whispered in his ear, "if that gossip about that little milkmaid in the village is true." He reached to yank one of her curls, but she danced out of his reach. "Did old Angus MacDonnell truly pay court to you, Mama?"

A smile softened her mother's lips. "Indeed he did. The gallant fellow offered me a side of beef from a stolen cow, Cameron I suspect, and his own black heart. I've always felt a bit guilty. When I chose your father over him, it broke a peace of almost"—she counted on her fingers—"six hours."

Sabrina's cousin Enid, who was visiting from London, trotted from the room, clutching two Ming dynasty fluted vases that had braved stormy seas and rutted roads to travel from Peking to Cameron. A thump and the sound of shattering glass was followed by a muffled "Oh, dearie me." Sabrina winced.

Sighing wearily, her mother sank back on her heels and surveyed the drawing room. Stripped of its exotic treasures, the hall was a barren shell that hearkened back to another era, when the tower had been the heart of a primitive fortress instead of the drawing room of an elegant manor house.

They all knew that even now Dougal Cameron was in the courtyard instructing their clansmen on the finer points of courtesy that would allow them all to survive this night. One overturned wine goblet or upset pepperbox could result in a massacre that would destroy the illusion of civilization Elizabeth Cameron had devoted a lifetime to preserving. Her fierce passion had coaxed both her genteel children and her precious English roses from the harsh Highland soil. Her dejection wounded them all.

Hoping to cheer her, Sabrina stood on her tiptoes and plucked a crystal rose from its vase on the mantel. "The Belmont Rose, Mama. Shall I hide it in the buttery with the rest of your things?"

Her mother rewarded her with a smile. "No, princess. 'Twas a gift from King James to my father for saving his crown at the battle of Sedgemoor. Carry it up to the solar, where no one will be tempted to crush it." Spirits restored, she wiped her hands on her skirt and began firing off commands. "Bestir your lazy self, Brian, and help Alex with that chest before I take the starch out of your ruffles. Enid, stop sniveling behind that fire screen, or I shall write William and tell him what a silly goose he's raised for a daughter."

Heartened by her mother's recovery, Sabrina climbed the curving stairs to the gallery, twirling the rose's smooth stem between her fingers. She'd always found the Belmont Rose an object of fascination.

Fragile and exquisite, the handblown glass glowed beneath the sunlight streaming through the oriel windows. Her fingertip traced a petal more delicate than all the teardrops she'd never shed for one MacDonnell. As she entered the serene gloom of the solar, a knot tightened low in her belly, a knot she'd thought to be long unraveled.

For five summers Morgan MacDonnell's shadow had fallen across her life. Five summers of waiting for the next hairy spider to drop down her back. Five summers of stumbling over the grubby foot that shot into her path. His final blow had landed the summer she was eight, when he had finally befriended her brothers and enlisted them in his pranks. Her wistful affection for the tall, proud boy had been slowly buried like a stone in her heart.

His father had summoned him home in his sixteenth summer after some fool MacDonnell got himself gutted stealing a Cameron sheep. Swinging on the garden gate, Sabrina had watched him go, mystified by the tears that choked her throat. Her fondest wish had come true. Morgan MacDonnell wouldn't be coming back to Cameron Manor. Not next summer. Not ever.

Until tonight.

With painstaking care Sabrina laid the rose on the crushed-velvet runner atop her mother's harpsichord. The wretch was probably dead by now, she thought unkindly, stabbed by one of his own treacherous kin or shot dead in the bed of some jealous crofter. When he was only fifteen, the maidservants had already begun to admire the broad flare of his shoulders and the bold invitation in his sleepy green eyes that had never looked at her with anything but cool disdain.

Sabrina wandered to the window. Her restless gaze followed the jagged crest of the mountains. Snowy white clouds raked their peaks. The MacDonnells might even now be lumbering out of their lair and down the rugged trails toward Cameron. Did the only son of Angus MacDonnell ride among them?

She shook off a sudden chill, hoping neither she nor her father would find the price of peace too high.

As Morgan MacDonnell rode out of the shadow of the mountains, he kicked his mount into a canter. Warm autumn sunlight breached the clouds and spilled over the meadow in defiant splendor. He narrowed his eyes against its brilliance. Pookah's hooves pounded the aroma of heather from the spongy turf. The wind tore at Morgan's hair, urging him forward, bending him low over Pookah's mane until he almost believed he could outdistance them all and ride to freedom.

"Morgan! Morgan me lad! Where's that blasted son o' mine gotten off to?"

At his father's roar, Morgan rolled his eyes heavenward, thankful God had given him shoulders broad enough to bear the weight of his clan. He reined in the horse and wheeled around. 'Twas just as well the harsh reminder had come so quickly. There was no place for a MacDonnell in this world of open meadow and soaring sky. Even on Pookah's wings, he could ride forever and never find a place where he belonged. The mountain cliffs were both his sanctuary and his prison, the only home he would ever know.

He nudged Pookah back up the trail, forcing him between two of his squabbling kinsmen.

"Eh, Morgan, this rascal stole my cheese. Mind if I shoot him?" his cousin Ranald asked, drawing his pistol.

Ranald had inherited his Gypsy mother's snapping dark eyes and raven hair. People tended to look twice at him as if to see if he was really as handsome as they thought or if the striking beauty of his features might have paled when they glanced away. Morgan felt like a homely gargoyle next to him.

"By all means," Morgan replied, smiling pleasantly. Ranald cocked his pistol at the young thief's paling face. "That is, if you don't mind me breakin' your neck when you're done."

Pouting, Ranald lowered the pistol. "Dammit, Morgan, I ain't killed nobody all day. My trigger finger is gettin' stiff."

Ranald's prettiness was surpassed only by his lack of judgment. Morgan plucked away the moldy hunk of cheese, fed it to Pookah, then knocked both the men's heads together hard enough to leave their ears ringing.

Shepherding the motley remains of Clan MacDonnell to Cameron was like herding a flock of quarrelsome children. During the eight-hour journey, Morgan had broken up three fistfights, thwarted two rapes, and buried a great-uncle. His uncle hadn't even the dubious honor of being dispatched by a relative. He'd simply fallen off his horse in a drunken stupor. Before his head had struck the rock that would kill him, his more resourceful clansmen had relieved him of both purse and boots. Morgan had dug the grave in stony silence while the others wept loudly, passed around a jug of malt whisky, and toasted the old man's journey to hell.

"Sorry 'boot your uncle, lad," one of the men

called out as Morgan picked his way up the rocky path. "Ol' Kevin was a bonny fellow, he was."

"Kerwin," Morgan growled under his breath.

"Aye," another agreed. "No one could spin a tale 'round the fire on a cold winter night like puir ol' Derwin."

Christ, Morgan thought, the man had been dead an hour only and they couldn't remember his name. He wondered if they would forget him so easily.

"Morgan! Damn it to blasted hell, where's that lad o' mine?"

Morgan ground his teeth. There were times when he wished his father would forget him altogether. He drove Pookah into a lope until he reached the old man's side.

Angus MacDonnell's eyes twinkled in their deep crannies as he gazed up at his son. "Ah, there's the fruit o' me loins." He nudged the hooded figure riding beside him. "Took a mighty oak to plant such a strappin' seed."

"Aye, but even the mightiest of oaks can wither with age," Morgan shot back.

His father cackled at the gentle jibe. "The lad's wit draws more blood than his ax. As sharp as his ol' da, he is."

Morgan grunted, refusing to commit himself. He'd never worn the mantle of his father's pride comfortably. It had been too long mixed with cunning, jealousy, and the willingness to use his only son as a pawn against Dougal Cameron. Since Morgan had last returned from being fostered by his father's enemy, he'd been the true leader of Clan MacDonnell, and they both knew it.

"Greedy wee bugger." Angus's voice rose with each word. "Never had a mother, so he just latched on to whatever comely teat he pleased."

"Still does," Ranald called out, evening the score for Morgan's earlier interference.

The men burst into bawdy laughter. Morgan aimed, cocked, and fired his finger at Ranald. Ranald clutched his heart in mock distress and weaved in his saddle.

Angus's shoulders were hunched beneath the weight of his moth-eaten plaid. A yellow pallor tinged his leathery skin. "A glorious day this is," he called out, "when those scoundrel Camerons come crawlin' to us on their bellies, beggin' for peace!"

A cheer rose from his clansmen. Angus took advantage of the pause to tip an earthenware jug to his lips. Morgan exchanged a glance with the hooded figure at his father's side. The hood bobbed in understanding, and Morgan winked gratefully. The faithful shadow had ridden at his father's side for as long as Morgan could remember, tugging off Angus's boots when he lapsed into stupor, covering him from the damp night chill and watering his whisky to keep him from meeting the same fate as the unfortunate Kerwin.

His father had an audience now. He no longer needed a son. Morgan sent Pookah cantering down the hillside, leaving his clansmen to their dreams of remembered glories and imagined victories. He preferred the warm, sinewy reality of Pookah. The approaching twilight shed cooling pockets of air in their path.

As badly as it chafed him to admit it, Morgan knew the Cameron's invitation was an errand of pity, not humility. The MacDonnells had wenched, robbed, and skirmished their way into too many graves, leaving Morgan master of little more than a band of rash outlaws. Only the tattered armor of their ferocious reputations kept the Grants and Chisholms to the north from declaring open warfare. Their last hope for survival lay in allying with the Camerons. But Morgan had no intention of crawling to Dougal Cameron on his belly. Not to save his clan. Not even to save his life.

He topped a rise to find the Cameron's domain spread across the glen below like a checkered quilt. The disparity between their lives struck him a harsh blow.

The MacDonnells skulked in the mountains like rabid wolves. The Camerons presided over a spacious valley dotted with fat livestock and ringed by well-tended fields. The MacDonnells lived in a crumbling

ruin in imminent danger of sliding down a cliff. The
Camerons lived in a manor house nestled among rolling
hills and crowned by a castle tower.

The bloody Camerons even had a princess.

A rare smile touched Morgan's lips. Would
Dougal's daughter remember him? For five summers
the stubborn child had remained true to her pledge.
She had never once tattled on him, not even when his
mischievous tricks bordered on cruelty. Upon discovering he had picked all the threads out of her embroidery,
she had simply tilted up that wee prim nose of hers,
telling him silently that she expected no better from a
no-count MacDonnell.

If a pistol ball exploded through his heart before
he reached the manor gate, Morgan would know whose
dainty hand had wielded the weapon.

Oddly cheered at the thought, he thundered down
the slope, letting loose a jubilant Highland cry that
would give the villagers of Cameron Glen nightmares
for months to come.

Sabrina wiggled forward on her elbows to peer over the
edge of the gallery, bunching her cumbersome nightdress beneath her.

"Careful," Enid whispered, nibbling nervously on
one of her fat braids. "My brother Stefan once got his
head caught in the banister and we had to saw it off."

"His head?"

"No. The banister."

Enid, Sabrina's Belmont cousin, had arrived on
their doorstep that spring with a trunk and an apologetic letter from Uncle Willie, hinting at some sort of
disgrace. Sabrina found it difficult to imagine the docile
girl being involved in anything more sordid than hoard-
ing sugarplums from the dinner table. Her only vice
seemed to be her craving for the lurid scandal pamphlets her brother sent from London. Tonight her round
face was flushed with excitement at the prospect of
being ravished and murdered by a clan of Highland
savages.

The drawing room had been stripped to spare medieval splendor. Braces of candles and bowls of oil had usurped her mother's ornate lamps. Hazy light flickered over the faded tapestries that had been carried down from the attics to adorn the walls. At each end of the hall, banners emblazoned with the Cameron crest fluttered from the massive rafters. Sabrina found the effect enchanting.

The Cameron men milled below—Sabrina's uncles, cousins, and brothers, lean and resplendent in their stylish cravats and waistcoats. Her father had draped a narrow shoulder plaid over the sleeve of his velvet coat in deference to his heritage. Most of the men had wisely left their women at home, but as mistress of the manor, Sabrina's mother flitted among them, exotically defiant in a shimmering *saque* gown that would have served her equally well during her days as a lady-in-waiting for Queen Anne. Pride swelled in Sabrina.

"Mama looks like a queen, doesn't she?"

"Quite," Enid dutifully agreed, although her hands were pressed over her eyes in terrified anticipation.

Fists thundered on the massive door at the end of the hall. Enid almost bit her braid in two. Sabrina gave her cousin's icy arm a squeeze.

Total silence reigned below. The doors swung open with an agonizing creak. Sabrina swallowed a knot of trepidation. Even Enid dared to peek through her fingers as the Camerons turned as one to greet their guests, her father flanked by the tense forms of Alex and Brian.

An old man strutted into the hall, trailed by a parade of ragged but forbidding men. Most were dressed as their chieftain was in mismatched tartans and trews. Sabrina shuddered, wondering how many people had died to clothe them. From what she had heard of the MacDonnells, she suspected their victims had found themselves stripped before their bodies had even cooled. The wilted plumes of their bonnets danced in the breeze from the open door.

The old man's gnarled fingers clutched the hilt of a rusty claymore that dragged the ground with each step. Sabrina's father had a similar antique mounted on his chamber wall.

"Dougal Cameron, ye worthless son of a whore!" the MacDonnell bellowed. Enid gasped and shifted her hands from her eyes to her ears.

Sabrina's father swaggered forward, hands on hips and legs splayed in arrogant challenge. "Angus MacDonnell, you foolish goat-spawned bastard!" he roared in return.

The chieftain of the MacDonnells cocked his head like a canny parrot. "Is that any way to greet an ol' friend?" he whined before throwing his arms around her glowering father and drawing him into a crushing embrace.

The hall resounded with alarmed cries. Brian and Alex rushed forward to ensure the wily old man wasn't hiding a dirk in his knobby paw.

"The Glasgow stage lost a great actor in that one," Sabrina whispered.

"I once read of an actor whose wig caught afire and—"

"Shhhh," Sabrina hissed, not wanting to miss a word of her father's reaction.

Dougal waved back his would-be rescuers and slapped Angus on the back. "Friend or enemy, Angus MacDonnell, welcome to Cameron Manor. Tonight we lay down our old grudges to feast together." He stepped back and spread his arms wide. "As a sign of our goodwill, my men have laid down their weapons as well." Arching his eyebrow, he gave the MacDonnell's ancient claymore a pointed look.

A rumble of discontent and profanity rose from the motley band of Highlanders, but when their chieftain drew out his claymore with a flourish and tossed it down, they had no choice but to follow suit. An arsenal of broadswords, pistols, harquebuses, dirks, muskets, and clubs emerged from scabbards and hidden pockets to rain down on the stone floor. The clatter was deafening.

Sabrina took advantage of the confusion to search their ranks for Morgan's slender form. But all thoughts of her old nemesis fled as a man who had been hanging behind the others stepped through the door in a swirl of night mist.

"Holy Hannah," Enid breathed. "The legends are true! They *are* giants!"

Sabrina's breath caught in her throat. The MacDonnells were tall, but this man towered head and shoulders over every other man in the hall. He neither strutted nor swaggered as his clansmen did. He didn't have to. He wore no bonnet and his sun-burnished mane hung well past his shoulders. A belted hunter's plaid of misty blue and black hugged his massive form, and Sabrina realized with shock that he was not only bare-kneed, but barefoot as well. He made the Cameron men in their European dress look effete by comparison. Sabrina wouldn't have been surprised to hear a mad skirl of bagpipes herald his arrival, wailing in time to the throbbing drumbeat of her heart.

His back was to the gallery and she could see the tension knotted in the massive breadth of his shoulders as he drew a monstrous Lochaber ax from his belt. A primitive thrill of fear clutched her heart. It was too easy to imagine his muscled arms swinging the gleaming blade, cleaving off the heads . . .

Enid nudged her, already fumbling for the bottle of hartshorn she carried in her pocket to avert potential swoons. "You're deathly pale. You're not going to faint, are you?"

Sabrina wrinkled her nose and shoved the pungent spirits away. "Of course not." She shook off a shiver, trying to convince herself revulsion had prompted it. "I just don't fancy large men. Especially large men with such enormous . . . muscles."

A dreamy sigh escaped Enid. "I shouldn't be so hasty to dismiss him if I were you. I know girls in London who would say he's everything a man should be."

And more. The words rose unbidden to Sabrina's mind. Furious at herself, she dug her chin deeper into her hand.

The man stepped up to the pile of weapons, the haft of the ax poised in his palm. He hesitated, the motion fraught with deliberate insolence. Sabrina frowned. That lethal combination of grace and arrogance chimed an elusive warning in the back of her mind.

Although her father was tall, he had to tilt back his head to meet the stranger's gaze. Sabrina couldn't fathom the long, enigmatic look that passed between the two men, but suddenly the tension in the hall shot even higher than it had been upon their enemies' arrival.

The eyes of every MacDonnell lifted to the stranger, and Sabrina realized that for all of Angus's posturing, this man was the true master of their clan. And the true danger to the Camerons.

The ax slid from his fingers and thunked down on the pile. Sabrina's breath escaped in a relieved whoosh.

As if realizing he was losing his audience to a more masterful player, Angus MacDonnell bustled toward her mother. "Beth!" he cried, his wheedling tones ringing through the hall. "Ah, me beautiful Beth, would that e'er a face so fair had graced me own table!" He brought her clasped hands to his lips.

Sabrina stiffened, outraged. "Why, that disreputable rascal! Nobody but Papa dares to call her Beth."

Her mother, gracious as always, curtsied before him, then took his arm to lead him to the table. Sabrina noted with satisfaction that her mother towered several inches over the wizened gnome. A man shrouded in a hooded plaid followed in their wake, dragging his left leg behind him.

"Eerie creature, isn't he?" Enid whispered.

Sabrina nodded her agreement, not finding him nearly as eerie as the muscled barbarian squeezed between her brothers.

Three long trestle tables had been arranged in a U shape. Her father and the MacDonnell sat side by side at the center of the connecting table, their backs to the heavy tapestries strung along the wall. Elizabeth took her place at her husband's side, while the hooded man hovered like a cloud of doom behind the MacDonnell's bench.

After perfunctory grumbling over the fact that all the knives had been removed from the table, the MacDonnells fell upon the feast prepared for them. The hall resounded with satisfied grunts and growls, but very little conversation. The Camerons exchanged amused glances. A striking MacDonnell with an aberrantly dark tangle of hair plucked up the entire haunch of venison intended for that table and began to gnaw on it. Sabrina's mother gave the gaping maid a frantic signal.

Enid's eyes softened with sympathy for a kindred soul. "The poor dear must be starving!"

As goblets and bellies were filled and refilled, the mood mellowed. Snatches of song and bursts of good-natured talk came drifting toward the gallery. Sabrina's gaze was drawn back to the blond behemoth. Unlike his clansmen, he picked at his meat and drank only water, leaving his goblet of wine untouched. Perhaps he feared it was poisoned, she thought. But then, why would he allow his clansmen to partake of it? He sat in the midst of them, yet apart, resisting all of Brian's and Alex's attempts to draw him into conversation. Wariness tautened his massive shoulders, stretching the worn tartan to dangerous lengths.

A pang of empathy tugged Sabrina's heart. She knew how it felt to be surrounded by others yet feel alone. As an only daughter blessed with two rowdy brothers, adoration had been her birthright. But adoration did not always mean acceptance. Her brothers still tended to treat her like a child, but she accepted it as the price she must pay for their love.

A snore tickled her ear. Enid had dozed off, her head pillowed on folded arms. Leave it to her cousin to choose a sound slumber over the most thrilling night in Cameron history. Shaking her head in bemusement, Sabrina peeled off her woolen shawl and laid it over Enid.

In the hall below, Angus MacDonnell had raised his goblet. His slurred voice began an endless litany of toasts to the MacDonnells, the Camerons, and the entire Scottish race. Sabrina wouldn't have been surprised to see the flamboyant little rooster jump on the table.

Her gaze slid away against its will. The bench was empty. The tawny-maned barbarian was gone. A hollow feeling opened deep in her belly.

Then a flicker of movement caught her eye. She slammed her cheek against the floor, praying the shadows beneath the banner would hold. The stranger had taken advantage of his chieftain's boasting to slip up the stairs undetected. Her heart thundered in her throat as she peered toward the opposite end of the long gallery to see him disappear into the sanctuary of her mother's solar, his stealthy grace a disquieting contrast to his size.

Her hands knotted into fists. The wretch had to be up to no good. Leave it to a MacDonnell to use her father's hospitality as an excuse for thievery or ambush. Indignation flooded her, tempering her fear. She cast Enid a frantic glance, knowing already that her stolid cousin would be of no help.

Her lips tightened. She might never have a better chance to earn her brothers' respect. Alex and Brian might believe her too callow to face a banquet hall of MacDonnells, but she wasn't too callow to face one MacDonnell caught in his treachery. She envisioned her brothers' mouths dropping open as she marched the sneaky giant down into the hall at the end of a Cameron blade. Let the crafty Angus charm his way out of that one!

Refusing to give herself time to lose her nerve, she leapt to her feet and sprinted for the darkened corridor that led to her father's chambers.

Morgan slipped into the solar and drew the door closed behind him, shutting out the raucous merriment below. Soothing fingers of peace and dark enveloped him. Leaning his back against the door, he drew in a hungry breath. His nostrils tingled at the attar of roses that lingered on the air. This room had haunted him for seven years, and he had to see it one more time if only to banish its charms from his memory.

His eyes slowly adjusted to the dark. Misty moonlight trickled through the casement windows, spinning a delicate web of light and shadow over the solar's treasures. A muffled chirp and rustle warned him he had awakened the tiny yellow finches that always hung in a golden cage beside the door.

"Hello, wee fellows," he whispered. "No need to set up a squawk. 'Tis just Morgan. Remember me?" He lifted his finger to the cage, only to discover it had grown too big to fit between the bars.

Unaccountably chagrined, he left the birds to their mutterings and padded toward the bookshelves. If the hall below was the head of Cameron Manor, the solar was its heart. This was where the family had gathered each night to share stories and laughter and songs. To Morgan it had seemed the gateway to another world, a world of books and music and paintings, a world where a man could dare to dream.

His summers at Cameron had served only to set him apart from his own kind. They had trimmed the rough edges from his speech, rendered his ideas more dangerous. Upon returning to his clan each autumn, he'd been forced to parry the taunts of his clansmen and fight for his very survival until eventually there was no one left to best. His father had watched his battles with ill-disguised glee and savage pride, knowing his future as chieftain was assured.

He drew out a leather-bound volume. Already half in love with Elizabeth Cameron by the summer he was fourteen, he had proudly spurned all of her offers to teach him to read. But that hadn't stopped him from skulking in the shadows while she read aloud to her children each night. He would grip his knees in excitement as her cultured voice recited tales of bold warriors and cunning gods who sailed the seas in mighty ships. He would sneak back the next morning to caress those same books in his reverent hands.

The book fell open to a richly illustrated woodcut. It was his old friend Prometheus, nailed to a rock, his face contorted in agony as the eagle dove down to peck at his liver. Sometimes Morgan felt a bit like poor beleaguered Prometheus, eternally chained to a bleak cliff while his clan ate him alive. He slammed the book shut. He'd do well to remember its words were only gibberish to him, its pictures only childish fables.

A hand-carved clarsach was propped on a table beside the harpsichord. Morgan plucked one of its gossamer strings. A delicate note shivered on the air, jarring the silence. He jerked his hand back. He had often wondered if his own life would have known such genteel pleasures if Elizabeth had chosen to wed his father instead of Dougal Cameron. Or would Angus have eventually crushed even her indomitable spirit?

Morgan knew nothing of his own mother except what his father had told him—that in his own crude, violent struggle to enter the world, Morgan had killed her. The note of pride in Angus's voice had both appalled and shamed him. His father hadn't even troubled himself to remember her name.

A sparkle of light caught his eye. A crystal rose lay nestled on a wing of velvet atop the harpsichord. A strange ache caught in his throat. A rose, sweet and feminine, like a charm from one of Elizabeth's beloved fairy tales, fragile, yet enduring enough to change even a beast like him into a prince.

He chuckled at his own whimsy, but was still helpless to keep from lifting it, from twirling the delicate stem between his callused fingers to watch its luminous petals capture the moonlight.

Without warning the door behind him crashed into the opposite wall. Morgan swung around to find himself facing yet another exotic creature of myth.

A princess, her cloud of dark hair tumbled loose around her shoulders, the light behind her throwing every curve beneath her ivory nightdress into magnificent relief. Her slender fingers were curled not around a scepter, but around the engraved hilt of a ceremonial claymore.

Silvery fingers of moonlight caressed the five feet of steel that lay between her hands and his heart.

"Hold your ground, rogue MacDonnell," she sweetly snarled. "One false move and I'll be taking your head back downstairs without the rest of you."

Morgan didn't even feel the pain as the rose snapped in his hand, embedding its stem deep into his palm.

Chapter Two

"Why, you clumsy oaf! Look what you've gone and done now!"

Morgan's gaze automatically dropped to his hands. A jagged shard of glass protruded from his palm. Warm blood trickled down his wrist and forearm to puddle on one of Elizabeth Cameron's precious rugs. Before he could quench it, the old shame flared. Shame for being a MacDonnell. Shame for being such a crude ox. Just as quickly on its heels followed rage—the crushing rage that shielded his tattered pride from every blow. But before he could unleash it on the hapless girl, she dropped the sword and rushed to his side.

Tossing the splintered remains of the rose away, she cradled his hand in hers and dabbed at the wound with a wad of her nightdress. Her hand was warm, soft, and silky-smooth beneath his own.

"You really should take more care," she chided him. "Had you struck your wrist, you might have bled to death."

Morgan was too dumbfounded to point out her illogic. Had she cut off his head, he most certainly would have bled to death. Still scowling over his hand, she dragged him toward the pale arc of light at the window.

"Be very still," she commanded. "I'm going to fish out this piece of glass. It's bound to be painful. You may scream if you like. I shan't think any less of you."

Since she'd never thought much of him to begin with, Morgan wasn't concerned. He didn't even flinch when she pressed his palm with her thumb and snagged the sliver of glass between the polished crescents of her fingernails.

Thoroughly bemused, Morgan studied her in the moonlight. The top of her head barely came to his breastbone. The spiral curls he used to yank with such relish now tumbled down her back in inky waves. Her skin was fair except for the faintest hint of color, as if God had brushed rose petals across her cheeks and lips. A fringe of ebony silk shuttered her eyes.

Her scent filled his nostrils. He was shocked to feel his throat tighten with a primal hunger. She smelled like her mother, but fresher, sweeter somehow. Some primitive male instinct warned him this was a bloom still on the vine, fragrant and tender and ripe. He scowled. She might be nectar to another man, but to a MacDonnell, Dougal Cameron's daughter would be more deadly than nightshade.

Her teeth cut into her lower lip as if to bite back a cry of her own as she drew forth the shard of glass and staunched the bleeding with another wad of her nightdress. Morgan feared there might soon be more of it twined around his arm than around her body. But an intriguing glimpse of a slender calf silenced his protest.

Grimacing, she laid the bloody splinter on the windowsill before glancing up at him. His hand was in moonlight, but shadows still hid his face. "A rather ignoble end to the Belmont Rose, wasn't it? Perhaps when King James gave it to my English grandfather for his loyal service, he intended it as a weapon, not a trinket. If he'd have realized it would end up in a Highlander's hands, I'm sure he would have tipped the thorns with poison rather than gold."

Sabrina Cameron's baby fat might have melted and realigned in a very enticing manner, but one thing hadn't changed. She still loved to chatter.

A low chuckle rumbled from his throat.

Sabrina frowned. The sound was unfamiliar to her—rich and deep, a mere octave above a growl. Yet if she were a cat, every hair on her head would have bristled in warning.

At that moment he cocked his head to the side, giving her an unobstructed view of his face. Moonlight melted over its harsh planes and angles, etching its alien virility in ruthless lines. He was a stranger, yet so hauntingly familiar she couldn't stop her hand from lifting, her fingertips from brushing the stubborn jut of his jaw. His eyes were guarded like the forest at dusk.

"Hello, brat," he said.

Sabrina felt that old familiar kick in her stomach and realized she was standing face-to-face in the moonlit tower with Morgan MacDonnell, his boyish promise of masculine beauty come to devastating fruition.

Mortified by her boldness, she snatched back her hand, remembering the first time she had touched him in tenderness and been rebuked in anger.

A wry grin quirked his lips. "I suppose if you'd have known it was me, you'd have let me bleed to death."

Terrified that she was going to revert to a stammering six-year-old, she snapped, "I'd say not. You were dripping all over Mama's Flemish rug."

To hide her consternation, she lowered her gaze back to his hand. Another mistake. She could not help staring, fascinated by the blunt size of his fingers, the warmth of his roughened skin, the rhythmic throb of his pulse beneath her thumb. She had the absurd thought that it must take a mighty heart indeed to fuel such a man.

"You've grown," she blurted out accusingly.

"So have you."

His low, amused tone warned her. She looked up

to find his gaze taking a leisurely jaunt up her body, finally coming to rest with bold regard on her face. A splinter of anger twisted in her heart. She had yearned for so long that he might look at her with affection. Why did he have to choose now, when she sensed his admiration might be even more lethal than his enmity?

Hardly aware of her actions, she tore a strip of priceless Chinese silk from her mother's drapes and wrapped it around his palm. "So what were you doing up here? Plotting a massacre? Trying to find a way to lower the harpsichord out the window? Searching for a mouse to stuff into my bed?"

Lucky mouse, Morgan thought, but wisely refrained from saying so. "If you must know, lass, I was searchin' for a moment's peace."

"Ha!" She knotted the bandage with a crisp jerk that finally drew a flinch from him. "Peace and the MacDonnells hardly go hand in hand."

"Noble sentiments from a lass who just burst in here, threatenin' to carry my head to her papa on a platter."

Sabrina could hardly argue with that.

He nodded toward the door. "Why aren't you down there with the rest of your kin, lordin' your noble gestures over the peasants?"

Morgan's size might have changed, but he still had the uncanny knack of making her feel ashamed of who she was. She snorted daintily. "Peasants indeed. Barefoot savages, the lot of them. Mama would have been better off serving them at a trough."

Morgan's voice was quiet, its very lack of emotion a rebuke. "If their table manners aren't to your likin', it might be because most of them won't see that much food again in their lifetimes. And their feet are bare because they're savin' the rotted soles of their boots for the cold winter months. They don't lose as many toes that way."

Shame buffeted Sabrina. Morgan had always brought out the worst in her. She dropped her gaze, then wished she hadn't as it fell on the stark lines of Morgan's bare feet. Golden hair dusted his muscular calves. His soles must be as tough as leather to bear the stony soil of the mountain without protection. Her own toes curled sheepishly into the plush cashmere of her stockings.

"If you must know, I begged Mama to let me join the festivities," she confessed.

"Why didn't you appeal to your dotin' papa? Are your pouts failin' you? As I recall, he never could resist a flutter of those ridiculously long lashes of yours."

Sabrina's gaze shot to his face. Morgan had never given her any indication that he'd noticed her lashes, or anything else about her. "Even Papa was adamant this time." A soft chuckle escaped her. "It seems your reputations for lechery preceded you. He was terrified one of you might hit me over the head and drag me off by my hair."

Morgan was silent for so long that she feared she'd offended him again. Then he reached down and lifted a skein of her hair into his uninjured hand, rubbing it between thumb and forefinger. A dreamy languor stole across his features. The cadence of Sabrina's heartbeat shifted in warning.

He let the stolen tendril ripple through his fingers in a cascade of midnight silk before turning the dusky heat of his gaze on her. "I can't say I blame him, lass. If you were mine, I'd probably lock you away too."

If you were mine . . .

The words hung suspended between them, far more awkward than the silence. In a breath of utter lunacy Sabrina wondered how it would feel to belong to a man like him, dared to ponder what came after being dragged off by her hair.

Caught in the same spell of moonlight and solitude, Morgan's gaze dropped to her parted lips. His starving senses reeled, intoxicated by the scent of roses that flared his nostrils and the cling of her hair against his callused knuckles. He'd long ago resigned himself to the harsh life of a Highland warrior. But this girl's softness awakened old hungers and weakened his resolve. He hadn't touched a drop of wine, yet he felt drunk, reckless. What harm could it do to steal one taste of that tender rosebud of a mouth? Resisting the temptation to plunge his tongue between her unwitting lips, he leaned down and touched his mouth to hers.

At the press of Morgan's lips against her own, Sabrina's eyes fluttered shut. His kiss was brief, dry, almost tentative, yet a melting sweetness unfolded deep within her. She felt the leashed power in his touch. Such gentleness in a man his size wove a spell all its own. Only in the last brief second of contact did he allow himself the wicked luxury of dragging his lips across hers, molding her beneath him in perfect harmony.

Sabrina's eyes drifted open to find herself clutching a handful of Morgan's plaid as if to keep from sinking to her knees at his feet. She could feel the warmth of his skin beneath the worn tartan, the dizzying thud of his heart against her palm. But too soon the smoky mist fled his eyes, banished by a predatory glint she recognized only too well.

"What now, princess?" he asked, the endearment a mockery on his tongue. "Shall you behead me yourself or demand your father toss me in the dungeon for my boldness?"

She awkwardly untangled her fingers from his plaid. "Don't be ridiculous. 'Twas only a kiss. I've been kissed before," she lied.

A shock raced through her as he brushed his fingertips against her lower lip. It felt swollen, ripe beneath his touch. "I don't think you have. But with lips like these, I can promise you'll be kissed again."

Afraid he was going to do just that, and even more afraid he wasn't, Sabrina tossed back her head in defiance. "I won't tell my father you kissed me. I'm not a baby anymore. I swore you'd never make me tattle."

He caught her chin in the broad cup of his palm. "And that I'd never make you cry." Even he seemed taken aback when the husky words came out more promise than taunt.

Surprised that he even remembered her childish oath, Sabrina stepped away from him, desperate to escape the moonlight, the crisp musk of pine wafting from his skin, the strange intimacy of having his blood stain her nightdress.

Sensing her retreat, Morgan folded his arms over his chest. "Would you be callin' an end to our truce, then?"

She tilted her nose in the air. "I am."

"Verra well. Take up your battle stance."

Sabrina eyed him suspiciously. What was the rogue up to now?

Humor flickered through his eyes, as irresistible as sunlight through a summer glade. "Go on with you," he commanded. "As pleasant as it might be, I haven't all night to dally in your company. As I recall, you were standin' over there. By the door."

Puzzled yet captivated by this more playful Morgan, she marched to the door. He nodded. "Now take up your weapon."

Morgan watched, lips twitching, as she struggled to heft the massive sword, muttering something about "almost never getting the cursed thing off the wall." After three tries she still hadn't lifted the blade more than a few inches off the floor. She'd have better luck cutting off his feet than his head, he thought. Panting with exertion, she finally faced him, the blade trembling in her hands.

He allowed the smile he'd been swallowing to shine on her full force. "Aye, that'll do it. You were there, threatenin' to behead me, and I was just about to do this."

Reaching into his plaid, he drew forth a pistol and leveled it at her comely bosom.

The tip of the blade clunked to the floor. "You dirty cheat! You swore to lay down your arms. Have you no common—"

"—decency? Sense?" He shrugged. "I'm a MacDonnell, lass. You didn't expect me to play fair, did you?"

Her eyes darkened for an elusive instant with old hurts, old resentments, and Morgan knew a brief tug of regret that he hadn't allowed her this small triumph.

"No," she said softly. "You never have, have you?"

Forced into surrender, she propped the claymore against the wall and stood aside to let him pass. He slid the pistol back into his plaid.

"Morgan?"

"Mmm?" He paused in the doorway. Their bodies brushed in the near darkness.

She held out her hand. "The pistol, please."

He was almost as startled as she was by the peals of laughter that rumbled up from his chest. Always a man to admit when he'd been bested, he laid the weapon across her palm and folded her fingers around it like the creamy petals of an orchid.

He bent to press his lips to her ear and whispered, "I don't trust just any lass with my gun. Be gentle with it, won't you?"

As Morgan descended the stairs, his step much lighter than when he'd ascended, he wondered if perhaps the time hadn't long passed to call a permanent truce between one bullheaded MacDonnell and one luscious Cameron princess.

Sabrina slumped against the door frame, dazed. She finally looked down to find Morgan's pistol cradled tenderly against her breast. She jerked it away, dangling it between two fingers.

Be gentle with it indeed! She should have shot the wretch. It would have served him right to be done in by his own pistol.

She stared down at her nightdress. She felt branded, marked with Morgan's blood like some sort of primitive trophy. Lord, she thought, what sort of hysterics would Enid pitch if she woke to find her beloved cousin spattered with blood and cosseting a loaded pistol? At least Sabrina assumed it was loaded. Morgan didn't seem the sort to go around waving an empty pistol. Pointing the flared muzzle at her face, she closed one eye and peered into it, but saw nothing but darkness.

"That's of no help at all," she muttered.

Refusing to attribute the languid weight of her limbs to the lingering effects of Morgan's kiss, she stuffed her father's sword under the settee and tucked the pistol behind a Venetian mirror. She cast a wistful look back at the moonlit solar before pulling the door shut. In the harsh light of morning she knew their encounter would seem to be only a dream.

Hugging the shadows, Sabrina slipped around the gallery, fully intending to bundle both Enid and herself off to bed before anyone else discovered their flummery. But a burst of laughter—rich, deep, and compelling—stopped her in her tracks.

She drifted to the railing and sank to her knees, lured by the unfamiliar sound and the ripple of gold as Morgan tossed back his head at one of Brian's jests. A boyish smile transformed his face, erasing its weary lines and crinkling the taut skin around his eyes. Sun, wind, and responsibility had aged him far past his years. Some men would always be boys, but Sabrina sensed that Morgan MacDonnell had been born a man.

The intensity of his raw masculine beauty struck her anew; her heart spasmed as if someone had reached through her chest and squeezed it. Her hands clenched on the balusters.

On Morgan's other side, Alex filled his own goblet with fresh wine and lifted it in a toast. Morgan's gaze flicked to the gallery, catching Sabrina unawares. A more intimate smile teased his lips as he lifted his mug of water in a silent tribute that made all the noise and chaos between them fade to a meaningless hum. Brian slapped him on the back and Morgan lowered his gaze and his mug, taking care not to alert the others to her hiding place.

A fragile happiness welled in Sabrina's heart. Fearful of betraying an emotion so new and precious, she forced her gaze away from him. As she watched, the dark-haired MacDonnell rose and slipped out the main door, clutching his stomach. A burst of night wind fluttered the banners.

Probably ill from too much venison, Sabrina thought, grinning.

Their animosity softened by wine and camaraderie, Angus and her father seemed to be faring as well as their sons. The hooded servant who had hovered behind Angus had disappeared, probably to curl up in some forgotten nook of the manor. Sabrina's glassy-eyed mother looked as if she would like to do the same.

From the corner of her eye Sabrina saw the tapestry behind them ripple. She glanced toward the door, expecting to see the hoggish MacDonnell stumble back in, mopping his mouth with the back of his hand. The door remained closed.

Sabrina frowned. Almost without realizing it, she rose to her feet, beset by a terrible premonition that something was wrong. She leaned over the rail, staring hard at the tapestry. Was that a flicker of movement she saw, or just a trick of the guttering candles? Of their own volition, her feet dragged her toward the stairs, drawn as if magnetized to the source of her unease.

"Sabrina! What in heaven's name are you doing out of bed at this hour?"

Her mother's cry jerked her out of her reverie. She realized she was standing at the foot of the stairs. A rush of half-formed impressions buffeted her. Her father's worried frown. The open leers of the MacDonnell men as they nudged each other under the tables. Morgan's black scowl.

Brian's words carried through the hall. "Good God, Alex, is that blood all over her gown?"

Sabrina had forgotten about the condition of her nightdress. Feeling naked and exposed before them all, she opened her mouth to explain, but before she could speak, Angus rose to his feet, weaving dangerously.

"Ah, this must be the bonny Sabrina! Word o' yer beauty has spread to the farthest reaches o' the Highlands." Even in his drunken state he managed to leer at her mother and wink at his men at the same time. "If me Beth had been blessed with better taste in husbands, ye might have been me own daughter."

His men burst into lusty laughter. Sabrina's father nodded, his good-natured smile strained. She felt a painful blush creep up her throat. Scowling even more fiercely, Morgan began to tug at the bodkin holding his plaid pinned as if he had every intention of whipping it off his own naked form and wrapping it around her.

"To Sabrina!" Angus bellowed. "The tenderest bud of my fair Beth!"

The men cheered wildly as their chieftain hefted his goblet in a mighty toast before pitching forward dead in his plate, the jeweled hilt of a dagger protruding from between his bony shoulder blades.

Chapter Three

Morgan's roar of anguish shook the rafters, drowning out everything but Sabrina's shrill scream.

Dougal Cameron shoved his wife down the nearest corridor to safety, then bent to cradle Angus's body. He lifted his hands, staring at his fingers as if bewildered to find them stained with blood. The MacDonnells fumbled for their scabbards and reached into their plaids, only to have their hands return empty.

Morgan had seen too many dead men fall to waste time coddling his father's corpse. His wide-eyed gaze lit on Sabrina. Alex and Brian reached for his arms, but he flung them away as if they were no more than puppies nipping at his heels and bounded over the table. Everyone thought he was diving for the pile of weapons.

Everyone but Sabrina. She had seen the murderous flare of accusation in his eyes. She knew what he believed as surely as if he had shouted it. That she had been a lure, a distraction to draw his attention from his father's impending assassination.

She was mesmerized by his charging approach. There was nowhere to run. Nowhere to hide. No time to beg for mercy. If he had snatched up his ax in that moment and swung it, her feet would have remained rooted to the stone long after her head had flown.

His arm circled her waist. He jerked her against him and turned them both to face the hall. Sabrina felt his hand dip into his plaid, reaching for a pistol he'd surrendered to her only minutes before. Bereft of any other weapon, his big hand closed over her jaw, tilting her face upward to show them all that the slightest twitch of his fingers would break her neck.

A strange calm flowed through her. Even hanging helpless in Morgan's grip, her weight braced against his splayed thighs, she knew she would bear no bruises from his touch. His hands were almost gentle, their violence restrained by a ruthless competence more terrifying than cruelty. She had little doubt that her death at his hands would be as brutally tender. One jerk of his blunt fingers and her life would wink out like a star at the approach of dawn.

Every man in the hall, even Morgan's clansmen, stood frozen with shock. Impotent fury glazed Brian's eyes. Alex was breathing hard, his face flushed redder than his hair.

"Your hospitality leaves much to be desired, Dougal Cameron," Morgan snarled, his hot breath fanning Sabrina's hair.

Dougal lifted his bloodstained hands in plea. "Don't do this, Morgan. I had no hand in killing your father. If you'll give me the chance, I swear I'll help you find the scoundrel who did."

"My father gave you a chance. And look what it got him. Gather your arms," he commanded his men.

The MacDonnells fell on the weapons like a pack of ravening dogs. Their greasy hands snatched the rusted hilts of swords and dirks, caressed the scarred butts of their pistols. As each man straightened, his eyes narrowed to hungry slits at the thrill of approaching bloodshed. They were in their element now, poised for open warfare and prepared to kill the men they'd just so amiably dined with.

Sabrina's own eyes narrowed as she spotted the bonny dark-haired MacDonnell among them. How had he gotten back into the hall? Had she simply overlooked him in the chaos? Her questions were swallowed along with her dread as she realized her own clansmen stood before the MacDonnells as unarmed and helpless as lambs for the slaughter.

Morgan backed toward the door, using Sabrina as a shield.

Dougal slammed his fist on the table. "Damn you, Morgan, free her! She's only a child! This fight is between you and me."

Morgan's voice rumbled down Sabrina's spine, his words meant only for her ears. "You killed the wrong MacDonnell, brat. You should have cut off my head when you had the chance."

Morgan rarely made tactical errors in the heat of battle, but indulging himself in that taunt proved to be a costly one. For Sabrina, time swept backward. He was no longer a dangerous stranger who held the fragile thread of her life in his hands, but that same vexsome, arrogant boy who had trod upon her tender feelings at every turn.

"Always have to have the last word, don't you?" she said, her voice deceptively soft.

Every snippet of ruined embroidery, each of her tarts he'd so gleefully fed to Pugsley, every tear she'd never shed was in the force of the blow as she swung her fist behind her and smashed it into his face

Morgan's eyes crossed at the pain, and he knew she had broken his nose. "Why you wee bi—"

Suddenly he was holding a flailing dervish in his arms. Her sharp little heels tattooed on his shins. Between grunts and pants of exertion, she managed to choke out, "If you'd . . . use . . . that thick skull of yours for something other than hanging a . . . b-b-bonnet on, you'd listen to my . . . father." She bit the hand he shoved over her mouth, drawing blood.

His men exchanged uneasy glances. None of them had ever bested Morgan in any contest, and they had the scars to prove it. Now this half-English slip of a girl actually seemed to be holding her own with him. Her black hair streamed over her face; her white teeth snapped at the air in a quest for fresh flesh.

"Want me to shoot her, Morgan?" Ranald suggested hopefully, cocking his pistol.

Morgan saved him the trouble by slamming her to the floor and pinning her beneath his weight. His men cheered, thinking a new sport was in the offing. What better revenge for Angus's murder than to defile the Cameron's daughter while he and his sons were forced to watch? They licked their lips in anticipation, hoping for a turn of their own when Morgan was done with her.

Brian lurched forward only to find a MacDonnell dirk pressed to his throat. Alex cast his father a desperate glance, but Dougal stood silent, his expression almost pensive as he watched the two locked in a battle of wills on the floor of his hall.

Morgan had trapped Sabrina's thighs between his own and captured her slender wrists in one of his hands. Both of their chests were heaving as their gazes locked. Morgan tasted blood where the back of her head had split his lip.

"Shag her once for me!" one of his men called out.

Morgan saw the color drain from Sabrina's cheeks. Yet even now, when they both knew he had the power to leave her broken, bleeding, and debased on the stones, she refused to beg, refused to cry.

"Give the wench a taste o' yer blade, Morgan. I'll wager 'tis heartier than the one that killed yer da."

Morgan drew back his fist, knowing he had no choice but to cuff her unconscious before his clansmen's ugly mood veered beyond his control. Her struggles were only whetting their lust. She wasn't going to make it easy on him. Her soft body trembled beneath his, but her unflinching eyes taunted him, dared him to strike her.

Her hair fanned around her face in silky black waves. It was the kind of hair a man dreamed of wrapping his hands in and pinioning to his pillow. The kind of hair . . .

Morgan hesitated, praying his blow wouldn't be hard enough to shatter the defiant tilt of her jaw.

That brief flicker of compassion cost him dearly. He felt the cold muzzle of the pistol jammed against the base of his skull an instant before he heard the click of its hammer being raked back.

Elizabeth Cameron's cultured tones were crisp with fury. "Get off my baby, Morgan MacDonnell, or I'll send you to join your father in hell."

Chapter Four

Sabrina felt Morgan's grip tighten for an implacable instant as if even the threat of death weren't enough to make him let her go.

Had she not been riveted by the smoky green of his eyes, she would have seen the desperate glances exchanged by his men. Ranald could take out Elizabeth Cameron with one shot, but if her finger so much as twitched on her own trigger, the MacDonnells would be less not only one blustering figurehead, but also the man who bound the remnants of their clan together. A costly price to pay even for a meal as hearty as the one the Cameron had provided.

Morgan made the decision for them.

Staring straight ahead, he surrendered Sabrina's wrists and lifted his hands. He slowly rose, unfolding his large frame with measured grace. Sabrina remained sprawled on the floor, mesmerized by his arrogant stance and the unrepentant quirk of his lips. She was beginning to wonder if she was destined to spend her life at this man's feet. She could now clearly see the pearl-plated pistol shoved against the side of his throat.

"Anythin' to please a lady," he drawled, daring a rueful smile.

Her father braced his palms on the table, looking as weary as Sabrina had ever seen him. The gray in his hair fanned out from his pallid temples in stark wings. "Brian, Alex, escort our guest to the dungeon before your mother kills him." His voice trembled with suppressed fury. "I want the rest of you out of my home. Now!"

"Murdered our poor chieftain before dessert," Ranald muttered, tucking his pistol down the front of his kilt. He pilfered a mutton leg from a table as he passed. "Bloody rude lot if ye ask me. No manners a-tall."

"Aye," another MacDonnell dared, scooping up a flagon of ale and a handful of silver spoons. "Angus was a fine man. He deserved to meet death face-to-face, not be stabbed in the back by some miserable Cameron coward."

Grumbling like disgruntled children at being deprived of the anticipated bloodshed, the MacDonnells trailed out. The women of their acquaintance were as likely to shoot a man as bed him, and they had no reason to believe the Cameron's wife was any different. They weren't willing to risk Morgan's life to salvage either pride or pudding.

One of the larger men heaved Angus's corpse over his shoulder. Morgan didn't even blink as his father's body jostled past, although Sabrina would have sworn she saw a muscle twitch in his granite jaw. She shuddered to imagine her own papa's body being bounced about with such lack of ceremony.

Brian and Alex caught Morgan's wrists, twisting them behind him with more force than was necessary. Bronzed slabs of muscle rippled in his forearms, a harsh reminder that it was only by his grace and the pistol still trained on his head that they were being allowed to restrain him at all. Her brothers' faces were taut with rage as they bound the hands of their former friend.

As they marched him from the hall, Morgan allowed himself one last sweet taste of rebellion. He twisted around and leveled a long, inscrutable look at Sabrina.

His eyes marked her more plainly than his blood ever could, promising plainly what his lips could not.

Later . . .

A dark shiver raked her. Brian gave Morgan a shove. Then they were gone and her father and mother were kneeling beside her, her father wrapping his frock coat around her shoulders, her mother enfolding her in a perfumed embrace.

"Did that wicked beast hurt you?" Elizabeth smoothed the hair from Sabrina's face.

"Not yet," she answered absently, still staring at the empty doorway.

Dougal lifted her wrists to the light as if searching for far more than just the circlet of bruises that should have branded them. They were unmarked, as smooth and creamy as they had been when she crept out of her bedchamber. A strange mixture of triumph and sorrow knitted his brow.

"So, my wee princess, have you had enough excitement for one night?" he asked.

She laughed shakily. "Enough for a lifetime, I do believe. Wherever did you get the pistol, Mama?"

Elizabeth frowned at the weapon as if seeing it for the first time. "A German clockmaker made it for my father in thanks for a generous donation to his Lutheran church." She pointed it at the ceiling and pulled the trigger. A colorful shock of feathers burst from the muzzle.

An odd sound gurgled up in Sabrina's throat, half sob, half giggle. "Bested by roses and feathers all in one night. Poor devil."

Her parents exchanged a troubled look over her head. Dougal reached to stroke her cheek, but was stopped by the sight of the ugly bloodstains on his hands.

"Who would dare to work such wickedness?" Elizabeth asked.

Dougal's hands closed into determined fists. "I don't know. But I've every intention of finding out."

"Perhaps some enemy of Angus's, neither Cameron nor MacDonnell, slipped into the manor undetected," Sabrina suggested.

Her parents both stared at her as if they'd forgotten her presence.

"Don't you worry your comely wee head about it, princess," Dougal commanded.

"Your papa's right. We were thoughtless to discuss it in front of you. Come along, lamb," her mother coaxed, helping her to her feet. "I'll tuck you into your bed and brew you a nice hot cup of tea."

Sabrina surprised both her parents and herself by pulling away and forcing her weak knees to support her. "Thank you, Mama, but I believe I shall take myself off to bed. If I'd have stayed there to begin with, I might have spared everyone a great deal of bother."

Sabrina didn't want to be coddled. She didn't want to climb between her crisp linen sheets, sink into her warm down mattress, and think of Morgan, chained below the layers of stone and wood in the chill, damp dungeon.

Her parents watched her climb the stairs, her diminutive frame swallowed by her father's knee-length coat. Dougal's natural optimism prevailed. A thread of excitement twined through his dismay over Angus's death. Perhaps the crusty old chieftain hadn't died for naught. Perhaps the opportunity for Dougal to realize both his hopes for Clan Cameron and his dreams for his beloved daughter had just fallen into his lap along with Angus's body.

He shook his head, marveling at the sweet irony of fate. "Not a mark on her. Extraordinary."

Elizabeth's eyes narrowed. She had seen that angelic expression on her husband's face before and had every reason to distrust it. "Not a mark you can see," she muttered.

Sabrina's steps had already begun to drag before she reached the top of the stairs. She rounded the corner of the gallery only to stumble over Enid's prostrate form.

Her cousin rolled to a sitting position, knuckling her reddened eyes. "Dear heavens, I must have dozed off. I didn't miss anything, did I?"

It took Sabrina three days to muster up her courage. Three days of being ruthlessly cosseted by her mother. Three days of watching her father, brothers, and the elders of their clan stomp and swear about the manor in search of a solution to their dilemma. Three days of listening to the MacDonnell bagpipes keen in protest outside the manor walls. At least, she thought, the sunken earth of the dungeon would muffle their endless drone.

The tapered heel of her slipper caught in a crevice in the stone. She braced her palm against the damp wall to keep from pitching down the winding stairs into blackness. She could well imagine her parents' horror to find her broken body crumpled at the foot of the stairs. Her breath rasped from her throat, echoing eerily in a silence broken only by the torturous drip of water on stone. A stale draft licked at the flame of her candle. She loosed her grasp on the wall to cup her hand around it. She would rather go tumbling headfirst than to be left alone in this stygian darkness.

Her teeth chattered as she inched her foot from one step to the next, thinking it a fine time to discover she was more cowardly than Enid.

She stepped off the last stair into the belly of a serpentine corridor. The air hung dank and chill. She slipped her hand into the pocket of her gown just long enough to squeeze a measure of valor from the warm, linen-wrapped package within.

The maze of passages twisted, digging Sabrina deeper into the earth with each bend. She passed empty cells layered in limp straw and refuse, iron doors hanging off rusted hinges, manacles dangling from domed ceilings, their tangled chains marred by a coppery stain she feared was not rust. The walls wept oily tears that trickled into dank pools at her feet, soaking the ruched silk of her slippers. Squeaks and rustles greeted each of her shy footfalls, and once a sinuous slither caused her to jerk up the hem of her skirt and stand paralyzed for a faltering heartbeat.

For decades the dungeon had slumbered vacant beneath the ancient tower of Cameron Keep. Remembering Morgan's taunts, Sabrina wondered if another MacDonnell might have been its last occupant—perhaps his grandfather or his contentious great-great-great-uncle christened Horrid Halbert by both enemies and clansmen for his unfortunate habit of skinning his foes alive. A draft raked icy claws down her exposed nape, making her shiver.

She hurried around a curve she would have sworn she'd passed only moments before. She didn't know how much time she had. She'd been able to steal away only because the men had rushed from the manor to keep a drunken MacDonnell from setting fire to the village kirk.

This gloomy cavern seemed a world away from the graceful wings of the manor house. The corridors narrowed. The skirts draped over her wide paniers brushed the walls. The weight of the stones pressed in on her until she could almost hear the ghosts of booted footsteps and hellish screams of torment. She fought panic, afraid to admit she was lost. Remembering the look of warning Morgan had given her in the hall, she realized she must be lost indeed to willingly seek him out.

Just as she was ready to succumb to the temptation of plopping down on the filthy stone and bawling like a baby, a tunnel sprang into her path. A blast of chill wind moaned through the yawning passageway. Her candle guttered, then winked out.

Sabrina slammed her eyes shut. Better a dark of her own making than the cloying murk of panic. But she quickly realized she couldn't just stand there forever with her eyes closed. Not only was it futile, it was boring. She pried one eye open, then the other. The useless candlestick slid from her hands to clatter on the stones.

The faintest spark of light would have blinded her to the glow at the far end of the tunnel. Only utter darkness revealed it. The floor slanted beneath her feet. She crept forward, hugging the wall for comfort, afraid she might not ever find Morgan and more afraid she would.

The light revealed iron bars rooted between floor and ceiling and a man so still he might have been sculpted of the massive slabs of rock that entombed him. A fat candle sputtered in a wooden sconce, its spare light flirting with the shadows. Sabrina's relief that her father had not been so cruel as to leave him in darkness was buried beneath a fierce surge of anger as she saw the thick chains that manacled his arms and legs to an iron stake embedded in the floor. No wonder her father hadn't seen fit to post a guard.

Primitive outrage tore at her. Morgan shouldn't be imprisoned in this miserable hole. He should be galloping across the glen, a breeze winnowing his wheaten hair. He should be sleeping beneath a crisp net of stars, his only shelter the rustling boughs of the pines.

He sat on a narrow shelf that jutted from the wall. Not even the greedy shadows could dull the sheen of the hair that veiled his face. He slowly tipped back his head, dispelling the image of beaten prisoner with one motion.

A bruise smudged the skin beneath his left eye. The decadent fullness of his lower lip was marred by a cut as if he'd been caught there by a blow from a heavy ring. Recalling the fiercely protective looks on her brothers' faces as they'd led him away, Sabrina suspected they had sought their own private retribution after Morgan had been safely chained.

But instead of eliciting sympathy, his injuries only made him look more dangerous. Sabrina's lips tightened. She'd do well to remember that this man neither warranted nor needed her pity.

He unfolded his heavy frame, transforming the confining space from cell to cage. His plaid was knotted around his waist. His bare chest gleamed like buttered steel. He padded toward her, leashed animal power in every movement. Had he charged her roaring and rattling his chains, he would have no more resembled a warrior spawned from some barbaric hell. As he approached the bars, Sabrina backed instinctively against the opposite wall.

At first Morgan thought captivity had driven him mad. He had paced every inch of the cell before sinking down on the bench to fight despair. Then into this dank, foul-smelling prison had come a whisper of roses and an even more incongruous aroma of ginger and spice. His groin and his stomach tightened with hunger, each vying for his attention.

He couldn't believe Sabrina was really there, so prim and clean-smelling, her skin glowing like alabaster in the thin light. A coronet of braids graced her fair brow. Still playing the princess, he thought, and he might have grinned if his torn lip hadn't hurt so damned much.

He closed his fingers around the bars, ignoring the abrading tug of the chains. "Come to gloat, have you? To gawk at the pretty beast and enjoy your revenge for all those nasty tricks he played upon you?"

The chains would never allow him to reach her, yet his very proximity robbed Sabrina of all her wit. Against her own best intentions she blurted out the truth. "I was afraid you might be hurting."

"I am. My nose hurts like hell. You broke it, you know."

She tilted her head to study him. Not even a broken nose could damage the ruggedly asymmetric magnetism of his features.

He shrugged off her scrutiny. "It's been broke before. Probably will be again if I live long enough. Of course, your lovin' da will see to it that I don't."

"I wasn't talking about your nose. I was talking about your father."

He shrugged again, although the lazy glitter of his eyes sharpened. "Nothin' to talk about. The old rogue is dead."

Sabrina had expected to find him wild with grief, roaring with rage. His icy calm was even more unsettling. She wondered if he kept all his emotions in such merciless check.

Breaking away from his gaze, she began to pace before the cell, still maintaining a wary arm's length between them. "I don't see how you can believe my father killed yours. If he had, don't you think he would have armed his own clansmen? Why would he risk the lives of his family for such a petty, malicious trick?"

"You tell me."

She stole a glance at him to gauge his reaction. He yawned, shaking his mane out of his eyes like a big, sleepy lion.

She paced faster, refusing to let him goad her. "Before Angus was murdered, I saw the tapestries ripple as if someone were hiding behind them. What was to stop the assassin from sneaking in by the side corridor, then fleeing the same way? You can't deny your father had enemies enough. Why, it could have been anyone! Someone from the village. A passing Grant or Chisholm who would relish the idea of starting a fresh war between our clans."

Or even one of your very own clansmen. Sabrina bit back the words, knowing he would see them only as a ruse to clear her father's name.

He braced the back of his forearm against the bars above his head. "Anyone but you, my sweet. We all know where you were, don't we?"

His mocking tone shamed her. She could almost feel the gentle stroke of his lips against hers and felt as if she'd been caught strolling naked through a regiment of MacDonnells. Tendrils of heat twined up her throat to her cheeks.

Morgan glared at the fragile incline of Sabrina's neck, choking back a growl. The girl ought to be made to wear her hair loose, he thought, if only for his own self-preservation. The sight of her bare nape twisted something deep inside him, something best left untouched. He'd rather see her angry than vulnerable. Perhaps that was why he'd spent so many years teaching her to hate him.

"Where are my men?" he barked. "No one in this godforsaken hole will tell me."

Sabrina wasn't supposed to tell him either. She shot him a look from beneath her lashes, trying to decide how far she would go to earn even a crumb of his trust in the hope of averting further tragedy for both their clans.

"They're camped on the hill across from the manor," she finally said, sighing in defeat. "But no one can tell if they're planning a siege or celebrating. They dance and swill whisky all day, then terrorize the village by night. Oh, and they play the bagpipes. Incessantly. If this were Jericho, the walls would have crumbled the first day."

"That would be Ranald. He's a bloody wretched pipe player."

"At least we agree on something."

Morgan paced away from the bars, dragging his chains behind him. He couldn't afford to let Sabrina see the excitement flaring behind his eyes. If his men were still nearby, there might be a chance of escape. Perhaps even now they awaited some signal from him.

When he swung back around, Sabrina recoiled with fresh horror.

Morgan was smiling.

As if that weren't enough to stun her, this was no ordinary smile. It held not even a trace of the mockery or maddening arrogance she had come to expect from him. This was a boyish grin, devastating in its openness. It crinkled his face in all the right places and cut to her heart faster than a blade. It was the smile Hades might have given Persephone before sweeping her off to the underworld. The smile Satan might have leveled on Christ to tempt him in the wilderness. Neither chains nor bars could contain it. A woman would do anything for a smile like that. Anything at all. He padded toward the bars and the fear that she was being stalked turned to terror.

His voice softened to a husky purr that stroked her staggering senses. "I thought I was dreamin' when

I looked up to see you standin' there. Or that I'd died and gone to heaven."

Sabrina couldn't resist cocking a skeptical eyebrow. Had she not been blistered by the intensity of his charm, she would have burst into laughter at his sheer gall. But some mischievous part of her wanted to see just how far he'd take this charade.

She shuffled her feet modestly. "You more likely thought you'd been banished to hell to find such an ugly imp peering through the bars at you."

His palm flew to his heart as if her words had wounded him. "Don't dare to jest so, lass. Even the angels must weep with jealousy at your loveliness."

Sabrina was tempted to peer behind him to see if Angus's ghost was talking while Morgan moved his mouth. "The angels need have no fear of me. As a certain boy once took great delight in reminding me, I am far from lovely." The lightness of her voice belied the pain of the memory as she counted off her faults on her fingers. "My lips are too puffy, my neck too scrawny. My ears point heavenward like the basest of elves, and my nose puts one in mind of Pugsley."

His remorseful gaze never made it past her lips. "Ah, but those were the taunts of a foolish boy. I'm not a boy anymore, Sabrina. I'm a man."

Her name rolled from his lips like song. She wasn't sure what jolted her more—hearing him address her as something besides brat, or his blunt stating of the obvious. With the plaid draped low across his narrow hips and the taut knitting of bone and muscle in his chest exposed, the nature of his sex could have been no more evident had he let the plaid fall in a pool at his feet.

Her heart thudded into a traitorous rhythm at the vision. She lowered her eyes, hating that she wasn't as immune to his cunning as she'd hoped. She wanted to end it. She didn't want to know how far he'd go to achieve his mercenary ends. She feared she already knew.

Tilting her head, she affected a winsome smile

and played her final card. "I didn't come here to gawk or gloat, Morgan. I came to offer my help."

He crooked a finger at her, luring her nearer the cell. She sidled toward him as if it were only maidenly shyness keeping her out of his reach. His hands closed over the bars, his fingers sliding up and down in a calculated stroke that made her skin dance.

"I'll not ask much of you, lass. If you'll just bring me the pistol I entrusted to your tender care, I'll be out of your da's hair in a trice." His voice softened to a rough whisper. "Please, Sabrina. I need you."

His words reverberated through her soul like the echo of a forgotten dream. How many times had she risked his scorn for the chance to hear them? And if she brought him his precious pistol, what would he do? Probably shoot her through her foolish heart with it. Wry anger spilled through her.

"I swear I'll take care not to hurt any of your kin," he continued, coaxing and seducing with that glib devil's tongue of his. "I'll just put the gun right here under my plaid—"

"May I suggest a better hiding place?" she inquired sweetly. "It won't be quite as comfortable, but I can promise you the guards won't think to look there."

Morgan looked as shocked as if an angel had snapped her wings at him and started spewing profanity. His smile vanished. A black scowl split his brow. His fists clenched on the bars, looking more inclined to throttle than caress. Despite her trepidation, Sabrina wasn't surprised to learn she liked this Morgan far better than his duplicitous twin.

She took a step backward, wary of the flex and ripple of his chest muscles. "It seems in your past perusal of my chubby lips and pointy ears, you forgot one thing—a brain. I have one. Tell me, does that oily pandering actually work on the ladies of your acquaintance?"

"Don't know any ladies," he admitted, managing to look sulky, sheepish, and thoroughly dangerous at the same time.

"Then with what tender phrases do you woo the lasses?"

" 'Bend over' usually does it," he snapped.

Sabrina's hand fluttered to her throat as if it could stymie the disturbing images his words provoked. "I'm not playing games with you, Morgan. I came here to help you. But not to offer pistols or knives or even keys. Aren't you sick of all the bloodshed? What's going to happen when the rest of your clan marches out of the mountains and lays siege to Cameron? More fighting? More dying? If you'd only give my father time to prove his innocence, you'd be able to convince your clan of it as well. They'd listen to you. You're their chieftain now. If you weren't so blasted stubborn—"

A choked sound from the cell stopped her. Morgan had covered his head with his folded arms. His big shoulders quaked. He threw back his head and roared with a laughter so black and devoid of mirth that it raised the hairs at Sabrina's nape. Tears streamed from his eyes, but when she saw the hopelessness reflected in their depths, she wondered if they weren't tears of another kind altogether.

"The *rest* of my clan?" he echoed. "Oh, that's rich, lass. It seems the Camerons will have the last laugh after all, because there are no more of us. Those prancin', pipin' fools on the hill are all that's left. All died off, the others have, and now my own da's gone to join them. He's probably wenchin' in hell right now and havin' a good laugh at my expense. I'm the chieftain, all right. The chieftain of nothin'!"

Sabrina was stunned. She couldn't even fathom the death of her clan. Clan Cameron numbered in the hundreds, each man farming his own plot in the glen, swearing fealty to her father, even taking his name as their own before God and man in a ceremony as quaint and timeless as that of the tenderest wedding.

To be clanless in the Highlands was to be no less than the basest of outcasts.

Morgan's gaze met hers. "I believed I wouldn't crawl, but I was wrong. I would have crawled for them.

I would have died for them. They're all I have. All I am."

Would any man ever declare himself for her with such passion and fervency? she wondered. Her heart lurched to realize Morgan wanted peace even more than her father did. His very existence depended on it. And now all his hopes had died at the brutal, cunning hands of Angus's murderer.

She started for the cell, wanting to offer him comfort even if it was only the press of her fingers through the bars.

"Don't!" he roared.

Sabrina froze. Here at last were the grief and rage he'd kept leashed inside him, boiling from his eyes in molten warning. His chains rattled, the manacles no more than fragile iron bracelets as he flexed his mighty arms.

"Don't," he repeated. "Don't come near the bars." Then more softly, "Don't you know what I could do to you?"

Sabrina thrust her hands into her pockets to hide their trembling. A faint warmth still emanated from one of them. She drew out the linen package she had wrapped with such care.

Morgan stood unmoving as she took one step toward the bars, then another, refusing to meet his eyes lest she lose her courage. Another step would put her within his reach.

She took it, bracing herself for the whip of the chain around her throat. When it didn't come, she knelt and laid her offering just outside the bars, where he could reach it without straining. The angular flare of his calves and wide boned feet filled her vision.

She smoothed back the edges of the crested napkin, freeing the spicy aroma of ginger and molasses. "I remembered how gingerbread was always your favorite. You used to drive the cook mad, stealing it from the kitchen before it cooled."

Fearful of the scorn she might read on his face, she turned and started up the tunnel. A mouse was already creeping out of his nest to investigate. He stood up on his hind legs, whiskers twitching as he whiffed the air. At least someone would benefit from her folly, she thought, dashing away a stray tear before Morgan could see it.

Morgan's fingers bit into the bars as he watched Sabrina go. His gaze dropped to the generous slab of cake at his feet, then shot back to the end of the tunnel, where Sabrina paused to peer both ways before plunging into the darkness. His gaze drifted to the cake again. His nostrils twitched at its pungent scent. His stomach contracted with hunger. The mouse inched toward the napkin, its tiny claws skittering on the stones.

Sabrina darted past the mouth of the tunnel again, flitting like a ghost through the oily blackness. Morgan watched her patter past three more times before growling an oath under his breath.

"Woman!" he barked.

Silence, then she reappeared, her face a pale oval against the darkness. Morgan wrenched his candle from its sconce, tearing loose its tallow moorings, and thrust it through the bars.

"Take it."

"Oh, but I really couldn't. You'd be left in the dark until the guards returned and—"

"Take it!" he repeated. "I want you the hell out of here. You're ruinin' my bloody appetite."

Their fingers brushed as she took the candle from him. Neither of them paid any attention to the spatter of hot tallow against their skin. She cupped her palm around the flame, stubbornly refusing to let the draft seize it.

"Brat?" he whispered, wanting to give her something more for all she had given him. A grimy candle couldn't compare to the courage it must have taken for her to creep into this damp hell and offer him comfort for his grief.

"Yes, Morgan?" she answered primly.

"Tell your mother the next time she points a gun at a MacDonnell, she'd best take care 'tis loaded with more than feathers. Alex ambushed me countless times with that toy when we were but lads."

Sabrina blinked up at him, her eyes so wide and confounded, he was afraid he might kiss her. He reached through the bars and gave her a gentle shove toward the mouth of the tunnel.

Then she was gone, taking the light with her.

Morgan gripped the bars, haunted by the seeds of doubt she'd planted in his mind. Had his hatred of the Camerons blinded him more surely than the darkness? What if she were right? What if it was not a Cameron hand that had wielded the blade that killed his father, but the hand of a treacherous stranger? Even as he pondered her words, he cursed her beauty. If it hadn't been for the distraction of her comely face, he would have been noting the comings and goings in the hall prior to his father's death with his usual thoroughness for detail.

Part of him still could not believe Angus was dead. His grief was tinged with bitterness. In his mouth lay the ashes of a lifetime of words bitten back and left unspoken. Now that his father was gone, he had no choice but to swallow them.

Morgan crouched and groped through the bars until his fingers found the warm, crumbly mass of cake. A furry body brushed his hand and shied away, squeaking in protest.

"Hush now, wee fellow," he murmured. "I'll not rob you of your fair share." He tore off a corner of the gingerbread, then smiled to hear the satisfied scrabbling that followed.

For the next few minutes Morgan hunched against the bars, cramming fingerfuls of gingerbread into his mouth. Long after it was gone, he found its taste still tempered the bitterness of his grief with sweetness.

Chapter Five

Dougal was in the solar a week after Angus's murder, polishing the blade of the claymore he'd found mysteriously stuffed beneath the Egyptian settee, when his wife stormed in, slamming the door behind her with enough force to waver the candle flames.

She blew a coppery tendril out of her eyes. "I do hope you're sharpening that blade to use on Morgan MacDonnell's thick neck."

Dougal lifted an eyebrow, half wishing his clansmen could see her now. As their mistress, she was the very model of genteel decorum. Her soft-spoken commands brooked no disobedience, yet only in his presence did all of her fire leap to the surface. Dougal delighted in it, for with that fire came the bright, burning passions of a woman, not a lady.

He removed a gilded mirror from above the mantel and hung the sword in its place, admiring the addition of its clean masculine lines to this feminine domain. "Is there something you wish to discuss, dear?" he asked mildly.

With a wordless exclamation of rage, Elizabeth whirled to pace the room, her pagoda sleeves rippling with each step. Her hands darted out, caressing her delicate treasures as if to derive comfort from them.

She had beautiful hands, their tapered lines broken only by his ruby betrothal ring. They were an artist's hands, God-designed not for painting or sculpting, but for nursing the living things in her garden. Dougal would have sworn he'd seen roses unfurl their petals toward the sun at the faintest brush of her fingertips. After twenty-three years of marriage, her touch still had the same effect on him.

She spun around. "It's been seven days and you've done nothing. A hundred years ago you might have been master and king of these lands, but we are under English law now. Why haven't you summoned the soldiers and had him taken away?"

Dougal wished he were a king. He needed the wisdom of a Solomon to make the decision confronting him. Some stubborn ancestral spirit recoiled at the image of English redcoats invading his home. "On what charge, Beth? Grief? Helpless rage at watching his own da cut down before his eyes? Those are transgressions in neither the eyes of the king nor the Lord."

"What about the transgression he committed against your daughter? She's hardly touched her food since. I hear her pacing her chamber at all hours of the night. Why, she may never recover!"

Dougal suspected his wife was right, although his reasons differed drastically from her own. "What would you have me do? Flog him publicly? Hang him?"

Her smooth brow furrowed. "My brother William has connections. I'm sure the British Navy would be delighted to accept such a strapping creature into their service."

Dougal rarely raised his voice to his wife; his even tone conveyed his disappointment much more effectively. "So you propose I have him impressed into the navy against his will. As I recall, you were always the first to champion the lad. 'Starved for a mother's touch,' you'd say, 'but too stiff-necked with pride to accept it.' Why this sudden vindictiveness?"

Elizabeth dropped her gaze. They both knew her proposal had less to do with vengeance than fear. Fear of the way Morgan had looked at her daughter. The way he had touched her.

"Free him, then. Send him home," she whispered.

Dougal's own frustrations erupted in a hoarse oath. His burr thickened as he rose, dragging a hand through his hair. "Then what, Beth? Morgan believes we committed 'Murder under trust,' the most heinous crime known to any Highlander. His men think we're no better than those wretched Campbells who massacred the poor MacDonalds in their beds at Glencoe. Do you think he'll just trot home with his tail tucked betwixt his legs?"

Elizabeth shook her head mutely. Tears shimmered on her lashes.

Fearful of being swayed by them, Dougal paced to the window. The bonfire raging on the opposite hill brought the hellish stench of smoke and ashes wafting into the chamber, chased by the ceaseless wail of the bagpipes. Angus's plaid-shrouded corpse presided over their dark merriment.

"Barbarians," Elizabeth whispered. "They won't let us bury him, yet they had the nerve to steal a barrel of brine and vinegar to soak his wrappings." She shuddered. "Why, if the days weren't getting cooler . . ."

"From the looks of him, I suspect Angus was already well pickled before the blade found its mark." Dougal jerked the window shut hard enough to rattle the beveled panes. "The rest of the MacDonnells might be more concerned with revelry than revenge, but Morgan's a Highlander through blood and bone. He won't rest until he's had retribution. Not on the tidy confines of a battlefield, but in a moonlit glade when Alex is riding home from a stag hunt or in a deserted alley when Brian is sneaking out the bedroom window of that milkmaid he's been courting." He faced his wife. "I'm not willing to shed the blood of Morgan or my sons for the sake of stubborn pride. Not Cameron pride or MacDonnell pride."

Elizabeth straightened her shoulders with visible effort. "Very well. If we don't convince the MacDonnells we're not murderers, I'll be setting an empty table for my fancy suppers. I doubt Lady Fraser or the MacPhersons would care to dine with us if they fear we might poison their pudding or skewer them with the poultry pick."

Dougal would never have belittled her civilized fripperies. They were the very interests that made her so feminine—so essentially his Elizabeth.

He reached for her hand, but she allowed him only the briefest squeeze before withdrawing it. "I concede to your wisdom. Do what you must, Dougal, to preserve your precious peace." She lifted her skirts in a regal curtsy, then left him, closing the door softly behind her.

Dougal sank against the windowsill, rubbing his beard. Whoever had struck this blow against both Cameron and MacDonnell had struck well and deep. All of his inquiries had turned up nothing. In the chaos following the stabbing, the villain had fled without leaving a single clue to his identity.

Surely even Elizabeth would understand that Angus's assassination had forced Dougal's hand. If he wanted to hold up his head in the Highlands and safeguard the future of his clan as well as the future of his children, he had only one choice. He must give the chieftain of the MacDonnells an irrevocable emblem of his trust—a treasure of such exquisite value that Morgan could never again doubt his goodwill. A treasure Dougal had been holding in trust for the lad for twelve sweet years.

He gazed at the closed door, praying his decision wouldn't cost him his wife as well. God might forgive him for his scheming, but he wasn't sure Elizabeth ever would. Behind him, the wild, haunting notes of the pipes pierced the Florentine glass as if to taunt him about what the morrow would bring.

· · ·

Frantic to escape the maddening skirl of the bagpipes, Sabrina dragged the comforter over her head and burrowed beneath her pillow. From the foot of her half-testered bed, Pugsley lifted his head and growled deep in his throat. Still the pipes played on, their untamed melody luring Sabrina far beyond the sturdy walls of the manor that had enclosed her all her life. Ignoring Pugsley's snarl of protest, she threw back the blankets and padded barefoot to the window.

She drew it open. A frosted pearl of a moon dipped low over the foothills. Her breath caught in her throat at the sight silhouetted against its luminous backdrop.

Tongues of flame from a roaring bonfire licked at the night. Sparks shot skyward only to be caught by the wind and tossed like a handful of rebellious stars back into their heavenly fold. Shadowy figures cavorted and danced within its halo of light, their tartans flapping behind them like wings.

Sabrina knew that had she stood among them, the scene would have lost its romance. She would have heard the profanity, seen the drunken stumbling and recoiled in horror from Angus's shrouded corpse laid out like a pagan sacrifice in their midst. But from the cozy distance of her second-story window, their revelry wove its own dark enchantment.

The Highlanders danced wild and free, unfettered by the manners and conventions so prized by her mother. All of her life Sabrina had been lovingly snipped and pruned like one of Elizabeth's blooms, groomed to someday travel to England and take her rightful place in the illustrious Belmont family. But sometimes when the thunder came down from the mountains in mighty drumrolls, her soul yearned to ramble like the wild Highland roses that tangled their thorny briers through fern-choked glens and stony rills.

The song of the pipes made her ache to flee the staid silence of the manor in these wee hours of night. Her feet itched to caper across the dew-drenched meadow. To dance and leap across the fire and risk being engulfed in its ravenous flames to win a taste of its heat and magic.

She sank down on the window seat. Morgan should be among his own kind, not buried beneath the same stones that sheltered her. For a week he'd been deprived of the crisp autumn breezes and the precious warmth of the sun that spent the shortening days baking the heather to vibrant purple.

Several times since she'd visited him she had found herself teetering on the edge of those steep stairs as if on the brink of some momentous decision. Once she had awakened as if from a daze to find Morgan's pistol hidden in the folds of her skirt.

His last words still haunted her. He had known her mother's gun was a bluff, yet he had allowed himself to be taken, to be caged like an animal at her father's mercy. Why? she wondered. Then she would remember the leering faces of his clansmen. They had been whipped to a lust-crazed frenzy even Morgan might have been hard pressed to dampen. But why would Morgan make a sacrifice as dear as his freedom for a girl he could hardly tolerate—a Cameron no less? Guilt and doubt plagued her, poisoning her dreams until she feared to sleep.

She laid her cheek against the cool wood of the timbered frame. A lone figure stood silhouetted on the crest of the hill, coaxing a plaintive wail from the ponderous pipes. A cloud gusted across the horizon, then raced on. The moon poured its liquid beams over the player.

Sabrina blinked in astonishment. She would have almost sworn it was not a man, but the slender figure of a woman playing the pipes, her unbound hair whipping molten silver in the wind.

The tune was no longer the discordant wheeze that had tormented them for days, but a raw and melodious plea to a goddess older than time itself. Sabrina drew the window shut, but still the song wept on, crying for Angus, crying for Morgan, as only the heart of a woman could.

She clambered back into bed, surprised to find her own cheeks bathed in tears.

The next morning a polite tap sounded on Sabrina's door. She moaned a protest and nestled deeper into the mattress. The sky had melted from black to gray before she had finally cried herself into an exhausted slumber. Pugsley aided in the efforts to rouse her by snagging the comforter with his tooth and dragging it off her upturned rump.

She sat up, rubbing her eyes. Before the knocking commenced again, another sound assailed her.

Silence. Pure, blessed silence. Fear and excitement tightened her chest. She plunged from the bed and ran to the window.

The hillside was deserted. Ribbons of smoke curled from a mass of charred firewood to mingle with the morning mist.

Her mother poked her head around the door. "Dress with haste, darling. Your father is convening court and he requests your presence."

"Court? But why?"

Elizabeth frowned. "I honestly cannot say. But we should all be there to support him if that is his wish."

Sabrina knew better than to disobey that dulcet note of command. Terrified she might miss something of interest, she wasted no time ringing for a maid, but instead buckled the tapes of her own paniers and left off her corset altogether. After sliding a gown of deep lavender silk over her starched petticoats and struggling with the tiny buttons of the bodice, she twisted her hair into a severe knot. Her reflection in the mirror gave her pause. With her dark gown and the matching shadows beneath her eyes, she looked as if she was already in mourning.

A shiver touched her spine. Her father had never before convened an old-fashioned Highland court of justice. It was surely a slap in the face to the MacDonnells to remind them that as long as they trespassed upon Cameron lands, her father was both lord and master of their fates, his word more sacrosanct than any English magistrate's could ever hope to be. She could not help but envision her papa accused of murdering Angus and tossed on the mercy of a MacDonnell court. She suspected most of their justice would be meted out by the honed blade of an ax. Her heartbeat quickened. Was her papa about to condemn Morgan to some fate even more terrible than imprisonment?

"Don't forget the time the rascal poured honey in all of your slippers," she reminded her worried reflection. "Hanging would be no better than he deserved."

She jerked out a sprinkling of saucy tendrils before sailing from the room with Pugsley huffing and puffing at her satin-clad heels.

After leaving Pugsley in the kitchen to gum a saucer of gruel, Sabrina entered the hall to find its face transformed yet again. Her mother's graceful furniture had been shoved aside to make room for rows of crude benches and a raised dais crowned with a single carved chair. The hall was thronged with the elders of the clan and several ancient villagers. In their dour, wrinkled visages she read memories of other Cameron courts and judgments. Sabrina wondered if her father was breaking the English laws by daring to convene a court that boldly placed his authority as laird of Clan Cameron over the king's.

One of Sabrina's uncles twisted around to give her a fond wink as she slid onto a bench next to Enid. "Have I missed anything?" she whispered.

Enid shook her head, her face flushed with excitement. "Not a word. It's as if they've been waiting for something."

Sabrina had no further opportunity to question her cousin. At her father's signal, the main door was flung open.

Sabrina's heart fluttered like the fragile wings of one of her mother's finches. Morgan stood in the doorway, proud and free, his plaid draped in folds across his mighty shoulders like the mantle of a king. The morning sunlight slanted behind him, wreathing his hair in gold and sheening the blade of the ax hanging from his belt to dull copper.

Enid leaned over to whisper, "From what I can gather, Uncle Dougal freed him at dawn and commanded he appear before the court with his kin. There was a terrible row when your brothers tried to convince your papa the MacDonnell would take his clansmen and flee to the mountains for reinforcements."

No, Sabrina thought. Morgan was one MacDonnell who would run from nothing. And she was the only Cameron who knew that there were no reinforcements waiting in the mountains.

Morgan's clansmen clustered in a protective knot around him, their hands resting on the hilts and butts of their weapons. Some were obviously still suffering ill effects from the night's revelry. One pale lad stumbled over the stoop and would have fallen flat had his nearest companion not righted and cuffed him in the same clumsy motion.

Morgan stepped forward. Sabrina had never seen a man surrounded by so many look so alone. She squelched a pang of empathy.

For an elusive instant before he spoke, Sabrina would have sworn she felt her father's gaze brush her. Then his lilting burr filled the hall, unwittingly echoing the words she had spoken to Morgan twelve years earlier. "Welcome to Cameron, Morgan MacDonnell."

The greeting was given as if the man hadn't spent the previous week imprisoned beneath this very hall. There was a long pause, then an audible sigh of relief from the benches when Morgan curtly inclined his head in acceptance. Brian and Alex stepped forward from the crowd to escort him to the dais. Escort or guard? Sabrina wondered, noting the way Morgan dwarfed her lean brothers. The crowd gave way like water before their path. Morgan's gaze passed over her without so much as a flicker of recognition.

Sabrina squirmed on the bench, ignoring Enid's

puzzled look. Morgan was obviously going to be judged for daring to accost the laird's daughter.

How could she allow Morgan to march so stoically to his fate without speaking even a word in his defense? Perhaps if her father knew the true circumstances of his surrender, he might soften his judgment. As Morgan had so unkindly but truthfully pointed out, Dougal Cameron had yet to deny his only daughter anything.

Before she realized she was going to do it, Sabrina jumped to her feet and cried out, "Wait!" Instead of the forceful command she'd envisioned, her voice came out as a mere yelp.

Morgan pivoted on the stairs to the dais. His green eyes blazed, warning her that he cared for nothing she had to say, be it condemnation or defense. Surely he would scorn her pity even more than her rancor. Could she blame him? How could he ever hope to lead a group of rogues such as these if they realized he had surrendered himself to an unarmed woman? He would become a laughingstock, all of his hard-earned respect lost.

She cleared her throat, feeling as if she'd swallowed a mouse. "Pardon me. I sat on a splinter."

"I've got somethin' the lass can sit on!" came a cry from the back of the hall.

"Aye, Fergus, but 'tis smaller than any splinter!" yelled another, eliciting a burst of ugly sniggers from the MacDonnells.

Sabrina sank down on the bench, wishing she could crawl beneath it. Her cheeks burned beneath the heat of her mother's disapproving gaze.

As Morgan sat in the chair on the dais, Dougal swept out a hand toward an empty bench near the front of the hall. "I've cleared a bench for the MacDonnell elders. Their wisdom and opinions are welcome in my court."

There was a flurry of pushing and scrabbling of feet along the back wall. A thin, graying man stumbled from the MacDonnell ranks, propelled forward by his clansmen. He shuffled to the front of the court and took a seat, only to be dwarfed by the long, empty bench. Morgan ignored the embarrassing display. The MacDonnell way of life must not be conducive to longevity, Sabrina deduced. Had Angus been their only elder?

Dougal locked his hands at the small of his back, commanding the court's attention. "As laird of Clan Cameron, I have convened this court today to see that justice is served."

An approving murmur rose from Sabrina's clansmen. Justice, they believed, would surely mean the downfall of the heathen MacDonnells.

Dougal continued. "We are here today to arbitrate a fine to compensate the chieftain of the MacDonnells for the shameful and untimely slaying of his father."

A shocked buzz rippled through the room. Sabrina's mouth fell open. It was not Morgan, but her father who had come to be sentenced by his own court. His request for arbitration was tantamount to a confession of guilt. Her mother looked as stunned as she; Brian and Alex both paled until their freckles stood out in sharp relief.

The Cameron lifted his hand. The resulting silence was immediate and fraught with tension. "I maintain my innocence in the murder of Angus MacDonnell. 'Twas not my doing nor that of any of my kin. But since the MacDonnell was under the sacred protection of Cameron hospitality when his death occurred, I will pay the fine required by our ancient and revered laws."

Sabrina could almost read her mother's mind. Gaelic laws. Not English laws.

An anonymous cry came from the benches. "Aye, and if the ol' villain had stayed home, where he belonged, he might yet be alive!"

A MacDonnell sword flashed, but Morgan's warning glance stayed it.

"'Twas by my invitation that Angus MacDonnell came to Cameron," Dougal replied. He turned to Morgan. "Morgan Thayer MacDonnell, are you prepared to accept the judgment of this court for the slaying of your father?"

Morgan leaned back in the chair, resting his ankle

on his opposite knee with arrogant grace. "What choice do I have?"

I would have crawled for them. They're all I have. All I am.

As Morgan's words rushed back through her mind, Sabrina twisted to see the men scattered along the back wall. What did Morgan see when he looked into their jaded eyes? A shadow of remembered pride? A shred of former glory?

Dougal faced the lone old man trembling on the bench. "And the MacDonnell elders?" he said with respect as if the man's opinion bore the weight of emperors' and kings'.

"Aye," he whispered timidly, then broke into a toothless grin as a cheer went up from his clansmen.

An irreverent smile played around Morgan's lips. "Go on, Cameron. Do your worst. I'll get two goats, you'll get a slap on the hand, and we can all go home."

Sabrina's great-uncle Robert climbed the steps to join them. Sabrina was surprised that her father did not intend to pronounce the judgment himself. Robert stood before his nephew. "Do you in turn agree to abide by the judgment of this court, Dougal Cameron?"

"I do."

Her father left the dais and went to sit beside his wife. As he gripped her hand, his knuckles went white with tension.

Robert unrolled a sheet of vellum even longer than his snowy beard and adjusted his gold spectacles. "Very well. All listen carefully to this judgment. It will stand with the authority granted it by these two chieftains. The following is paid by the Cameron and awarded to the MacDonnell—two hundred sheep, a hundred head of cattle . . ."

As her uncle's quavering voice droned on, Sabrina studied Morgan. He yawned, then drew out a menacing dirk and began to pare his fingernails. His affectation of boredom did not fool her. His eyes glittered behind his curtain of hair.

". . . two hundred chickens, three cases of fine Scotch whisky . . ." This drew a cheer from the flagging MacDonnells. ". . . his ceremonial claymore, the Cameron betrothal ring . . ."

Sabrina flinched in sympathy. She'd never in her memory seen that ring leave her mother's hand.

". . . and his daughter, Sabrina, in holy matrimony."

Morgan's dirk clattered to the dais. A deathly pall of silence fell over the hall. The sole MacDonnell elder went blue around the lips. Sabrina lifted her head, not even daring to breathe as Morgan came out of the chair, his hands still braced on the carved arms as if for support. Their gazes met across the sea of people between them.

A staccato burst of laughter escaped him. His words were for Dougal, but his eyes were all for Sabrina.

"For God's sake, man, show me a wee bit of mercy! Can't you give me four hundred chickens and spare me the bloody daughter?"

Chapter Six

The court erupted in chaos. Elizabeth gave an agonized cry and burst into tears. Brian unsheathed his sword and dove for Morgan. Alex caught his brother around the waist before he could reach the stairs. Swords and dirks cleared sheaths with a steady hiss. The MacDonnell elder took advantage of the confusion to creep back into his clan's fold. Dougal stroked his beard, his eyes impassive as the hall teetered on the brink of war.

For the first time, Sabrina understood the wrenching betrayal Morgan must have felt when he believed her father had deceived him. Her papa could have cut her no deeper had he plunged a dirk into her heart. At least Angus's wound was fatal. She had been given a life sentence.

Morgan sank back in the chair, his hearty laughter dying to a chuckle. He grinned stupidly at Sabrina, making her wonder for an instant what it might feel like to fight *for* this man instead of against him. For years she'd tried in vain to wring a smile from his surly countenance. But only the prospect of being bound to her in unholy wedlock was enough to awaken his latent good humor. A devilish twinkle lit his eyes, forcing a shiver of reaction through her. Her worst nightmare was coming true. If her father had his way, she would be completely at Morgan's mercy.

And she knew from past experience that he had none.

Sunlight flashed on an ax hefted by a MacDonnell with even fewer teeth than Pugsley. Dougal leapt to the dais and roared, "Enough! Restrain your men, Morgan. They can ill afford a battle pitched in the midst of Cameron lands."

Morgan subdued his clansmen with a choked command.

Dougal turned to him. "I believe we'd both prefer to continue this discussion in private."

"Don't do it, Morgan! 'Tis a trap!" one of his men cried out.

"Aye, and a canny one at that," Morgan said, his gaze almost admiring as he assessed Dougal. "Ranald, take the men and await me on the hill. I'll send word."

His clansmen hovered on the brink of rebellion, but when they saw the Cameron's own men rising to leave, they obeyed. Sabrina saw a slender figure shrouded in a tattered plaid hang back for a moment before limping after the others. Enid rose and tried to tiptoe away, her terror of conflict even stronger than her devotion to her cousin.

"Oh, no, you don't!" Sabrina said, jerking her back by the box pleats of her skirt. "You'll not abandon me too."

After a hissed exchange with Dougal, Elizabeth joined them, wrapping a protective arm around her daughter. Brian and Alex stood near the dais, Alex simmering and Brian shooting looks of open fury at Morgan.

Sabrina was not immune to the frank glances of sympathy her kin gave her as they filed past. She was the one condemned by this court to life with a man who despised her.

Pride infused her spine. She lifted her head to find her father standing in front of her. She fixed her gaze on the sapphire brooch pinning his jabot at his throat, unable to look at the face she had loved so well and so long.

"'Twould be best if you left us alone, daughter," he said gently. "Morgan and I have affairs to discuss."

She locked her chin to keep it from quivering. "Since I am part and parcel of those affairs, I choose to remain."

"Does that suit you, Morgan?" Dougal asked.

Morgan lifted his shoulders in an expansive shrug. "As long as she is prepared to hear what I have to say."

He jumped down from the dais and paced before the benches, his long, restless strides betraying the fury rumbling beneath his humor. "What makes you think I'd care to be saddled with your brat, Cameron?"

Dougal steepled his fingers under his chin. "You find her beautiful, don't you? I've seen the way you look at her."

For the second time that day, Sabrina wanted to dive beneath the bench. Morgan turned on his heel. He had obviously expected fluent political arguments. Dougal's candor disarmed him.

He cast Sabrina a look as provocative as it was insulting. Her skin heated beneath a lazy assessment that swept from the tiny silver buckles that adorned her slippers to the crown of her head. "The lass might be a pleasant enough diversion for an afternoon. But not for a lifetime."

Brian growled. "Why you son of a—" Alex caught his brother's hand before it could reach his sword hilt.

Dougal refused to rise to Morgan's baiting. "Your clan will not survive a war."

"And war is what they'll get if I don't wed your daughter? Are you so eager to be shed of the lass? Can't you foist her off on one of her more desperate Cameron cousins?"

Sabrina shook off her mother's embrace and

jumped to her feet, trembling with rage. "I'll have you know, Morgan MacDonnell, I've been fending off proposals since I was thirteen. But unlike the MacDonnells, we Camerons frown on wedding our cousins." She sat, then popped back up. "Or our sisters!"

Her mother drew her down. Morgan and her father returned to their discussion as if she had not spoken, infuriating her further.

"The Grants and the Chisholms have been breathing down your neck for months, lad," Dougal said. "If you're to preserve what your ancestors built, you need an ally. A powerful ally. With Sabrina as your wife, you'll have one. Me."

Morgan turned his back on them all, his fists clenched as if he were waging some private war that had little to do with clans or allies. He finally swung around, giving Sabrina a dark look. "Verra well." Sarcasm laced his words. "My *bride* and I will leave Cameron tonight."

"That you will not," Dougal said. "You will spend your first night as man and wife beneath my roof."

Morgan arched a mocking eyebrow. "Why? The better to hear her screams?"

Brian's sword cleared its sheath, but Sabrina pushed past him before he could wield it. "Pardon me. May I interrupt you gentlemen for a word with my betrothed?"

Dougal and Morgan exchanged a look, unexpected allies at that moment. They had expected female hysteria. Sabrina's icy dignity plainly unnerved them both.

Her father nodded and stepped back, leaving her to face Morgan alone. He stared down his nose at her, legs akimbo, hands locked at the small of his back.

Sabrina tipped her head back to look him in the eye, giving him the full effect of her regal sniff. "Make your decision with care, Morgan MacDonnell." She mimicked her mother's flawless British diction without realizing it. "For I swear I will not give you an afternoon's pleasure. I'll not give you even a moment's pleasure."

He rocked back on his heels. "I expected no more from a spoiled shrew. Why do you think I asked for the chickens?"

"If you marry me, you'll wish you'd got them."

Morgan could not resist baiting her just as he'd done as a boy. He leaned down until his nose almost touched hers and gave her an infuriating grin. "I already do."

Sabrina resisted the urge to plant her fist square in the middle of his smug face. The fragile truce they had forged in the solar lay scattered at her feet like the shards of her pride. She snapped her skirts around and marched from the hall, knowing in her heart that she had already made one fatal mistake.

She should never have stopped hating Morgan MacDonnell.

Dougal longed to press his palms over his ears.

Between Enid's blubbering and the rhythmic sniffling of the maids laboring over Sabrina's wedding gown, he wished himself anywhere else in the world. He would have gladly faced a legion of MacDonnells, all armed and roaring for his blood, before spending another moment in this solar of hysterical women.

But worse than the keening of the servants, most of whom had adored his daughter from birth, was his wife's accusing, dry-eyed stare. It impaled him to his place by the window, challenging him to stay and witness the havoc he had wreaked. Elizabeth's graceful hands flew, jabbing a needle through a thick slab of leather as if she wished it were his heart.

With her usual aplomb she had thrown the entire household into the frantic preparations for the wedding to be held that night, as if hoping mindless bustle might stave off panic. Even Enid had been swaddled in an apron and handed a bowl of vegetables to chop. Dougal doubted they would require salting. Enid's tears were running in a steady stream down her quivering chin and into the bowl.

Elizabeth rose from the settee to snap off a fresh

volley of commands. "Aggie, run and fetch a sharp pair of shears." She peered into the bowl braced between Enid's ample knees. "Good heavens, child, those aren't mushrooms. They're toadstools. Fish them out or we'll have another dead MacDonnell on our hands tonight."

Enid obeyed with a fresh wail. The fragile legs of the Turkish ottoman teetered beneath her weight.

Elizabeth paused before the shimmering blue confection that had once been her own wedding dress. "Careful, girls. I won't tolerate a single water spot on that satin." She jerked a lace handkerchief from her bodice, held it to the pinkened nose of a dimpled young maid, and snapped, "Blow!"

Dougal gritted his teeth. The maids were handling the pearl-studded satin as if it were a burial shroud.

The door flew open. It was not Aggie returning from her errand, but Sabrina, her eyes brimming with tears. Dougal saw his own dread mirrored in their sapphire depths. Enid's wails died to sniffles. The maids' trembling fingers dropped stitches, unraveling the work they'd done.

She flung herself across the solar and clutched his ruffled shirtfront. "Papa, you must relent. You cannot force me to marry such a hateful man. You heard him. He despises me. He despises us all. Why, he'd as soon wed Pugsley as me!"

Dougal gently caught her wrists. "I have no choice, lass. Perhaps someday you'll understand."

She turned away from him. "I shall never understand."

He rested his hands on her shoulders. "Aye, my princess, there will come a day when you shall."

Sabrina pulled away from him and ran to Elizabeth. "Please, Mama, surely you can soften his heart. He would do anything for you."

Elizabeth cupped her daughter's cheek in her palm. "I've already tried, darling. His mind is set."

Sabrina slowly turned, her eyes overflowing with mute entreaty. She walked toward him—the man who had carried her on his shoulders through the village, who had tickled her cheek with his beard until she squealed with laughter, who had devoted his life to granting her smallest wish—and dropped to her knees at his feet. Dougal wondered if the others could hear the crack of his heart breaking.

She bowed her head. A solitary tear splashed on his buckled shoe. "If you do this thing, you'll have your peace, Papa. But you'll doom me to a life of battle."

Sabrina was the only one who didn't see his hand reach toward the softness of her hair, then veer away. He yearned to make her understand, to tell her of the hopes and dreams he'd cherished in his heart for years, but he knew that some truths were better discovered in their own time. "I am as bound by the laws of the court as any other man. I swore to abide by them, and as my daughter 'tis your duty to do the same." His voice softened. "Go now and prepare to make your vows."

She rose and walked to the door. As she faced him, a current as palpable as lightning flashed between their eyes of identical color. "How will I ever forgive you for this?"

Even after she was gone, her helpless question hung like a torn thread in the air. Enid broke into fresh sobs, flung her apron over her face, and fled the solar, trailing vegetables in her wake. The maids politely withdrew. Dougal sank against the windowsill, rubbing his aching temples.

Elizabeth's eyes blazed a cold fire. "How dare you speak of duty to that child? 'Twas your idea to wed her to that heathen, and no one else's. Tell me—have you nursed this plot in your cunning brain since they were but children? How will she survive life with a man who detests her?"

"Morgan does not detest her," he said wearily. "You know it as well as I."

"But does he know it? And will he destroy her before he discovers it? Sabrina is like the rarest rose— sweet-natured, gentle, docile. We've never taught her to fight for herself."

A wistful smile touched his lips. "She was doing an able job of it this morning."

Elizabeth swept up her scraps of leather. "If you'll excuse me, I'm going to prepare your lamb for the sacrifice. You swore you wouldn't shed the blood of your sons, but you seem only too eager to shed the blood of your daughter." She wrenched his betrothal ring from her finger and hurled it at him. "Give that to your precious Morgan as well. *'Tis your duty.*"

The door slammed behind her, rattling a miniature family portrait from the wall.

Dougal toyed with the ring, stroking the beveled planes of the glowing ruby. "Ah, Morgan, if my wee princess is half as docile as her mama, 'twill take far more than a ring to bind her."

Sabrina and Enid lifted their tear-streaked faces to find Elizabeth standing in the doorway of her daughter's bedchamber.

She nodded to Enid. "'Tis best you go now, dear. I must speak to your cousin alone."

Still gripping her bowl of wilting vegetables, Enid stepped outside the door, only to have it slammed behind her. It seemed an eternity before her aunt emerged to stalk off down the corridor without another word for her.

Enid crept back into the room. Sabrina sat on the edge of the bed, eyes glazed and mouth ajar. She had gone stark white, her cheeks robbed of the roses that usually bloomed there.

Enid set aside the bowl and passed a hand over her cousin's line of vision. Sabrina didn't even blink.

Truly frightened now, Enid gave Sabrina's shoulder a harsh shake. "Cousin! What is it? What did she say to you?"

Sabrina blinked. Her voice was barely audible. "She told me what I could expect from the marriage bed."

"Oh, is that all?" Enid plopped down on the bed, then remembering herself, affected a look of wide-eyed horror. "Is it so dreadful?"

Sabrina shuddered. "Horrible!" Her eyes finally

focused. She cupped a hand around Enid's ear and whispered into it.

Enid gave a satisfying gasp. "No! She must have been jesting. He couldn't possibly put . . . that"— her voice rose to an excited squeak—"*there*."

Sabrina nodded solemnly, then whispered something else.

"Oh, dear Lord!" Enid felt her eyes roll back in her head at the thought. Sabrina fished in Enid's pocket, pulled out the bottle of hartshorn, and waved it under Enid's nose. Enid fanned herself with her hand, hiding her dreamy smile. "Imagine doing that with such a strapping . . . male . . . animal."

Shaking off her shock, Sabrina jumped down from the bed to pace. "Oh, that's only the beginning. It gets worse. Much worse. Perhaps I should kill myself. After I'm dead, they can lay me out in the drawing room in my wedding gown. Papa can kiss my wan, cold cheek if he dares."

Fresh tears sprang to Enid's eyes at the vision of her noble cousin meeting such an ignoble end. "Perhaps Morgan's not the monster you imagine. Might some part of him not be amenable to taking a wife?"

"No doubt. And thanks to Mama, I now know exactly which part."

Her burst of energy spent, Sabrina dragged herself back to the bed and sank down beside Enid. "I swore I wouldn't give him a moment's pleasure, but it seems a man will seek his pleasure how he chooses and a woman's will means nothing. Even before Morgan believed the Camerons murdered his father, he despised me. What's to stop him from slaking all of his rage on me? What if he decides to make me pay for all the Cameron crimes against his family, both real and imagined?"

Enid saw Morgan's face in her mind—stern, forbidding, beautiful even at its most mocking. She shivered. "How you must hate him!"

Sabrina bowed her head. "Would to God that I could."

It was not her cousin's lack of tears that rent

Enid's heart, but her quiet despair. She touched Sabrina's hair. It was soft and thick and so much more lovely than her own wispy blond strands.

Sabrina was the brave one. She had been Enid's friend from their very first meeting. Shamed at being banished from London, Enid had been sniveling in her bedchamber when a fat, hairy spider had cornered her on the bed. It had been Sabrina who calmly scooped up the puzzled little fellow and escorted him to the window before drying Enid's hysterical tears. Frustration now swelled in her. Even if there was something she could do to help Sabrina, she knew she would lack the courage.

Helplessly she patted Sabrina's shoulder, forgetting the bowl of vegetables, which tumbled to the rug. A plump toadstool bounced across Enid's foot.

As she bent to pick it up, her pale eyes narrowed with a fierce determination Sabrina wouldn't have recognized. "Perhaps your Morgan will find his taste for revenge more bitter than he expects."

Morgan stumbled over the stoop, biting off a blasphemy that caused every head in the candlelit kirk to swivel in his direction. Ranald stepped on his heels. Morgan threw back his shoulders, tacitly warning every Cameron who had come to witness this farce of a wedding that their first chuckle at this MacDonnell's expense would be their last.

It was a miracle he could walk at all with the damnable leather flaps cinched to his feet. He had no need of sandals! His own soles had been toughened to callused hide by traipsing over heath and hills, stones and briers, all his life. Had his future mother-in-law not braved the derision of his men to deliver them, he would have given in to his temptation to fling them into the baptismal font.

He should have known his men were up to no good that afternoon when they'd lapsed into stunned silence. They'd been teasing him mercilessly ever since he'd laundered both himself and his plaid in the icy waters of a rushing burn.

He had parried their taunts as he hung the plaid over a tree branch to dry.

"Och, Morgan's near as pretty as Ranald when he's clean, ain't he? He'll make a bonny bride for the Cameron wench."

"Careful, lad, that staff twixt yer legs'll shrink if ye get it wet."

"Is that what happened to yours, Fergus?" he replied pleasantly before swinging around to face his tormentors, hands on hips, naked, dripping, and exhibiting bold evidence that Fergus was a shameless liar.

Only it wasn't Fergus standing at the crest of the hill, but Elizabeth Cameron, a basket hanging over one arm and a maidservant cowering behind her. The mistress of Cameron Manor neither blinked nor blushed at the sight of him.

Morgan barely had time to yank the cold, wet plaid around his hips before a pair of sandals slapped him in the chest.

"I cannot find any shoes in the village to fit those slabs of beef you call feet, but I'll not stand by and watch my only daughter wed a barefoot savage."

With those words, she had turned on her heel and marched back toward the manor, regally oblivious of the whistles, applause, and appreciative hoots that followed her.

Morgan's ears burned at the memory. He wondered if Sabrina had inherited her mother's talent for making him look like a bloody fool.

He concentrated on putting one foot in front of the other. He hadn't set foot in a kirk since his last summer at Cameron. Its atmosphere of hushed reverence unnerved him.

Ranald echoed his thoughts. "Too bloody quiet in here," he whispered. "Should have brought me pipes."

"Shhh," Morgan hissed. "Take off your bonnet."

Ranald jerked off the jaunty hat and crumpled it against his chest, eyeing the narrow stained-glass windows as if he expected Jesus and his apostles to stage an ambush. Morgan had wisely left the rest of his clansmen to the casks of ale Dougal had provided. With Angus dead, Ranald was the closest thing he had to true family, and it had been Morgan's choice to have Ranald by his side to witness the vows.

An unexpected pang of loneliness touched him. He missed his da's canny wit and tart tongue. His men cared for nothing but revelry, their chief concern being where their next flagon of ale would come from. At least if Angus were still alive, Morgan would have had someone to discuss his decision with. But if Angus were alive, Morgan wouldn't be traversing this seemingly endless aisle to the altar.

Dougal Cameron stood at the end of that aisle, his bearded face as serene as an angel's. Morgan bit back a growl, torn between suspicion and uncertainty. Was this marriage only a clever ploy to divert attention from Dougal's complicity in Angus's murder? But a father would have to be mad to entrust his daughter into the keeping of a man who would have the legal power to exact the cruelest sort of retribution with no fear of reprisal. And Dougal Cameron was no madman.

His men might be willing to condemn Dougal and gleefully anticipate the revenge Morgan would wreak on the Cameron's fragile daughter, but Morgan found too many flaws in that theory for his satisfaction.

Dougal had also spared them an audience, inviting only his immediate family. As Morgan drew nearer, a blotchy-eyed blond woman crushing a bouquet of wilted flowers stepped aside to reveal his waiting bride.

Suddenly panicked, Morgan froze in his tracks, provoking another stumble and grunt from Ranald. *A bride*. What in God's name was he supposed to do with a bride? His men had given him ample suggestions in the past few hours, none of which bore repeating in the house of the Lord. But not one of those men would appreciate the sacrifice he was about to make. Uniting with Clan Cameron in this unholy alliance would buy them both peace and the time they needed to build Clan MacDonnell to its former glory.

Sweat broke out on his brow. Dougal should have

left him to rot in the dungeon. His life was surely over now, severed not by chains of iron, but of matrimony.

The irony did not escape him. Unlike most of his clansmen, he'd always taken great care where he spilled his seed, lest his freedom be curtailed or his life be ended by an outraged papa waving a musket. Now, due to Dougal's twisted idea of fair compensation, he was being sentenced for a crime he had not committed. Yet.

Fighting the urge to flee, he strode boldly down the aisle. Let no man say Morgan MacDonnell was afraid, especially not of some dainty scrap of a girl. As he approached the altar, Sabrina glowered at him fiercely. It puzzled him until he realized she was only mirroring his own scowl. A cloud of blue satin enveloped her, the color of the sky over the heath on a spring day.

The minister commanded them both to kneel. Morgan stood stiffly at attention. A MacDonnell knelt before no man. Not even a man of God. Sabrina bobbed, then straightened when she realized Morgan had made no move to obey. They glared at each other, neither willing to be the first to bend the knee. The minister rolled his eyes heavenward as if seeking some divine assistance.

It was not God, but Dougal who laid a firm hand on both their shoulders and drove them down.

"Would you join hands? Please?" the minister added, a cajoling note creeping into his tone.

Morgan had spent half his life holding this girl at arm's length. Her unbound hair hid her expression as he lifted her hands in his own. A chaplet of autumn roses crowned her brow. Their haunting fragrance stirred far more than just Morgan's senses.

As the minister rambled on above them, Morgan studied Sabrina's hands. They were cool and smooth in his callused embrace, so delicate he feared he might break them out of sheer clumsiness. An image rose unbidden to his mind—those same hands stroking, gliding, dancing like velvet wings against his heated flesh.

She recited her vows, her voice prim and passionless. As her generous lips compressed to a thin line,

Morgan felt a twinge of regret. If at their first meeting he had scooped her up, dried her baby tears, and accepted her extended hand of friendship, this day might be a day of celebration for both Cameron and MacDonnell. Instead, he had chosen to make her hate him. And judging by her grim expression, he had met with rousing success.

But perhaps it wasn't too late to woo her, he thought. Wouldn't tenderness be his most effective weapon, since it was the last thing she would expect from him? He was already congratulating himself on his shrewdness, when the minister asked him to recite his vows.

Morgan stumbled over the unfamiliar words, then chilled in fresh horror when he was asked to bind their oaths with a ring. He had no ring to give.

"Here you are, lad," Dougal whispered, pressing the Cameron betrothal ring into his hand. "It belongs to you now."

The heavy gold weighted Morgan's palm. He stared down at it, the symbol of everything he hated. It was gaudy, ostentatious, and valuable enough to feed his entire clan for a year. The ruby gleamed like a fat drop of blood. MacDonnell blood shed over the centuries by the Camerons. His first impulse was to throw it right back in Dougal's smug face.

But Sabrina was already holding out her slender finger. A fierce surge of possessiveness seized him. Tenderly or not, tonight it would be Cameron blood shed as he gave her something more binding than any oath or lump of gold. He shoved the ring on her waiting finger more roughly than he intended.

They stood, and the minister gave him leave to kiss his bride.

Morgan was tempted to laugh. Sabrina had squinched her eyes shut and wrinkled her face in such dread that it was obvious she expected a punishing assault to brand her as MacDonnell booty before her family and God.

'Twould be as good a time as any to test the keenness of his weapons, Morgan decided. Ignoring her brothers' baleful glares, he framed Sabrina's face in his hands and gently laid his lips on hers. Caught off guard, they parted at his coaxing. He flicked his tongue against hers in a subtle promise of pleasures to come. As he drew back, the misty wonder reflected on her face made him feel as if he'd just transformed from ogre to prince before her very eyes.

Like *La Belle au Bois Dormante* stirred by her first kiss in one of her mother's favorite nursery tales, Sabrina awoke from the numbing spell of her father's betrayal to find herself wed to a towering heathen who smelled of sunlight and pine. She stared dumbly at the bone bodkin that secured his plaid.

"What is it, lass?" he bent to whisper. "Have you never seen a bodkin before?"

"Is that a human bone?" She ran her fingertip across it.

Morgan's lips touched her hair, snuggling deep to find her ear. His burr deepened. "Aye. Belonged to me first wife, it did. Terribly curious, the lass was. Always pokin' her wee fingers where they didna belong."

Sabrina snatched her hand back, curling it into a protective fist before she realized Morgan's eyes were twinkling with suppressed laughter. The unfamiliar weight of the Cameron betrothal ring cut into her flesh.

Then they were torn apart, Sabrina to endure her mother's tearful embrace and Morgan to accept the grudging congratulations of Alex and Brian. Dougal stood back, beaming in paternal pride.

Ranald took advantage of the chaos to bend Enid over his arm and kiss her wildly. Morgan suspected the poor girl was near swooning, for she didn't seem to be struggling at all. He snatched a handful of his cousin's kilt and heaved him toward the door, leaving the dazed blond gasping for air.

"Eh! What's the bloody rush? I haven't kissed the bride yet!" Ranald protested.

"Nor will you," Morgan snapped. "Not in my lifetime." He hastened after Ranald, believing there might still be a chance of escaping this barbaric ritual with a scrap of his pride intact.

His hopes died as the minister stepped into his path and shoved a quill pen into his hand. He was steered toward the leather-bound register lying open on the altar.

"There you go, lad. Sign your name and 'twill all be official."

Sabrina wiggled out of her mother's hug to find Morgan standing motionless before the altar, a pen gripped like the haft of an ax in his fist. A dull flush suffused his throat.

She had seen that flush before. One rainy summer afternoon when Brian had thrust *The Iliad* at him and insisted it was his turn to read. She had quickly piped up, protesting that her brother had skipped her. But the damage had been done. Morgan had knocked the book away before striding from the solar, never to return except to skulk in the shadows, where he believed no one could see him. But Sabrina had seen. And remembered.

Shoving the startled minister out of her path, she rushed to her husband's side and bestowed an impish grin on him. "It's too late to change your mind now. You're stuck with me."

Beneath the guise of patting his hand, she rearranged his fingers around the pen, dipped it in the ink, and guided his fist in the motion of writing his name. Then she pried the pen from his stiff fingers and signed her name below his with a flourish.

Still scowling, Morgan bent to examine the clumsy loops and elegant spirals that encompassed their names. Sabrina scattered a handful of sand across the signatures before his nose could collide with the fresh ink. Her chaplet of roses tilted, sliding over one eye.

Morgan slowly straightened. Acutely aware of the curious stares of the others, Sabrina kept her smile bright and braced herself for the damning rejection that had always greeted her shy attempts to befriend him.

He cocked his head to the side, studying her from beneath his sandy lashes before reaching down and gently righting the chaplet of flowers. A stray petal caught on his fingertip. The severe line of his lips never wavered, but one brilliant green eye closed and then opened in silent regard, sending Sabrina's mind reeling.

God in heaven, help her! she prayed. Morgan MacDonnell had winked at her.

Morgan's wink was only the beginning of Sabrina's torment.

She lay flat on her back in the strange bed, the thick quilts drawn up to her chin. The canopy vibrated in time with her shivers as she awaited the arrival of her bridegroom. Outside the closed door, Pugsley whined a mournful refrain. Undoubtedly horrified at the prospect of her daughter's virginal bed being defiled by Morgan's overwhelming maleness, her mother had tucked them at the far end of the east wing. Morgan had made his earlier boast in vain. From there, no one would hear her scream.

All his boyhood cruelties had paled in comparison to the diabolical kindness he had shown her that night. Her first bittersweet taste of perdition had come when he had pulled out her chair at the supper table. She had sat slowly, fully expecting to go tumbling when he whisked it away at the last second. Instead, he had smoothed her napkin over her lap and polished her silverware on his plaid before pronouncing it fit for her bonny lips.

He pilfered choice morsels of mutton and grouse from her brothers' plates for her. He dabbed imaginary droplets of wine from her chin. He was even polite to Enid, coaxing a wan smile from her by praising the stewed mushrooms she shyly pressed on him.

Finally, when he had leaned over and innocently inquired if she might care for a lick of his sausage, Sabrina's frayed nerves had snapped. Overturning the goblet he had so graciously refilled, she had jumped up and fled the table, ignoring his cry of concern.

He had even given her ample time to prepare for his arrival in their bedchamber. But Sabrina knew she could prepare for a lifetime and never be truly ready for the big, dangerous stranger who was now her husband. The minutes ticked away, measured by the hollow thump of her heart. Her toes twitched beneath the blankets. When Morgan came, she would calmly and coolly suggest they discuss the terms of this marriage, a marriage they had both agreed would be devoid of the pleasures and intimacies usually shared by wedded couples. She frowned. He had agreed, hadn't he?

Against her will her mind dwelled on the things her mother had spoken of earlier. She could hardly believe that a minister of god had given Morgan the right to work those dark and mysterious acts on her body. Images flitted past. Brazen. Masterful. Shocking. But even more disturbing was the tender magic her mother had suggested she cast on Morgan. Spells to soften his temper, to bend him to her will. Charms she might weave around that big, intractable body of his with her hands, her legs . . . her mouth. Sabrina fanned herself with the blankets, then jumped from the bed as if her shameful thoughts had ignited it.

She drew open the window; a rush of cool wind soothed her burning brow. Autumn was fast fleeing, shoved aside by the relentless hand of winter. The MacDonnells were reveling again. From this side of the manor she had to strain to hear their merriment, but then the wind shifted, carrying on its wings a drunken voice braying in song—

Aye, me son, 'tis no trick to satisfy the wenches!
Toss up her bonny skirts, me lad, an' give her all ten—

Sabrina slammed the window and raced for the bed, once again chilled to the marrow. She jerked the blanket over her head in a vain attempt to drown out the deafening thud of the footsteps approaching the door. After several minutes she realized it was only her heart pounding in her ears.

She peeked out from beneath the blanket. Even Pugsley had ceased his vigil. The rumble of his untroubled snores drifted through the door. She collapsed against the pillows, exhaustion seeping through her body like a drug. As her lids drifted down, one last thought pierced her consciousness.

Perhaps Morgan wasn't coming.

Perhaps he was out making merry with his clansmen, toasting his final cruel jest at Sabrina Cameron's expense. She knew she should be relieved, but instead she hugged herself, hoping sleep would dull the peculiar ache in her heart. Her chin had just nudged her chest, when the door crashed open.

Her husband filled the width and breadth of its frame.

He slammed the door in Pugsley's puzzled face and lurched across the chamber. His arm came up in one fluid motion. Before Sabrina even saw the claymore in his hand, its lethal point was pressed against the hollow of her throat.

"Disrobe, you treacherous witch," he snarled. "I'm goin' to make you my wife tonight or bloody well die in the tryin'."

Chapter Seven

Sabrina had married a madman. The tip of the claymore trembled. Morgan swayed dangerously. She pressed herself into the pillows, leaning away from the cold blade, and wondered if the church would recognize murder as grounds for annulment.

"You treacherous witch," he repeated, growling under his breath. "How dare you sit there and blink at me so innocently! Have you nothin' at all to say for yourself?" He squinted as if having difficulty bringing her into focus. A glassy sheen dulled his eyes.

Sabrina's mind raced. She had seen Morgan drink only water with his supper. Had he gone off later and gotten drunk with his men? "Perhaps you'd best decide in which order you'd like to rape and murder me," she said evenly. "If you don't remove your sword from my throat, you're going to impale me."

" 'Twould be my pleasure, lass. Sword or no."

She took the blade gingerly between two fingers and pushed it away. The simple movement unbalanced Morgan. He stumbled back, flailing the claymore before steadying himself on the bedpost. His bronze skin had gone ashen. His other arm was wrapped around his stomach as if to hold it in place.

Perhaps your Morgan will find his taste for revenge more bitter than he expected.

The memory of Enid's cryptic words and her cousin's sudden craving to cook mushrooms suddenly spawned a terrible suspicion in Sabrina's mind.

Morgan straightened with visible effort. "Tell me, princess, did your papa use you only to bait the trap or did your own delicate hands mix the poison?"

She wanted to recoil from the accusation he spat out. But when he swayed, she climbed to her knees and reached for him.

He jerked away from her outstretched hand. "Stay away from me, you bonny she-devil! If you won't give me any answers, I'll wring them from your father's bloody neck."

He lunged for the door, but in the brief respite, the claymore had grown too heavy for his arm. He dragged it behind him, gouging plugs in the polished wood. Sabrina flung herself from the bed, tripping on the quilts, and caught the nearest part of him she could reach—his leg.

"Morgan, don't! You mustn't!"

He dragged her a few steps, but she hung on with all her strength. "Listen to me, Morgan! My father had naught to do with your poisoning!"

Morgan rubbed his brow as if he could massage the words into his foggy brain. His gaze slowly lowered to meet her own. His eyes focused with an icy clarity that froze her soul. Sabrina swallowed. She'd had no time to prepare for this moment. Her nightdress had ridden up. The flat side of Morgan's blade rested against the inner curve of her calf. The iron muscles of his thigh convulsed beneath her grip.

The hair at her nape stood erect as he said softly, "You?"

Sabrina bowed her head. How could she let her timid cousin brave this man's wrath? Enid wouldn't survive even one scorching blast from his temper. Aside from that, Enid had acted only in a misguided attempt to protect her.

"Believe what you will, Morgan MacDonnell," she said softly. "You always have."

Morgan's gaze bore into the back of her neck. A curtain of curls sheltered her burning cheeks as she awaited the bite of his blade. She opened her mouth to plead for his mercy but found the words would not come. She had bitten them back too many times before.

"I knew you hated me. But never this much," Morgan whispered. He sank against the door as if her unspoken confession had robbed him of the last of his strength.

The sword clattered to the floor. He slid to a sitting position, his long legs sprawled around her own.

Sabrina gathered the skirt of her nightdress to rise, thankful for any excuse to escape his bleak gaze. "I shall summon my father's physician."

His hand shot out to grasp her wrist. "No! I'll not give those Cameron butchers the chance to finish me off." His fingers tightened as another spasm of pain racked his features. "Just tell me one thing. Am I going to die?"

Remembering the time Brian had inadvertently fed Alex a similar mash of toadstools, she grimaced. "No. But you may wish you had."

He groaned. "I already do." His face had gone from gray to green. Sweat beaded his brow. "Oh, God." He tottered to his feet, holding the wall for support. Panic touched his gaze. When he swayed forward and would have fallen, Sabrina threw herself against him, bracing her shoulder against his chest.

He staggered away from her. "Get out!" he bellowed. "Leave me be!"

She hesitated.

He took a menacing step toward her. "I'm warnin' you, lass. I'll not give you the satisfaction of gloatin' over your handiwork!" His threat was spoiled as he tripped over the claymore and crashed headlong to the floor. His big hand curled into a helpless fist. "Please," he whispered. "Go."

Torn by the sight of the fallen giant, Sabrina slipped out and shut the door behind her. She leaned against it, flinching as another deep groan rended the silence. Pugsley's tongue snaked out to lick her toes. She crouched down, burying her fingers in the dog's brindle coat.

Once she might have laughed at Morgan's predicament. Now she ached with misery that he believed her cruel enough to poison him.

The tortured sounds finally stopped. Sabrina touched the doorknob with hesitant fingers. She knew her father too well to believe in the privacy he had afforded them. It would not do for Alex or Brian to wander past and find her cowering outside her own wedding chamber. A more terrible thought entered her mind. What if the hapless Enid had fed Morgan a fatal dose of toadstools? Perhaps even now he lay stiffening upon the cold floor, his lush green eyes fixed forever in an accusing glare.

She threw open the door. Morgan lay slumped in the floor where she had left him, his wheaten hair dampened with sweat. She knelt beside him, daring to part the folds of his plaid and flatten her palm against the smooth, sculpted muscles of his chest. Its shallow rise and fall wrung a ragged sigh from her. She dropped her cheek to the rigid warmth of his breastbone, trembling with relief.

"Get off me."

Sabrina lifted her head, paralyzed by the contempt in his hoarse command.

"I have a wee bit of pride left. Even we MacDonnells aren't lecherous enough to want a wench who'd rather murder than bed us."

His body was coiled with tension, but he made no move to shove her away. What would he do if she chose to practice her mother's lessons now? Would it soften his temper if she dared to nibble the generous satin of his lower lip? Would it melt his anger to feel the teasing swirl of her tongue against his throat? Or would he consider it a mockery? An affront to that dangerous pride he held between them like a shield.

"What do you want from me?" she whispered, her question more heartfelt than he would ever know.

"The sword."

His blunt words snapped her back to reality. To Morgan, this was a battle and she was the enemy. Hoping she wouldn't lose her head for her obedience, she dragged the weapon over to him, not realizing until she'd folded his fingers around the hilt that it was her father's ceremonial claymore.

His voice, musing and bitter, mirrored her thoughts. "Not my sword. Nor my betrothal ring. Not even my bloody wife."

Grunting with the effort, he scooted his back against the door.

"You can't spend the night on the cold floor," Sabrina protested. "You've been ill. You should be in bed."

"With you?" His bark of laughter rendered the very suggestion profane. "No, thank you. I'd rather live to see the dawn." He arranged the massive blade across his knees.

Sabrina didn't know if he intended the claymore to defend him from ambush or from her. After several tense minutes during which he showed no sign of relaxing his vigil, she curled into a miserable knot on the edge of the bed, blinking back tears. She'd sworn never to cry for him, and she wasn't about to start now. Her last image before drifting into restless slumber was of Morgan glaring at her from beneath his thunderous brows. A dark mutter that would be forgotten by the morrow pierced her troubled dreams.

"If I can't have you, princess, then, by God, neither can they."

The next morning found Morgan gazing down at the sweet assassin curled on the bed. He was reluctant to believe that her father had no hand in his poisoning. Robbed of the leadership of their chieftain, the MacDonnells would have quickly dispersed, leaving the Camerons, Grants, and Chisholms free to tear apart the mountain like a flock of hungry vultures. But why would Dougal have gone through with the pretense of a wedding, when he could have murdered him outright or left him to rot in the Cameron dungeon?

Morgan sighed, forced to accept that Sabrina had probably acted alone. He had believed himself well armored against Cameron betrayal, but the realization grated like salt over the fresh wound of his father's death. He could only imagine what might have happened had she dared such a betrayal while surrounded by his clansmen. They might have killed her while he was still too weak to protect her. It pained him to imagine the roses in her cheeks fading to ashen gray.

Her dark hair swirled across the pillow in striking contrast to the cream and pink of her skin. She'd slept with no blankets, and a dawn chill had permeated the fireless chamber. His gaze drifted downward. The bodice of the nightdress clung to the puckered tips of her breasts. Her skirts had ridden up to her thighs. It was only too easy for Morgan to envision one of his callused fingers stroking her pert nipple, another slipping into the warm, inviting cleft between her legs.

He swung away from the bed, swallowing an oath. She was his wife, yet like his ring, his claymore, and his very life, she belonged to him only by the grace of Dougal Cameron. And no MacDonnell had ever settled for charity. Especially not the charity of his enemy.

But he had a more immediate problem than the wild and needy throb of his groin. Did he dare give Sabrina the chance to tell them all that their marriage had not been consummated? Was casting aspersions on his manhood yet another of her and her papa's clever ploys? One of a chieftain's most important duties was providing an heir for his clan. His face darkened as he imagined her glibly blurting out the shameful details of their wedding night.

He could see them tearing her from his arms, casting him back down into the dank hole beneath the tower, or, worse yet, tossing him out on his ear to face the scorn of his clansmen.

Morgan swung back around, his hands clenched into fists. She was his bride. He must deflower her. 'Twas more than his right; 'twas his duty. Once he'd consummated their marriage, not Dougal Cameron, the king of England, or almighty God himself would dare take her away from him. The peaceful future of his clan would be assured.

Sabrina stirred, curling her fist against her parted lips. She looked so small, so helpless and trusting in sleep. He knew he could have his hand over her mouth and her thighs spread to accommodate him before she could draw breath to scream. But unlike some of his clansmen, Morgan had little stomach for rape.

His eyes narrowed. He mustn't think of it as rape. He must think of it as duty. He would remain cool and detached, as if he were simply carrying out a painful but necessary procedure as he'd done for his clansmen hundreds of times. Like cauterizing a wound or digging a pistol ball from a festering shoulder.

Or ravishing his wife's tender, unsuspecting body, driving himself deep into her silky sheath until she writhed and moaned beneath him.

His mouth went dry and his shaking hands felt less than detached as he sank down on the bed beside her. He stroked his fingers across the silken temptation of her hair, weaving it around his hands as he'd dreamed of doing all those chill, lonely nights in the dungeon.

Morgan might have recovered from Sabrina's eyes fluttering open to catch him at his folly. But he stiffened as if from a mortal wound at the shattering tenderness of the smile that followed in the wake of their discovery.

Chapter Eight

Sabrina awoke to find herself trapped in a web forged between her hair and Morgan's fists. There was no violence in his grip, only gentle determination, pinioning her to the pillow and preventing an escape she wasn't sure she desired. His hearty tan had returned, washing away all traces of illness. Only the lingering red rimming his eyes betrayed his sleepless night. His plaid was draped around him in neat folds, and his breath smelled spicy, like cinnamon and cloves.

She smiled in genuine pleasure to see him looking so fit. But her smile faltered beneath the somber weight of his gaze. She sensed she was teetering on the razor-sharp edge of a dangerous brink.

"Sorry to disappoint you, lass. I fear you're not a widow yet."

"Not did I intend to be."

"Then your cookin' leaves much to be desired." He wound her hair a coil tighter, still not pulling, just letting her know he was there. "Just what did you intend?"

His drowsy gaze held her captive. Mere inches separated their lips. A stammered near-truth was all she could manage. "I—I—I was afraid to be alone with you."

He frowned. "Do you believe me such a monster?"

His unexpected sincerity only increased the breathless cadence of her voice. "Have you ever given me reason to believe otherwise?"

He tilted his head. "Perhaps 'tis far past time I did."

His lips descended on hers, their firm, silken contours molding her mouth beneath his. His fingertips stroked her cheeks, coaxing her to open for him, to answer the swirl of his tongue with a teasing stroke of her own. The crisp scent of him filled her senses; his tongue plunged deep into her mouth.

From the corridor outside the door came a stealthy footfall and canine whine of welcome, quickly muffled. Morgan's head snapped up; his eyes hardened. His palm replaced his mouth over her lips, stifling a questioning cry.

Morgan knew his time had run out. He stared into the tremulous blue eyes above his hand, knowing he had only seconds to make a choice that could win him his wife's everlasting hatred. She might have eventually forgiven him for dipping her braid in the ink bottle or using her first corset as a slingshot, but he suspected raping her within earshot of one of her brothers would be a sin not so easily absolved.

He lifted his hand from her mouth. "Moan," he whispered.

"Have you lost your—?"

"Dammit, woman, moan!" he snapped.

Sabrina emitted a faint sound, more squeak than moan.

He dropped his head in disgust. "I was makin' the lasses squeal louder than that when I was twelve years old."

It was the wrong thing to say, and Morgan knew it the instant he saw anger flash in her eyes. Her lips tightened to an intractable line as if she might never again part them to utter a sound.

He hesitated. The corridor was quiet. Too quiet. The listening silence was palpable.

Shaking his head, he said, "Verra well, lass. You leave me no choice."

With those words of rueful warning, Morgan determined to use every trick he knew to wring a convincing cry of passion from Sabrina's stubborn throat. Lacing his fingers through hers, he pinned her arms above her head and rocked between her legs, mimicking the motions of lovemaking until the bed creaked wildly with it and her moans were coming in earnest.

The down mattress provided Sabrina no escape from Morgan's provocative assault. She felt as if she were drowning beneath his big, hard frame. The consequences of his rash actions manifested themselves with devastating swiftness. A breathless whimper escaped her as the rigid evidence of his own need rubbed against the tender mound between her thighs, nudging and stroking until neither plaid nor nightdress could stop the waves of pleasure fanning out from her lower body to ravish her brain.

"Say you want me, Sabrina." Morgan's hoarse voice flooded her ear, scraping her livid senses.

She shook her head in mute denial, fighting to hold the tatters of her will intact.

"Say it!"

He plundered her ear with his wet, rough tongue, and the words spilled out of her, her cry cresting on a broken note.

Morgan went still. Tears trembled on Sabrina's lashes but did not fall as she waited for him to gloat over his mastery, to finish the wicked seduction that would leave her more battered and debased than an outright beating. He did neither. After listening for the pad of Pugsley's paws in the corridor, he simply rolled off her dazed body and pulled a tiny dagger from the folds of his plaid. Her eyes widened.

She sat up on her elbows in horrified fascination as he clenched his hand into a fist and drew the blade across the inside of his forearm, slicing the flesh without so much as a wince. He held his arm up, spattering droplets of blood over the pristine sheets.

His gaze met hers. "Evidence of your virginity. I'll give them no excuse to take you back. If bein' wed to a princess is the price of peace, I've no choice but to pay it. Even if I have to shed every last drop of my blood." He staunched the bleeding with the hem of the sheet, then caught her chin between his fingers. "If you dare to contradict me in front of your father or any of my clansmen, I'll drag you to the nearest private corner and make it true. Then there'll be no doubt in anyone's mind, includin' your own, that you belong to Morgan MacDonnell."

His cold efficiency appalled Sabrina. Her heart and body were still throbbing to the compelling rhythm he had set. Her lungs pumped out air like a set of tattered bellows.

He rearranged the folds of his plaid, as cool and unmoved as a green-eyed glacier. "Be packed and ready to travel by midday. I won't spend a moment longer than needed under your father's thumb." He stole a glance at her. "Don't look so broken-hearted, lass. I'll send you home to Cameron as soon as you give me a son. Not even Dougal Cameron would dare make war on his own grandson."

Outrage mingled with Sabrina's horror. "You expect me to just drop a babe like a litter of puppies, then run home to Papa. Did it ever occur to you that a child needs his mother?"

Morgan shrugged, but avoided her gaze. "I never did. The lad can spend his summers at Cameron just as I did."

"How generous of you. And if I do you the grave dishonor of presenting you with a daughter? What then? Will your MacDonnell pride be able to withstand the blow?"

He didn't even bother to answer. With a swirl of

his plaid he was gone, leaving Sabrina to stare at the door in disbelief.

She flopped back among the pillows, trembling all over. How could he just walk away and leave her like that—aching, empty, starving for a touch that would not come? But what better way to punish her than to stoke the flames of a desire she could never allow him to fulfill? She had vowed not to give him a moment's pleasure, only to discover it was not his pleasure she feared, but her own.

She shied away from the stained sheets, despising the hateful lie they represented. Was she so repugnant to him that he preferred maiming himself to sharing her bed? He had made it painfully clear what he wanted from her—her son, not her body. She hugged a pillow to her breast, trying vainly to soothe the wild throb of her heart, the hollow ache between her legs. She should have expected no more from a man like Morgan. A mockery of a marriage, a crude parody of the tender act that should bind wife to husband.

The bloodred ruby in the betrothal ring winked knowingly at her. She had been wrong all of those years. Morgan MacDonnell was crueler than any monster.

Morgan made it down to the deserted garden before the cost of his control betrayed him. He staggered blindly to the nearest bench and sank down, a fresh fever roaring through his veins. Dougal needed no assassin to finish him off. Sabrina was poison enough—sweet, potent, and deadly, reducing him to shivering, primal need with only the sound of his name on her lips.

I want you, Morgan.

The shock of her cry reverberated through him anew, losing none of its power for being coerced by the rough chicanery of his body. Its raw honesty had struck him a harder blow than the innocent abandon of her response. He had expected her to stiffen at his assault, to turn her face away in prim distaste. Instead, she clung to him, lips trembling, eyes awash with a glisten that might have been tears in another woman. He'd seen that look on her face before.

Once when she'd caught him splinting the broken wing on a fallen sparrow and again when he'd thrown himself in front of a Cameron groom who had been determined to destroy a lamed mare who needed a warm poultice more than a pistol ball. The look she had given him on those occasions had both warmed and terrified him. Unable to bear the illusion that he might ever be anything more than a worthless MacDonnell, Morgan had taken great care to wipe it from her face.

Even then he had sensed that Sabrina was the only Cameron who could reach through the impenetrable armor of his pride and seize his heart. The only Cameron with the power to break it.

When she flung the challenge of bearing him a daughter into his face, Morgan was forced to flee the chamber before she saw his icy façade crack. He had been unable to bear his unexpected hunger at envisioning a giggling, ebony-curled little girl lifted high above his head—Sabrina as she had been the first time he had laid eyes on her, before his rejection marred the sparkle in her pretty eyes. To have a second chance at such a treasure was more than he or any other man deserved.

He swept his hair out of his face, letting the cool fingers of morning mist caress his flushed brow. As a lad, he'd been able to resist Sabrina's gap-toothed grins and coltish charms with no more than a pang of regret. But remembering her wounded expression, he now feared the cost of his resistance might be more than he was willing to pay.

At exactly thirty-three minutes past midday, Sabrina swept into the courtyard, trailed by a subdued, red-nosed Enid and a parade of servants bearing trunks. A hooded velvet pelisse enveloped her. A matching muff dangled from the royal blue ribbon circling her wrist. She tilted her nose to a regal angle and measured each step as her mother had taught her, wishing she'd have thought to have the maids carry her ermine-trimmed train.

If Morgan MacDonnell believed he'd wed a princess, then a princess he would have.

During the night an icy wind had blown down from the mountain, wiping the face of autumn clean. It whistled around the stone walls, gusting the hem of Sabrina's pelisse and whipping roses into her cheeks. Pewter-tinted clouds roiled above the courtyard, their swollen underbellies boding ill for their journey. Like a vast mirror, the bleak sky reflected the winter chill seeping into Sabrina's heart.

A clash of bass voices drew her attention. Brian and Alex were arguing in the corner, fiery head to fiery head. Their clenched hands and flushed faces warned that their quarrel was threatening to deteriorate into one of their old shoving matches.

Morgan's man Ranald stood at the courtyard gate, holding the reins of a horse. The dappled gray bared its yellow teeth and rolled its eyes at the sight of her. A web of scars crisscrossed its massive haunches. Sabrina thought it was surely the largest, most forbidding creature she had ever seen. Except for her husband.

A brief flare of heat banished her chill as she saw Morgan leaning against the wall, arms crossed and brows drawn together in a glower that was already becoming painfully familiar. Her father wore an identical scowl. Her mother stood between the two men with Pugsley in her arms, beaming with feline smugness.

Morgan's sulky scowl dissolved into a mocking grin as he moved to meet her. "Good morn, sweet flower of Scotland." The honeyed words dripped like acid from his tongue. "I'm delighted you deigned to join us. Your family was beginnin' to wonder if perhaps I'd murdered you in our bed."

Enid paled and dropped an entire armload of glove boxes. Flipping the horse's reins to a Cameron groom, Ranald hastened to help her retrieve them. The groom kept a wary distance from the snapping teeth of the prancing gray.

"Nonsense," Sabrina replied airily. "You were the very spirit of consideration and forbearance."

Morgan wrapped his fingers around her wrist in subtle warning. Searing warmth emanated from his touch. "Perhaps we should delay our journey, lass, so I can give you another taste of my forbearance."

His gaze dropped to her lips. The devilish sparkle in his eyes promised her he was only too willing to make good on his threat.

"That won't be necessary," she assured him, lowering her eyes. It had taken all her courage to face her family, knowing what they believed had transpired between her and Morgan the previous night, without having it become reality in the nearest empty cupboard.

A fresh thread of anger wove through his words as he led her toward her family. "It seems your father neglected to mention another of his . . . conditions. One of your kin is to accompany us to MacDonnell. That way, if I'm cross to you over supper, they can cut off my head and bring it back to your father on a pike."

Judging from the beleaguered roll of her father's eyes and her mother's triumphant grin, Morgan wasn't the only man who had spent a sleepless night at Cameron.

Elizabeth stroked Pugsley's coat. A pale band marked her finger where Dougal's betrothal ring had rested. "Don't be so dramatic, Morgan. I simply wanted my daughter to have some company."

Morgan drew himself up with the painful dignity he had always shown Elizabeth Cameron. "I can promise you, my lady, that my wife will not suffer from lack of company. However, I will respect your wishes." He swept out his arm toward Sabrina's waiting brothers. "Go on, my dear. Choose your poison."

The glove boxes went tumbling again and Enid swayed beneath Morgan's sudden piercing gaze. Ranald cupped her elbow to steady her.

Sabrina knew why her brothers had been arguing. As she approached, they threw back their shoulders like troops awaiting survey by their general. Brian ruined his military posture by sneaking her a wink. Clever, mischievous Brian. He'd never grown too old to tease her. She adored his wit and spirit of mischief.

Alex's high cheekbones colored beneath her perusal. Had it been his step they'd heard outside the bedchamber that morning? Dependable, staid Alex. When she fell, he had always been the one to pick her up and dust off her ruffles.

They'd both inherited their mother's temper in different guises. Brian's fiery rages would subside as quickly as they flared, while Alex quietly simmered until the inevitable explosion. Neither of them would survive a day with the MacDonnells. She favored them both with a tender smile before facing Morgan.

His tawny hair whipped in the wind, partially shielding his expression. He doubtlessly saw this as a fresh betrayal on her part. She refused to let her mother's well-intentioned scheming drive yet another wedge between them.

Meeting his gaze squarely, she announced, "I choose Enid."

Enid fainted dead away. Ranald caught her before she could hit the flagstones. A dazzling grin split his face. "Sound choice, lass. There's nothin' I love better than a bonny fat girl."

"Enid's not fat," Sabrina protested absently, transfixed by the glint of approval in her husband's eyes. "She's"—Ranald staggered beneath her cousin's weight—"pleasingly plump."

"I dare say she'd please me," Ranald said, peering down Enid's bodice in the guise of loosening her lace collar.

Protesting bitterly, Brian, Alex, and Elizabeth all stormed toward Sabrina.

Dougal stepped into their paths. "We all agreed this was to be Sabrina's choice. God knows she's had little enough say in all of this. I won't take this much away from her."

Her papa's familiar figure blurred before Sabrina's

eyes. She knew instinctively that this was the last time he would have the right to champion her.

"How will I explain this to my brother?" Elizabeth cried. " 'Dearest Willie, did I mention I've sent your daughter off to live with a band of thieves and cutthroats without even the dubious protection of matrimony?' Why he shall have an apoplexy!"

"I shall answer to William myself," Dougal replied sternly. "'Tis only until Sabrina is settled. I'm sure Morgan can provide for Enid's safety until we come to retrieve her."

Elizabeth's face crumpled in a moment of rare vulnerability. "And who will provide for my Sabrina's safety?"

Morgan's hands closed over Sabrina's shoulders. She shivered at the possessive mastery of his touch. His rich voice reverberated down her spine, oddly devoid of mockery. "The lass is under my protection now."

Enid's pale blue eyes fluttered open. She almost swooned with fresh excitement to find herself cradled across the lap of a Highlander with the face of an angel and the leer of an imp.

Sabrina knelt beside her. "You don't have to come if you don't want to. It must be your choice."

Enid grappled visibly with her decision. During their tearful conversation that morning, she had learned that it was Sabrina's sacrifice that had protected her from Morgan's wrath.

Swallowing hard, she mustered up a brave smile. "Of course I'll come. 'Twill be a grand adventure." She held up her hand and locked fingers with Sabrina. Morgan's shadow fell over them.

Enid snuggled against Ranald's broad chest, obviously preferring an unknown threat to a known one.

"We shall await you on the hill while you pack," Morgan said. "Ranald, stay and see to the lass's needs."

"Wouldn't I love to?" Ranald muttered under his breath as he assisted Enid to her feet.

Morgan caught Sabrina's arm, his dubious patience at an end. She found herself being tugged along, past her brothers, past her parents, to the prancing nightmare of the steed that awaited them.

"Steady now, Pookah," Morgan murmured, his voice low and soothing. The horse's nostrils flared.

Sabrina thought the horse looked every bit as demonic and perverse as his faerie namesake. She threw the snorting beast a look of pure terror.

"I can provide a carriage," her father offered, a note of desperation climbing in his voice.

"I've no need of Cameron charity." Morgan caught Sabrina by the waist and swept her into the saddle as if she weighed no more than a feather. Before the skittish animal could bolt, he swung himself behind her. "I'll take only what's mine by law. We MacDonnells take care of our own." His arm circled her waist, its possessive strength reminding her that she was no more to him than a herd of sheep or a flock of chickens. Or a brood mare.

Her mother rushed forward and shoved Pugsley up into her arms.

Sabrina hugged his warm, compact weight. "I can't take him, Mama. He belongs to you."

Elizabeth smiled through her tears. "He's always loved you best. You'll take good care of him, won't you? He's very precious to me. I should never replace him if he were lost." But her eyes were not on Sabrina. They were on Morgan, asking far more than that he allow her daughter the comfort of her childhood pet. Morgan gave her a curt nod in reply.

Sabrina leaned down and her mother pressed a soft, rose-scented kiss to her mouth. Then her papa was there, his face stricken, arms hanging empty at his sides.

Sabrina stiffened. She longed to fling herself into his arms, to bury her face in his prickly beard and beg him to make her understand. But if not for his manipulations, she wouldn't have been given to this forbidding stranger. She wouldn't be leaving behind all that was dear and familiar to battle this Highland beast in his lair.

Her papa stood on his tiptoes to kiss her. At the

last second she turned her face away. His lips collided with her cheek, lingering there for an instant before he stepped back, accepting her rejection as his due with a grace that nearly shattered her. As she straightened in the saddle, Morgan's arm tightened, its unyielding strength all that kept her from breaking into a thousand pieces.

He gathered the reins. Dougal stepped forward and grasped his bare calf. His dark blue eyes snapped with challenge. "Take care of her, man. Or you'll answer to me."

Morgan neither acknowledged nor disputed her father's threat. He simply urged the horse into a walk. Sabrina dared one look back before they passed through the manor gates. Her parents clung to one another, so entangled that it was impossible to tell who was supporting who. She knew they would recover in time. They had each other. It was she who must go on alone, robbed forever of her girlish yearning for a love such as theirs. Her father had destroyed that dream with a ruthlessness that belied everything she had ever believed about him.

As they left the shelter of the manor walls, a blast of icy wind snatched her breath away. A tear rolled slowly down her cheek to splash like a molten diamond against Morgan's hand.

His voice against her ear was both soft and bitter. "You'll cry for him, but not for me. Damn you."

But even as Morgan cursed her, he reached around with a corner of his plaid and gently dried her tears.

PART TWO

If thou canst but thither,
There grows the flower of Peace,
The Rose that cannot wither,
Thy fortress and thy ease.

—Henry Vaughan

Chapter Nine

Sabrina was thankful for the shelter of her hood. If she dared a glance to the left, she saw Angus's mummy bumping along, tied to his saddle in macabre imitation of a rider. If she twisted right, she was subjected to the leers and chuckles of Morgan's bolder clansmen. So she stared straight ahead, keeping her eyes fixed on the narrow road twining up toward MacDonnell lands and clutching the slumbering Pugsley like a talisman against the unrelenting gloom and Morgan's stony silence.

Bone-chilling tendrils of mist seeped from the forest floor, coiling like serpents poised to strike around her ankles. She stole a nervous look at Angus, thankful they were riding upwind from him. Despite his small stature, he had once seemed larger than life itself. Now his plaid-shrouded form looked tiny and withered. Sabrina recognized the gaunt, hooded figure who led his horse as the servant who had tended him at the ill-fated banquet.

As if sensing her curiosity, he swiveled in his saddle, piercing her with a hostility she could sense even beneath the shadowed folds of his plaid. Her gaze shot back to Morgan's big-boned hands wrapped around the reins.

Desperate to break a silence disturbed only by the nervous cackling of the crated chickens and the mournful lowing of the livestock, she blurted out the first thing that came to mind. "My father would have granted him a proper burial if you had but asked."

"I won't have him buried on Cameron lands," Morgan replied.

"I doubt he would have noticed. Do you miss him?" she dared, her own papa's stricken face fresh in her memory.

Once again came that implacable shrug. "If the Camerons hadn't got him, the whisky would've."

Knowing she was badly outnumbered, Sabrina swallowed a defense of her family. "Is that why you don't drink spirits?"

"Whisky makes me surly."

"'Twould be a pity to temper your gregarious nature," she muttered beneath her breath. If Morgan grew any surlier, it would be like holding conversation with a rock.

A MacDonnell who sat his mangy horse like a squat bull took their terse exchange as an invitation. "Ye're lookin' a trifle bit pale, Morgan. Rough night?"

"Aye, but his bride looks rosy eno'," another chimed in. "What ails ye, lad? Did the wee she-devil suck all the blood out o' ye?"

"With a mouth like that, I'll wager 'twas not his blood she was—"

Morgan's look was threat enough to stifle the man in midsentence. He and his companion nudged their horses out of their chieftain's reach, still muttering among themselves. Their words carried clearly to Sabrina's ears.

"I suppose 'tis fitting revenge for Angus's death, but the lad's a bloody fool if ye ask me. Why, I'd as soon bugger lame ol' Eve as bed a Cameron!"

Sabrina ducked as a shadow went flying past her

and into the tart-tongued MacDonnell. A murderous cry tore from its throat. Pookah half reared, but Morgan controlled the horse with only a shift of his thighs, bringing him to a shuddering halt. Sabrina gaped to discover Angus's grim escort straddling the hapless Scot.

A low, virulent voice sent a shiver down her spine. "Shall lame ol' Eve bugger ye a new windpipe, Fergus, me man?"

Fergus's beady eyes crossed as he perused the rusty dirk pressed to his throat. "I'd rather she didna, if ye please."

The blade twisted; a trickle of blood skated across the man's bulging Adam's apple. "Perhaps ye'd rather go bugger yerself."

His voice cracked. "If ye like."

The figure rose and threw back its hood, shaking down a coarse silver braid. Sabrina recoiled to find herself staring into a striking pair of gray-green eyes. A woman's eyes. Even more shocking was the unguarded hatred poisoning their depths. It rendered poor Fergus a foolish nuisance while impaling Sabrina with malice. The woman stabbed the dirk back into her belt and lurched back to her horse, her awkward gait betraying her limp.

"And who might she be?" Sabrina whispered.

"My guardian angel." A wry note of pride tinged Morgan's voice. "Eve was my da's servant. She'd been with him for as long as I can remember. The MacDonnells won't stomach any show of weakness. They've no tolerance for cripples. When Eve was only a lass, the clan voted to cast her out. Before they could stone her, my da championed her. She's been wild with grief ever since he died."

Sabrina swallowed. "So it appears." If she'd have been any wilder, Fergus would have been choking on his own blood instead of sheepishly climbing to his feet.

Sabrina could not help staring as Eve dragged herself back on her mount. She was unlike any woman Sabrina had ever known. A cumbersome set of pipes was strapped to the back of her saddle, reminding

Sabrina of the beautiful dirge that had haunted the final night of Morgan's imprisonment. Perhaps Eve's flinty shell only shielded a woman's heart.

Catching Sabrina's perplexed stare, Eve spat on the ground, then drew the back of her hand across her mouth in a gesture of pure contempt. She kicked her horse into a canter. She and her grisly companion disappeared around a bend, riding far ahead of the motley party. Sabrina's spirits sank further. There went one more MacDonnell who blamed her for their chieftain's death.

She was beginning to wonder if she would survive to see the morrow. Tonight there would be no one to care if she screamed.

No one but Enid. As Morgan nudged Pookah into motion, a shrill giggle reminded her that Enid was faring far better than she. Her cousin was perched on a rickety wagon bench beside Ranald. With each rock of the wagon up the rutted trail, their shoulders collided, eliciting a fresh trill of giggles. Enid's wan cheeks colored prettily as the dashing Gypsy-Highlander popped a sweetmeat pilfered from the Cameron kitchen into her mouth.

Sabrina discovered Pugsley was awake and worrying Morgan's hand with his tooth. "Bad doggie," she scolded, prying Morgan's finger out of his mouth.

"Leave him be." Morgan stroked the loose folds of skin beneath the dog's chin. "I've found animals to be better company than most people."

She averted her eyes as Fergus, now roaring a Highland ditty, adjusted his plaid to relieve himself without bothering to dismount. "Considering the company you keep . . ." She trailed off, cringing to realize she sounded as sanctimonious as her mother.

As if to complement her flagging spirits, the sky unfurled a sodden gray curtain of rain to slow their journey up the treacherous mountainside. The wind drove icy needles of water into her face. The damp wasted no time in penetrating the fashionable thinness of her pelisse. Shivering, she huddled against Morgan, grateful to be wedged between the warm cradle of his thighs.

"Lean up," he snapped.

Sabrina shot to attention, mortified to have been caught relaxing her guard against him for even an instant. But instead of scolding her, he unwound a voluminous length of plaid from his shoulders and draped it over their heads, forming a cozy tent to shield them from the rain. Pugsley snuffled his approval.

Morgan urged her back and she found herself snuggled against his bare chest. Helpless to resist, she turned her cheek to its warmth. Both her father's and brothers' chests were sprinkled with hair. But Morgan's was smooth, his skin heated satin stretched taut over granite. The horse swayed beneath them and Sabrina felt herself succumbing against her will to the rhythmic lullaby of Morgan's heartbeat against her ear.

Sabrina awoke several hours later to find herself being borne by another beast whose long strides carried her irrevocably toward his den.

Her empty hands batted at the air. "Pugsley?" she mumbled without opening her eyes, fearing she had dropped him somewhere along the road.

Morgan's voice rumbled in her ear. "Your dog is fine. One of my men is findin' the wee rascal somethin' to eat."

She screwed her brow into a puckish frown and muttered something under her breath.

Morgan chuckled. "No, lass. I won't let him eat your dog. We MacDonnells eat only people."

"I'm relieved," she said, rooting against his shoulder like a sleepy piglet.

Morgan knew if she could have seen the hungry look on his face at that moment, her silly smile would have vanished. His arms tightened around her, savoring her damp weight against his chest. He slowed his strides, knowing the sooner they reached their destination, the sooner she would awaken and he would be forced to relinquish her trust.

But as they passed beneath the shadow of a broken arch, her eyes fluttered open. Morgan braced himself, waiting for her to turn up her prim little Cameron nose at his home.

Sabrina's drowsy gaze traveled up. And up. And up. Finally, it stilled on the crumbling ramparts of Castle MacDonnell.

An ethereal smile broke over her face. "Oh, my," she breathed. "'Tis magnificent."

"Don't mock me," he growled. "I may be unschooled, but I'm not stupid."

She blinked at him as if she had awakened to discover an ogre mauling her, then returned her gaze to the castle. "Not stupid perhaps, but blind indeed."

Morgan would have thought it impossible to be jealous of a chunk of stone, but he was. He already knew what would happen to him if she dared look at him with such longing. And what would happen to her. He glared at the forbidding edifice, wanting desperately to see what was putting the stars in the sapphire sky of her eyes.

Darkness had fallen and the rain had melted to a fine mist, blurring the harsh edges of the castle's silhouette.

Sabrina had simply been caught off guard by mist and exhaustion, he decided, just as she had been caught off guard by a mysterious stranger in the moonlight of her mother's solar. By day she would see the ivy sinking its talons into the crumbling mortar, the collapsed ceilings, the gaping holes torn by cannonballs fired by her own Cameron ancestors. By day she would see what he had always seen—a gaunt ruin poisoned by centuries of warfare and neglect.

Then she would laugh at her own romantic folly and realize the castle, like its master, possessed too many chinks in its armor to ever survive redemption.

Sabrina's hand curled around his nape, winding lazily in his damp hair. "I'm so sleepy. Will you take me to bed, Morgan?"

He gazed down at her, unprepared for the rush of thunder through his loins, and damned Dougal

Cameron anew for making him feel like a rapacious thief for wanting his own wife. His lips took on a mercenary twist that would have done Angus proud. Would it truly be possible to get her into his bed, disrobed, and under him before she realized the consequences of her innocent request? She had vowed never to give him a moment's pleasure, but if he could catch her off guard as he had done that morning, he might coax her to break her vow with artful tenderness instead of force.

His da's naughty chortle rolled through his mind. *MacDonnell blood will out, me son. Ye canna fight it forever.* Surely he and his bride deserved one night when they were neither Cameron nor MacDonnell, but simply man and woman seeking the pleasures the darkness could give.

"Aye, lass," Morgan whispered. "I'll take you to bed. If that's what you desire."

"Thank you," she murmured primly, resting her cheek against his chest.

"Save it for the morn," he answered, touching his lips to her brow. "Then perhaps we'll know if I'm deservin' of your thanks."

With his bride in his arms, Morgan strode through the darkened corridors of Castle MacDonnell. He might have run if he hadn't feared jostling Sabrina into both wakefulness and sanity. Despite the inky blackness, his steps never faltered. He knew precisely where to duck beneath a splintered lintel, when to step over a pile of battered stone when another man might have stumbled and fallen.

Now that he'd committed himself to the low road, he plunged down it with utter surrender, determined to wring what pleasure he could from his own destruction. He'd wanted Sabrina Cameron before he'd been old enough to know what wanting meant. Tonight he intended to have her. Without counting the cost to either of them.

He hesitated before the closed door of his chamber. Surely tomorrow would be soon enough to humble himself, to plead prettily for her forgiveness and remind her that the vows she'd made before the minister of God were more binding than the angry words they'd snapped in her father's court.

Bracing her weight with one arm, he twisted the rusty doorknob. The door creaked open. A smoky peat fire snapped on the grate and he silently blessed Eve's intuition. Even in her grief she had not forgotten him.

He eased the door shut and pivoted just in time to see a frowsy blond head emerge from the bedclothes.

"Morgan, me darlin', I thought ye'd never come!"

At this rate he never would, Morgan thought despairingly as he looked down to find his bride blinking up at him, her eyes as bright and wary as a baby owl's.

Chapter Ten

At the adoring melody of Morgan's name on another woman's lips, Sabrina had snapped awake. The rumpled creature in her husband's bed did not cling to false modesty. She didn't even trouble to pull the sheet up over her naked breasts. An unexpected burst of starch infused Sabrina's veins. She stiffened, sliding from Morgan's arms like a wooden plank.

His jaw worked as if in time to his thoughts, but Morgan was a man of action, not words. He strode to the bed, wrapped a sheet around the intruder, and guided her toward the door without so much as an if-you-please.

The statuesque blonde dragged her feet as she stumbled past Sabrina. "Who the bloody hell is she?"

Feeling short, damp, and bedraggled, Sabrina tried not to wither beneath the woman's hostility.

Morgan deposited her in the corridor. "My wife," he replied, closing the door gently but firmly in the woman's dumbfounded face.

Without turning around, he leaned against the door, weight braced on his splayed palms, one knee cocked forward. Silence crackled between them, louder than the fitful sputter of the fire.

Sabrina applauded lightly. "Gracefully done. Brian would have admired your technique. You tossed her out as if she weren't any more consequence than a cooled bed warmer."

"She's not."

"You owe her no explanation?"

"I explained." He swung around to face her, crossing his arms in a stance that might have been warning or challenge. "Shall I call her back? I'm a bit weary, but the day hasn't yet arrived when I can't handle the both of you."

Sabrina ignored the heat rising in her cheeks. Morgan seemed determined to miss no opportunity to remind her of the kind of man she had wed. "I couldn't help but notice a family resemblance. Who is she? Your paramour? Your cousin?" She paused for an insulting beat. "Your sister?"

"Alwyn is Ranald's cousin."

"But I thought Ranald was your cousin." When Morgan's own brow clouded with confusion, Sabrina pressed her fingertips to her temples. "Oh, never mind. I'm too exhausted to untangle the twisted branches of the MacDonnell family tree. I suppose you're fortunate to know who your mother was."

When she opened her eyes, she was alarmed to find Morgan stalking toward her. He backed her toward the hearth, firing off each word like a pistol ball. "I haven't slept in over thirty-six hours, lass, and it's beginnin' to tell on my judgment. So unless you're willin' to expand my family tree right here and now, I've no wish to discuss it with you."

Morgan's temper exuded more heat than the brooding fire. As Sabrina tipped her head back to meet his gaze, all the fears she'd forgotten while cradled in his arms came flooding back. The MacDonnells were notorious for three traits—their savagery, their voracious carnal appetites, and their hatred of the Camerons. She feared she was about to learn about all three at the merciless hands of this disgruntled giant.

His arm came up, casting a shadow over her face. She shrank against the warm stones, biting back a flinch. In her entire life no one had dared to strike her. Not even when she deserved it. But having been warned that the MacDonnells despised any show of weakness, she pressed her eyes shut and prayed she could keep from crying when that big hand descended.

A chunk of peat hissed on the flames. Warm fingers sought her cheek, easing back her hood and freeing the wavy tumble of her hair. Sabrina opened her eyes to find Morgan gazing down at her, his eyes shadowed as if she had struck him a mortal blow out of pure cruelty.

"I've taught you well, haven't I, lass?"

Sabrina couldn't tell if the note of wry contempt in his voice was for her or for him. She inclined her head, ashamed that he had read her fears so easily. He turned away from her, his steps weighted by weariness.

She hugged back a shiver. In Morgan's absence, the fire was a poor shield to ward off the misery and chill she'd been fighting all day.

As if oblivious of her presence, Morgan drew the bodkin from his plaid and began to painstakingly unravel its drapes and pleats. Sabrina was riveted by his unselfconscious display. He shrugged the plaid from his shoulders. Firelight licked at the rugged slabs of sinew and muscle in his chest. Tendrils of heat danced down Sabrina's spine, chasing away her chill. The tartan unfolded over his taut abdomen and she caught herself holding her breath like a child on Christmas morning, eager to see what new treasures might be revealed.

But when without warning the plaid spilled into a pool at his feet, Sabrina got more than she'd wished for. Much more.

As Morgan padded nude to the bed, she stared so hard at the wall that her eyes crossed with the effort. The bed creaked beneath his weight. His satisfied groan made the hair on her nape tingle.

"Aren't you comin' to bed, lass?"

"No," she said hastily, scrambling for any excuse not to prostrate herself on the altar of that magnificent male animal. "I won't sleep there. Not on the same bedclothes as your . . . that . . . woman."

Hr grunted. "Suit yourself."

She dared a peek over her shoulder. As if it were of no import to him where she slept, Morgan had rolled away from her, dragging the ragged quilt over his nakedness.

She stood for a long time, half hoping he would comment upon her wounded sniffs. Her knees started to ache, so she drew off her pelisse and made a tidy nest of it on the stone floor, balling the hood beneath her head as a pillow. She was lying on her back, watching the unfamiliar shadows writhe on the ceiling and wondering if that might be a rat scratching outside the door, when Morgan's quiet voice pierced the silence.

"You've no need to flinch from me. I'll not lay a hand on you, Sabrina Cameron."

"Sabrina MacDonnell," she whispered to the darkness, but Morgan's soft snores were her only reply.

Sabrina awoke the next morning to watery sunlight and the distant drone of bees. Hundred of bees. Thousands of bees. All clamoring for a taste of her tender flesh. Her fingers plucked at the nubbed fabric of the quilt. A nasal wail assailed her ears.

Not bees. Bagpipes.

Nothing had changed, she thought. She was nestled in her cozy bed, waiting for her mother to bring her morning chocolate. Morgan was entombed beneath her, his life hanging by the tenuous thread of her father's mercy. She opened her eyes. Her elegant half-tester was gone. The murky recesses of a stone ceiling loomed high above her, reminding her that she was now the one entombed at Morgan's mercy.

She sat up. Her pelisse lay trampled on the dusty floor. Morgan must have carried her to the bed before he arose that morning.

Pugsley trotted into the chamber and jumped on the bed, his mud-caked paws leaving tiny footprints.

"You're looking quite pleased with yourself," she exclaimed as he dropped his offering into her lap. She held the grimy cylinder up to the light. It was a bone. A bone that looked suspiciously and alarmingly human. "Probably belonged to Morgan's last wife," she muttered.

Leaving Pugsley to gum his treasure, she climbed down from the high bed, wincing as her pinched toes hit the floor. She had never slept in her shoes before. The nearest window was a gaping hole in the stone shielded by warped glass. As she drew aside the drapes, the rotted silk shattered in her hands.

Far below, the woods parted to reveal a grassy knoll where the MacDonnells had gathered to bid their chieftain a final farewell. As Augus's body was lowered into the shallow cairn, Sabrina's gaze unerringly found his son in their midst. Morgan's shoulders were unyielding even in grief. The last bittersweet skirl of the pipes trembled on the wind. Sabrina shivered at the melancholy sound. Eve might be rough and crude, but she could make the bagpipes weep with a skill that would have been the envy of any music master from London to Edinburgh.

The MacDonnells slowly dispersed, leaving Morgan alone. He didn't follow their path back to the castle, but mounted Pookah and melted into the dusky gloom of the forest.

A stab of grief tore through Sabrina's heart. She was Morgan's wife now. She should be at his side. But he did not need her, she reminded herself. He had made it painfully clear that there was only one reason a man like Morgan needed a woman at all.

She shoved open a window on the opposite side of the chamber. Wind battered her, stinging her eyes and tearing her hair away from her face to reveal the raw magnificence of the view. Snowy mountains adorned the cloudswept horizon like a pearl-studded crown. Jagged cliffs hugged the mountainside in a sheer drop to the heath below. A narrow road snaked along their edge. Sabrina shuddered, thankful that she had slept through the nightmare of Morgan's high-strung mount prancing along that narrow ribbon of stone and dirt.

Her hands clenched on the stone in nameless longing, responding to the untapped wildness that beat in her heart. Morgan must have found the gently rolling hills and rock-enclosed pastures of Cameron unbearably tame. She imagined him growing up here, surrounded by impenetrable forest and unscalable cliffs. Was it any wonder his heart was no less unbreachable?

Sighing, she turned back to the bed. Its cozy invitation was spoiled by a lurid image of Morgan entangled in Alwyn's sun-bronzed arms.

Fueled by indignation, she stripped the musty quilt from the thin tick and hurled it out the window. It billowed down to sink into the dank, bracken-choked moat without a trace. She tossed the bone after the bedclothes, grabbing Pugsley before he could hurtle himself out the window after it.

"Oh, no, you don't. Yours is the friendliest face I'm likely to see today."

His tongue laved her nose. She noted that someone had already pried the paste gems from his collar. Her trunks were probably meeting the same fate, being meticulously unpacked by Morgan's clanswomen. She shuddered to imagine the busty Alwyn squeezing herself into one of her own delicate corsets. On the heels of that came another shudder, this one prompted by both horror and guilt.

Enid!

Good Lord, how could she have abandoned her cousin to those lusty barbarians! The poor dear was probably cowering under some cobweb-festooned bed, praying for deliverance. Or death.

Without bothering to straighten her rumpled clothes, Sabrina dropped Pugsley on the bed and shot out of the chamber at a dead run.

•   •   •

Sabrina careened around a blind corner, slamming her toes into a pile of rubble. She hopped up and down, massaging her throbbing foot, then raced on, refusing to squander precious seconds when her cousin's virtue might hang in the balance. The jagged windows cut at irregular intervals puzzled her until she realized they weren't windows at all, but holes torn in the mortar by enemy fire.

After passing Morgan's chamber twice more, she heaved a sigh of relief to find a broad staircase winding into the belly of the castle. She ran down the stairs, flying past a handsome woman garbed in Swiss-dotted muslin.

"Good morning, love. You'd best do something with that hair. Aunt Elizabeth would have fits if she knew you'd gone to bed without braiding it."

Sabrina teetered on the edge of a crumbling step, then pivoted on her heel. "Enid?"

Her cousin was picking her way over a fallen rafter. A white lace cap perched on her bobbing ringlets.

"Enid! Where do you think you're off to?" Sabrina cried.

Sabrina recognized the straw basket draped over Enid's arm as containing the food her mother had packed for their journey. "Ranald and I are dining outside this morning. He's promised to show me some sights I've never seen before."

"I dare say he has," Sabrina muttered. "Do you think it wise to go off alone with him? You've known him for less than a day."

"Oh, pooh! Ranald is like a cuddly little bear cub. He wouldn't harm a flea."

"But I was hoping the two of us might—"

A wheedling burr floated up the stairs. "Oh, Enid? Where's me plump sweet pumpkin? Yer furry bearkins is hungry and waitin'!"

Sabrina laid a hand over her churning stomach, thankful she hadn't eaten yet.

"I'm coming, dear," Enid called. With her eyes sparkling and her cheeks glowing like polished apples,

Sabrina realized her cousin was almost pretty. "I'll find you as soon as I return," she promised Sabrina. "I'll tell you all about Ranald and you can tell me about Morgan."

That shouldn't take long, Sabrina thought grimly.

She sank down on the steps and watched her cousin teeter off on her narrow heels. Loneliness gripped her. Even Enid didn't need her anymore.

Her stomach began to rumble with genuine hunger. Knowing it would do her no good to sit on the dusty steps feeling sorry for herself all day, Sabrina rose to seek the kitchens, absently working her hair into a knot at her nape as she walked.

After passing through a deserted hall, she pressed her palm to the first door she found. As it swung inward, a burst of harsh masculine laughter assailed her.

"He'll tire o' the Cameron whore soon eno', I'll wager. It won't take a man like Morgan long to wear out what's betwixt those frail thighs."

A dark shiver crawled over Sabrina's skin.

A raspy voice said, "Aye, and when he sickens o' her mewlin', he'll toss his scraps to us. I, for one, will be ready and waitin'."

"Ye were born ready, Fergus. What makes ye think they'll be anythin' left o' the lass when he's through with her?"

"Cedric speaks the truth. Ye know what the women say about him. Bullheaded and—"

Sabrina gently pulled the door shut before she could discover what her husband's lovers thought of his prowess. She flinched as another wave of black laughter crashed like thunder against her skull. Despite her most valiant attempts at optimism, her day seemed destined to go from bad to worse.

Stiffening her spine, she marched away from the door, unwilling to face the niggling fear that Morgan truly hated her enough to use her, then toss her to that pack of rabid wolves.

An arched corridor led her through a buttery into a poorly lit cavern that must serve as the kitchen. Milky sunlight trickled through arrow slits set high on the wall. Sabrina hesitated in the shadows, her hands knotted even tighter than her stomach to discover women draped over the tables and benches in various states of slovenly undress.

There was no bustle of activity here as there had been in the Cameron kitchens, no mouth-watering scents of pork frying or porridge bubbling. The twin hearths gaped like toothless mouths, their ashes dark and cold.

There was no sign of Eve, but Sabrina had no difficulty recognizing the woman Morgan had cast out of his chamber the previous night. Alwyn straddled a scarred bench as if it were a bucking stallion. A tangle of golden hair hung well past her buttocks.

"Saw the wee bitch myself, I did." Alwyn snapped a bite out of a shriveled green apple. "A haughty thing. Ugly too. Pale as milk with thick, dark brows that looked like slugs." Sabrina absently traced the arch of one eyebrow with her fingertip. "I felt nothin' but pity for me Morgan. Left alone all night with that pathetic bag o' bones."

An old woman cackled, revealing a mouthful of rotted teeth. "Maybe he put the pillow o'er her face 'afor he did the dirty deed. I 'spect a Cameron bitch is the same as any other when the candle's blown out."

The other women giggled, but Alwyn took another ruthless swipe at the apple, her gray eyes hardened to smoky flints. "I'd like to put a pillow o'er her face. One less Cameron would do this world proud."

Golden juice trickled down her chin and Sabrina's stomach betrayed her. Its fearful rumbling drew Alwyn's gaze like a magnet. The woman's sulky lips thinned to a malevolent smirk, but instead of pointing out Sabrina to her cronies, she simply flexed one of her long, shapely legs, revealing the wicked-looking dirk strapped beneath her gown. Sabrina was transfixed by the throaty venom of her voice.

"The Cameron wench may be a lady, but me Morgan needs a woman who can give as good as she gets. A lady won't be able to handle a man like him."

She looked Sabrina dead in the eye. "He'll tear her apart."

Sabrina retreated into the shadows of the buttery. She was beginning to understand why her mother had always warned her against eavesdropping. At Castle MacDonnell, it was less a matter of manners than survival.

Whirling around, she darted blindly down the nearest passage, feeling her way along the rough stone when the sheen in her eyes blinded her. The hollow ache in her gut was worse than hunger. She wandered the deserted catacombs for what seemed like centuries until she passed beneath a fluted arch and turned down a corridor that ended in a massive stone wall.

A dead end. A passage to nowhere. Just as her feelings for Morgan had always been.

But a glimmer at the far end of the corridor drew her forward. The wind moaned through a row of shattered windows, stirring rotted tapestries that looked as if they'd been shredded by giant claws.

Sabrina found herself face-to-face with her own reflection in a full-length wall mirror framed by tarnished bronze. A jagged crack severed her head from her throat. Mesmerized by the stranger peering back at her, she slowly unwound her hair, letting it fall in a dark cloud around her face. The warped glass distorted her features just as the past week had distorted her life. It was as if she'd tumbled into some nightmarish realm where everything she'd been taught to believe was only cruel illusion.

Her fingers sought the familiar arch of her brows, the slant of her nose, the trembling fullness of her lower lip. She'd never considered herself vain. She'd never had to be. Her beauty, like her wealth and the love of her family, had simply been a fact of life, as indisputable as the rich sable of her hair or the pearly evenness of her teeth. All her life, people had told her she was pretty.

But what if they had lied? What if they'd told her only what she wanted to hear? Had they been laughing behind her back, or, worse yet, pitying her? Only one person had ever remained untouched by her beauty.

Morgan.

Her vision clouded. Her dark hair and blue eyes shifted into the dear and familiar image of her papa, his expression as bereft as it had been in the moment she had denied him her farewell kiss.

The harsh whisper tore from her lips. "Oh, Papa. Why have you done this to me?"

But even as she condemned him, she pressed her palm to the mirror, seeking the prickly warmth of his beard but finding only the stark betrayal of cold glass.

Sometimes Morgan felt that Pookah was the only freedom he had ever tasted. The horse picked its way through the ferny bracken, docile beneath his control. Only on Pookah could Morgan escape the constant demands, whining, and clamoring of his clan.

He'd been sixteen when he had wrested the stallion from the drunken son of a wealthy laird who had been beating the horse into insensibility. After being given a taste of his own riding crop, the arrogant whelp had been only too eager to yield the horse to Morgan. He had saved his pride by proclaiming the horse stolen by one of those "thieving MacDonnells." The outraged laird had hanged the next MacDonnell caught poaching on his land—a lad of twelve.

Pookah still bore the scars of his first master's abuse, both outwardly and in the fierceness of his disposition. Morgan sometimes felt they were brothers beneath the skin.

Leaving the horse to root in the sparse grass, Morgan dismounted and entered a stone crofter's cottage nestled in a glade. The thatch-roofed cottage was a quaint reminder of a time when the MacDonnells still had sheep and the crofters to tend them. Morgan often came here to think when he could no longer bear the crushing weight of the castle.

He cocked back a chair and propped his feet on

the windowsill. His father's body now slumbered eternally beneath a blanket of stones.

Morgan knew in his heart that Angus had never loved him for who he was but for what he could do. The old man had taken great glee in provoking fights so Morgan could prove his worth with his fists. It was Angus's mercenary games that had made Dougal Cameron's affection so intolerable all those years ago. How could Morgan accept a regard not bought at the price of his own sweat and blood? Now Angus's murderer had gone free, leaving Sabrina Cameron to pay the price for his treachery.

He let the chair thump down. Damn the Camerons anyway! Even when he should be mourning his father, all he could see was Sabrina's face at the moment she believed he would strike her. Didn't the wee fool know he could kill her with a single blow?

Morgan had never struck a woman, no matter how sorely tempted. He had learned long ago not to use his strength recklessly—at seventeen, while standing, chest heaving and blood streaming from his broken nose, over the crumpled corpse of a clansman who had been his friend. His father had provoked the good-natured brawl, then taunted Morgan's rival into an enraged frenzy. Alarmed at the bloodlust gleaming in his friend's eyes, Morgan had sought to end the bout before one of them was maimed. But the single blow designed to do so had ended his clansman's life instead.

Angus had rushed forward to slap him on the back in congratulations. For the first time, Morgan had knocked his father's hand away and towered over him, fists clenched in rage. The flare of fear in Angus's eyes had sent Morgan reeling through the crowd to find a quiet place where he could relieve the churning of his stomach and his mind.

An uneven footfall struck the dirt floor behind him. Morgan didn't turn around. Only one person would dare invade his sanctuary.

"Are you sorry to see him go, Eve?" he said softly.

"We both know he would've been dead before the first snowfall. But, aye, it galls me to know a Cameron blade cut him down. I hope ye'll make that worthless wench o' theirs pay."

"Why? It wasn't her hand that wielded the blade."

"It might as well have been. I know her sort. She's poison, like any other fancy lady. Cloudin' a man's mind with soft talk and sweet perfumes."

Morgan swung around to face the stony jut of Eve's jaw. "I've already killed one woman just by bein' born. I've no intention of killin' another. Shall I butcher the sheep Dougal gave me as well? And the chickens? Have they no other worth than vengeance?"

Steel clashed between their eyes before Eve dropped her gaze. The two of them had always shared respect, if not tenderness. A bond of intelligence ran between them, deeper than blood, stronger than even the strangling chains of clanship. They had long ago joined in unspoken agreement to do whatever it took to keep the faltering flame of Clan MacDonnell burning.

Eve tossed her braid over her shoulder and drew a chair around to straddle it. "Verra well, lad. If ye won't kill the lass, then do somethin' else for me own peace o' mind."

Morgan repeated the promise he had given Elizabeth Cameron, fully aware of the irony. "Anythin' to please a lady."

"Put yer babe in her."

Morgan rose and paced to the barren hearth. He braced his hands on the crudely hewn stones. It had taken iron control to resist doing just that when he'd found Sabrina curled on her pelisse that morning. Had it not been for the smudges of exhaustion beneath her eyes and the arm she'd slipped so trustingly around his neck when he'd lifted her to the bed, they would have been waiting to bury his father while he buried his seed in his wife.

A wheedling note sneaked into Eve's tone. "I know what care ye've taken, lad. Ye're the only man 'round these parts without a passel o' green-eyed bastards trottin' on yer heels. But what if Dougal changes his mind? What if he claims ye stole his daughter and brings the redcoats down on our heads?"

"Let him come. He'll not take back what's mine."

Eve limped over and slapped him on the back, reminding him eerily of his father. "That's the spirit, boy. Swear ye'll put yer brand on the lassie before 'tis too late."

Eve was tall for a woman. Tall even for a MacDonnell. Her hot breath stung the back of his neck. He swung around to face her. "I'll see to the matter in my own time. With no interference from you or any of my kin."

Eve stepped aside to let him pass, a lifetime of battling Angus teaching her when to retreat.

"Oh, and, Eve?" he added. "I might meet with more success if you'd kindly keep Alwyn out of my wife's bed."

She crinkled her nose in a moment of rare mischief. "I just wanted to remind ye what ye'd be missin' by sleepin' with the enemy, lad. Shall I tell Alwyn ye'll be comin' to her from now on?"

"No." He strode to the door, offering no further explanation.

"Morgan? Ye won't disappoint yer da, will ye?"

He threw a humorless smile over his shoulder. "I never have, have I?"

Sabrina buried her nose deeper in *The Pilgrim's Progress* in a vain attempt to ignore the rumbling of her stomach. Its next rabid growl sent Pugsley whining into the corner.

She tossed down the book, wearying of the long-suffering Hopeful and Faithful when her own burdens seemed so unfair. She felt more like Christian in the Valley of Humiliation, forced to fight the giant devil Apollyon, whose body was covered with shining scales of pride. She rose to pace, fighting back a wave of light-headedness.

She'd been barricaded alone since her first disastrous foray into enemy territory. She had found her way back to the chamber to discover her trunks piled neatly in the floor with no sign of being pillaged.

She'd passed the rest of the day stubbornly devoting herself to the tasks that had always given her pleasure: reading, sewing, writing a letter to her mother full of false cheer and humorous anecdotes about her new family. She had sanded and sealed it before realizing it made no mention of the two men who haunted her thoughts.

A rosewater sponge bath and a fresh gown had helped stave off melancholy, but now the shadows of gloaming were creeping over the windowsill. Her spirits fell with the darkness.

She lit six of the expensive wax candles her mother had packed, scattering their light across the gloom. She was being shamefully wasteful, but frugality seemed less urgent than holding the encroaching shadows at bay. Juniper scented the air, the fresh, pungent aroma reminding her of Morgan.

A rush of anger rendered the crisp fragrance more bitter than sweet. For all Morgan cared, she might have starved by now. She swept across the room, startled by how heady the anger made her feel. It flooded her veins, shoving aside her trepidation with a mocking jeer.

Her slippered footsteps drummed to the cant of her mother's teachings. A true lady must never show her anger. A true lady must turn the other cheek. A true lady should starve politely in her chamber without inconveniencing anyone else in the household, least of all her husband.

Morgan could carve it on her headstone after he tossed her skeletal body into its rocky cairn. *Sabrina Cameron MacDonnell—A True Lady.* But since Morgan couldn't write, she supposed she'd be deprived of even that modest tribute.

Pugsley cocked his head to the side as she marched past. She would have sworn she saw a gleam of hunger in his beady little eyes.

"Don't fret, Pugsley. You'll have my bones to gnaw on soon enough."

She snatched a hand mirror from a trunk she'd upended to serve as a dressing table, half expecting to see a sunken skull peering back at her. Her reflection differed greatly from the one that had greeted her that morning. A tidy coronet of braids graced her brow. Bright spots of anger stained her cheeks. The dark wings of her eyebrows were drawn into a forbidding line.

She slammed the mirror down. She was a Cameron, by God! She'd be bloody well damned if she was going to let those barefoot savages hold her prisoner in her own chamber! It was far past time they learned that MacDonnell had a new mistress.

Storming to the door, she threw it open . . . then sneaked her head out and peered both ways before tiptoeing into the corridor.

Sabrina was sidling toward the stairs when a sharp cry, half smothered, stilled her feet. Frowning at its familiar cadence, she crept toward the nearest closed door. The sounds of muted scuffling drifted into the corridor. She pressed her ear to the door. A low moan pierced the silence. A cold sweat broke out over Sabrina's skin as she recognized it as the same terrified keening Enid had made when cornered by the spider at Cameron.

Someone was hurting her cousin.

Sabrina shoved at the door. It was bolted from within.

Her frantic fists pounded the wood, but at that moment something within the room began banging in rhythm, drowning her out. An agonized groan was followed by a hellish caterwauling that made the hair on Sabrina's nape writhe in horror. Dear God, they weren't just hurting her cousin! They were killing her! It was all her fault for turning Enid loose in this nest of vipers. They wouldn't care that she was an innocent Belmont. They would see her only as another Cameron, deserving of their tortures.

She beat madly at the door. Tears streamed from her eyes, blinding her. When her throat went raw from screaming, she shoved her knuckles between her lips, tasting blood, and eyed the unyielding oak.

Morgan. Morgan was the only one who could help her.

Lifting her skirts, she tore down the stairs, screaming her husband's name. Her lungs ached as if they would burst as she shot through the archway leading to the hall and into a dank cloud of peat smoke and unwashed men.

They reeked of stale sweat and malt whisky. Her empty stomach spun. She shoved her way through them, calling for Morgan.

She stumbled. One of the men caught her by the arm to steady her and shoved his face into hers, giving her a toothless leer. "Och, lass, if Morgan ain't around, won't I do?"

The anger she'd nursed earlier infused her. She whipped her arm out of his grip with surprising strength. Ignoring the smirks and catcalls, she fought her way through their ranks. They were practically drooling at the unexpected bounty of discovering a hysterical Cameron in their midst. A wave of relief surged through her when she finally broke out of the throng, but it faded quickly as she realized there was still no sign of Morgan.

The jeers and hoots subsided to mocking silence.

Sabrina could feel dozens of green and gray eyes boring into her back, all sharpened by predatory amusement. Alwyn chose that moment to detach herself from a sniggering circle of women. She sauntered forward to plant herself in Sabrina's path.

She stared down her aquiline nose at Sabrina. A triumphant smile curved her lips. "What ails ye, lass? I never had no trouble keepin' Morgan in my bed."

Sabrina didn't see the massive iron-banded doors at the end of the hall swing open. All she saw was red.

Alwyn's smile vanished as Sabrina curled both fists in the bodice of her filthy gown and drove her back until she slammed into a wall.

The MacDonnell women gaped as Sabrina Cameron, a true lady born and bred, jerked Alwyn's face down to hers and snarled, "I've had just about enough of your sass, you ill-mannered strumpet! Where the bloody hell is my husband?"

A masculine voice, rich with suppressed laughter, cut through the shocked silence. "Turn around, lass. He's right behind you."

Chapter Eleven

Morgan filled the doorway, his presence a living, tangible thing in the unnatural stillness of the hall. Mist beaded his plaid and glistened in his hair. A tantalizing hint of a smile carved brackets around his mouth. Sabrina had never in her life seen a sight so welcome.

For an elusive moment he was as precious and familiar to her as the handsome, stubborn boy he had once been. Emotion welled in her throat.

Leaving Alwyn to slide to a trembling heap in the floor, she rushed over and caught his big, warm hand in hers. She squeezed his fingers as if she'd never let them go.

Her words spilled out in a panicked rush. "You've got to come, Morgan! Someone is murdering Enid. Please hurry, before it's too late!" At the puzzled hesitation in his eyes, she dropped her pride and brought his hand to her lips, only too aware that she was humbling herself before a pack of wolves who would like nothing more than to scent her blood. "Please, Morgan, I'm begging you! Say you'll help her. I'll do anything. Anything at all."

His lashes veiled the quizzical glitter of his eyes. He brushed his knuckle against her lips, gently nudging them apart, and said softly, "I'd say that was an invitation a man would be a fool to refuse."

Keeping a frantic hold on his hand, Sabrina dragged him through the hall and up the stairs. A gawking parade of his clansmen followed, eager for the next entertainment in what had begun as a typical eve of drinking and wenching.

Sabrina shoved him toward the offending door. "There. Someone has her in there. And they won't open the door."

Morgan didn't have to lay his ear against the door. Everyone in the corridor and stationed up and down the stairs could hear the wild thumping and howling coming from the chamber. A choked gurgle floated out, sounding like someone caught in the throes of an agonizing death. Morgan's clansmen exchanged baffled glances.

Sabrina wrung her hands. "Hurry, please! Before it's too late!"

An odd expression crossed Morgan's face. "Are you absolutely sure—?"

"Yes! Yes, I'm sure! Please!" She gave him another desperate shove. "Open it now!"

He shook his head ruefully. "Verra well, then. Stand back."

Sabrina pressed herself to the opposite wall as Morgan splintered the bolt with one mighty kick from his bare foot. The first sniggers should have warned her. She darted forward, ducking under Morgan's arm when he threw it out to block her.

The rocking bed frame creaked to a halt. But it was not Enid lying crumpled on the thin tick. It was Ranald, his eyes screwed shut in ecstasy. Enid perched quite comfortably astride him, revealing an impressive amount of creamy flesh that was growing steadily pinker beneath the fascinated gazes of their audience.

The MacDonnells wasted no time on mercy.

"Who's killin' who, lass? It seems yer cousin has the upper hand, in a manner o' speakin'."

A dirk skittered across the floor toward the bed. "Here's me dagger, Ranald. Save yerself before 'tis too late!"

"Aye, but don't the lad look natural! At least he died with a smile on his lips."

Their hearty guffaws spread into roars of laughter.

Enid tumbled off Ranald and snatched the blanket over her flaming breasts. Her mortified gaze met Sabrina's.

As Morgan watched the color drain from his wife's face, his nostrils flared in anger. He crossed the room in two strides. A whimper escaped Enid as his towering shadow fell over the bed. The laughter died to nervous snickers.

He snatched Ranald up by his nape. "I asked you to look after her, you whelp. Couldn't you keep your randy hands to yourself for even a day?"

Ranald lifted his hands in sheepish defense. "A man can stand only so much temptation, Morgan. I gave it me best effort."

A sly voice shot out from the crowd. "Aye, and a fine one it was if all that bellerin' was for real."

Disgusted, Morgan dropped Ranald back to the bed.

"Forgive me." Sabrina's words were a mere whisper, but they cut straight through the ugly laughter to Morgan's heart. Her bewildered gaze traveled from Enid's stricken face to his. "Forgive me," she repeated simply before gathering her skirts and turning away.

Her fragile dignity shamed the crowd into silence. As his clansman parted to let her pass, Morgan's hands clenched into helpless fists.

Sabrina stood at the window and let the night wind ripple across her heated brow, cooling her shame. It didn't bother her that she'd been made a fool of. Lord knows she'd been a fool in Morgan's eyes ever since she'd landed at his feet with her skirt over her head. What ate at her now was the brief expression that had passed over Enid's face in the moment their gazes had locked. Pity.

Even plain, timid Enid was more of a woman than she. She was nothing more than a trophy of war. She rubbed her arms against a ruthless shiver.

Morgan watched his wife from the doorway. The rugged stone framed her, making her look small against the unyielding blackness of night. The breeze teased the tendrils of hair that had escaped her coiled braid. After the humiliation she had endured, another woman would have thrown herself sobbing on the bed. Perhaps if she had, he would have known how to comfort her. As it was, his hands hung useless at his sides.

She spoke first, surprising him. His stealth was almost as legendary as his size. It was whispered he could cut an enemy's throat and be halfway back to MacDonnell before the body hit the dirt.

Her voice whirred across his senses like velvet wings. "I'm sorry if I embarrassed you before your clansmen. This hasn't been a good day for me. I'm not accustomed to being disliked. Everyone I ever met has adored me." She stole a glance at him over her shoulder. "Everyone but you."

At her wry smile, a dagger of shame twisted in Morgan's heart, but he kept his face carefully impassive.

She turned back to the night, her voice musing. "I never really had to *do* anything to earn their affections. I just grinned and giggled, and if that didn't work on my father's more fierce clansmen, I'd sing them a clever ditty Brian had taught me or crawl into their laps and tug their beards."

Morgan folded his arms over his chest. "I don't recommend crawlin' into the laps of any of my clansmen."

"Oh, I don't know." She trailed her fingertips over the windowsill. "It seems to have worked for Enid." Swiping the dust from her hands, she faced him. "If my behavior seems odd to you, it's because I haven't

yet gotten the knack of being despised simply for who
I am."

"It doesn't take long."

She was wise enough to know he wasn't asking for
her pity. Their gazes met and held through the soft
shimmer of the candlelight.

Candlelight. Morgan suddenly became aware the
air was absent the sputter and hiss of tallow, the stench
of melting animal fat. The clumsy candles had been
replaced by tapers as slender and graceful as their
mistress. Their flames burned bright and true, as if
steadfast enough to bear even an icy onslaught of winter rain.

Their light cast lustrous pools over the Brussels
lace draped over an upended trunk. It sparkled across
the mysterious bottles of scents and cosmetics littering
its surface. It gleamed over the burnished wood of the
stringed clarsach propped against the wall. It caressed
sheets of ivory linen turned back over the wooden bed-
stead in an invitation that made Morgan's throat close
with hunger. He ached to shed the scratchy tartan and
pull Sabrina down naked between them.

Sheafs of creamy vellum were scattered over a
three-legged stool. The jaunty plume of a quill pen protruded from a bottle of ink. A chess set carved from
jasper sat in the middle of the scarred table. The
Cameron claymore hung over the hearth. Now Morgan
knew what had been in the heavy trunks he had carried
up the stairs that morning—civilization.

Sabrina followed the path of Morgan's gaze,
growing more nervous by the second. Her decorations
now seemed childish to her, like the folly of an
overimaginative child pretending a hawthorn bush was
a castle. "I should have asked before changing anything. If you don't care for it, I'll . . ."

Morgan held up a hand, and she trailed off, transfixed by the shy wonder dawning in his eyes.

Morgan wanted a moment to savor what she had
done. Within a few meager hours she had transformed
a lonely, gloomy animal's den into a palace fit for a

prince. Or a princess. A slow smile curved his lips. Aye, the lass had her mother's touch after all.

Morgan's smile frightened Sabrina. Without conscious volition, she took a step backward.

The crisp aroma of juniper flooded Morgan's senses, chasing away memories of women perfumed with sweat and peat smoke instead of roses. Delight threatened to overwhelm him. He wanted to toss down the Cameron claymore and dance a wild fling around it. He wanted to scoop Sabrina up and twirl her in his arms. He wanted to rumple those pristine bedclothes with the weight of their straining bodies. He hid his emotions the only way he knew how—behind action.

Clearing his throat gruffly, he drew his eyebrows together in a glower he hoped was convincingly stern. "As I recall, lass, you made me a promise when I agreed to help your cousin."

Here it comes, Sabrina thought, already regretting her foolish oath. This was the foot shooting out to trip her, the garden snake slithering down the back of her gown. How could she have trusted herself to this man's mercy? Her words rushed back to haunt her. *I'll do anything. Anything at all.*

She took another step away from him. "Now, Morgan, there's no need to be hasty . . ."

He wheeled to pace the chamber in long strides. "The days are gettin' shorter and the nights longer. I've a passel of work to do readyin' our new livestock for winter. I expect sundown will find me weary, cold, and surly."

"Imagine that," she murmured.

He pivoted on his heel to give her a penetrating look; she summoned up a meek smile.

"All the day long I'll be forced to suffer slothful work habits, crude jibes, and ill-natured companions. When I join you in this chamber at night, I'll expect a smile, a bit of pleasant conversation, and a fire to warm my feet. You may sing to me if you like or show me the sewin' you've done durin' the day." He pointed at one of the unopened trunks. "There are books in there, I suppose."

She nodded, knowing her eyes were probably wide enough to swallow her face.

"Excellent," he snapped. "I will be read to every night. When the snows come, there'll be time for you to teach me some letters and figures. Oh," he added, "you'll also teach me to play chess. I'd appreciate it if you'd endeavor to lose. I haven't the stomach for it myself."

Sabrina opened her mouth and closed it again, robbed of all speech by shock. She'd never imagined Morgan's brain storing so many words, much less uttering them. His masculine arrogance both astounded and fascinated her. She resisted the temptation to drop down and genuflect at his bare feet.

He took advantage of her stupefaction to stride toward the door.

"Where are you going?"

He tilted his jaw to an imperious angle as if explaining something to a rather stupid child. "To my chamber. Your parents kept separate chambers, did they not? All the fine folk do."

Sabrina massaged her temples, wondering if hunger had driven her mad. Morgan was not a man given to graceful surrender, yet there he stood, giving her exactly what she had wanted. A marriage of convenience. So why did she feel so inconvenienced? And how did the man expect to get a son from her if they slept apart? Surely he wasn't *that* unschooled. A disgruntled glance at him vanquished that question. This was a man born knowing what to do, a green-eyed rogue destined to be every lass's forbidden fantasy and every papa's nightmare.

"Most have separate chambers, I suppose," she muttered. "Although often in the winter, Mama and Papa would—"

"Verra well. Good night." His hand closed on the doorknob.

Sabrina was shocked to realize she didn't want him to abandon her to the bleak solitude she had suffered all day. A note of desperation touched her voice. "Morgan!"

He paused.

She could think of only one way to postpone their parting. If he had so generously accepted the terms she had offered, then what harm would there be in making a small concession to his own ego?

She darted her tongue out to moisten her lips and sidled toward him. "There's more to marriage than chess and singing, you know. A true gentleman would never bid his wife good night without first offering her a parting kiss."

His brows drew together in a wary line. "Your father *kissed* your mother?"

She nodded primly. "Every night. Without fail."

"His own wife?"

Sabrina resisted the urge to kick him in the shins, knowing she'd only get a broken toe for her effort. "His very own wife."

A groan escaped Morgan as if he were suffering mightily beneath the weight of civilized custom. "If 'tis the proper thing to do . . ."

Sabrina had no time to prepare herself. His arm snaked around her waist, snatching her clear off the floor. His mouth clamped down on hers. His attack ended as abruptly as it had come, leaving her staggering.

She shot him an accusing look and knuckled her lip. "You bit me!"

He ducked his head. A grin lurked behind his rakish fall of hair. "Now, lass, you can't expect a MacDonnell to know how to kiss. Barefoot savages we are, the lot of us."

Sabrina remembered only too well that the insult he threw back in her face now had preceded a kiss of drugging tenderness in her mother's solar.

"Perhaps I should let you do the honors," he said, crossing his arms over his chest and staring straight ahead.

Sabrina approached the flesh-and-blood monolith with trepidation, unable to forget that a man's heart beat hot and strong beneath his golden skin. Her teeth worried her tender lip. Drawing in a breath for courage, she closed her eyes, pursed her lips and . . .

. . . kissed his plaid.

Scowling, she plucked a wool fuzz from her lip and tried again. Even by arching her neck and bouncing up and down on her tiptoes, she could do no more than graze his throat. Morgan remained impervious to her struggles; his stony jaw cracked in a yawn.

Determined to wring a response from him, Sabrina dragged the stool over and climbed on top of it. Morgan's lips were set in a stern line, but his eyes glittered with mischief. Remembering her mother's wedding-night lesson, Sabrina softened her demure pucker. Framing his rugged face in her hands, she pressed her lips to his. Their firm, silky contours parted beneath her coaxing, and she allowed him a teasing taste of her tongue.

Morgan's growl blended with a roar of warning in her ears. The world swayed, but Morgan caught her before she could fall. "What is it, lass? Are you ill?"

She laughed shakily, clinging to his plaid. "Just hungry, I fear. I haven't eaten today."

His face darkened with displeasure. "Damn Alwyn anyway. The lazy wench was supposed to bring your meals to your chamber."

Sabrina had to do no more than arch one eyebrow before he nodded sheepishly, conceding it an ill-conceived idea from the start.

He gently set her on her feet. "I'll have somethin' sent up right away."

"Morgan?" she asked shyly. "Will you be expecting a good-night kiss every night?"

It seemed a much greater struggle for him to affect a stern expression. "Aye, lass. Every night. Without fail."

The door closed in her face, then swung back open, giving her barely enough time to hide her triumphant grin. "I'll strike a bargain with you, lass. I'll keep Alwyn out of the kitchen if you'll steer Enid clear of the garden. Her stewed mushrooms are pure murder."

She snatched at the door before he could close it

again. "But how did you know it was Enid who poisoned you?"

His grin took on a devilish slant. "I didn't. Until now."

Morgan was gone before Sabrina realized he had tricked a confession of innocence from her. She didn't know whether to bless or curse his canny wit. She slumped against the door, pressing her cheek to the rugged wood and knowing it wasn't hunger making her heart beat with such wild abandon.

On the other side of the door, Morgan fought every masculine instinct that commanded he march back into the chamber and seize what was his. Patience was a virtue a true warrior must possess. But the sweet, intoxicating taste of Sabrina still flavored his mouth, making him hunger for more. Much more. He would have sworn her ethereal scent had followed him into the corridor. He bunched his plaid beneath his nose. The haunting fragrance of roses clung to it, planted there in the moment she had swooned in his arms, not from ardor, but hunger.

His hand clenched the tartan as if mere brawn could preserve such an elusive prize. He could not afford to let Sabrina know how badly he wanted her. A MacDonnell could never humble himself before a Cameron. Tonight had been a small triumph to savor, but others would soon follow, he promised himself. Damn his own pleasure for now. He would court her and tease her until she was begging for the pleasure he could give her. Never had the prospect of battle loomed so gloriously; never had victory been so wickedly anticipated.

When Sabrina's surrender finally came, it would be made all the sweeter for the waiting.

Sabrina awoke the next morning to the beguiling sensation of someone stroking her hair. "Mama," she mumbled, rolling to her back.

But when she opened her eyes, she saw the rounded blur of her cousin's face.

Enid twined a stray tendril of Sabrina's hair around her finger. "My hair has always been too thin to curl."

Sabrina sat up and leaned against the headboard, hugging her knees. Wary silence hung between them.

"I never meant—"

"I came to tell—"

They both lapsed back into silence.

Enid twisted a loose fold of the coverlet. "There's something you should know. There was more to my being sent to Cameron than my father let on."

"I thought it was simply so we could get to know each other before my visit to London in the spring," Sabrina lied, wanting to spare her cousin's feelings.

She was surprised to realize how distant her dreams of London seemed. She had spent hours envisioning handsome suitors falling at her feet. Now she would trade all of their imagined gallantries for the shadow of a smile from one man.

Enid shook her head. "I had a suitor in London," she confessed shyly. "Philip Markham. A Cambridge graduate. Tall. Handsome. Very proper, even a bit severe, but Mother and Father were delighted. They had begun to despair of ever marrying me off." Her faint shrug revealed more than she intended it to. "I truly believed he cared for me. Perhaps he did in the only way he knew how."

As she continued, Sabrina took her hand. It was clammy and cool. "The day he came to ask my father for my hand, he did the only unconventional thing I'd ever known him to do. He waited until the family had gathered in the salon. Then he tore the ribbon off a box and drew out a gown, a stunning gown with a narrow waistline stitched into gathered pleats." Enid's fingers tightened. "He told them all that the day I could fit into that gown was the day we would wed."

Tears of anger and empathy stung Sabrina's eyes. "That wretch! I hope Uncle Willie sent him packing."

"They were all very quiet for a moment, then

they jumped up to offer their congratulations. Not even Stefan could look me in the eye. It was the longest evening of my life. I managed to smile my way through supper, then I retreated to my room."

"Where I hope you wrote a scathing letter dressing that scoundrel down to his stockings!"

"I vomited," Enid said starkly. "Then I ate an entire box of chocolates. The day the engagement announcement appeared in the *Gazette*, I ate the turkey the cook had dressed for Sunday's dinner." A sad, triumphant smile played around her mouth. "Within three weeks I couldn't fit into my own gowns, much less the one Philip had chosen. So he broke off our engagement in disgust." A fierce pride lit her pale eyes. "But I learned something in those weeks. I learned there were men in the world who cared nothing about a woman's weight. Underfootmen. Delivery boys. Barbers."

The light in her eyes died. "When my father caught me on the desk in the library with his very own solicitor, he banished me to Scotland until the scandal of Philip's rejection could die down."

Swallowing her shock at her cousin's blunt confession, Sabrina stroked Enid's downy cheek. "Oh, Enid. I'm so terribly sorry."

"All my life I've been told how pretty I would be if I weren't fat."

"But you're not fat," Sabrina dutifully protested. "You're—"

Enid laid two fingers against her lips. "Fat. Not pudgy. Not plump. Fat. But Ranald is one of those men who finds me pretty anyway." Patches of pink tinted her cheeks, but Sabrina sensed that she needed to say what would come next. "When I expressed a fear that in my ardor I might crush him, he only laughed and said that any man who couldn't handle a magnificent lass such as I was was no man at all."

Sabrina had a thousand questions to ask, but was ashamed to admit she hadn't allowed her own husband to teach her the answers. Enid stiffened as she awaited her response.

Sabrina tucked a wispy strand of hair behind her cousin's ear. "I don't think you're pretty." Enid's eyes darkened. Sabrina started to smile. "I think you're beautiful."

Enid opened her arms and Sabrina fell into them. Their tearful embrace was interrupted by a bloodcurdling scream from Enid. Her hand trembled as she pointed over Sabrina's shoulder.

Clutching her ringing ear, Sabrina swiveled to find a huge black beetle frozen on the wall behind the bed. His antennae quivered in apparent terror.

A giggle burst from her. She met Enid's eyes and they both started to laugh as they realized Enid possessed the courage and recklessness to bed a wild Highlander but could still swoon at the sight of a harmless bug.

The chamber door flew open to reveal a corridor of curious MacDonnells, rabid for excitement. They gaped at the puzzling sight of the two young women collapsed in each other's arms, howling with mirth. Their dumbfounded expressions sent Sabrina and Enid into fresh gales of laughter.

An old man, bald except for a shock of white hair above each ear, scratched his shiny head. "Why, I'll be damned! Ye never know which bed ye're goin' to find these young lassies in. And they say we MacDonnells are a randy lot!"

Chapter Twelve

Sabrina chose the following night to teach her husband the intricacies of chess.

She didn't even blink when Morgan's fist came down on the board, overturning it and sending the pieces rolling to all corners of the chamber. With a long-suffering sigh, she knelt to gather them into her skirt. It was the third time he'd upset the board and she'd yet to explain the movements of bishop or rook.

Morgan paced the chamber in angry strides, his hand clenched around the object of his contempt. "How?" he raged. "How can the king be so bloody powerless? Has he no honor? No pride? Where lies the glory in hidin' behind a woman's skirts?"

Pugsley stretched out his little legs, rolled over on the hearth, and yawned.

"You're missing the point." Sabrina plucked the toes of a hapless knight from the fire. "The king is the most important player on the board. You can play without a queen, but you can't play without a king. When he is captured, the game is lost. He must be protected at all costs."

"Protected? By a handful of foolish pawns and a mere woman! What manner of chieftain is he? He should be stoned and cast out of his clan." To illustrate his point, Morgan hurled the cowardly monarch toward the fire. Pugsley caught the piece and worried it between his merciless gums.

Sabrina rolled her eyes as Morgan absently helped her flip over the heavy board. "A mere woman? There have been many women throughout history who have given their lives protecting their own. What of your very own Queen Mary?"

He slammed his palms on the table, his scowl deepening. "Whose head was forfeit to *your* very own Queen Elizabeth "

Sabrina thumped down a rook. "She wasn't *my* Queen Elizabeth. I'm as Scottish as you are, Morgan MacDonnell!"

"Then why do you talk like a bloody Sassenach?"

They found themselves leaning over the table, nose to nose. Sabrina's breath caught as Morgan's gaze dropped to her lips, his eyes the minty color of a raindrop suspended on a new leaf. His gaze held her mesmerized for a timeless moment before falling to the chessboard. He picked up the graceful figure of the dark queen.

His burr softened, losing the sharp edges of anger. "Women are delicate creatures. Fragile. Gentle. Made by God to be sheltered from the harshness of this world."

Sabrina was riveted by the sight of his hands, impossibly large, impossibly gentle, caressing the translucent jasper. She had seen his hands move with that same dreamy grace over the petals of the Belmont Rose an instant before it had snapped.

" 'Tis a man's duty to protect his woman. To cherish her."

Considering Eve and the other MacDonnell women Sabrina had met, she found it extraordinary that Morgan was speaking from the heart. His notions of

honor and pride confounded her. They were contrary
to everything she had been taught to believe about his
clan.

"Are you certain you're not a changeling?" she
asked softly. "Perhaps the fairies left you in a basket on
your father's doorstep."

A wry smile twisted his lips. "My da accused me
of the same thing on occasion. But I had a mother. She
died when I was born."

His thumb stroked the carved folds of the queen's
skirt. An emotion akin to jealousy unfolded within
Sabrina. She shivered at a vision of those bronze hands
moving against her own skin with such aching tenderness.

Unable to endure any more of his sweet, unwitting torture, she snatched the queen away from him
and sat to sort the pieces. " 'Tis only a game, Morgan."

He dropped into his chair, arms crossed. " 'Tis
not seemly. I won't play."

Sabrina folded her own arms, and they sat in sullen silence. Pugsley lost interest in the disgraced monarch and spit him out. Morgan finally leaned across the
table. "I suppose there's no help for it, then. I'll have
my good-night kiss now."

Sabrina closed her eyes and dutifully puckered.
When nothing happened, she opened them to find
Morgan surveying her, his own eyes narrowed to lazy
slits. He cupped her face in his hands much as she had
done his own the previous night. Her heart thundered
against her ribs in warning as both of his thumbs
brushed her lips, probing, stroking, testing their softness, their resistance to his will.

She felt them melting like warm wax beneath the
startling intimacy of his touch, opening for him in
shameless invitation to pierce her yet deeper. His breath
was warm and sweet against her skin. Still, he continued his persuasive stroking, ravishing her mouth with
nothing more than the broad, callused pads of his
thumbs.

She writhed in her chair as tendrils of flame licked
through the dark, mysterious passages of her body,

tightening her breasts and slicking her secret folds with an unfamiliar dew. Then and only then did Morgan's tongue delve into her, caressing her own with a single deep stroke that rendered her mindless.

Ignoring her agonized moan, he drew back to plant a brisk kiss on the tip of her nose. "Good night, brat."

Dreading the breathless sound of her voice, she waited until he'd reached the door to say, "I thought you MacDonnells weren't well versed in the art of good-night kissing."

"Ah, but that's why we must practice with such diligence." He gave her a devilish wink. "Sleep well, lass."

When he was gone, Sabrina let her head fall limply on her folded arms, her body so inflamed with the potent seeds of desire he'd planted that she doubted she would ever sleep again.

Sabrina chose the next night to introduce her husband to Homer, hoping the Greek bard was clever enough to hold Morgan's attention and too dry to stir his passions, passions that had proved devastating to both her sleep and her peace of mind. She had lain awake half the night, aching and tossing until the sheets were twisted around her like the tendrils of Morgan's unbreakable hold.

She curled her stocking feet beneath her and began to read, feeling a bit like Scheherazade entertaining the emperor. Only it wasn't her head she risked losing to Morgan, but her heart.

Her fears were unfounded. Morgan was soon perched on the edge of his chair, listening raptly as the fearless Odysseus outwitted his enemies and battled his way back to his beloved Penelope. Sabrina stole a look at Morgan over the top of the book. Boyish wonder had softened his rugged features. When Odysseus blinded the terrible Cyclops, he leaned forward so far, she feared he might tumble out of the chair. She found herself caught up in the ancient tale as if hearing it for the first time.

She began with relish the story of Odysseus and the clever enchantress Circe. Morgan shifted his weight back in his chair, her first clue that something was amiss. The telltale lines of his scowl deepened. Sabrina began to read faster, stumbling over simple words as her concentration faltered and her mind danced ahead to their impending kiss.

"Fool!" Morgan's fist crashed on the table.

The book snapped shut in her hands.

"Damnation! The man's a bloody fool! I would never have made such a mistake. The canny witch turned his men into pigs and now he's fallen into her bed? Hasn't he an ounce of pride?"

Morgan's obsession with pride was beginning to wear thin on Sabrina's nerves. She met his gaze boldly. "Circe enchanted him with her beauty. Perhaps he was willing to forsake his pride for a taste of her pleasures."

"Any man who forfeits his pride for a woman is a bloody fool."

Sabrina read the warning in his stormy eyes clearly. If she allowed him, he might someday give her his body, even his son, but he would never give her his heart. To her horror, unexpected tears stung her eyes.

Letting the book slide to the floor, she moved to the window, where the breeze could burn the tears away. The wind bore the crisp threat of an early snow. "Perhaps you're right. Odysseus's decision cost him dearly. According to Homer, he was killed by one of the offspring of that union—his very own son." She faced him, dry-eyed and confident now in her anger. "But if you'd have let me finish the story, you would have understood. Odysseus shared Circe's bed only to free his men. He valued their lives above his paltry pride. Surely you of all men would understand such a sacrifice."

Morgan understood only too well. Circe wasn't half the enchantress Sabrina was. She had woven a spell around him with her mellifluous voice, binding him tighter with each shy smile she had stolen at him, each gentle shaping of her lips around Homer's words. He wasn't sure if he had erupted in fury over the magnitude of Odysseus's folly or his own.

She faced him now, no less magnificent in her defiance than Circe. Her delicate features were taut with emotion; the night wind coaxed strands of hair from her prim coronet. He could envision her on a sea-washed rock, her unbound hair shimmering with spray, boldly meeting any challenge the sea could offer. Perhaps Odysseus wasn't a fool for surrendering to Circe. Perhaps he was a fool for leaving her.

When Morgan crooked a commanding finger at her, Sabrina considered refusing his summons. But curiosity won out and she marched over to him. He patted his knee in invitation. After a moment's hesitation, she stiffly sat, feeling like a puppet dancing from Morgan's strings.

His warm fingers curled around her bare nape, eliciting a shiver of pleasure. "Perhaps your cunning Odysseus only soothed his pride by pretendin' it was a sacrifice."

Sabrina knew that was the closest Morgan might ever come to an apology. He drew her down until their lips touched and ignited in the pure, hot flame she was coming to both crave and dread. She slid inexorably down his thigh into the unyielding cradle of his lap. He gently laved her lips, flicking and nibbling at the sensitive skin until she parted them in a plea for more.

This time he did not deny her. His tongue swept out in a flare of heated satin, exploring the tender crevices of her mouth and evoking a response that sent her own tongue dancing over the strong, even line of his teeth. She kneaded his plaid like a satiated cat, squirming in his lap without realizing it. A hoarse rumble of reaction escaped him, sending both exaltation and fear roaring through her veins. If she ever truly broke Morgan's control, she wondered, would she be woman enough to handle him?

She buried her burning brow against his throat, wishing he would make the choice for both of them, wishing he would rise, carry her to the bed, and make her forget her foolish vow to deny him. She didn't know whether to feel relieved or disappointed when he stood and set her gently on her feet.

"Will you read to me again tomorrow, brat?"

She reached up to toy with a silky strand of his hair, hoping her mischievous smile would hide the helpless need hazing her vision. "Oh, indeed I shall. I have just the story. It's about a bold warrior named Samson and a spirited lass called Delilah."

Sabrina emerged from her chamber the following afternoon, her steps sharpened by purpose. As mistress of MacDonnell, she could hardly spend the rest of her life skulking in her chamber, awaiting Morgan's sporadic attentions. She was already beginning to chafe at being treated like an exotic pet—albeit a pampered one.

As she passed the mouth of a crumbling stairwell, the sound of voices drew her attention. Voices lifted in anger were a common occurrence at MacDonnell and were usually followed by the thud of fists and the clatter of falling teeth. But these voices were lowered to hissed growls, and Sabrina sensed this was more than a simple quarrel. She wavered, remembering the cost of her earlier inadvertent snooping, but the next words held her riveted.

"How could ye have been so damn clumsy, woman? He should've never trusted ye with the task."

"Trusted? 'Twas my idea in the beginnin', or have ye forgotten? God knows a dimwit like ye couldna have mastered such a plot. The chieftain pronounced it a bold stroke o' genius."

"Aye, and look what it got him. Ol' blind Galvin could have done as well! I knew yer leg was faulty, but in truth, I thought yer eyes were sound."

"Go to hell!"

Before Sabrina could pretend to be doing anything more than eavesdropping, booted feet clattered up the stairs. She was dismayed to see Ranald emerge. His swarthy face paled at the sight of her. Doffing his bonnet, he mumbled, "My lady" before dashing off down the nearest corridor like a startled hare.

Eve appeared and leaned against the stone wall, her lips twisted in a contemptuous smirk. Her hair was loose now, and Sabrina realized with a shock that Eve was not as old as she had first believed. Although wind and sun had weathered her skin and washed the gilt from her hair, she couldn't have been much older than Sabrina's own mother.

"You have lovely hair," Sabrina said, maintaining her wary stance. "You should wear it down more often."

"Ah, but that I canna do." Eve circled her like a wildcat scenting its prey. "Long hair ain't nothin' but a noose in battle. I once caught a foolish Grant lassie by her curls and split her from stern to gullet."

Sabrina gave the neat coil anchored at her nape a nervous pat. "Do tell."

"Aye," she pronounced proudly. "Angus always said I could slit a man's throat and the fool wouldna know it till he arrived at the gates of hell."

"I'm sorry about Angus. Morgan tells me the two of you were very close."

Eve shrugged, her stoic response reminding Sabrina more of Morgan than she would have liked. "He died as he lived. By the blade."

"But by whose blade?" Sabrina dared softly.

She started as Eve drew a callused finger across her cheek, her touch surprisingly gentle. "So pretty. So smooth. Morgan likes it that way, don't he? Smooth skin. Soft voice. Just like yer ma, ain't ye? Just like Angus's precious Beth."

Eve's eyes had taken on a dim haze and Sabrina began to suspect the real reason for the woman's hatred of the Camerons. Conflicting emotions assaulted her. Fury at Angus's thoughtlessness. Compassion for the girl Eve had been—homely, crippled, forced to live in the shadow of the fine lady Angus had failed to woo.

But before she could speak, Eve's face hardened. "Has the lad even troubled to bed ye, lass? Morgan's more like his da than he cares to admit. He'd rather pine for what he canna have than pleasure himself with what he can. After all, ye're nothin' but a pale imitation o' the woman they both wanted."

Sabrina backed away, desperate to escape the taunt in Eve's eyes. They seemed to see inside of her, to pierce her darkest and most secret fears. "What are you saying?"

"More than I should. Ye'll find out soon enough." A pity more terrible than contempt flickered through her eyes. "Don't give yer heart to him, lass. He'll only feed it back to ye, piece by piece, until ye damn near choke on it." She shuffled away, her lame foot dragging on the uneven stone.

Sabrina stared after her, the cryptic words echoing through her brain. She had not forgotten that Eve and Ranald had been the only MacDonnells conspicuously absent from the hall when Angus was murdered. Did she dare share her suspicions with Morgan? Would he believe her, or would he accuse her of seeking a scapegoat to clear the Cameron name? She sighed. It was simply too soon to jeopardize their fragile regard with accusations. She abhorred the notion of once again drawing the line of Cameron and MacDonnell between their divided hearts.

Shoving aside her lingering unease, she continued on her mission.

As Sabrina entered the smoky hall, she resisted the urge to rub her hands together in gleeful anticipation. Homer had given her an idea. If Circe had woven her enchantment to turn men into pigs, why couldn't she use her own particular charms to turn pigs into men? But even Circe would have been challenged to choose a victim from so many delicious prospects.

She found it ridiculously easy to imagine snorting, snuffling pig heads perched on the broad shoulders of the MacDonnell men. Three of them slouched before the fire, tossing dice. When one of them shot a stream of tobacco into his partner's matted hair, a scuffle ensued. At another table, a wrestling match over a haunch of venison ended with one man crashing a jug of whisky over another's head, knocking him out cold.

A snorting roar of laughter from the center table drew her attention. Ah, now, there was a challenge worthy of a mighty enchantress!

Mr. Fergus MacDonnell himself, swilling ale and making ribald toasts, his grimy hand shoved down the bodice of the giggling woman draped across his lap. His bulbous nose even had a porcine tilt to it.

Sabrina lifted her skirts and picked her way gingerly over the bones and ominous stains that littered the floor. The other men at the table quietened uneasily at her approach, but Fergus was too busy fondling the girl's breast to notice. He tilted a jug to his lips, wearing its earthenware handle as a pinkie ring. Ale trickled down his grizzled whiskers into the thick, bullish folds of his neck.

"Och," he grunted, leering at the girl. "Ain't nothin' finer on a chill day than a jug of ale and a warm tit."

When his crass remark failed to garner the laughter he expected, he slammed the jug down on the table. "What's got into the lot o' ye? There's tits eno' to go 'round, ain't they?" He peered down the girl's bodice. "Last time I checked, ever' wench had two." He roared at his own jest.

One of his companions cleared his throat. "Eh, Fergus . . ."

It was too late. Sabrina tapped Fergus gently on the shoulder. "Pardon me for interrupting your charming and poetic discourse on the merits of a woman's bosom, Mr. MacDonnell, but I have need of you in my chamber."

The flailing dice players rolled to halt. The man who'd been knocked unconscious by the jug of whisky stirred with interest.

Fergus swiveled on the bench, dumping the occupant of his lap to the floor. "Me, lass? Ye've need o' me? In yer chamber?"

She smiled sweetly and crooked her finger at him. "In the worst way."

Giving the men a wide-eyed look that clearly said *How did I get so bloody lucky?* he tucked his thumbs into his kilt and strutted after her like a bantam cock about to raid a henhouse.

Enid had prepared the chamber as Sabrina had requested. A delicate china tea set was laid out on a tablecloth of Valenciennes. A piping hot pot of tea sat on a starched doily. Steam wafted from its graceful spout.

"Mr. MacDonnell?" Sabrina gestured toward the nearest chair. Fergus acted as if he hadn't heard, so she repeated herself.

Starting with surprise, he ducked his head shyly. "Ain't no one e'er called me mister before. Me friends call me Fergie, but ye can call me darlin' if ye like." He winked at her, but without the bracing presence of his cronies, the gesture lost some of its leer. Sabrina deliberately overlooked his impudence.

He perched on the edge of the chair and peered around, obviously intimidated by the feminine trappings of the chamber.

Sabrina poured him a cup of tea. "Do you take sugar in your tea, sir?"

"Don't know," he admitted. "Ain't never had no tea. Malt's always been me drink o' choice."

Sabrina dropped in three of the grainy lumps, suspecting his jaded tastes might veer toward the sensual. She pressed the wafer-thin cup into his hand. His florid palm dwarfed it. He took a hasty slurp, then crinkled his nose in a poorly hidden grimace.

Sabrina hid her own smile behind a sip of tea. As Fergus lowered the cup, his hand shook violently. The cup rattled against the saucer; tea sloshed over its rim. His broad face flushed. His gaze darted toward the door as if to seek escape.

Sabrina stared, fascinated, into his beady, red-rimmed eyes, seeing for the first time the panic in their depths. The revelation stunned her. Why, this crude, blustering man was afraid of women! No, not afraid. Petrified! He'd simply chosen to hide that fear behind crass jibes and a randy reputation. Pity welled in her heart.

Knowing she was taking a terrible chance, she reached over to pat his trembling hand. "It's all right, Mr. MacDonnell. There's nothing to be afraid of. I swear I'll be gentle with you."

Early that evening as a crisp wind blew down from the north and the slate sky began to spit snow, Morgan dragged his exhausted body into the buttery. He'd spent his entire day wrestling with the Cameron sheep, penning them into the narrow glen that would serve as their home during the harsh winter to come. The rock walls would shelter them from the worst of the weather. Come spring, they would be freed to roam the heathered heath as a sign of fresh hope for his clan's prosperity.

He had never dreamed sheep could be such befuddled creatures. He and his men would barely get one hemmed in before another would wander away.

He peeled his plaid from his shoulders, stripping down to the waist. His muscles throbbed in protest. Groaning, he cupped his hands in a barrel and splashed cool spring water over his face, slicking back his hair as the water ran in soothing trickles down his chest. No matter how exhausted he was, he always stopped to wash before joining Sabrina in her chamber. Too many times in his life he'd heard the words "filthy, stinkin' MacDonnell" hissed behind his back by those not bold enough to say them to his face.

As he patted his face dry, his gaze flicked upward to the beamed ceiling. The pleasure he took in knowing Sabrina awaited him both delighted and alarmed him. Her chamber had become his sanctuary after grueling hours of bellowing orders at men so unaccustomed to a decent day's work that they lapsed into naps over their shovels and staffs. Oddly enough, it wasn't her stories he anticipated, but the teasing melody of her voice. It wasn't the games, but the matching of his mind to her clever wit. He had thought to find solace and peace in her chamber only to discover a challenge more exhilarating than battle had ever been.

He straightened, wincing as fresh pain shot across his shoulders. Perhaps Sabrina would use her supple fingers to work out the kinks in his muscles. She had refused him nothing yet. An unbidden smile stole across his face. If he continued to prove to her a MacDonnell could be more than just a rutting beast, she might soon invite him into her bed, not out of charity or duty, but out of desire. Then he had every intention of sliding between those crisp sheets and her milky thighs and making her his own.

Morgan's groin grew hot and heavy at the thought, pulsing in time to his anticipation. He closed his eyes, allowing himself a moment to savor the raw power of the enticing vision. A shock jolted him as an arm snaked around his waist. Grubby, chipped fingernails raked his bare abdomen. Another hand slithered up his thigh to grope crudely beneath the plaid. Long hair tickled his back.

"Alwyn," he muttered.

"Aye, Morgan. 'Tis yer own bonny Alwyn." An excited coo escaped her. "Right and ready, ye be. But ye always were, weren't ye, love?"

Dodging her persistent fingers, he swung around. He could smell the fresh taint of another man's sex on her. It withered his desire faster than a dash of icy water.

She was already drawing up the skirts of her gown. He shoved them back down. "I thought I'd explained myself, lass. You can't go around droppin' your drawers every time I walk into a room. 'Tis not seemly. I've a wife now."

"Go on with ye, Morgan. Ye know I don't wear drawers." She stalked him like a big, blond Highland wildcat, backing him against the barrel and shoving her ample breasts against his chest. "The timin' is near perfect. Yer precious wife willna disturb us. If she can entertain another man in her chamber, what's the harm in us stealin' a wee bit o' fun for ourselves?"

"Another man?"

The ominous note in Morgan's voice sent Alwyn into a cautious retreat. "Aye. I thought ye knew. Eve told me he's been up there for hours."

"Hours?" A haze of red descended over Morgan's eyes. His ears roared.

Alwyn backed away, her eyes widening in alarm. Her own numerous dalliances had never troubled Morgan. How was she to suspect his wee, monkey-faced wife could provoke such a fury?

Morgan wasn't furious. He was rabid. Tripping over his trailing plaid, he shoved past Alwyn and burst into the hall. Smoke and silence hung over the cavernous chamber, both too thick to be cut with a claymore. Sweet Christ! Did they all believe he had been cuckolded by his Cameron bride?

His clansmen gazed into the fire, shuffled their feet, swirled their whisky in their mugs. Not one of them would look him in the eye. Only Eve dared to heft her chipped mug in a mocking toast.

As he crossed the hall, Morgan slowed his strides to a more dignified pace, feeling their gazes bore into his exposed skin.

Behind him, the wagers flew in frantic whispers and hushed tones as his clansmen speculated on whether he would strangle his fickle wife or plant a pistol ball in her black little heart.

Chapter Thirteen

As soon as Morgan was out of sight of the hall, he thundered into a run. He took the crumbling steps two at a time, then stopped dead outside the door of Sabrina's chamber. Over the gently plucked notes of the clarsach and the thud of his heart in his ears, he could hear a man's deep baritone and a woman's sweet soprano blended in a melody so poignant it would have made the most ruthless of warriors weep.

The man sang:

> I might have had a king's daughter,
> Far, far beyond the sea.

Sabrina countered with:

> I might have been a king's daughter,
> Had it not been for love o' thee.

Another man was singing with his wife. Morgan didn't realize it was the first time he had thought of her not as Sabrina, or brat, or a bloody Cameron nuisance, but as *his wife*. Rage and helplessness buffeted him. The sheer intimacy of their melded voices was somehow more damning than fornication itself.

He threw open the door. Two startled pairs of eyes surveyed him. He suddenly realized what a fool he must appear—half naked, hair dripping, jaw dropped in astonishment.

He could not help but gape to discover the angel's baritone belonged to a man with a soul more charred than Satan's.

Fergus MacDonnell hefted his squat bulk from the pillow at Sabrina's feet and offered her a rusty bow. "Thank ye for the tea, me lady. I'm much obliged."

She laid the clarsach aside. Fergus's crude paw swallowed her dainty hand. "Thank *you*, Mr. MacDonnell, for sharing those charming Highland ballads. My husband will appreciate them during the long winter nights to come. Won't you, dear?"

It took Morgan a full minute to realize she was addressing him. "Huh?"

Fergus paused in the doorway to give him a chiding frown. "Don't grunt at yer wife, lad. Ye're not a bloody swine." He tossed the dangling tail of the plaid over Morgan's shoulder. "Ye shouldna go about half dressed in the presence of a lady. Did yer da teach ye no manners a-tall?"

Fergus slapped him fondly on the back before swaggering off down the corridor. Sabrina bustled around the chamber, humming under her breath and blithely gathering teacups as if there weren't a hall full of MacDonnells below waiting for the thundering report of his pistol.

"Charming man, isn't he?" She blew a speck of dust off the cream pitcher. "Beneath all that bluster lies the soul of a gentleman."

Morgan snapped his jaw shut. He'd once seen Fergus suck a mutton bone clean while cleaving off an enemy's head with his other hand. "Aye, a regular poet, he is."

At Morgan's even tone, Pugsley wiggled under the bed until nothing but his curly little tail was showing.

Morgan gently shut the door behind him. "Would you care to explain his exalted presence in your chamber, lass?"

She polished a teacup on her sleeve, rubbing away Fergus's grubby fingerprints. "What is there to explain? I invited him to partake of tea with me. He was kind enough to teach me some of your lovely Highland ballads. I knew you would tire of Mama's English songs rapidly enough." Her nose wrinkled. "Too many references to routing the shiftless Scots, I fear."

"Is it an English custom to take tea with a strange man? Alone in your bedchamber?"

"Well, no. But I hardly found the hall suitable for . . ." She trailed off at the full implication of his words. The teapot slid from her hand and struck the table edge, chipping off the porcelain rose that adorned its surface. Incredulous pain darkened her eyes. "Are you accusing me of . . . ?"

"I'm accusin' you of nothin', lass. It's just that when Alwyn told me—"

"Oh. Alwyn." Her voice turned dull and lifeless, belying the fierce sparkle of her eyes. "You would believe Alwyn, wouldn't you? After all, she's a MacDonnell, isn't she? Not a sly, deceitful Cameron. And where were you and your darling Alwyn when these accusations were made?"

A flicker of guilt danced across Morgan's face as he remembered the greedy feel of Alwyn's fingers around him. The wounded gleam in Sabrina's eyes deepened.

He swore beneath his breath. "I didn't lay a hand on her, lass, I swear it."

Sabrina didn't even seem to hear him. A shaky laugh escaped her. "I should have expected as much, shouldn't I? Why should you trust me? After all, there is no depth to which we Camerons will not sink—

murdering our dinner guests, poisoning our bride-grooms. Why should it be such a stretch of the imagination for you to believe I'd whore for your men?"

She turned her back on him, her slender shoulders rigid with fury. Morgan shook his head in grudging admiration. Sabrina had managed to turn both his anger and his jealousy against him. None of his clansmen would dare lift their voices to him in genuine anger, but once again this slip of a girl had proved them all cowards and himself a bloody fool.

He picked up the rose that had chipped from the teapot. If only he had stopped to ponder the absurdity of the accusation. He was always charging in without counting the cost, destroying something precious and fragile in his rash clumsiness—his mother's life, the Belmont Rose, Sabrina's pride.

Laying the rose on the table, he padded over to stand in front of her, so close he could feel her breath against his bare chest. Its sweet whisper stirred him as Alwyn's touch never could. She kept her head bowed, stubbornly refusing to meet his eyes.

"I don't suppose you'd read me that story you promised? The one about the bonny lass Delilah?"

"I don't suppose so," she whispered.

"A game of chess? I swear I won't toss the board. Not even if you win."

She shook her head. The silence stretched between them.

Morgan ran a hand through his damp hair, feeling the dead weight of regret settle into his bones. He sank heavily into a chair.

Sabrina had decided her husband was impossible to please, so she decided to please herself. Ignoring Morgan, she sat upon the stool and began to pluck a melody from the clarsach. Inclining her head, she toyed with the bittersweet words of the ballad Fergus had taught her.

Her attempt to pretend Morgan didn't exist soon failed her. Even motionless and silent, his raw masculine presence commanded the room. Six feet three inches of brawny Highlander was impossible to ignore, even to someone oblivious of his charms, which, Sabrina regretted keenly, she was not.

She stole a look at him. Her voice faltered, stumbling over a puir lassie's pledge of undying love to her faithless suitor. Longing closed her throat. Morgan's eyes were closed, his gilt lashes resting flush on his cheeks. His muscled legs were stretched out before him and his plaid had ridden up to reveal bronze thighs dusted with sandy hair. Sabrina drank him in like a tall, cool swallow of water on a hot summer day.

She stroked the strings of the delicate instrument, weaving an old English melody, one her mother used to sing to them on cold winter nights when icy bits of snow tapped against the windows of the solar. She loved watching Morgan relax his fierce guard. She could almost see the tension seeping out of his muscles, the wary lines of his brow melting in contentment. She longed to fan her fingers along his rugged jaw, to touch him as she was touching the clarsach, with tenderness and reverence and joyous hunger.

He stirred in the chair, sighing drowsily, and murmured, " 'Tis a lovely melody, Beth."

Sabrina's fingers froze. Morgan's eyes drifted open, but she could read nothing but bewilderment in their depths. She held her breath. Perhaps she had only imagined his lapse.

He rubbed his brow. "I must have dozed off. I'd best get to bed before you have to call Fergus to carry me off."

He lumbered to the door, then stopped. Sabrina felt his continued presence like a vise squeezing her heart. She was desperate for him to leave, desperate to be alone so she could give herself over to the doubts lodged like a stone in her throat.

Finally, when she could bear it no more, she swung around to face him. "For God's sake, man, *what* are you waiting for?"

He stood like a Greek statue, his arms folded over the pagan span of his chest. "My good-night kiss, of course."

Sabrina was flabbergasted by his nerve. She rested her hands on her hips. "It seems I've neglected to educate you fully on civilized custom. If a husband has behaved badly and wounded his wife's tender feelings, they do not share a good-night kiss."

He took another moment to digest that bit of lore. Then he strode over and lifted her by the shoulders until her feet dangled a full foot off the floor. His mouth claimed hers in a slow, gentle mating of tongues until all the nether pulses of her body began to beat to his dark, erotic rhythm. The resilient satin of his lips almost made her forget Eve's warning, almost drove everything from her mind but the lazy promise of passion in his eyes. Almost.

"Stupid custom," he pronounced, lowering her to her feet. "Good night, brat." He shut the door behind him with a gentleness that mocked the thundering of her heart.

"Good night, Morgan," she whispered to the silence. "No wonder he always calls me brat. He probably can't remember my name."

Pugsley emerged from beneath the bed at her words.

Sabrina threw the edge of the tablecloth over the chipped teapot, sickened somehow by the sight of it. Had Eve been right? Was Morgan no different from his father? Had he truly nursed a vain infatuation for her mother all these years? She searched her memories, finding Morgan's face, its lean planes drawn with boyish longing as he listened to Elizabeth sing.

Sabrina pressed a hand to her stomach as if she could stop the dull ache spreading through it. The irony did not escape her. While she had propped her own little chin on her pudgy fist to gaze adoringly at Morgan, he had been watching her mother in that same worshipful stance.

She had thought nothing of it at the time. They had all looked to Elizabeth. Hers was the gentle pulse that beat at the heart of Cameron Manor. Sabrina had struggled her entire life to emulate her.

When Sabrina would have had every excuse to be the spoiled, vain brat Morgan believed her to be, she had striven instead to be graceful, generous, and well-mannered.

She had dutifully squelched the raw passions trembling in her heart. She had sat in the window, her embroidery in her lap, and watched wistfully as Morgan and her brothers went cantering over the heather-strewn hills on their shaggy ponies. To please her mother, she had even been willing to travel to London and marry some staid Englishman, secretly knowing that her heart would always belong to the Highlands and to the wild, stubborn boy who had stolen it.

Sabrina had been Mama's dainty rose.

Papa's perfect little princess.

And now she was Morgan's charming pet, hopping to attention each time he jerked her leash.

But she'd never been a woman. And never a wife.

While Enid had found the courage to break the chains of the past, Sabrina had fallen into the same old trap, seeking to charm Morgan's clansmen, hoping that if she won their hearts, she might win their chieftain's as well.

Flattening her palms on the table, Sabrina surveyed the chamber with smoldering eyes washed clean of childish illusion. There was nothing of Sabrina Cameron here, no hint of her character, no clue to her personality. Her mother's elegant hand was everywhere. On the porcelain tea set shipped from London at her expense, on the graceful tapers dipped per her orders, on the virginal bedclothes hemmed by her precise stitches.

Everything in Sabrina's chamber, including her dog, had belonged to Elizabeth first. And now she had reason to believe her husband's heart had as well.

Sabrina loved her mother. Admired her. Respected her. But she could not *be* her. Not even for Morgan.

All those years ago, Morgan had taken such perverse delight in knocking her crown askew. Now the time had come for her to relinquish it willingly.

Pugsley growled his approval as she drew the pins from her hair, sending it tumbling around her shoulders in a dark, smoky mass.

It was nights like this that made Morgan wish he were a drinking man. Not even the iciest of spring waters could quench the fire roaring through his loins. His exhaustion had fled before the sweet acquiescence of Sabrina's lips beneath his. The prospect of sleep was now as removed as earning a spasm of precious release for his lust-battered body.

In a moment of savage weakness, he wished he could be the man Sabrina believed him to be. He envied the moral poverty of his notorious ancestor, Horrid Halbert, who would have simply chained the beautiful Cameron girl in his dungeon to rape at his leisure.

Groaning, Morgan tossed back another draft of water. He had sought the hall, hoping to find both solace and anonymity among his boisterous clansmen. As their numbers had dwindled over the past few years and the sporadic raids of the Grants and Chisholms had grown bolder and more bloody, most of the MacDonnells had abandoned their decaying cottages and sought the refuge of the castle. They took their meals together in the hall and huddled on the benches wrapped in their plaids to sleep each night just as their ancestors had done five centuries before.

The skipping notes of the flutes and the rhythmic throb of the tambours kept time with Morgan's restless heart.

"Heave ho, there he goes!" came the warning cry as one of his clansmen took a good-natured punch and went sailing down the table.

Morgan caught the lad by the scruff of his plaid and heaved him aside without blinking an eye. Fergus sat next to him on the bench, nuzzling a lass's neck with far more tenderness than he might have shown a few hours earlier. Another afternoon tea with Sabrina and Morgan feared the grizzled rascal would start spouting Shakespeare. Eve perched at the end of the table, surrounded by four MacDonnells too distant from Morgan in kinship to even have earned the dubious honor of being called cousins. Their whispers and sly glances nagged at him, and he found himself once again obsessing over the frustrating mystery of Angus's death. It galled him to know that he might never learn who murdered his father.

He yearned for that taste of sweet oblivion when Sabrina had eased him into slumber with her song, slipping him back in time to the peace of the Cameron solar, where Elizabeth's rich soprano had finally drowned out the shouting, cursing, and violence that had punctuated his young life. But when he had awakened, Beth's daughter had been watching him, a quizzical pain darkening her eyes. His elusive peace had shattered beneath a flood of blinding need.

It was snowing harder now. Glittering flakes drifted through the arrow slits and into the hall like a sprinkling of banished stars, melting as they reached the heated air.

Morgan stiffened as a sinuous pair of arms circled him from behind. "I hate to see ye lookin' so grim," Alwyn purred in his ear. "Gi' me a moment o' yer time and I'll put a smile back on those bonny lips o' yers."

As tight as his loins were wound, Morgan suspected a moment was all it would take. His hand clenched around his mug. For one bleak instant he was tempted. Sabrina would never have to know. But as he met Eve's wise, amused gaze down the length of the table, something in him resisted, knowing instinctively that he would feel worse after the soulless coupling. Dirtier and even more unworthy of the girl he had married, a girl as fragile and pure as the fresh flakes of snow pouring into the hall.

He was forming his rebuff when the music died. The flutes shrieked into silence. The tambour player thudded to a halt. Fergus choked on his whisky, spewing it across the table in the face of a lad too dumbfounded to bother wiping it away.

Morgan followed their stunned gazes to the archway. When he saw what had captivated them, he reached over, blindly pried the mug out of Fergus's hand, and killed its contents in a single convulsive swallow.

Chapter Fourteen

Morgan wheezed as the pure malt whisky seared a path down his untried throat. For an eternity he could neither breathe nor swallow, but he suspected both efforts would have been futile anyway as Sabrina came scampering into the hall, looking for all the world like a mischievous wood nymph.

The skirt of her rose-colored gown had been slashed into so many ribbons, it made even Alwyn's attire seem modest. She wore no underskirt, petticoats, or paniers, and with each jaunty step she took, an alarming expanse of milky thigh was revealed.

Her feet were bare, her hair unbound. It tumbled down her back in a wild mass, crowned by a circlet of satin roses that looked suspiciously like the ones designed to bind her bodice at a decent level. She wore no powder. The flush tinting her cheekbones was natural. Only the bee-stung pout of her lips had been rouged in invitation.

Morgan wanted to do things to those lips. Tender

things. Unholy things. A pulse throbbed to life in his groin, beating a rhythm of warning.

His beady eyes twinkling with mirth, Fergus splashed more whisky into the mug. "Drink up, me man. I've a feelin' ye'll be needin' it before this night is done."

Morgan drained the mug, his gaze never leaving Sabrina. The whisky wove fiery tendrils all the way down to the pit of his belly, where he feared his heart was now residing.

Sabrina wound her way through the frozen dancers, pausing at intervals to bestow an impish grin on a gaping face. The silvery peals of her laughter rippled through the taut silence as she approached Morgan's table, her hips swaying in an invitation older than time itself. From the corner of his eye Morgan saw Alwyn hop into Fergus's lap.

Sabrina planted a hearty kiss on Fergus's grizzled cheek, then straddled the bench, facing Morgan. "Was your bed too cold for your liking, my lord?" Her gaze strayed to Alwyn, making it obvious she had witnessed the woman's defection from Morgan to Fergus. "Perhaps you came to seek some warmth?"

Morgan's hands clenched around the mug, gouging fresh scars in the crude earthenware. He kept his voice low, so low that even Fergus would have to strain to hear it. "Guard your tongue, lass. My clansmen believe we share a bed, and I'd prefer to keep it that way. So why aren't you in yours?"

Her blue eyes widened to ingenuous saucers. "I wasn't aware my chamber was to be a cell. Or a cage. Am I your prisoner now, Morgan? Or your pet?" She offered him her upturned wrists. "Perhaps you would care to bind me?"

Her words and posture conjured up pagan images made none the less erotic for their barbarism. Morgan shoved her hands back into her lap, struggling to ignore the tantalizing drape of her thighs over the rough wooden bench and the crushed velvet pooled at their enticing V.

He covered the shaken note in his voice with

sternness. "This is not the way a chieftain expects his wife to behave."

"Ah, but I've behaved all my life, and where has it gotten me? There's no point in letting the naughty girls have all the fun." To his shock, she arched her graceful neck and caught his earlobe between her sharp little teeth before whispering, "Your clansmen aren't nearly as stupid as you'd like to believe. If you were sharing my bed, you'd have better things to do than brood."

Before he could recover, she was dancing out of his reach. He glowered, entranced against his will by the provocative sparkle of her eyes. Wary of his still-ness, Morgan's tablemates were already edging out of his reach.

Sabrina clapped her hands in a bid for an attention she already had. "I should like to propose a toast." She swept a chipped goblet from the nearest table and hefted it high. "To my newfound family—the MacDon-nells!"

A dubious cheer rose from the hall. Although the MacDonnells feared their chieftain's stony counte-nance, they couldn't resist drinking to anything. This time when Fergus offered him the whisky, Morgan took the bottle instead of the mug. He quaffed it, then dragged the back of his hand across his mouth.

Sabrina tipped the goblet to her lips. Morgan was transfixed by the convulsive arch and ripple of her throat around the potent liquor.

The shock of it lowered the fabric of her voice from creamy silk to husky velvet. Her eyes glittered with tears of reaction. "I promised Fergus I'd teach you a new song, and contrary to what your chieftain be-lieves, we Camerons always keep our vows." She began to clap her hands and tap her foot in rousing rhythm.

Her enthusiasm was infectious. After throwing an uneasy glance at Morgan, the boy manning the tam-bours began to pat out a beat on their warped skins. Other hands and feet picked up the rhythm, clapping and stomping until the hall resounded with it.

The playful clarity of Sabrina's voice rose above the din:

Ride hard the MacDonnells wi' their wild golden locks,
Fierce their long claymores, but nary as fierce as their—

"Sabrina!" Morgan roared.

The whisky bottle exploded in his hand. He shook off the amber bits of glass as if they were of no more consequence than rose petals. The rhythm of the tambours faltered and died. The clapping hands stilled in mid-motion.

" 'Tempers?' " Sabrina whispered, mesmerized as Morgan lunged to his feet and started toward her.

She had hoped that goading any response from him would be better than none, but his predatory grace reminded her that she had been tweaking the tail of a dragon. And judging from the feral glitter of his eyes, a hungry one.

The crowd melted before Morgan's thundering strides. Sabrina fought to hold her ground, but her feet had other ideas. They lured her back until her rump struck the edge of a table and she could flee no farther. Morgan's shadow towered over her. For a terrible instant, she wondered if he might break his vow and strike her there before them all.

She mustered her defiance by tossing her hair out of her eyes. "I hope my humble tune did not displease you. I thought you would be honored at such a tribute to the MacDonnell . . ." She trailed off, her husband's resolute expression robbing her of words. Her teeth worried her lower lip.

"Stamina?" he offered. "Prowess?"

He caught her arms, his fingers stroking her flesh in a caress rendered more brutal by its mocking tenderness. The wicked slant of his lips reminded her that some punishments could be far more diabolical than a mere cuffing.

She forced her gaze away from the awesome

breadth of his chest. " 'Twas only a song. There was no insult intended."

"None taken." He released her, but her sigh of relief caught in her throat as one of his hands slipped beneath her hair to cup her nape. His deft fingers worked their way through the thick mass of her hair. "I feared you might believe the bard had flattered us, lass. Perhaps you'd care for a private demonstration?"

Morgan's fingers sought and found the tingling nerves buried in her scalp. Sabrina's head fell back of its own volition, arching against the beguiling pressure. "No, thank you. I'll take your word for it."

Morgan angled his body to block the avid gazes of his clansmen. "Then perhaps you'd prefer a public one?" The silkiness of his tone warned her that she had pushed him too far too fast, that he was fully capable, equipped, and willing to live up to his dangerous reputation.

That still didn't prepare her for the shock of his other hand slipping into her drooping bodice and closing gently over her bare breast. He kneaded the tender globe in his palm, his thumb stealing out to rake its sensitive peak. Her body responded with humiliating swiftness. The raw triumph in Morgan's expression warned her that he knew it.

This betrayal was far worse than the bullying he had done as a boy. His impersonal caress violated not only her body, but the deepest, most tender secrets of her heart.

All the wounded pride and hurt she'd suppressed for years was in her voice when she bit off, "As you wish, Morgan MacDonnell. I expected no more from the likes of you."

"Then I shouldn't wish to disappoint you."

Without betraying even a flicker of remorse, he freed her breast and laced his fingers in hers, hastening her from the hall as would any husband eager to share a tender moment with his wife. Sabrina threw a helpless glance over her shoulder to discover Eve watching them go, a satisfied smirk carved on her lips.

• • •

Sabrina resisted the urge to drag her feet like a truculent child as Morgan whisked her through the darkened maze of Castle MacDonnell.

But she could not resist a rebellious mutter. "Isn't walking a bit civilized for your tastes? Shouldn't you throw me over your shoulder or drag me by my hair?"

He stopped so fast that she stumbled into his back. As he swung around, his breath scorched her like a blast of dragon's fire. She was surprised it didn't singe her curls. "Don't tempt me," he said between clenched teeth.

"Why, you've been drinking," she accused him, primly sniffing the air.

"You're enough to drive a monk to it."

"Ah, but you're no monk, are you?"

His low-pitched growl made the hair on her nape tingle. "No, but I've been livin' like one. And I'm damned weary of it."

He pulled her along, slowing only when she stumbled over a pile of crumbled mortar and would have fallen had he not reached back to steady her. As they careened around a blind corner, Sabrina recognized the dead-end corridor she had discovered her first day at MacDonnell.

Snow unfurled through the shattered windows, sparkling like motes of fairy dust in the brittle air. Gusts of wind whipped the shredded tapestries into a frenetic dance. The snow cast a luminous curtain against the night. The cracked mirror threw back their looming reflections.

Leaving Sabrina standing in the middle of the corridor, Morgan marched to the mirror. "Damn it all! I would have sworn there was a door here."

It seemed their mad flight had been a flight to nowhere. A hysterical giggle welled up in Sabrina's throat. She tried to smother it with her palm, but failed.

Her mirth faded at the sight of Morgan's expression. "It's all just a joke to you, isn't it? My crumbling castle. My pathetic clan. Just like that foolish ditty someone wrote to keep the MacDonnells in their proper place. Beneath your dainty Cameron feet."

His anger didn't shock her as much as the depth of the other emotion lurking in his eyes. She couldn't have hurt him, she reassured herself. She didn't have the power.

"So did you decide to sink to our depths tonight?" he asked. "Is that why you're dressed like a—a—" He sputtered to a halt.

"Slattern?" she generously offered. "Those are obviously the sort of women you prefer in your arms."

"*Alwyn* approached *me*," he thundered.

"And how many times has she *approached* you since we were wed?"

A predatory smile touched his lips. His voice softened. "Jealous, brat? Guard your words well or I just might think you care."

"God help me if I did!"

Her impassioned declaration seemed to catch him off guard. He cocked his head to the side and studied her.

Sabrina shivered beneath his regard, suddenly aware of how cold the drafty corridor was. She had never realized how much warmth her voluminous undergarments provided. Without them, she felt naked, exposed, vulnerable to the cold wind licking up her thighs and the heat simmering in Morgan's eyes. As his gaze dropped, the contrast between the two extremes tightened the peaks of her breasts. Protectively she crossed her arms over her chest.

Morgan's jaw tightened. He paced away from her. "What would your mother say if she could see you now?"

"Who gives a damn!"

At Sabrina's choked cry, Morgan swung around, both provoked and fascinated by a glimpse of a passion he had only suspected. She snatched up her tattered skirts and paced into the path he had abandoned.

"I'm not my mother. I can't behave like her. I can't bear to be polite to idiots, I've never seen the point in embroidering those teeny little flowers on the bedclothes, where no one will ever see them, and a drawing room full of ladies who talk of nothing but babies and sewing bores me to tears."

She switched paths, brushing recklessly past him. Morgan closed his eyes, soaking up the fragrance of her unbound hair. It struck him harder than the whisky, making him weave on his feet.

"Cursed roses," he muttered beneath his breath.

"Roses!" Sabrina snatched the word as if he'd tossed her a rope on a stormy sea. "Why, that's it exactly! Mama wants her roses imported from England. She wants them to have pedigrees longer than Pugsley's. She plants them in precise arrangements, and if one of them dares to rebel, even to stretch its poor thorny limbs toward the sun, then *snip!*" Sabrina snapped the air with a pair of imaginary shears. "She whacks its head off."

An odd weight curled in Morgan's chest. Sabrina's eyes were shining. A wistful smile played around her lips. It was the same look he had seen on her face when she had first laid eyes on Castle MacDonnell, the same look that had devastated him as a boy.

Her Scottish lilt deepened, slurring the precise echo of her mother's tones, giving her voice a resonance all its own. "Aye, but I love wild roses with prickly thorns that rip your sleeves and scratch you bloody. I love to spot a flash of pink or yellow on a barren hill and to climb until I arrive at the top all dirty and out of breath to find a single spray of roses tangled among the stones, too stubborn to be choked by the rocky soil."

She caught his plaid in her balled fists and gave him a gentle shake. "Those blooms are glorious and free. You have to shed your blood just for the privilege of touching them. They won't bloom in captivity." She inclined her head, lightly resting its crown against his chest. Her voice softened to a whisper. "Neither will I, Morgan. I can't spend my life in a gilded cage to please you."

Sabrina pleased him more than she would ever

know. It pleased him to know that being dressed like a whore did not make her one. Even barefoot, her hair hanging in a wild tangle around her face, her lips stained a lush scarlet, she was as much a lady as she had been as a six-year-old child. Her purity transcended the carnal. Even his selfish masculine possession would not destroy it.

He smoothed a stray snowflake from her hair. "Sabrina?"

"Yes, Morgan?"

"You still chatter too much."

Sabrina shivered as Morgan's arms slipped around her waist, turning her away from him to face the mirror. The sleepy glitter of his eyes made her mouth go dry. The smoky tang of the whisky on his breath mingled with his crisp scent, enveloping her in an intoxicating cloud. The warmth of his body was an alluring contrast to the chill of the air. It took all Sabrina's resistance to keep from sinking against him in surrender. Their entwined reflections shimmered in the hazy glass.

"You don't have to be anyone but yourself, Sabrina. You're pleasin' enough for any man." His voice tainted with the huskiness of desire, he stroked the sun-browned backs of his hands down her cheeks. "You're white where I'm dark." Mesmerized, she watched as his hands continued their provocative descent, easing her bodice down until it clung precariously to the rosy tips of her breasts. His knuckles grazed the skin between them. "Smooth where I'm rough. Soft"—the fall of his hair veiled his expression as he reached down and gently cupped her feminine heat in his hand, then dipped low to mold his hips to the curves of her bottom —"where I'm hard."

Sabrina gasped at the bold evidence of his regard. Her head fell back and Morgan emblazoned whisper-soft kisses along her throat. She could hardly recognize the woman in the mirror—a wanton creature, moist lips parted in need, splayed against the masterful body of a man who held the very heart of her in his hand.

Their gazes met in the mirror. Was this how

Alwyn had felt? she wondered. Was this how all the other women had felt in Morgan's arms?

A memory assailed her, so sharp she could smell the tart aroma of baking gingerbread. A leaner, younger Morgan sitting on a stool in the kitchen of Cameron, a flushed maid no more than fifteen herself, straddling his lap and kissing him avidly. Sabrina had walked in on them, then turned around and walked back out without either of them seeing her. She had skipped supper that night and the next, unable to meet the besotted eyes of the maid without losing her appetite.

Morgan gave her a gentle squeeze; his hoarse groan resounded with triumph. Panic spilled through Sabrina. Was Morgan making love to his wife or was she just another woman, a fresh conquest for the victory-starved MacDonnells? She couldn't bear it if her innocence was no more to him than another bloody trophy to sport on his belt.

Biting back a cry of denial, she stiffened and arched away from the coaxing pressure of his fingers. Morgan sensed her withdrawal immediately. His hand stilled; his head lifted. His eyes darkened in the mirror with an emotion Sabrina might have thought was betrayal in another man.

Before she had time to form an excuse, a lie, or a plea, Morgan swung her around and pushed her back against the mirror, imprisoning her between the unyielding glass and the tempered steel of his body.

His eyes sparkled, reminding her once again of that wicked boy she had known. "What ails you, lass? Afraid I might steal a moment's pleasure? You cringe from my touch. Don't you want your husband's filthy MacDonnell hands on your precious flesh?"

Sabrina clutched her gown closed at the throat. "Please, Morgan . . ."

"Please what? Please don't dirty me with your unworthiness? Or are you only doin' what the Camerons have always done best. Flauntin' somethin' of unspeakable beauty before our eyes only to jerk it away when we finally choke up enough courage to reach for it!"

Sabrina blinked in miserable confusion. *Unspeak-*

able beauty? How dare he mock her now! A battle raged in Morgan's eyes, as if his intelligence and control were warring with the centuries of savagery bred into his massive frame. Sabrina turned her face away to hide her fear. In the past, his cruelty had held only the power to wound. Now she knew it would destroy her.

He caught her shoulders in his implacable grip. "You've always hated me, haven't you, lass? Maybe it's far past time I gave you a real reason."

The injustice of his words struck Sabrina a harsh blow, shattering the silence of thirteen years. She tossed back her hair, baring far more than just her face to him. "I never hated you! I adored you! I worshipped the ground beneath your arrogant feet!"

For a timeless moment the only sound was the muffled whisper of snowflakes striking the stone floor. Morgan was frozen, paralyzed by the luminous glitter of Sabrina's eyes. Tears, he realized. Tears he'd been waiting for for half his life. They were stunning, like liquid diamonds trembling on her lashes, slipping down her pale cheeks. She'd finally broken her oath. This beautiful girl was crying for him. For Morgan MacDonnell, the no-good, overgrown son of a ruthless scoundrel.

His hand shook as he lifted it to her cheek, bathing his fingers in the silky wetness. A shudder passed through her at his touch. Her lips trembled; the tip of her nose pinkened. Morgan had never seen anything more lovely. A single teardrop caught on his fingertip and he brought it to his lips, savoring its salty warmth. He took a step backward, staggered by the taste of her courage. Even his most fierce enemy would never have dared to lay such a weapon in his hands.

Horror washed over Sabrina as the echo of her impassioned confession reached her brain. Her hand flew over her mouth as if she could somehow snatch back the words. But it was too late. A dazzling grin was spreading over Morgan's face, a tantalizing blend of boyish triumph and wonder.

"I'll be damned," he breathed. "Can you imagine that?"

She scrubbed at her cheeks with both hands, bracing herself for his roar of laughter, his mocking taunts.

But his bemused smile remained, underscored by a rumbling chuckle. "Fancy that, won't you? Who would have thought it?" Sabrina blinked, wondering if he wasn't drunker than she'd realized. The brilliant glamour of his grin nearly blinded her.

She remained frozen in shock as he turned and marched away, still shaking his tawny head. Eve's warning echoed through the empty corridor.

Don't give yer heart to him, lass. He'll only feed it back to ye, piece by piece, until ye damn near choke on it.

Sabrina collapsed against the mirror. "Oh, dear God," she whispered. "What have I done?"

Chapter Fifteen

"Enid, wake up! Enid, please!"

The hissed whisper barely penetrated Enid's fuzzy brain. She was dreaming, floating naked and weightless in a lake of sweet cream. Ranald waited for her on the opposite shore, plump, juicy strawberries dripping from his outstretched hands.

"Mmmm," she moaned, anchoring her arm around Ranald's lean waist. He burped in his sleep.

"For heaven's sake, Enid, would you wake up?"

It wasn't so much the desperation of the plea as the frantic hand clawing at her shoulder that finally roused her. Freeing Ranald, she rolled over and pried open one bleary eye.

"S'brina?" she mumbled to find her cousin crouched on the floor beside the bed, all but hidden by a voluminous pelisse and hood.

Sabrina laid a warning finger to her lips. "You mustn't wake Ranald. I need your help. Something terrible has happened."

Enid scrambled in her pocket for her bottle of hartshorn, forgetting she was nude. "What is it? Are we being attacked by the Chisholms? Is the castle on fire?"

"It's worse than that. Far worse." Sabrina paused dramatically. "I told Morgan that I loved him."

Enid smiled dreamily and rooted back into the pillow. "How very nice. I was wondering when you were going to get around to it."

Sabrina shook her violently. Enid's eyes flew back open. "It's not nice," Sabrina hissed. "It's horrible. Morgan knows I'm vulnerable to him now."

Sabrina's panic finally began to seep into Enid's consciousness. Even in the scant firelight, Sabrina's face was stark white, her eyes shadowed. Enid propped herself up on one elbow, suddenly wide awake. "Have the two of you never—"

"No! Never!"

They both held their breath as Ranald shifted to his back, mumbled something about roast mutton, then lapsed back into soothing snores.

"It's really not as bad as people lead you to believe, you know," Enid whispered. "At least not after the first time. Of course, with a man of Morgan's incredible . . . um . . . stature . . ."

"Enid!" Sabrina wailed. "You're not listening."

Enid gasped at the sudden insight. "Why, you're not afraid he'll hurt you! You're afraid he won't!"

Sabrina lowered her eyes, remembering the feel of Morgan's warm hand cupping her, the melting pleasure that could drive even the proudest of women to her knees. She had no choice but to flee before he discovered her girlish infatuation had burgeoned into a woman's love.

"I can't stay," she said softly. "I have to get back to Cameron before it's too late, before I'm no better than one of Morgan's besotted doxies hanging around the great hall, praying I'm the one he'll choose to warm his bed that night."

"You don't honestly think he'll let you go?"

"I'm going now. Tonight. But I can't go alone."

Enid's despairing gaze traveled between Sabrina

and Ranald. Ranald's beautifully sculpted mouth hung open, making him look no more than twelve.

Sabrina squeezed her cousin's hand. "I know I'm asking too much of you, but I can't make it down the mountain alone."

Enid smoothed the quilt over Ranald's chest before throwing back her side. "Sometimes I think this husband of yours is more trouble than he's worth."

Sabrina managed to smile through a warm sheen of tears. All of her brave words to Morgan had been a lie. She was the one too cowardly to risk bloodying her hands by reaching for the wild rose growing just out of her reach. "He's trouble, all right. But I suspect he's worth it. I'm just too afraid to find out."

She quickly bundled the grumbling Enid into a heavy gown and cloak and herded her out the door.

Ranald's eyes popped open.

Sighing heavily, he propped the back of his head on his folded hands and glared at the ceiling. "Damn ye anyway, Morgan. If ye'd keep the wee chit in yer bed, where she belongs, a man might get a decent night's rest and a mornin' cuddle to boot."

After long and thoughtful deliberation, he crawled out from beneath the warm quilts and slid into his trews, shivering and swearing under his breath with a flare that belied his lack of schooling.

Tossing Pugsley through the narrow aperture of a broken window proved to be far easier than shoving Enid after him. When her cousin's hips hung and her grunts escalated to muffled squeals of alarm, Sabrina knew a brief flush of horror at the prospect of once again becoming the object of MacDonnell ridicule. No wonder Morgan hated to be laughed at.

She gave Enid's rump a desperate shove that sent them both tumbling out the window into a fresh mound of snow. Pugsley danced around them, yapping and trying to bite their ankles through their thick stockings.

Enid rolled to a sitting position wearing a frothy

white beard. "You didn't have to push me. You might have broken my neck."

Sabrina scooped up the squirming dog. "If Morgan catches us running away, he'll spare me the trouble."

That dire reminder brought Enid lurching to her feet. They trundled toward the stables, their steps slowed by the weight of their cumbersome cloaks. The wind had slowed, giving the sky time to lace the icy crystals into plump feathers. The drifting snow muffled their steps, but made the aching thud of Sabrina's heart seem obscenely loud.

The rickety stables crouched beneath the snow-laden branches of a pine thicket. Sabrina and Enid exchanged a nervous glance before each one tugged one of the handles that would swing wide the rough-hewn doors. A warm, musty blast of air hit them, punctuated by the drowsy whickers of the horses. Pugsley's deep-throated growl was their only warning before a satanic gleam split the shadows.

The stables exploded in a flurry of rolling eyes and flailing hooves.

Of one accord, they slammed the doors and threw their backs against them. The entire structure shuddered.

"Pookah," Sabrina whispered, smothering Pugsley's alarmed yips beneath her hand.

Robbed of their plan to *borrow* one of the MacDonnell mounts, they trudged back around the castle only to find themselves shivering on the edge of the cliffs. A billowing sea of white had swallowed the heath below. The wind roared across its vast emptiness, whipping Sabrina's hood from her head and biting tears from her eyes. The road to Cameron twined along the cliff's edge like a narrow ribbon of glass.

"It can't be the only way, can it?" Enid asked doubtfully.

"Of course not," Sabrina said with more conviction than she felt. "We're on a mountain, aren't we? All we have to do is head downhill and we'll be safe and warm in front of the fire at Cameron by the morrow."

Cheered by her words, they wheeled around and marched toward the welcome shelter of the forest. Against her better judgement, Sabrina allowed herself one last hungry look at Castle MacDonnell.

With loving hands the sky had laid its blanket of snow over the crumbling edifice, shrouding its flaws and hiding the heartrending neglect that had stripped the mighty structure to a husk of its former glory. Firelight flickered in scattered windows, winking like knowing eyes against the dark. In the hazy half-light, it looked romantic, ethereal, a kingdom suited to a rough-edged prince of Morgan's intense pride.

Enid tugged her arm. "If you don't come on, you're going to turn into a pillar of salt like Lot's wife."

" 'Twould be no more than I deserve."

It would be no more than she deserved if Morgan found her in the morning, her feet rooted in ice, her face frozen in pathetic yearning. She tore her gaze away from the castle. Hugging Pugsley to her breast, she plunged into the forest, resolving to look only forward from then on, no matter how lonely and bleak the path before her.

"I once saw two beggar children frozen in an alley," Enid said, ducking beneath the spiny arm of an ice-glazed branch. "It was quite ghastly, really. Their faces were all black and their lips curled back. I'd read that freezing to death was quite a pleasant way to die, not as nice as drowning can be after you cease to struggle, but peaceful nonetheless."

Sabrina stumbled over the sodden train of her pelisse, mercifully distracting herself from her cousin's gruesome anecdote. Between huffing and puffing for breath, Enid launched into another tale of a Belmont great-uncle who had lost two toes after being caught in a blizzard on the Prussian slopes. He had kept the shriveled digits in a jar on his mantel, whipping them out to rattle at his terrified grandchildren.

Sabrina began to stamp her feet with each step. Was she only imagining the numbness creeping toward

her shins? She gave her arm a sharp pinch, nearly pan-
icking at the absence of sensation until Pugsley's offended yelp told her she had pinched the dog instead of
herself. He had long ago become a dead weight in her
arms.

Enid shambled along behind her like a rotund
snowman, nothing visible above her muffler but a pinkened nose and a pair of watery, accusing eyes. Her
glum demeanor increased with each step that carried
her deeper into the forest and away from Ranald.

The jagged snap of a branch sent her stumbling
into Sabrina's back. Sabrina's feet shot out from under
her. She couldn't break her fall without dropping
Pugsley, so her rump was forced to absorb its impact.
She sat there, feeling the miserable wetness of the snow
sink through her pelisse and swallowing the urge to
burst into childlike tears. She wished desperately for the
sturdy warmth of Morgan's plaid, the sturdy warmth of
Morgan himself. But she knew if she started thinking
like that, she might never get up.

Compelled to fight Enid's gloominess with an optimism she did not feel, she struggled to her feet,
brushing the snow from Pugsley's muzzle. "Nothing to
be alarmed about. Simply a branch breaking under the
weight of the snow."

"I hope so," Enid whispered, peering high above
them, where the ebony branches clicked and swayed
like the fuzzy legs of a giant spider.

"If we keep putting one foot in front of the other,
we'll eventually reach Cameron." Sabrina tramped on,
restating her plan as if to assure herself she had not just
made the most terrible mistake of her life. "I shall explain to Papa that although Morgan was quite kind to
me, we simply did not suit. Then I shall apply for an
annulment." She glanced over her shoulder at Enid,
hoping to discover a lifting of the girl's fear. "As long
as the union wasn't consummated, an annulment
should present no problem."

Sabrina slammed into something warm and solid.
For a dazed moment she thought she had walked into
a tree trunk. Her eyes crossed as they traced the intri-

cate pattern of the tartan before them, following it upward like a checkered map to find a jaw hewn in stone, lips tilted in arrogant amusement, and lush green eyes lit by a mocking sparkle.

A tree would have been more pliant, more relenting, and infinitely less smug than the brawny arms her husband folded over his chest.

"Now, lass," he rumbled, "it seems you've got yourself a wee problem."

Chapter Sixteen

Sabrina did not consider six feet and three inches of smirking Highlander a wee problem. A momentous obstacle seemed a more apt description. Since she had just outlined for his obvious amusement her entire cowardly plan of retreat and abandonment, she chose to attack rather than wait for his own sally.

"You followed us," she accused him.

"Aye, and a wee bit dizzy we were gettin'."

"Dizzy?"

Morgan stepped aside and swept out an arm toward the ground. Enid managed to look both miserably guilty and shamelessly happy to discover Ranald standing behind him, holding Pookah's reins. Sabrina would have sworn she saw a maniacal gleam of satisfaction in the horse's eyes.

Puzzled, she studied the path they would have bisected if Morgan hadn't stopped them. The sugary snow had been flattened, baring the twigs and bracken beneath as if someone had taken a broom and swept them clean. Sabrina glanced over her shoulder at the sodden, unwieldy train of her pelisse.

Morgan nodded, confirming her sinking suspicion that they'd done nothing but amble in a wide circle since leaving the castle, drawing him a map so unmistakable, he could have followed them all the way to Cameron had he chose.

"Proud of yourself?" she asked.

"You might have made it more of a challenge." He plucked Pugsley out of her arms. The dog arched his back, wiggling madly to lick Morgan's face.

"Traitor," she muttered.

He handed the dog to Ranald. "Take the dog and the woman back to the castle."

Pretending he was talking about her, Sabrina headed for the relative sanctuary of her husband's cousin. Morgan caught her by the hood. "The *other* woman."

Sabrina twisted around to glare at him. "She has a name, you know."

Morgan sighed. "Mr. MacDonnell, would you please escort Lord Pugsley and Lady Belmont back to the castle?"

"Aye, that I will." Ranald leered. "With pleasure."

Casting him an apologetic look, Enid ducked beneath Ranald's outstretched arm and threw her arms around Sabrina. "I won't let you take her."

Morgan rolled his eyes skyward and locked his hands at the small of his back. His tone was almost painfully reasonable. "Miss Belmont, I have been very patient with your interference in my marriage, even choosin' to forgive what I suspect was your rather clumsy attempt to murder me." Enid blanched. His gaze shifted to Sabrina, afire with an unholy light. She clung to Enid, feeling her frozen knees melt beneath its heat. "But no one, not you, nor a regiment of Camerons, nor the devil himself is going to stop me from *takin'* my wife tonight."

With those words, Morgan bent and neatly hefted Enid over his shoulder. Ranald staggered as Morgan handed her off. Dodging Pookah's snapping teeth, he heaved Enid headfirst over the horse's back. Enid pulled a handkerchief from her cloak and gave Sabrina a forlorn little wave as Ranald led the horse away. They melted into the trees, leaving her alone with her husband.

"You're not . . . ?" she said, backing away.

"I am."

He did.

Sabrina bounced along over his shoulder, hands fisted as if she could somehow deny the indignity of being carted off like a sack of turnips. But when his long strides nearly upended her into a snowdrift, he took it upon himself to anchor her rump to his shoulder. The possessive heat of his hands molded the wet pelisse to her vulnerable curves.

"Your plan impressed me, lass."

"It did?"

"Aye, but there was one thing you overlooked."

"Aside from the fact that we were never more than thirty feet from the castle?"

He nodded. "Aside from that. If you'd have succeeded in reachin' Cameron, I'd have been forced to declare war on your father."

She tried to twist around to see his face, but his grip prevented her. "Over me? You'd have risked your clan over me?"

His shrug almost dislodged her. "I couldn't have the Camerons sayin' a MacDonnell couldn't hold on to his wife, could I? 'Tis a matter of pride, lass."

Everything was a matter of pride to Morgan, Sabrina thought bitterly. His reputation. His clan. His marriage. She just prayed she'd have enough pride of her own to resist him. A fat feather of snow drifted down to tickle her nose. She irritably brushed it away. They should have reached the castle long ago. Perhaps he was going to toss her off the icy cliffs to punish her for running away. A quick death would be preferable to a slow, lingering one beneath the blunt artistry of his hands.

They emerged in a clearing. Sabrina peered under Morgan's arm to find a darkened stone cottage thatched with snow. "How quaint," she murmured. "And to think I expected a cave."

He gave her rump an infuriating squeeze. "Ah, but even we savages enjoy our creature comforts."

The door thumped open to a cozy blast of warmth. The world righted itself as Morgan lowered her gently to her feet. She barely noticed when he shut the door, unfastened her damp pelisse, and plucked off her frivolous slippers. Nor did she see his hungry gaze rake her, noting with obvious pleasure that above her thick stockings she wore only the tattered gown she had worn in the hall.

She was too busy staring. The cottage wasn't dark after all. Luxuriant furs had been pounded over the windows, imprisoning them in a gauzy web of firelight and warmth. The air danced with the scattered light of tall, familiar tapers. A heather tick had been dressed with crisp sheets and laid beside the stone hearth. Dried rose petals simmered in a pot over the fire. Their heady fragrance wafted to Sabrina's nose, making her feel reckless and drunk. She was in far more peril than she had realized. This was no scene of rape, but of seduction.

Morgan's possessive gaze caressed her.

"Why, you scoundrel! You had this planned all along." She spun around for the door.

His hands reached it first, splaying on either side of her. "You've left me little choice, lass. I can't risk you sneakin' off to get an annulment every time we quarrel."

She swung around to face him, half afraid he could hear the wild beating of her heart. "What are you going to do to me?"

His expression was resolute but not cruel. "What I should have done the night we were wed."

Sabrina was unprepared for the shock of his big hand coming down to frame her abdomen. Its unexpected gentleness was somehow more intimate than his earlier caresses. Ribbons of heat unfurled from his fingertips like the tender sprouts of a new bloom.

"I'm goin' to put my child in you, Sabrina

Cameron. 'Tis our duty to preserve the peace between our clans by givin' your da a MacDonnell bairn for a grandson." He nudged her chin up with his knuckle. "Don't look so crestfallen, lass. If I'm willin' to suffer through it, so should you be." Their breath mingled as his lips lowered. "Remember the sacrifices your brave Odysseus made for his clansmen."

Panicked not so much by what he intended as how he intended to accomplish it, Sabrina ducked beneath his arm. All the warnings she'd never heeded about him flashed through her mind. She knew he was accustomed to being savage in his own needs, heedless of his mate's pleasure. He had the power to tear her apart without meaning to, to break both her body and her heart. For a moment she feared she was going to swoon like the terrified virgin she was. How could she have ever thought herself woman enough to handle a man like him?

He took a measured step toward her.

She took a step back. "I'll scream."

A roguish grin curved his lips. He drew the bodkin from his plaid. "Aye, lass. That you will before this night is done."

A rush of longing mingled with her fear. Morgan tossed a fold of the plaid over his shoulder, revealing an alluring expanse of golden skin. "No need to be afraid. I'm a patient teacher. Ask any lad who's trained on sword or ax beneath me."

The potent masculinity of his swagger sent her backing against the warm stones of the hearth. "What of the many women who've trained beneath you? Did they find you patient as well?"

His reproachful gaze failed to shame her. Another fold of the plaid unraveled, exposing the sun-gilded planes of his chest and abdomen. As if beset by sudden modesty, he left the plaid hanging low on his hips, anchored by his fist. Sabrina knew it would take only a tug to make it fall. She tried to swallow, but her throat had gone bone dry. Once again Morgan MacDonnell wasn't playing fair. She found herself with no refuge but the past.

"Damn you!"

Morgan ducked as a lit candle went sailing toward his head. Melted wax spattered the wall behind him. His eyes widened. "Was it somethin' I said?"

Sabrina turned her profile to him. "It was some-something you did. Something mean and spiteful and unforgivable. Do you remember Isabella?"

He frowned, obviously at a loss.

"She wasn't one of the Cameron maids you dallied with. She was my kitten."

A dim memory stirred in Morgan. Scraggly, paint-spattered fur. A comic, wobbly gait. "Isabella! The wee tiger who used to nibble my toes."

"So you do remember! Papa told me she ran away, but I saw you talking to the traveling peddler on the morning she disappeared." To her horror, Sabrina felt long-forgotten tears clog her throat. Her hands curled into fists. "I know you sold her to that awful man. But I kept my vow. I never told Papa. I never said a word."

Without giving Sabrina a chance to resist, Morgan gathered her against him, rubbing his cheek against her hair. "I'm sorry, lass." One of her tears slid down to tickle his abdomen. "But, Sabrina?"

Her palms flattened against his chest, making his heart leap. "I've nothing more to say to you."

"I've somethin' to say to you. I didn't sell your kitten. She choked on a bug and your da thought it'd be easier if you thought she'd run away. I bought a nice cheroot box from the peddler and helped Brian and Alex bury her in your mother's garden."

For a lingering moment Morgan felt nothing but the stunned whisper of her breath against his skin. A faint shudder raked her, then another. Her shoulders convulsed beneath his hand and he realized she was laughing. "All these years . . . I thought it was the worst thing you ever did . . . why, I almost hated you!"

Morgan was unprepared for the rewards of being absolved of a sin he had never committed. A wild shiver danced across his skin as her hands stroked and explored the rigid definition of muscle in his chest.

Even more jarring was the rush of tender emotion that seized him as she flowered her soft lips against his breastbone, over his pounding heart, across the turgid bud of his nipple. A groan escaped him.

He had never known how tender a woman's touch could be. The women he had known had all wanted to be subdued, conquered, dominated beneath the punishing weight of his body. Not one of them had ever dared to make love to him with their hands, their mouths, the luminous eyes Sabrina lifted to his face. The pure emotion he saw restrained in their depths devastated him.

Growling deep in his throat, he plunged both of his hands into the sable mass of her hair and tipped her head back. "I may not have sold your kitten, Sabrina, but I've wronged you in many a way. I'm no gentleman."

"I never asked you to be."

His effort to seize control failed dismally as her lips melted beneath his, letting his tongue have its way with her in all its rapacious greed. The wet, yielding silk of her mouth tempted him, tormented him, made him ache to wrap every honeyed inch of her around him.

Sabrina felt the downy wool of Morgan's plaid slide down to cover her feet. She took a startled step backward.

Another man might have appeared vulnerable, diminished by his nakedness, but not Morgan. Nothing her mother had told her could have prepared her for the sight of his sleek warrior's body honed by blades of firelight.

"Sabrina?" His husky plea let her know just how close he was to begging a Cameron for her favors.

She stretched out a trembling hand in invitation. Morgan knew how much that simple gesture cost her, knew how many times he'd rebuffed the hand she'd offered him. He bridged the distance between them in one stride, tugging greedily at her clothes until she stood before him as naked and graceful as the flames that crowned the candles.

His eyes devoured her, drinking in the tumbled

fall of her hair, the elegant flare of her hips, the ripe shade of rose that tipped her breasts and stained her cheeks beneath his hungry perusal, the ebony curls nestled at the juncture of her milky thighs.

"I don't deserve this," he muttered, pressing a kiss to the hollow of her throat.

Her cheek dimpled in a shaky smile. "I know."

Sabrina hadn't expected a man like Morgan to waste precious time on kisses or caresses, so when his hand pierced the shelter of those nether curls, the shock was doubled. She clung to his shoulders, fighting to remain on her feet. No one had ever touched her there before, and to have his big, blunt fingers stroking forth that liquid fire was almost more than she could bear. She writhed, maddened by the flood of pleasure and the coaxing Gaelic words he muttered against her lips.

When Morgan felt her satiny flesh glove his longest finger, sending tiny ripples of shock through her entire body, he did something he thought he would never do. He dropped to his knees at the feet of a Cameron. He pressed his mouth to her damp curls, never dreaming surrender could be so sweet, so utterly delectable.

Determined that his surrender would become her own, he curved his hands beneath her buttocks and lifted her, laying her back on the heather tick. Leaning back on his knees, he braced her thighs over his shoulders until she was completely vulnerable to the tender attack of his lips and tongue.

Sabrina squeaked, jolted into mortified shyness by the tickle of his hair across her belly. "Morgan, you can't do that! It isn't seemly!"

He lifted his head. His wolfish grin sent a shiver of reaction through her. "Do you remember all those horrible tales your brothers used to tell you about the MacDonnells?"

She fought a swoon as he stroked one finger in and out of her with paralyzing gentleness. Her words came in breathless gasps, punctuated by tiny whimpers. "They said you had great tufts of hair on your feet and that you"—her voice broke on a groan as he pushed deeper, measuring, filling, laving her taut flesh for the pleasures to come. The words spilled out of her in a rush—"that you ate up black-haired little girls like me for breakfast."

" 'Twas a vicious lie, princess. I've just a scatterin' of hair on my feet and I eat up wee black-haired lassies like you only for dessert."

His teeth came down, nipping her most sensitive flesh with exquisite care. Sabrina cried out, twisting in his grasp as his tongue, his fingers, his lips, wove their own dark dance of delight over her flesh. She'd lost her heart to the boy he had been, but she was afraid she might lose her very soul to the tender, relentless mastery of the man he had become. Even as she tried to writhe away from him, his big, warm hands cupped her buttocks, arching, lifting, spreading, refusing to let her escape the maddening pleasure he would give her.

She hung, suspended on the tenterhooks of his sweet torture until his tongue took mercy on her and set her free. Then she was falling, her body convulsing, raked by shudders of pure ecstasy.

Morgan lowered her, covered her trembling body with the heat of his own. His lips touched her throat, luring her eyes open. She was surprised to feel the wetness of fresh tears on her cheeks.

"You're still a bully, Morgan MacDonnell," she whispered.

He captured a tear on the tip of his tongue. "Aye, that I am. And you broke your vow, lass. That's three times tonight you've cried for me."

She sniffed. "I don't intend to make a habit of it. I've just never . . ." A latent shudder rocked her.

"Neither have I."

Her eyes widened in misty shock. "Never? Not even with Alwyn . . . or any of the others?"

He shook his head, his gaze oddly intense. "I never even wanted to. Until you."

For a man of his experience, he couldn't have given her a more precious gift. Sabrina wanted to give him something in return. She locked her arms around his neck and pulled his lips down to hers, reveling in the fierce sweetness of his mouth, flavored with both the salt of her tears and the balm of her fulfillment. A deep-throated growl escaped him.

Sabrina thought that surely he would lose control now, mating her with the stark animalistic greed she had expected from him. But his hands softly stroked her breasts, then her inner thighs, coaxing them apart. She felt the heavy press of his flesh against hers. When she would have turned her face into her hair to hide her sudden panic, Morgan cupped her cheeks in his hands, his smoky gaze no less piercing than the blunt weight of his manhood.

The harsh tenor of his voice betrayed the cost of his restraint. "I want to see your eyes when I take you, Sabrina Cameron. I want to know you're mine."

Sabrina had been his for as long as she could remember. He was her first and only love. Her eyes glazed with both pain and pleasure as he filled her, inch by maddening inch, breaching the barrier of her innocence with relentless patience. She writhed beneath him, wanting to pull away, wanting to draw him deeper. Her fingernails scored his back, but he never flinched, never wavered in his determination to make her his woman. His wife.

His teeth clenched. "Take me. All of me. That's it, angel. More. Ah . . ." His guttural groan was both prayer and demand. "Just a wee . . . bit . . . more."

Sabrina moaned, believing the more of him would never end. But finally she lay fully impaled beneath him. She had witnessed examples of Morgan's iron control before, but never had she imagined a restraint so exquisite, a patience so consuming.

His jaw was locked, his eyes hazed with raw hunger. His muscles strained toward every primitive instinct, yet he remained utterly still, waiting until the wild nether pulses of their bodies began to beat in one accord. Each mad beat shuddered Sabrina, leapt in her throat, her heart, and between her legs, where the blunt weight of his flesh throbbed.

Only when Morgan felt Sabrina's taut sheath adjust to accommodate the full measure of him, only when he saw her eyes roll back in a half-swoon of naked delight did Morgan close his eyes and began to move.

He had never felt more like a man. He'd lost his innocence at the age of fourteen to an eager young Cameron maid, but all his previous dalliances now seemed nothing more than the clumsy fumblings of a rutting beast. His father had entreated him to "Be a man!" before he even knew what the word meant, but it had taken this beautiful, innocent woman to make him one.

Bracing his weight on his palms, he angled his hips, deepening his thrusts to let his ravenous body taste every delectable inch of her. It was becoming more difficult to temper his ferocious need with restraint, but still he hung back, knowing how easily he could bruise her with his size, his brute strength.

Sabrina's slight body absorbed each of Morgan's slow, heated thrusts like blows to her heart. They shattered the shell she had erected around it, leaving her totally vulnerable to this man whose magnificent body held her in thrall. His name spilled from her lips in a broken litany, only to be caught by the passion-roughened heat of his own mouth descending on hers. The pleasure was devastating. The wild, pounding tempo of his possession increased, driving her back until she reached behind her and braced her palms against the stones of the hearth, arching to take him deep into the very core of her.

A Gaelic oath escaped Morgan's lips, its reverent violence belied by the roar of pure masculine ecstasy that rumbled from his throat in the next breath as he suffered the sweetest death a MacDonnell had ever known at the hands of a Cameron.

Sabrina awoke to the provocative sensation of being tenderly bathed between her legs. Her eyes fluttered open to find Morgan silhouetted against the dwindling firelight. Unaware that she was watching him, he dipped a rag into a basin of water, then dabbed inward from her thighs, his hands unspeakably gentle as they soothed her fragile, swollen tissues.

Sabrina had witnessed more than once the tenderness his hands were capable of while he had nursed some small, wounded creature back to health. But she had never dreamed to experience it herself. The jarring intimacy of the act laid her heart bare. A haze of pleasure spread from his touch. A soft, helpless sound escaped her lips.

Morgan lifted his head. Their eyes met across her naked length. Her breasts swelled and tingled beneath his perusal. Heat crept up her body, half shyness, half arousal.

The tapers had melted to fragrant pools of wax, but Sabrina didn't need much light to see the unguarded vulnerability in Morgan's eyes. He lowered them quickly, staring at the rag in his hand. She realized it was a scrap of wool cut from his plaid, stained now with her blood.

He dipped the cloth into the water, water he'd warmed for her comfort. "I never meant to hurt you, lass. You're so damned delicate. I was half afraid I'd gone and killed you."

Morgan stroked the wool across her, but the innocent benevolence of the gesture was lost as their gazes met again. Sabrina's lips were parted, her cheeks flushed. Morgan felt his traitorous body responding against his will. Raw hunger flooded him. He knew it was too soon for her; her battered body couldn't possibly be ready to accept him again. He could only hurt her more.

"You should sleep, lass," he said gruffly, rinsing out the rag. " 'Twill be dawn soon enough."

Dawn, Sabrina thought, with its harsh winter light cast across their doubts and differences. She didn't care if dawn never came. She wanted to remain there forever, cloaked in nothing but the waning firelight and the heated regard of her husband's eyes. She wanted to stir the banked embers she saw in their depths to roaring flame. To break his rigid control and prove to him that she wasn't some fragile figurine that could be shattered by his touch.

When Morgan reached to draw the plaid over her, she sat up on her knees, caught his fist, and brought it to her lips. Her tongue played lightly over his knuckles.

She mocked his burr deliberately. "So ye think a puir wee Cameron lass too puny for a MacDonnell's legendary stamina? Perhaps ye've been takin' those songs about yer clan a mite too seriously, sir."

Morgan was stunned by the mischievous sparkle of Sabrina's eyes. He had expected more tears, perhaps bitter accusations. His gaze dropped to the pert tips of her breasts. They tightened to rosy nubs beneath his perusal. His breath caught in a near groan.

He jerked his gaze back to her face and cleared his throat. "Now, lass, I cannot blame you for bein' wary of me. 'Tis only natural. I was a wee bit rough on you."

"Och, is the big, bad MacDonnell worried about scarin' the Cameron lass?" She nipped his knuckles. "If you must know, I found you rather . . . civilized for my tastes."

"Civilized?" The word fell from his lips like the vilest of curses. She might as well have called him a eunuch.

She gave him a provocative glance from beneath her lashes. Morgan didn't know why she was playing such a dangerous game. But he could no more resist her teasing challenge than he could resist a generosity brave enough to unleash his most selfish lusts on her tender body.

He hid his grin behind a leer. "So you'd like a taste of what all the songs and legends are about, eh, lass?"

Sabrina braced her palms against Morgan's chest, her courage nearly deserting her at the open voraciousness of his gaze. "Only if it pleases you," she whispered timidly.

The devilish sparkle in his eyes deepened. "Nothin' would please me more."

Morgan pounced on her like a tawny beast. With

deft hands he turned her away from him and bent her over the tick in a position that gave her no choice but to obey every dark command of his majestic body. As he filled her, she arched against him by primitive female instinct, determined to prove she could take whatever he could give her. Her fingernails dug into the tick, freeing the heady scent of the heather. He wrapped his powerful fists in her hair, murmuring sweet, rough words against her ear.

Just when Sabrina believed the pleasure could grow no more intolerable, Morgan decided he could not bear to go to that place of wild release alone. So he reached around and stroked her, his artful fingertips an exquisite contrast to his crude ravishing of her body.

Spasms of ecstasy racked them both until they could do nothing but collapse as one into the welcoming folds of Morgan's plaid.

The cheery crackling of a freshly stoked fire lured Sabrina from sleep. A woolen fuzz tickled her cheek. She pried open her eyes to find Morgan straddling a chair backward and watching her sleep, his green eyes bright with an intensity that jarred her to total wakefulness. He was still naked. She didn't know if she would ever grow accustomed to his absence of shame regarding his body. But as he'd taught her twice in the night and again by the misty light of dawn, there was nothing about his body of which to be ashamed.

A cascade of erotic memories came flooding back. She averted her face shyly, hardly daring to believe he had tapped such a wild vein of passion in her civilized heart.

"I'm out of firewood, Sabrina, and it's gettin' a wee bit chilly in here."

She toyed with the soft folds of wool beneath her hands. "Then why don't you get dressed?"

He dragged a hand through his hair, his sigh fraught with patience. It was then she realized he was naked because his plaid had been lovingly tucked around her, enveloping her in a warm cocoon. Still painfully aware of his scrutiny, she unrolled herself and handed him the plaid, jerking her damp pelisse up to cover her.

Morgan arranged and belted the plaid with casual grace, then sank back down in the chair, crossing his arms on its ladder back.

Sabrina could bear it no more. "Why are you staring at me?"

His avid gaze dropped from her face to her belly. "I was wonderin' if you might be carryin' my child."

Tendrils of heat crept up her throat and Sabrina resisted the urge to pull the pelisse over her head. But the calculating light in Morgan's eyes froze her embarrassment to hurt and then to anger.

She snatched up her gown, only to discover it was beyond repair. "I certainly hope your efforts were successful." Holding the pelisse closed in the back, she crawled to retrieve her slippers. "I'd hate to think you made that terrible sacrifice for nothing." She shivered beneath the brief, cool caress of the air as she dared to drop the pelisse over her head. The hood covered her face and she realized it was on backward. She punched at the thin velvet, trying to right it, her words muffled. "We should know quite soon if you'll have to suffer through it again."

Strong, warm arms encircled her from behind. Morgan's husky lilt stilled her struggles. "A MacDonnell never quits workin' until he knows his task is done."

Her head emerged. She furiously raked her hair out of her eyes. "Forgive me. I've never known a MacDonnell who worked."

"You do now, lass." His lips grazed her throat.

Sabrina felt herself melting against him along with her anger. She closed her eyes, fearful of the power he wielded. If she had thought the night might weaken it or temper it with power of her own, she was wrong. It had only made it more potent.

"I intend to devote myself with great enthusiasm to the task of gettin' my brat on you."

"Your devotion to duty is inspiring." And irresistible, Sabrina thought, moaning as his hands glided up her sides, easing the damp velvet up with them. "You can't mean. . . ?" Her voice cracked. "Again?"

Each of his words was punctuated with a gentle kiss along her hairline. "And again. I wouldn't be much of a man if I gave up tryin' now, would I?"

Without bothering to remove either pelisse or plaid, her husband eased her to the tick and proceeded to show her just how much of a man he was.

Chapter Seventeen

Sabrina was the first Cameron to conquer Castle MacDonnell without firing a single cannon.

Embued with the confidence inspired by her husband's touching devotion to duty, and championed by the fierce Fergus, she watched with secret delight as Morgan's clansmen fairly flung themselves at her slippered feet in surrender. Those who still dared to mock or insult her were more like than not to find themselves scrambling across the hall in a vain search for their scattered teeth.

Only Eve remained immune to Sabrina's charms, but her mood was so despondent that neither Fergus nor Morgan had the heart to correct her.

Even Fergus required an occasional reminder that civilization had come to MacDonnell. Sabrina entered the hall one morning to discover his beefy fist raised to backhand a cowering boy who had spilled goat milk on Fergus's tartan. Morgan was reaching to box both their

ears, but the wry arch of Sabrina's eyebrow was all it
took to correct Fergus's lapse of manners.

"Aye, there's a bonny lad!" Fergus roared, fondly
ruffling the boy's hair as if it had been his intention to
do so all along. "Hell, he might even be me own son.
He's got me bonny fair hair, don't ye think?"

"A touch of your dimples too," Sabrina agreed,
pinching Fergus's grizzled cheek and making him
beam.

Morgan hid his own smile behind a hunk of the
steaming gingerbread Sabrina had baked for him, de-
clining to point out that half the children in the clan
had hair of that same sunny sheen. And half of them
were probably Fergus's.

Morgan approached Sabrina's chamber one chill
evening, anticipating a rousing game of chess and an
even more rousing tumble with his wife. Girlish giggles
drifted into the corridor.

He eased open the door, expecting to find Enid
and Sabrina engaged in one of the charming female rit-
uals he could never hope to understand. Instead, he
found Sabrina holding up a hand mirror so Alwyn
could admire her reflection. Alwyn caught his flabbergasted expression in the mirror and spun around, her
eyes wide with guilt.

Although Alwyn's leggy, big-bosomed fairness no
longer appealed to him, Morgan had to admit there was
much to admire. She wore a clean gown of cool blue
satin, marked as a castoff of Sabrina's by its brimming
bodice and ankle-length hem. Her face was fresh
scrubbed and a tidy braid hung over one shoulder.

Sabrina linked an arm in Alwyn's. Morgan felt his
stomach sink as would any man faced with two women
whose favors he had only too recently shared. Especially when one of them was his wife.

"Good evening, dear. I was just helping Alwyn
with her hair. Doesn't she look lovely?"

Alwyn could have been Helen of Troy and Morgan would still have been blinded by the impish twinkle
in his wife's eye. He scrambled wildly for an appropri-
ate answer, clearing his throat, coughing, and finally

settling for a grunt of approval. To his shock, Alwyn blushed. He wouldn't have thought her capable of it.

She bobbed a clumsy curtsy. "I'd best be gettin' along, me lady. I promised Mr. Fergus I'd dine with him tonight." Her toothy grin erased years from her age. "Thank ye for the bonny ribbon. Thank ye indeed." She scampered past Morgan, hugging the door frame to keep from brushing against him.

He stepped warily into the chamber, shutting the door behind him. " 'Twas kind of you to befriend the lass. She can learn much from you."

"On the contrary. Your Alwyn has much to teach me."

He scowled. "She's not *my* Alwyn. Never was. And I'm not sure I want you learnin' what she knows."

Sabrina's innocent blink made his blood heat. "Perhaps you shouldn't be so hasty."

With those teasing words, she hooked her hand beneath his belt and drew him past the waiting chess board to the bed, the mocking slant of her smile softened by the tenderness in her eyes.

If Sabrina ruled MacDonnell by day, then Morgan was master of the night. Never had a Cameron been so tenderly enslaved. He held her in bonds of pleasure forged stronger each time she shattered beneath the artful dominion of his body.

He proved every sly whisper she'd heard about the MacDonnells to be true. He was relentless in pushing her to the brink of ecstasy and beyond, unyielding in his demand of her satisfaction, merciless in extracting cries of surrender until she was begging for what he was only too willing to give her.

Only in the wee hours of dawn, when she lay with her head pillowed on his naked chest, her body still limp from its most recent sating, did she dare to wonder about the morrow. Although Morgan seemed to take perverse delight in wringing her own tender confessions from her lips, he had never once so much as whispered the three words she had hungered so long to hear. Never completely lost that rigid control imposed upon him by a lifetime of care and responsibility. He gave of his body with lavish generosity but kept his heart armored and intact, just beyond her reach.

Time, she promised herself. In time she would lay siege to his heart until he trusted her enough to lay it at her feet. For now, the thundering song of its rhythm beneath her ear would have to be pledge enough.

Morgan emerged from the forest late one afternoon, his muscles aching with the pleasant exhaustion of a job well done. He and his men had done the work of a full clan in the past fortnight. The last of the cattle had been branded that day and left to forage among the rich bracken of the forest floor.

A blast of northern wind struck him as he climbed the hill toward the castle, sending the shards of snow beneath his feet into a whirling dance. Let the winter come! he thought with savage satisfaction.

In the past he'd always hated to see the bleached bones of her fingers come creeping over the mountains. The taunting whisper of her snow-choked voice had brought the MacDonnells nothing but hunger and desolation. But this year promised to be different. He had fresh meat to feed his clan. He would fill out their pinched cheeks and wipe the dull film of despair from their eyes.

The chickens had been cooped, the sheep penned, and the Cameron claymore hung over the hearth in Sabrina's chamber. There remained only one task left unfinished in his dealings with the Camerons, and Morgan suspected the velvety darkness of the long winter nights would be ideal for its completion. Perhaps by spring Sabrina would bear his brand as well, marked clearly as his by the gentle swelling of the babe in her belly.

Morgan secretly wished for a girl child, not caring to contemplate being forced to honor his hasty and foolish promise to send Sabrina home if she gave him a son. If he had his way, God would bless him with a dozen daughters. He grinned to envision the miniature dark-haired, blue-eyed beauties hanging all over his plaid.

He topped a rise in the hill to discover why most of his men had deserted him earlier. Sabrina was wrapped in her pelisse and perched on a musty hay bale in the open courtyard, strumming the clarsach and surrounded by his clansmen. Fergus stomped out a jolly fling while Ranald kept time on a wheezy set of pipes. As he blew out a sour note, his audience hooted and jeered. Enid, her cheeks blistered pink from the cold, blew him a consoling kiss.

Morgan leaned against the scarred trunk of a Caledonian pine to enjoy Sabrina's triumph over his clan. He could have ordered their sullen respect from her first day at MacDonnell, but he knew that would have been a hollow victory at best. Harsh experience had taught him that a victory earned was a victory savored.

Her sweet soprano launched them into melody:

> Sweet William came whistling in from the plough,
> Says, "Oh, my dear wife, is my dinner ready now?"
> She called him a dirty paltry whelp:
> "If you want any dinner, go get it your—"

"Rider! Rider comin' from Cameron way!" The hoarse cry shattered their merriment as a boy raced into the courtyard, stumbling and gasping for breath. "Cameron comin'!"

Chapter Eighteen

Morgan's clansmen reacted to a lifetime of training by drawing their weapons and diving for shelter. The powdery snow flew as Ranald tackled Enid, rolling her to safety and leaving Sabrina standing puzzled and alone before the hay bale. Where before there had been dancing and laughter, there was only tension and the thud of rapidly approaching hoofbeats.

Morgan bit off an oath. He tempered his first savage impulse to rush into the courtyard and throw himself over Sabrina, knowing that MacDonnells were notorious for firing first and making their heartfelt apologies later. He didn't even dare risk startling them by calling out a command. Swearing steadily beneath his breath, he forced himself to walk slowly and evenly down the hill.

A lone rider cantered into the courtyard to find himself sighted down the barrels and blades of fifty weapons. Even from his distance Morgan could see he was a green lad, only a few years older than the boy who had warned them of his approach.

In the thick silence that followed his halt, pistols cocked, hands primed bows, swords cleared their sheaths, and eyes that had sparkled with mirth only seconds before narrowed in deadly intent.

Morgan saw Sabrina frantically searching the faces of his clansmen for some clue to their strange behavior. He already knew what she would find. He'd seen it often enough in their faces and in his own—the steely promise of death, as crude and irrevocable as the metallic stench of blood soaking into the thirsty soil.

She pasted on a shaky smile and gathered her skirts. As Morgan realized what she meant to do, his oath shifted to a single wordless prayer.

The stark image of her lying crumpled in the snow, her breast pierced by an arrow or pistol ball, almost staggered him. But he forced himself to keep moving, to keep closing the distance between them. Only a few more yards and he could put his hands on her.

He flexed them without realizing it as Sabrina darted forward, throwing herself into the path of every weapon trained on the Cameron rider.

Forced gaiety brightened her voice. "Why, look, everyone! It's Caden Cameron ridden all the way from home! Fergus? Ranald? Come out and meet my cousin Caden. He's the second son of my third cousin twice removed. We've been friends since we were only children, haven't we, Caden? Have you brought a letter or just come to visit?"

The reins jingled in the boy's unsteady hands. His face had gone milk-white beneath his mop of dark hair, and despite the chill, sweat sheened his fair skin. His raw voice cracked. "I've b-b-brought a letter, Miss Sabrina. Er, I don't believe I've the t-t-t-time for a visit."

Morgan's hand closed around Sabrina's forearm. He'd never felt anything so welcome as the warm resilience of her flesh beneath her sleeve. He squeezed it harshly as if to assure himself of its reality.

"You bloody wee fool," he bit off beneath his breath. "Haven't you an ounce of common—"

"—decency? Sense?" she hissed back at him. "It would not speak well of your hospitality to send this poor lad back to Cameron draped over his saddle and riddled with holes."

"Your da might have taken an even dimmer view of you bein' returned in like manner." Shaking his head in a promise of later retribution, he thrust her behind the shelter of his body. Her faint tremor betrayed the cost of her boldness.

The messenger swayed in his saddle at the sight of the towering Highlander.

"Hop down, lad," Morgan ordered. " 'Tis too late to return to Cameron tonight. That road is dangerous by day and deadly in the dark. You'll sup with us tonight and ride back on the morrow."

Caden shook his head, obviously fearing his chances of surviving a night with the MacDonnells were less than negotiating the treacherous road. "No, thank you. I'm not very hungry, sir."

From the violent green tinging his complexion, Morgan suspected the lad was in danger of losing his midday meal as well as his supper.

Morgan leveled a sweeping glare around the courtyard that saw every weapon sheepishly uncocked, lowered, and sheathed. Then he turned that same stern scowl on the rider, daring the lad to defy him. "My wife and I must insist you stay." He lifted an ominous eyebrow. "You wouldn't wish to displease my lady, would you?"

"Oh, no, sir. Not at all." The boy slid from his horse with such haste that he almost lost his footing. Morgan steadied him. Remembering his errand, Caden fished in his leather pouch for a cream-colored sheet of vellum sealed with the Cameron crest. "It's from your father, Miss Sabrina."

Danger forgotten, Sabrina reached around Morgan's shoulder and snatched the missive from Caden's hand. Her hungry expression tore at Morgan's heart.

As she studied the cryptic scrawl on the outer fold, he saw hope birth and die in her pretty eyes.

Disappointment dulled her voice. "It's not for me. It's for the chieftain of Clan MacDonnell."

She handed Morgan the letter and turned away. As Sabrina passed among them, his clansmen emerged from their hiding places, their own faces stricken with uncertainty at her retreat.

"Sabrina?" Enid said softly, plucking a piece of straw from her own braid.

"Ye forgot yer clarsach, lass," Fergus called after her, hefting the delicate instrument in his grimy paw.

Sabrina kept walking, melting into the shadows of the buttery as if she'd never existed in their world at all. Morgan shivered as an odd chill touched his spine.

His fist crumpled around the rich vellum. Damn Dougal Cameron to hell! With a single arrogant stroke of his pen he had once again made enemies of them all.

Sabrina picked her way over a pile of rubble, traversing the deserted corridors to her chamber. She should never have left its sanctuary. If she hadn't, she wouldn't now be haunted by the suspicion and bloodlust she had witnessed in the eyes of Morgan's clansmen, all incited by a boy's careless cry of "Cameron comin'!"

She swept past a shattered wall. Cold wind moaned through the crumbling stone and she shivered, chilled to the bone. She knew now how quickly the MacDonnells would turn on her to protect their own. Her foolishness and vanity shamed her. She had honestly believed she could fight centuries of hatred and distrust with nothing more than a few amusing ditties and a dash of reckless charm.

The truth battered her. No matter how hard she tried to win the MacDonnells' stubborn affections, she would never be one of them. She would never belong. Not to their clan and not to Morgan. A fresh knot of pain curled in her heart.

How long would it be before she saw that same look of cold distrust in Morgan's eyes? Let one of his clansman succumb to a stomach grippe or take a drunken tumble down the stairs, and who would he suspect? It would crush her heart to see the sunlit warmth of his eyes fade to steely wrath.

She had no clan of her own now. Her father hadn't even troubled himself to write her. She was outcast, nothing more than a political pawn in the long-standing feud between Cameron and MacDonnell and a willing slave to the sensual mastery of Morgan MacDonnell.

The hours passed with excruciating slowness as she paced her lonely chamber, waiting for Morgan to come. Well after midnight, she curled into the chair where they had once shared their good-night kisses and drifted into sleep, only to stir restlessly as the mournful wail of the bagpipes pierced her fragmented dreams.

Morgan's fist slammed down on Dougal's letter, cracking the seal. The wild skirl of the bagpipes drifted through the window of the crofter's cottage, the raw notes taunting him with their beauty. Damn Eve! She was like a Greek chorus of doom, an inescapable reminder of his own father's folly in loving a Cameron. Weren't Angus's last words in praise of Elizabeth's beauty, his final gesture a toast to her fairness?

He sank into a chair and dropped his head into his hands. The wee dark hours before the dawn clustered outside the cottage. He knew that all he must do to either banish his doubts or justify them was go to Sabrina and ask her to read him the letter. It was not pride that stopped him, but fear.

Morgan was no stranger to fear. He had stared it dead in the face countless times. The moonless night he'd been ambushed by seven Chisholm men. The morning his father had forced him to amputate the gangrenous leg of a dying clansmen with nothing but a bottle of whisky to dull the man's agony.

The first time he'd set his unworthy foot in the rose-tangled bower of the Cameron garden.

But this fear could not be mastered by a roar of

command or ignored by erecting a shield of indifference. It paralyzed him with an impending sense of loss. What if Dougal had had a change of heart? What if he'd decided a MacDonnell wasn't worthy of his princess and was demanding her return? What if he had found her another husband—a cultured gentleman who could play chess and sing clever duets with her? To hear those damning words read to him in Sabrina's dulcet tones would be his undoing.

Despising his ignorance, he tore open the letter and scanned the bold script, searching for any clue to its contents. If Dougal had wanted her back, wouldn't he have sent a battalion of English redcoats instead of one lone lad shaking in his boots?

Morgan smoothed the rich vellum beneath his fingers. It wasn't too late to pretend he'd never seen the letter. Angus wouldn't have hesitated to do just that. It was well within his power to make the Cameron boy vanish with Sabrina none the wiser. The Highland roads were narrow and treacherous, accidents common. A gunshot. A horse's fatal misstep. A plunge into an icy ravine. It might be spring before a rider's body was found.

Morgan strode to the hearth and cast the offending missive into the glowing embers. A tongue of flame licked at it, curling and browning its creamy edges.

Just before the greedy flames could engulf it, Morgan snatched it back, burning his fingers. Self-contempt flooded him. He was shaken to realize how low he would sink to keep his bride. 'Twas a plot worthy of Horrid Halbert himself.

Remembering the joyous hunger in Sabrina's eyes as she had reached for the letter and the bitter disappointment that had dawned in its wake, Morgan admitted it wasn't Dougal's summons he feared or even Sabrina's longing to return to the opulent manor house where she belonged. It was his own cowardice. He was afraid he wouldn't be man enough to let her go.

His lips set in a grim line, he tucked the letter back into his plaid, realizing in the eerie hush that

something had changed. The mocking voice of the bagpipes had stilled.

Sabrina sat across from Morgan and picked at her supper in oppressive silence, determined not to comment
on his absence of the previous night. Her melancholy
had deepened during the long day, matched by the oppressive snow-laden clouds brooding over the mountain
peaks. Both Enid and Alwyn had come knocking at her
door, but she had sent them away, pleading a genuine
headache. Pugsley had spent the day curled into a ball
in the corner, his brown eyes unusually soulful. He
slept now, twitching and whining at intervals as if troubled by dreams.

Twirling her spoon in her soup, Sabrina studied
her husband from beneath her lashes. Tiny lines of exhaustion fanned out from his shadowed eyes. He ate as
always, picking up his soup bowl to drain it, eating his
meat with his fingers, then licking them clean, stabbing
his bread with his dirk and bringing it to his lips.

But not once had he kissed her, called her brat, or
given her the contentious smirk he knew maddened her
to distraction.

Nor had he mentioned her father's letter. She suspected he had commanded one of his more educated
clansman to read it to him. But she refused to beg for
even a pathetic scrap of news from home. Her father's
messenger had been sent back to Cameron that morning, his pouch stuffed with the letters Sabrina had written her mother in the past few weeks. Letters that made
no mention of her papa.

When she could no longer bear the impassive
scowl hewn on her husband's features, she shoved back
her untouched soup. "Shall I read to you tonight?
Chanson de Roland, perhaps, or some more *Beowulf*?"

His hand slipped into his plaid, then back out
again. Sabrina wondered at the curious gesture. "My
head is already achin', lass. I've no desire to fill it with
a lot of fancy words."

She rose, helpless to keep from pacing like a nervous cat. "Shall we play a game of chess, then? Or I could teach you a new game. Loo perhaps? There are no queens to lose in loo."

His pained flinch was so brief, she might have imagined it. He slammed the dirk down on the table. "I'm not in the mood for silly games."

His cross words brought the childlike knot of disappointment she'd been swallowing all day welling up in her throat.

Shielding her face with the fall of her hair, she picked up the clarsach Fergus had propped outside her door earlier in the day. But her hands were clumsy, laden with the same heaviness that weighted her spirit. One of her fingernails caught on the strings, tearing down to the quick.

A passionate oath escaped her. She tucked the throbbing finger into her mouth.

Then Morgan was there, bringing it to his own lips to suck away the welling drop of blood. " 'Tis a good thing your mother didn't hear you swear. I've seen Brian get his mouth scrubbed with a ball of pomade for far less."

Sabrina snatched her finger back, unable to bear the erotic play of his beautiful lips around her flesh. She knew she was being petulant, but didn't care. "I'm sure these walls have seen worse atrocities than my feeble stab at profanity." She fled to the window, desperate to escape his puzzled scrutiny. "We mustn't forget the siege of 1465, when the Camerons starved your ancestors until they were forced to begin dining off each other."

Morgan frowned. "Aye, perhaps that's when we developed our taste for human flesh."

He had to strain to hear her soft, bitter words. "Then what a fine delicacy my heart must be." She stared off toward Cameron, her gaze tracing the glittering ribbon of road that snaked along the cliff's edge.

Morgan steeled himself behind an armor of apathy before asking softly, "Would you like to go home, Sabrina?"

Sabrina's breath caught on a broken exhalation.

She wondered for a dizzying moment if her heart would beat again. When it did, she felt no relief. Had Morgan tired of her so easily? Had her unskilled attempts to please him only slaked his appetite for her, or, worse yet, bored him? Perhaps this had been his intention all along—to wreak his sensual revenge on her pliable body, then send her home to her papa, marked with the shame of being a MacDonnell's willing whore. She hugged back a chill of pure misery, trying to work up the courage and the pride to coolly accept his offer.

Morgan slipped up behind her, his bare feet rendering him noiseless, but before he could touch her, she whirled on him, her eyes glittering like polished sapphires. "Don't touch me! There's no further need of it. I'm afraid I've failed both you and my father in your misguided attempts to provide an heir to cement your precious peace. *There is no child.*"

Morgan's initial stab of disappointment was blunted by a rush of possessive joy. Sabrina wasn't homesick for Cameron. She was grieving because she hadn't conceived a child. His child.

"How long have you known?" he asked.

She inclined her head. "Since this morning."

He was still too much of a MacDonnell to resist using his strength to his advantage. Before she could protest, he swept her up in his arms and carried her to the bed. He sat down beside her, his hip pressed to her own.

"Are you ill, lass? Do you hurt?"

Sabrina dashed a tear from her cheek. She knew she should feel embarrassed. She had never discussed such things with anyone but her mother. But Morgan's tender concern was irresistible. Unable to choke a word past the lump in her throat, she nodded and reached up to tap her brow.

His fingers stroked and probed her temples with infinite care, massaging until the tension began to ease from her neck and shoulders.

"Where else?"

She shyly patted her stomach. Stretching out full

length beside her, he rubbed her stomach with the flat of his palm, soothing away the dull ache.

Finally, propping his weight on one elbow, he surveyed her solemnly. "Anywhere else?"

Her hand closed into a fist. She pressed it to her heart, knowing it was the one pain he would be helpless to soothe. She was wrong.

His lips descended on hers, coaxing and nibbling until they parted for the tender, possessive stroke of his tongue. Even as his mouth wandered down the column of her throat, he was patiently opening the tiny buttons of her bodice, freeing the lush bounty of her breasts for the pleasure of his hands. Her fists caught in the fair silk of his hair as he inclined his head, sucking fiercely until her womb contracted with delight.

"Morgan!" she gasped. "Don't you understand? There's no need for you to do this. It's impossible for you to get me with child right now."

His hands pushed up her gown, slid her cumbersome petticoats down over her hips. The dark passion in his eyes robbed her of breath. "Humor me."

Sabrina was dazed by the impact of his words. Morgan MacDonnell had finally betrayed his own pride. Fierce joy spilled through her, tempered with triumph. This magnificent, arrogant man wanted her more than he wanted a son.

"Are you sure?" she whispered, arching boldly against him as his lips claimed hers again.

He lifted his head to give her a shameless wink. "You've been lax, lass, not to have studied the MacDonnell motto. 'Tis written in Gaelic, but it translates as, 'Any battle worth winnin' is worth sheddin' a wee bit o' blood over.' " The naughty twinkle in his eyes deepened. " 'Especially if it's not your own'."

Sabrina awoke to an empty bed. She lifted her tousled head to find Morgan at the table, his plaid knotted at his waist. A single taper burned, holding the shadows at bay and casting a golden sheen over his inclined head. She threw back the bedclothes and padded over to him, wearing the woolen nightdress he had tucked her into when the warmth of their bodies hadn't completely stilled her shivers.

A children's alphabet book lay open on the table in front of him. It had been Sabrina's favorite as a little girl and she planned to use it to teach some of the younger MacDonnells to read. Each of the letters was illustrated by a handsome woodcutting of an exotic animal. Morgan's lips moved with painstaking care as he compared its pages to a crumpled sheaf of paper.

Sabrina laid a hand on his shoulder. He started guiltily and slammed the book shut.

She clutched her pounding heart. "Mama always warned me never to sneak up on a MacDonnell."

He glowered at her. "Sound advice. You're lucky I didn't jump you."

A helpless giggle escaped her. "I thought you already did."

His sizzling glance told her he hadn't forgotten. She stood on tiptoe to peer over his shoulder. He cupped his hand around the paper, then relented. "Ah, hell, I can't read the bloody nonsense."

He exposed a shabby scrap of vellum that looked as if a rat had been chewing on it. As Sabrina smoothed it beneath her palm, bits of wax that had once belonged to the Cameron seal crumbled in her hand. Her heart quickened with excitement.

Morgan wearily rubbed his eyes. "As best as I can figure, your da, a bison, and an alligator are ridin' to MacDonnell to fetch their elephant."

Sabrina swallowed her grin with difficulty and hungrily scanned the letter. "No. My father, *Brian*, and *Alex* are coming for a visit. They wish to retrieve *Enid* and see how we are faring as husband and wife."

Morgan stroked his chin. "Checkin' up on me, eh? I'm surprised the crafty son of a"—he caught her reproving look and cleared his throat—"Cameron waited this long. When are they comin'?"

"Before Christmas." Her fingertip traced the bold line of script etched at the bottom of the page. A note of wonder dawned in her voice. "He didn't forget me after all."

Morgan quenched a childish flare of jealousy, wishing he'd been the one to make his wife's face glow with such serene joy. "What's it say, lass?"

" 'Tis from one of my mother's favorite poems by Robert Herrick." Thinking how odd it was that her father's enigmatic message mirrored the MacDonnell creed so aptly, Sabrina met her husband's wary eyes and softly whispered, " 'Ne'er the rose without the thorn.' "

Chapter Nineteen

With the ruthlessness of a warring chieftain, Sabrina prepared the MacDonnells for her family's visit. She blithely ignored their grumbling and muttered oaths, seeing through their hostility to the fear beneath. Fear they would be found lacking by the wealthy Cameron laird. Fear they would be laughed at, mocked for their poverty, their ignorance, they crudity.

Grudgingly blessing her mother's foresight, Sabrina delved deep into the trunks Elizabeth had packed, finding for each of them some talisman that might give them the illusion of courage.

For Fergus it was a handsome magnifying glass carved from African ivory, and for Alwyn a brass thimble. Alwyn put it to good use without delay, thumping Fergus on the head whenever his roving, magnified eye strayed to another girl.

Fearing the magical trunks weren't as bottomless as they seemed, Sabrina and Enid plundered their own wardrobes, sewing steadily to make gowns out of petticoats, lacy caps from drawers, and cloth slippers from the voluminous underskirts of one of Enid's ball gowns.

Even the gnarled crone who had claimed dominion over the kitchen proudly sported a girlish pink bow fashioned from one of Sabrina's garters. Eve remained resistant to Sabrina's overtures. Sabrina found her gift of a gold comb abandoned in a dirty mound of snow. She just shook her head, revising her opinion that Morgan was the most stubborn MacDonnell she had ever met.

The castle floors were swept clean, cobwebs peeled from the tarnished torch sconces, and the holes in the walls disguised by threadbare tapestries.

Morgan returned to the chamber late one night after spending the day clearing chunks of rubble from the narrow corridors. He picked his way over mounds of fabric only to discover his young wife asleep before the fire, her fingers still curled around her needle. Violet shadows tinted the delicate skin beneath her eyes.

She was doing none of this for her own benefit, he reminded himself. She had nothing to prove to her father. She was working herself to exhaustion so her husband could stand before Dougal Cameron and look him in the eye without the barriers of envy and shame erected between them.

Tenderness flooded him, tempering his lust with chagrin. His demands on her since learning of Dougal's impending visit had been both frequent and intense. He had made love to her with fierce abandon, a primitive possessiveness driving him to remind her that she was his woman now, a Cameron no longer. Her broken cries in that moment when she came apart beneath him were like song to him, an affirmation of the wild, sweet power that bound them. He yearned to sow his seed in her yielding body, to see their future shining in the eyes of their daughter.

A thread of guilt wove through his longing. He had made love to her with tender violence, yet still had not brought himself to say the words that would lay his heart bare and reveal his pride for the folly it was. His own cowardice shamed him.

Not trusting himself to carry her to the bed and let her sleep undisturbed, he lifted her in his arms, then sat, cradling her against his chest like a child. She nuzzled her cheek against his plaid, sighing with contentment.

He rubbed his chin against her hair. "I'll make you proud, lass. As God is my witness, I swear I will." Then he gently kissed her brow and whispered the words she'd waited more than half her life to hear.

Sabrina swore as a dense cloud of soot smacked her in the face. Dropping her broom, she backed out of the grate on hands and knees, coughing and wiping her eyes. Pugsley retreated beneath the bed, wheezing as if each breath would be his last. The chamber door swung open.

Morgan blinked down at her. "Pardon me. I was looking for my wife."

"Morgan!" Her annoyed cry stilled his retreating feet.

He crossed the chamber and hauled her to her feet, panic flaring in his eyes. "For God's sake, woman! Your father's expected at any moment. Do you want him to think I've made a charwoman of you?"

She rested her hands on her hips. "If you'd trouble to clean your chimney every century or so, I wouldn't be in this predicament."

They glowered at each other, both aware that this day would prove whether or not their newfound feelings could survive the past enmity of their clans. Then Morgan's stony lips began to twitch. Sabrina snatched up the hand mirror and glared at her reflection. Except for the angry blue sparkle of her eyes, her face was tinted solid black. Her pristine nightdress was streaked with filth.

A giggle escaped her. Still studying her reflection, she mopped her face with a wet cloth, washing away the worst of it. "I've a better idea. I'm going to tell him you've kept me manacled in your dungeon to ravish at your leisure."

"Don't think I haven't been tempted." He arched a wicked eyebrow. "Perhaps after he takes his leave . . ."

Sabrina tilted the mirror to peruse her husband's length, her heart quickening. His plaid was freshly laundered and draped in elegant ceremonial folds. He'd even donned a scuffed pair of boots for the occasion, having polished them to a dull sheen. She was touched both by his masculine vanity and his obvious desire to impress her father.

Their eyes met in the mirror. "Do I have your approval?" he said lightly.

If Sabrina had learned one lesson from her husband, it was that sometimes actions were more succinct than words. She threw herself into his arms, tumbling him back into a chair. She was melting against him, preparing to show him just how much she approved, when a sharp rap sounded on the door.

Morgan jumped to his feet, practically dumping her out of his lap, and jerked his plaid straight. "Sweet Christ, the rascal can't be here already."

But it was only Ranald who poked his hair around the door. His dark hair stood out in nervous tufts. His swarthy complexion had gone pallid. "There's trouble in the fold, Morgan. One o' them hardheaded sheep o' yers has wandered off and fallen through the ice on the loch. I got a rope 'round her, but I canna pull her out."

Sabrina wondered if it was her imagination or if Ranald was acting more twitchy than usual. Perhaps it was only her earlier hints that it was his duty to petition her papa for Enid's hand that was making him squirm.

"Damn it all!" Open dismay colored Morgan's eyes. "I wanted to be here when your father arrived, not wrestlin' with some witless sheep."

Ranald's words rushed out in a flood. He inched toward the door. "She was bleatin' somethin' turrible. I think ye'd better come quick. I'll try to keep her wee head above the ice until ye get there."

As Ranald fled, Morgan ran a distracted hand through his hair. Distress at the thought of an animal suffering was etched on his features.

"Go," Sabrina commanded, laying a soothing

hand on his arm. "If Papa arrives before you return, I'll simply explain. He's always been a firm believer in rescuing lost sheep."

"Are you sure? I know how much this means to you." His gaze searched her face. She hoped her bright smile erased any traces of disappointment.

"Go," she insisted, giving his immobile chest a push. "After all, we MacDonnells take care of our own."

She had hoped for one of the tender grins that had taken to cracking his stony features. She was unprepared for the intensity of his somber gaze.

He cupped her nape in his palm and crushed her mouth beneath his in a fervent kiss. "Aye, lass. And don't you ever forget it."

"Not likely, my love," she whispered after he was gone.

Sabrina knew she should sweep the hearth, and dress, but she couldn't resist stealing a moment to savor her happiness. Lured by the harsh, glittering beauty of the world beyond the window, she studied the narrow ribbon of road and wondered if she might be the first to sound the joyous cry of "Cameron comin'!" Frigid cold seeped around the warped panes, but she was warmed by the secret gifts she carried in her heart.

Morgan appeared below, wading through the drifts toward the meadow that bordered the road. He slid on an icy patch, nearly losing his balance, and Sabrina smiled, imagining the colorful oaths that were blistering the chill air. Unexpected tears burned her eyes. The man she loved wasn't the civilized chieftain with his polished boots, but the surly giant who went grumbling off in the snow to rescue a stranded sheep.

As Morgan disappeared over a hill, her hungry gaze was drawn back to the road. The two men she loved most in the world were about to meet for a fresh beginning. To one of them she would give her heart. To the other, forgiveness. She had torn up a dozen letters to her papa in the past week, deciding it braver to look into those blue eyes that were so like her own and tell him she understood the difficult choice he had made.

He had not given his princess to a beast after all, but to a prince in beast's clothing.

Suddenly eager to share their happiness, she flew into a frenzy of activity. She swept the hearth and laid a fresh fire on the grate. She scrubbed her hands and face and buttoned herself into a modest gown of ivory satin. Shaking out the skirts, she hoped her papa and brothers wouldn't be too disgraced by her lack of petticoats and corset. Fergus might find himself with a rival when Brian caught his first glimpse of the shapely Alwyn wearing nothing but his sister's discarded underwear.

Having given away her last ribbon, she decided to seek out Enid and see if her cousin had one to spare. Although Morgan loved to tangle his hands in her unbound hair, she felt a more dignified coif would suit a demure married woman such as herself. Grinning at the notion, she threw open the door.

Eve blocked her path, arms crossed and glee sparkling in her smoky eyes.

The very idea of a happy Eve terrified Sabrina. Without intending to, she took a cautious step backward, wishing even the toothless Pugsley were there to defend her. Eve pressed her advantage, stepping into the chamber.

Sabrina's nose twitched at the musty smell of the woman's plaid. Forcing herself to hold her ground, she tipped her head back to boldly meet the taller woman's gaze. "I've neither the time nor the patience for your predictions of doom, Eve. Nor will I let you spoil this day for Morgan."

Eve's lips parted in a toothy grin. "Nothin' could spoil this day for the MacDonnells. We'll not see the likes of it again."

"I'm glad we agree on something. You're fortunate to have a man of Morgan's vision to lead your clan into the future."

"Aye, and a grand and glorious future 'twill be. If only Angus had lived to see it." Her barren eyes reflected a more chilling emptiness of the soul.

Sabrina shivered at the sudden revelation. "Do

you know who killed him, Eve?" she asked softly, no longer able to bite back the question that had haunted her for weeks. What finer gift could she give both Morgan and her father than to see the Camerons absolved of blame?

Eve shrugged and began to pace the chamber, dragging her lame leg behind her. " 'Twas an accident. A slip o' me knife. Quick and clean. He never suffered."

Sabrina swallowed a knot of queasiness. "Would you like me to tell Morgan for you?"

"Don't you think he knows?" Eve snarled. "Didn't you see his face when Angus fell? Was it truly surprise you saw or only shock that the wrong man took the blade? The blade meant for yer father. Open those innocent blue eyes o' yers, lassie. Morgan's the one with the vision in this clan. A terrible and wonderful vision. 'Twas his idea to kill the almighty laird of the Camerons, and he's the man gone to finish the task today."

The chamber reeled around Sabrina. She reached out a hand to steady herself, but there was nothing there. Nothing but four centuries of suspicion and betrayal. She had found Morgan in her mother's solar minutes before Angus was killed. Had it truly been peace he was seeking or an alibi for his whereabouts while his clansmen murdered her father.

She remembered Ranald's untimely interruption only moments before, his wildly darting gaze. She and Morgan had planned to greet her father in the courtyard, standing shoulder to shoulder as husband and wife. Now Morgan was gone, leaving her at Eve's mercy.

We MacDonnells take care of our own, she had teased him.

And don't you ever forget it, lass.

Had his words been a promise or a warning?

She could still taste the flavor of his lips on hers. Surely no Judas kiss could have been so sweet, so full of loving hunger. Her spine stiffened. Someone had to be the first to believe, the first to cast aside the prejudices of the past and defend a future built on nothing more than the tenuous thread of blind faith.

Her papa wouldn't have chosen her for the task if he hadn't believed her worthy.

She faced Eve squarely, her voice quiet but filled with firm conviction. "You're lying. You and your cunning Angus might have plotted such treachery, but my husband wouldn't stoop to stabbing a man in the back *or* ambushing him. If he wanted someone dead, he'd at least have the pride to look him in the eye while he killed him. He is a man of honor."

"He is a fool!" At Eve's bitter declaration, fierce triumph burned through Sabrina's veins. The woman's next words tempered it with fear. "Morgan's simply blinded by what lies beneath those fancy skirts o' yers. I've sacrificed too much for this clan to just hand it o'er to the bloody Camerons without a fight. I'm not the only one who feels this way. Some of us aren't content to spend our lives tendin' sheep and pluckin' chickens. We were bred to fight, and if Morgan's not man eno' to go down fightin', there are those of us who are. He can make his choice. To stand with our guns or fall beneath them."

Sabrina dared a glance at the window. Her breath froze in her throat at the sight of a line of horses winding up the cliff road. Her father, her brothers, the Cameron party were no more than dark blots on the snowy horizon.

She flung herself at the door. But like the hapless Grant lassie before her, Sabrina was betrayed by the heavy fall of curls that had given her husband so much pleasure. Eve's hand twisted in them like a vise, jerking her back. Tears of pain stung her eyes.

Still gripping her hair, Eve shoved her across the chamber and threw open the window. Icy wind buffeted them both. Eve gave her hair a harsh yank, trying to force her to her knees. Sabrina bit back a cry of pain. Her hands clenched on the windowsill. She refused to crumple before this vindictive creature.

"I want ye to watch, lassie. Watch yer dreams die before yer eyes as I've spent me own life don'." Sabrina clawed at the sill as Eve forced her forward. The cobblestones below seemed to loom up to meet her. Vertigo made her head spin. " 'Twill be no surprise to Morgan that after witnessin' the massacre of her family, his spineless bride chose to end her life rather than wait for him to return and murder her himself."

Blinding calm flooded Sabrina. She pressed her eyes shut against the battering wind, knowing that Eve was mad. The woman's accidental murder of Angus and her own twisted devotion to Clan MacDonnell had unhinged her. She was willing to sacrifice them all, even Morgan, for her vengeance against the Camerons.

Images assailed Sabrina with shattering clarity. Her papa twirling her high in the air. Brian tickling her. Alex buttoning her cloak when her chubby little hands had been too clumsy. Bloodstained corpses in the snow. Morgan caught in the terrible aftermath of Eve's revenge. Morgan returning to find her body broken on the jagged cobblestones, believing in that black moment that she had doubted and feared him more than she loved him.

"No," she whispered, opening her eyes.

Ignoring the rending pressure at the base of her skull, she bucked against Eve. Forced to release her or fall, Eve stumbled backward, flailing her arms in a vain search for her ruined balance. Sabrina shoved past her, not even glancing back when a chair splintered beneath Eve's weight. The woman's howl of thwarted rage floated after her.

Sabrina flew down the stairs. The stone walls layered with the blood and sweat of Morgan's ancestors seemed to mock her frailty, her foolish optimism that one woman's heart could make a difference when weighed against centuries of senseless violence.

A stabbing pain tore at her side. She sped through the hall, ignoring the puzzled shouts and cries of alarm that rose in her wake. None of Morgan's clansmen could help her now. She had no way of knowing how many of them Eve had ensnared in her plot. There was no time to explain, and she wasn't sure enough of their fealty to know if they would believe her word against their own clanswoman's.

She burst into the snowy courtyard, gasping for breath. She had to warn Morgan. He was the only one with the power to avert the disaster that was about to befall them all. Knowing she could reach the meadow more quickly by taking the road that bordered it instead of cutting through the woods as Morgan had done, she plunged toward the stables, abandoning her slippers in a stubborn drift. Her frantic hands wrenched open the stable doors.

The warm must of horseflesh spilled around her as she examined the line of horses with the speed of desperation. Their placid eyes blinked back at her. Ribs protruded against their dull coats, and she knew most of them had been underfed not out of cruelty, but out of harsh necessity. Morgan would starve himself before he starved a horse.

She flinched as a pair of iron-shod hooves struck sparks off the back wall, demanding her attention.

Pookah tossed his mane in spirited defiance, eyes rolling in challenge. Slabs of sinew and muscle roiled beneath his shiny coat. Steam puffed from his flared nostrils, making him resemble a dragon more than he did the other horses.

Sabrina narrowed her eyes in determination. Refusing to give her fears time to root, she lifted her skirts and raced across the stable to throw herself, barefoot and saddleless, across Pookah's sleek back. Hooking her legs around him, she gave a wild cry of command and stabbed at his quivering flanks with her heels.

His body went completely lax. He stood like a statue, not prancing, not quivering, as far as Sabrina could tell, not even breathing. He was as docile as one of the fat, even-tempered ponies her mother had insisted she ride as a child. Sabrina couldn't believe she had come this far only to be defeated by another stubborn MacDonnell.

"Damn you, horse!"

Her heels flailed at him again, but he remained as unmoved by her blows as he was by her broken oaths.

As she saw her future slipping away, she was haunted by visions of a past that seemed determined to repeat itself.

She and Morgan, separated by iron bars. Morgan slamming her to the floor of her father's hall, cheered on by the jeers of his clansmen. Angus pitching forward, a jeweled dirk buried in his back. A golden-haired boy pushing her to the leaves, anger and pain flaring in his stormy green eyes.

Her curses died. Her legs went limp with exhaustion. She buried her face in Pookah's coarse mane, tears of despair spilling from her eyes as she whispered, "Please, God. Oh, please, not again . . ."

Pookah was no less moved by her tears than his master had been. Whickering softly, he tossed his dappled head. Hardly daring to hope, Sabrina clutched his slippery neck with both arms as he shot toward the open door. Snow exploded beneath his pounding hooves. Morgan's clansmen came pouring from the castle, their shocked faces nothing but a blur as Sabrina and Pookah thundered past.

The flying snow blinded Sabrina as she went careening down the icy road in search of the one man who held all their destinies in his hands.

Morgan stood waist-deep in the glacial waters of the loch, his numb arms wrapped around the belly of a terrified sheep. He'd arrived to find neither Ranald nor the rope he'd promised in evidence. Cursing his cousin's laziness, he had spent several minutes cracking the thick crust of ice that glazed the loch before plunging into its icy waters.

Holding the sheep's head above the water, he waded for the shore. Her pitiful bleating deafened him. One of her flailing hooves scraped his upper thigh.

"Easy, lass," he muttered, twisting his hips to a safer angle. "One more blow like that and my father-in-law'll be dinin' on mutton chops tonight."

His plaid tangled around his thighs in a sodden weight as he hefted the sheep from the water. He collapsed to his knees in the snow, holding the trembling creature against his chest to warm them both.

"There now," he soothed it. "You're safe and you'll soon be dry which is more than I can say for me." He freed her and she went trotting off without even a backward glance of gratitude.

"Just like a woman," Morgan said, shaking his head in bemusement. He climbed to his feet, flexing his raw hands. His only pair of boots were filled with water, and his feet were numb. Narrowing his eyes, he gazed down the distant road that ran adjacent to the meadow to see a party of riders approaching from the south.

His shoulders slumped. Here he stood to meet his illustrious father-in-law, soaked to the skin, his hair in a tangle, his plaid encrusted with muddy slush. He chuckled as his chagrin turned to amusement. The Cameron would simply have to understand that he was a workingman now. Dougal's beautiful, industrious daughter had seen to that.

Emboldened by the thought of her, Morgan strode toward the road to welcome their guests. The thunder of hoofbeats cracked like a whip across the brittle air. Morgan paused, frowning to realize they were coming from the wrong direction.

Shading his eyes against the glare of the snow, he gazed back toward the castle. Not even in his worst nightmare could he have envisioned the sight that greeted him.

Paralyzed with horror, he watched a gray streak barrel down the narrow road. A scantily clad figure clung low on the horse's neck, her own dark mane streaming behind her.

Sabrina. His wife's name was a soundless prayer on his lips.

Morgan lurched into a run, knowing his only hope was to somehow throw himself into Pookah's path. The horse took a torturous curve at a dead gallop, hooves skidding on the icy stones. Why didn't she fall off? Morgan thought wildly. Why the bloody hell didn't she just fall off? But even as she leaned back and tried to steer the horse away from the cliff's edge, her tenacious hold on Pookah's mane never wavered.

Morgan pounded across the meadow, arms and legs pumping, heart swelling in his chest until he thought it would surely burst. But the harder he ran, the farther away she seemed. He was twelve years old again, hurtling across a cloud-shadowed meadow, a little girl's hopeful cries of "Boy! Boy!" punishing him for ever being callous enough to flee her.

Morgan was halfway between Sabrina and the approaching riders when the Cameron party reached a cluster of tall rocks at the bottom of a steep hill. Shouts of warning and confusion rang out, followed by the shrill whinnies of terrified horses. Morgan's gaze never strayed from Sabrina. As she plunged down a straight stretch, he forced himself to run faster, knowing he had to bisect her path before she reached the next deadly curve.

There the road lay in a deceptively gentle ribbon, snaking only inches from the cliff's edge. At Pookah's speed the horse would never be able to make it. And neither would he, Morgan realized. There was only one way to give Sabrina a chance.

He dropped to one knee, drawing his pistol from his plaid in one fluid motion, praying its powder hadn't been dampened by his plunge into the loch. Stray gunshots rang out. The Camerons were thundering toward him. Hoofbeats bore down on him from all directions. His locked arm never wavered.

"I'm sorry lad," he whispered. Clenching his teeth against a frisson of anguish, he cocked the pistol, fixed Pookah's graceful head in his sights, and fired.

Before the horse could stumble, Morgan had dropped the pistol and was up and running. Pookah reeled in a macabre dance at the cliff's edge. Roaring Sabrina's name, Morgan launched himself from a towering drift.

For an impossible moment the horse teetered on the brink of the cliff. Morgan would have almost sworn he smelled the maddening scent of roses, felt the taunting whisper of Sabrina's hair brush through his fingertips before he slammed into the road with bone-jarring impact, his hands empty of all but air.

Pookah rolled, his legs flailing at nothing, before disappearing over the cliff's edge. Then there was nothing to break the winter silence but the shrill screams of horse and woman and the nightmarish sound of snapping bones.

Morgan hurled himself toward the cliff with every intention of plunging after her. A dead weight thudded into his chest, bringing him to the ground only inches from its edge. Arms and legs swarmed over him. Blinded with agony, he fought them like a madman for what seemed like an eternity. They straddled him, holding him down. Then a fist crashed into his jaw, slamming him into stillness.

Bewildered, he struggled to understand why a sweat-drenched Brian Cameron was lying across his legs while Alex Cameron, his freckles stark against his deathly pallor, held his shoulders. He blinked up at the man who had struck him. A bearded man whose lip was swelling and eye blackening from Morgan's frantic blows even as he watched. A man with Sabrina's dark-lashed eyes filled with a fierce anguish to match his own.

Dougal caught Morgan's plaid in his fists. "She's alive, lad! A ledge broke her fall. My men saw her chest move." Dougal gave him a harsh shake. "Do you hear me? I don't know for how long, but, by God, *she's alive!*"

Then Morgan did something he had resisted doing for twelve long years. He buried his face in Dougal Cameron's heaving shoulder and cried like a baby.

Chapter Twenty

Fergus MacDonnell had laughed in the face of death countless times, but if he lived to be a hundred, he would never forget the sight of his chieftain bearing his bride's broken body into the courtyard. A pall of silence hung over the clan, disturbed only by a muffled cry of anguish and a child's steady sniffling.

Their young mistress's neck hung limp, her dark hair streaming in a lank curtain over Morgan's arm. The ashen pallor of her face led many of them to believe she was already dead. Keening softly beneath her breath, Alwyn turned her face into Fergus's shoulder. He pressed her close, wanting to shield her from the even more terrible specter of Morgan's face.

His rugged features might have been hewn from rock. Their total absence of emotion was chilling. Nothing but the grimy tear tracks staining his cheeks even marked him as human.

Held in thrall by the grim spectacle, the MacDonnells hardly noticed the Cameron men who filed in after Morgan, some leading their horses, others limping, the fine wool of their garments torn and stained. Fergus gaped as their ranks parted to reveal Ranald stumbling between them, his hands bound by a frayed length of rope, fresh blood soaking the shoulder of his plaid. A questioning murmur rose.

Enid burst from the crowd only to find her frantic path blocked by Alexander Cameron. "Ranald!" she cried, jumping up and down to see over Alex's shoulder. "What happened? What in God's name have you done?"

Ranald stared straight ahead as if he hadn't heard her, his lips set in a grim line. Only after the doors closed on the grim procession and the massive bolt dropped, barring the clan from their own castle, did the whispers and rumors begin to fly.

Morgan refused to let anyone touch her. While the other men who loved Sabrina kept their own tortured vigil, he cut away her tattered gown, gently arranged her flaccid limbs, and bathed the numerous scrapes and gashes marring her smooth flesh. He wrapped her in clean sheets and brushed her tangled hair from her face. She lay as still as death beneath his tender ministrations.

Brian, the best rider among them, had been sent to fetch Dougal's physician from Cameron. Unwilling to risk his wife's life on the same road that had almost taken his daughter's, Dougal had given his son strict instructions to tell Elizabeth only that the physician was needed to tend a sick child. Dougal stared over Morgan's shoulder at his daughter's face, fighting sick despair. Their child.

His burning eyes raked the chamber. What sort of life had she shared with Morgan? Had it been one of love and laughter or bitterness and blame? Should he have come sooner, he wondered, or would his arrival only have hastened this tragedy? None of the clues fit. They'd arrived to find the chamber a charming portrait of welcome, marred only by a splintered chair. A merry fire had crackled on the grate. So why in God's name had Sabrina been charging barefoot down that icy road in little more than a nightdress?

Dougal's hands clenched into fists. He wanted to shake Morgan, to demand answers to the questions that tormented him. But as he watched Morgan draw a damp cloth across Sabrina's brow, something stopped him. He would have never believed hands so big and powerful could be so gentle, so fraught with the unspoken desire to cause no pain.

Alex appeared in the doorway, his bleak gaze avoiding the bed. Relieved by the distraction, Dougal listened to what his son had to say, then laid a hand on Morgan's shoulder. Morgan's eyes never left Sabrina's face; his hands continued their soothing motions.

Dougal withdrew his hand. "Two of the men who ambushed us are dead. Three others have scattered. Your cousin was wounded during the fracas. They've put him in the dungeon for now. He'll need attention."

Morgan's tone was low and vicious. "Let the bastard rot."

Tempted to agree with Morgan, Dougal shook his head at Alex, knowing Morgan might relent when the stench of betrayal wasn't so fresh in his nostrils.

The afternoon shadows deepened to twilight, then to full dark. The endless hours of the winter night ticked by, measured by the shallow rise and fall of Sabrina's chest. Morgan stroked his fingertips across the silk of her lashes, praying that she would open her eyes, longing to search their depths for some sign that she would not sleep forever.

But when she began to stir and thrash, Morgan had reason to regret his wish. Her eyes shot open, fixed sightlessly on horrors he could only imagine. A scream of agony tore from her throat, followed by another and another until Dougal buried his face in his hands and Alex rocked back and forth on the hearth, his palms clamped over his ears. Outside the chamber, Pugsley set up a mournful howling.

Sabrina's teeth tore at her lips until they beaded with blood. When Morgan tried to dribble whisky down her raw throat, she choked, and he was forced to abandon his efforts for fear his mercy might kill her.

As he threw his weight across her to keep her from harming herself in her violent struggles against the pain, he wondered savagely if he might have done her a greater kindness by planting the pistol ball in her brain instead of Pookah's.

Only when the pale light of dawn crept across the chamber did Sabrina collapse in a sweat-drenched heap against the tangled sheets. It was not relief but exhaustion that finally muffled her cries to whimpers.

A cheery footstep sounded outside the door. Dougal and Alex started to their feet.

A jovial British voice boomed out. "Don't you fret, Brian. I'll have her back on her feet in no time. Hearty as a heifer, the chit always was. Do you remember the time she got her fat little hand stuck in that beehive? And the morning she took that nasty tumble off the—"

Before the door could swing open, Morgan was there. He slammed Dr. Samuel Montjoy against the wall, pinning him by the lapels of his frock coat. The physician's steel-framed spectacles slid askew. His bewhiskered jowls quivered.

Befuddled to find himself the victim of such an attack, he could do no more than stammer an incoherent greeting. "G-g-good day, sir. I presume you are the—"

Morgan's words hammered the air. "Stop the pain. Do you understand? I don't care what it takes. Just don't let her hurt anymore. If you do, I'll kill you myself."

Morgan unclenched his fists. The doctor slid into a limp puddle, held on his feet only by Brian's bracing hand at his elbow. "Yes, yes, I dare say you will," he muttered, drawing off his spectacles with shaking hands to polish them on his ruffled stock. "Can't say I blame you."

As Morgan stormed from the chamber, Dougal

followed, doubling his pace to keep up with Morgan's long strides. "Damn you, Morgan MacDonnell, don't you dare go storming off! You owe me some answers! Brian almost killed you, you know. When he saw you drop and fire, he thought you'd shot Sabrina. If Alex hadn't realized you were going to fling yourself after her, I'd have shot you myself. As it was, I barely got there in time to stop you from throwing yourself over that cliff."

Morgan didn't slow his determined pace. "Don't do me any favors next time, Cameron."

"Dammit all, man! What happened? What in the bloody hell happened here yesterday?"

Morgan swung around. Dougal forced himself not to recoil from the murderous wrath in his narrowed green eyes. "I'm about to find out."

As Morgan vanished down the shadowed corridor, a wave of helpless exhaustion washed over Dougal. He sank against the wall, not knowing whether to pray for the hapless man in the dungeon or for his son-in-law's immortal soul. But when he closed his eyes, he found his mumbled pleas to God were all for Sabrina.

Ranald shielded his eyes against the blaze of torchlight. He looks like a rat, Morgan thought viciously, a scrawny rat caught in a trap of his own making.

His cousin huddled against the wall, his knees drawn up, his pale hand gripping his wounded shoulder. Noting that his plaid had been knotted in a clumsy bandage, Morgan felt a grim smile touch his lips. He was gratified to know that self-preservation was still the most consistent MacDonnell trait.

Ranald quailed before his mirthless grin. As Morgan dropped the torch into a rusted sconce, Ranald's feet scrambled at the floor as if he could somehow make himself part of the featureless stone. Shadows wavered across his handsome features.

His voice was raw. "Ye've always been more than just a cousin to me, Morgan. Ye've been a brother."

"As Abel was to Cain?" Morgan folded his arms

over his chest. His smile spread a dangerous degree. "With kin such as you, who needs the Camerons for enemies?"

From somewhere within the depths of his fear Ranald summoned up enough pride to push himself up the wall to stand and face him.

Morgan ruthlessly squelched a flare of admiration. "What did they promise you, cousin? Gold? A fresh mutton pie? The chieftainship after I was dead?"

"No! It was nothin' like that. I swear it. Ye know I'd never do anythin' to hurt ye. She said—" Ranald plunged into silence, fingering the bloodstains on his plaid.

"*Who* said?" Morgan's tone was ominous.

Ranald kept his silence.

The final thread of Morgan's control snapped. Ignoring his cousin's cry of pain, he caught him by the nape and gave him a savage shake. "The truth, Ranald," he roared. "Or do I have to beat it out of you?" He drew back his fist.

Their harsh breathing mingled, both of them knowing that if Morgan laid a fist on him, if he unleashed the terrible violence he'd restrained for most of his life, he wouldn't stop until it was done. But even more damning was the hopeful sheen in Ranald's eyes, willing Morgan's fist to fall, willing him to end his guilt with the punishment he deserved.

Shaken to the core, Morgan lowered his fist. Tears tumbled from Ranald's dark eyes. "It weren't my idea. I swear it weren't. Ye know I ain't ne'er been smart like ye. Eve said the Camerons were comin' to kill us all in our beds. That their visit was nothin' but a trick. That we had to get them before they got us. Yer lady was kind to me. I dinna mean to hurt her. I swear I dinna."

Taking care not to jar Ranald's wounded shoulder, Morgan wrapped an arm around his cousin and drew him into a fierce embrace, his own eyes dry and bleak. "I know, lad," he whispered. "Neither did I. God help me, neither did I."

· · ·

On the third day after the accident, Ranald appeared among his clansmen at Morgan's side, wearing a sheepish expression and a clean white sling. While the Camerons cast him contemptuous glances, the MacDonnells shunned him. Only Enid dared to approach him, her placid face alive with the fear that the terrible stories she had heard might be true. When Ranald kept walking, his eyes downcast, she turned away, smothering a broken cry into her handkerchief.

As the short winter days and interminable nights passed, the web of Eve's deceit untangled, the rumors slowly sifted through a skein of truth.

Eve had disappeared. Two of the renegade MacDonnells had been killed by the Cameron men who had closed ranks around their laird when the first pistol was fired. The other three had fled to the harsh northern mountains to escape Morgan's wrath.

The Cameron men passed among the MacDonnells unmolested, enmity forgotten as the two clans united their hopes and prayers for the woman who lay in a laudanum-induced stupor in the bed above them. Even the worldly Fergus was overheard mumbling a rusty prayer.

One morning near dawn Morgan sat at Sabrina's bedside, stroking her fevered brow and whispering Gaelic endearments only he could understand. Dr. Montjoy snored from his bench by the fire. Pugsley kept his own vigil at the foot of the bed, his brown eyes sorrowful. Dougal sprawled in a chair, an untouched book lying open across his lap. He and Morgan's eyes met in bitter accord across the splinted length of Sabrina's legs.

Ranald's confession had failed to answer the question that haunted them both. Why? Why had Sabrina plunged down that icy road on a horse that terrified her? Morgan had spent hours searching her lax features for the answer. He could not forget that elusive instant when she had pulled back on Pookah's mane. Had she been struggling to veer toward the meadow, or was it only a desperate attempt to slow the horse's wild flight? Had she sought to warn him of Eve's treachery or to save her family from a betrayal she believed to be his own?

Looking into Dougal's eyes chilled him. It was like looking into a mirror of his own emotions. He saw shock, rage, guilt, and a bitter accusation that made it even more imperative that he hear the truth from Sabrina's own lips.

She stirred against his hand, her delicate brow puckered in a twinge of pain. For now it would have to be enough that she lived. Stroking his finger across the downy curve of her cheek, Morgan began to sing softly, a child's lullaby from a memory he'd never realized he had.

Someone was singing.

A man's voice, rich and sonorous, endearingly off key, more compelling than the siren song that had lured Odysseus's ship toward the deadly rocks. Sabrina could make no sense of the words, but their tenderness was irresistible. She tried to turn her head to seek their source only to find herself, like Odysseus, bound against the temptation of surrender.

Dread heightened her struggle. She knew from harsh experience that after the voices would come the jagged edges of the pain. But worse than the pain were the gentle hands that would follow, familiar hands that smelled of camphor and peppermint, hands from her childhood pouring the thick poison, bitter and sickly sweet, down her unresisting throat. It made her want to gag, but she was robbed of even that feeble rebellion by the inevitable spiral into oblivion.

A callused palm cupped her jaw. The song faded to a weary mumble, its hoarse timbre striking a note of recognition. Morgan's voice. Morgan's touch. Morgan's hands on her. Her urgency escalated to panic. Dark slashes of memory battered her. Hoofbeats pounding down a twisting road. Glimpsing Morgan in the meadow through her streaming hair. Hauling back on Pookah's mane until the coarse strands cut like threads of steel into her palms. She must reach Morgan. Warn him about Eve. Assure him that her faith in him had never faltered.

She struggled against the shards of pain, fought the seductive whisper of unconsciousness. Clawing her way to the surface, she opened her eyes a slit to find herself dazzled by the firelight shining through the brilliant skein of Morgan's hair. After the infernal darkness, it was like a beacon, bathing the chiseled planes of his face in gilt. She lifted her hand, aching to touch him. A fierce joy seized her. She had succeeded! Morgan was alive! Tears of gratitude welled in her eyes as she struggled to form the words.

"Doctor. She's gettin' restless. You'd best come." Morgan's voice, harsh and implacable.

There was a frantic scrabbling as if of a large, nervous animal as someone else rushed toward the bed. Even as she screamed a silent denial, the first bitter draft hit her lips, burning like acid down her raw throat.

As she sank back into the sea of oblivion, a despairing moan escaped her, for she had failed to make them understand that feeling pain was better than feeling nothing at all.

Two days later Sabrina opened her eyes. Both puzzled and amazed at the ease of it, she squinted. The chamber was fuzzy, but not impossible. A narrow band of sunlight crept across the quilts, announcing the winter morning with simple grace.

Two men were silhouetted against the window, their unkempt hair haloed by the light. Their voices bumped and slurred to her unpracticed ears, finally separating into tones she could recognize: her papa's gentle Highland lilt; the other man's familiar rasp forever linked with childhood hurts and peppermint comfits pressed into her chubby hands. Dr. Montjoy's presence baffled her. She could not remember being ill or even having the sniffles.

So steeped was she in those confusing memories of childhood that her father's aged profile startled her. Haggard lines had been carved around his expressive mouth. The silver at his temples had cast its net over the rest of his dark hair. A wave of shock and pity washed over her, tempered by a thread of thanksgiving as she realized that Eve's ambush had failed.

"Papa?" Her lips formed the word, but no sound came forth. Her tongue was thick from disuse.

Her father rubbed a weary hand over his untrimmed beard. "We've waited long enough. He must be told."

Dr. Montjoy gave the door a furtive glance. "Would you be so kind? I don't think he cares for me. If he took it in his head that I were somehow to blame . . ." He trailed off on an ominous note.

"There's no hope at all?"

The physician shook his head sadly. "Her legs . . ."

His words slurred back into incoherence as icy fear paralyzed Sabrina's rediscovered senses. At that moment her legs seemed the most substantial thing about her, weighted with a dull ache. But even she knew there was only one commonly accepted cure for a badly broken leg. And hadn't she heard of soldiers who had lost their limbs on the battlefield and lived to complain of pain or even itching? Swallowing hard, she summoned up the strength to lift the quilt a furtive inch. A sigh escaped her to find her legs still there, splinted but intact. She couldn't quite swallow a rusty shadow of a grin.

Dr. Montjoy went on. ". . . The ledge broke her fall, but the horse's weight crushed the bones in her lower legs. Since her husband wouldn't let me amputate . . ."

Thank you, Morgan, Sabrina whispered silently. *Thank you, God.*

". . . Splints are being tried in London by the more reputable bone-setters, but no one knows if they're truly of any benefit. It's my opinion that the girl will live, but I'm afraid she'll not walk again."

Sabrina's grin faded.

The men were moving away from the window, turning to face her. There was no time to act, no time to think. She slammed her eyes shut, buying herself the only thing within her power—time.

Sabrina held herself motionless as Morgan stormed past the bed, pacing the confines of the chamber like a caged lion. "Shouldn't she be awake now, Doctor? You quit givin' her the laudanum three bloody days ago."

As her husband's steps retreated, Sabrina sneaked one eye open. Morgan's plaid flared around his broad shoulders. He had entered the musty sickroom in a jarring blast of juniper and winter sunshine. His very vitality hurt her eyes.

Exchanging a nervous glance with her father, the doctor shook his head. "I've seen cases like this before, son. The body simply shuts down, saving all its energies for healing. She'll come around when she's ready."

Sabrina slammed her eyes shut as Morgan approached the bed. She could almost feel the waves of suspicion rolling off him.

"I wonder . . ." he murmured. She heard his pause, the whisper of pages being turned. "I would have sworn this book was at the foot of the bed this mornin'."

Her pillow gave beneath the exacting pressure of Morgan's palms on each side of her head. The heat of his scrutiny scorched her. She was afraid to move, afraid even to breathe. His hair tickled her nose and she swallowed a tormenting urge to sneeze.

Her father bought her a reprieve, his calm, rational tone brooking no arguments. "Enid was in earlier for a visit. Perhaps she read to Sabrina."

Morgan snorted. "Aye. Or perhaps Pugsley was readin' to while away the hours."

Still shaking his head, he strode from the chamber, his absence more keenly felt than his presence. The other men trailed after him, Dr. Montjoy murmuring platitudes, her father strangely silent.

After they were gone, Sabrina propped her head up on the pillows, crossed her arms, and glared at her legs.

Hateful, useless things.

Morgan's own voice came back to damn her. *The MacDonnells won't stomach any show of weakness. They've no tolerance for cripples.*

Sabrina had learned from eavesdropping on her father and Alex that Eve had beat a coward's retreat. Yet it seemed the vindictive woman had won after all. 'Twas a pity she hadn't lingered to enjoy her handiwork. Wouldn't she have savored the irony of it all?

She heard Fergus's voice, thick with contempt. *Why, I'd as soon bugger lame old Eve than bed a Cameron!* Now she was both, Sabrina thought, lame and a Cameron.

She scooped up the book and hurled it at the far wall. It slid down to land in the floor, its pages rifled. Let Morgan figure out how it got there if he dared.

Her eyes burned hot and dry. Her legs throbbed dully. She welcomed the physical manifestation of her pain, all the while knowing it wasn't keen enough to distract her from the turmoil in her heart.

She'd had ample time to think in the past two days. Too much time. Time enough to know that from this moment on she would be nothing but a millstone around her husband's neck. He deserved a woman with two strong legs who could work for his clan. A woman who could give him the son he desired. Her hand fluttered over her stomach, refusing to give name to the one hope she still clung to.

Just by honoring their vows, Morgan risked losing the respect of his clan. She had borne the MacDonnells' enmity as her birthright, but their pity would kill her soul. Far worse would be the pity she would see in Morgan's eyes each time he looked at her, each time he touched her. The pity he might show a sparrow with a broken wing or a child who had fallen and skinned its knee. Her hands clenched the quilt. The MacDonnells weren't the only ones with pride.

She pressed her eyes shut, assailed by a memory of their last night together in the bed that had since become her prison. She could still see Morgan's magnificent body sprawled beneath her, burnished by the extravagant spilling of light from the tapers he insisted upon whenever they made love. She saw his beautiful face strained with pleasure as she surrendered her inhibitions, giving herself over with fierce abandon and knowing a surge of triumph in that instant when Morgan roared his own exultation, losing the very control he so prided himself on.

She opened her eyes, knowing what she must do.

When Dougal and the doctor returned, she was propped against the pillows, her hands folded in her lap.

"Princess, you're awake!" Her father rushed to her side, kneeling to clasp her hands. His hands felt almost feverish against the chill passivity of her own.

A joyous smile wreathed Dr. Montjoy's face. "Praise the good Lord! I knew he'd see us through. Stay with her, Dougal, and I'll go fetch the lad." A giddy laugh escaped him. " 'Twill be welcome indeed to have some good news to share with him." He trotted toward the door, rubbing his pudgy hands in anticipation.

Sabrina stopped him with a single word. "Don't." Dougal frowned. Even hoarse with disuse, Sabrina's voice dripped ice. "I do not wish to see my husband at present."

The doctor's smile faded. "But, girl, if you could only have seen him in the past fortnight. He's had near supernatural powers. I've never seen any man go so long without food or sleep."

"I do not wish to see him," she repeated. "If he protests, remind him that he owes me that much."

"But, lass—" Dougal started, aghast at her callous words.

"Tell him."

The doctor turned away, his jowls drooping like a disconsolate hound's. Sabrina gazed down at her father's hands. They still rested lightly over her frozen fingers. Eyes that knew her too well searched her stony face.

"Shall we talk about it, lass?" he asked softly, lifting his hand to cup her cheek.

Unable to bear his solace, she turned her face to the pillow. "No, Papa. I'm weary. I wish only to sleep."

As his hand withdrew in wounded silence, the throb of Sabrina's shattered legs was nothing compared to the agony in her heart.

Gulping the brisk air, Morgan clenched his hands on the crude stone of the battlement. He could not shake the terrible niggling suspicion that Sabrina was awake. He would have sworn she'd been watching him as he'd napped beside her bed the previous night. But when he had jerked his head around, her curly lashes had rested flush on her cheeks as innocent as a lamb's.

But what of the petulant quirk of her lips? he wondered. It hadn't been there before, had it? He had wrestled with the most absurd desire to cup her face in his hands and kiss it away. Perhaps guilt and lack of sleep were making him mad.

The wind stung his eyes and tossed his hair, bracing him with its icy purity. Surely nothing could be more healing than this breath of heaven blown down from the mountainside. As soon as she was well enough, he would wrap Sabrina in his plaid and carry her to this tower for a taste of it. He would carry her many places from now on. For the rest of his life, she would be the one burden he would gladly bear.

He had managed to sit calmly, Dr. Montjoy hovering in the background, while Dougal explained that Sabrina would never walk again. Would never dance down the stairs in those ridiculous little slippers of hers. Would never stomp out a Highland fling at Fergus's urging. Would never chase him across a meadow ripe with summer until he allowed himself to be caught and tumbled into a fragrant patch of heather and bluebells.

Would never run to greet him at the end of the day, a child on each hand and another clinging to her skirts.

It was the hardest blow Morgan had ever taken. But he hadn't allowed himself so much as a flinch. He hadn't sworn or roared or destroyed anything. He hadn't fixed his fingers around the hapless doctor's throat as he had longed to do. He'd simply thanked Dougal for his candor and excused himself, climbing the crumbling stairs to this tower, where he could endlessly relive the moment of Sabrina's destruction.

If only he had run faster, flung himself from the drift a second sooner, thought to sacrifice Pookah a dozen hoofbeats before he reached the cliff. If only he had failed to heed Ranald and let the damn sheep drown. If only he had seen the bitterness and twisted ambition in Eve's crystalline eyes.

Because of him, Sabrina was broken and couldn't be fixed. He couldn't splint her wing as he had the golden eagle that had once blundered through the tower window. He couldn't drip milk down her throat as he had the baby bird that had tumbled out of its nest at his feet. He couldn't tuck her beneath his plaid and warm her with his body heat as he had the half-frozen shrew he had found buried in the ice.

His despairing eyes searched the unforgiving vista of snow and rock. He should never have brought her to this place. Better to have left her in Dougal's plush demesne and adored her from afar.

A footstep sounded behind him. Morgan turned, wondering who would have braved the crumbling steps. Dr. Montjoy stood there, still huffing from the steep climb, an expression of abject misery on his face.

Morgan's mind spiraled crazily. Had Sabrina taken an unexpected turn for the worse? Died?

He took a step toward the man without realizing it.

Blowing out a nervous puff of steam, Montjoy held up his hand. "I've good news, lad. Sabrina has regained full consciousness. She's awake."

Morgan started for the stairs, unable to curb the joy pulsing through him. It recklessly shoved aside both guilt and grief.

With more courage than Morgan would have suspected, the doctor stepped into his path. He blinked up at him through his fogging spectacles. "I'm sorry, but your wife doesn't want to see you right now." He averted his eyes. "She said to remind you that you owe her that much."

Dougal's blunt honesty about his daughter's future had been no more than a reproving slap compared to the wallop Sabrina packed. Her dainty fist staggered him. It took all of Morgan's control to keep from reeling beneath its force.

He swung around to the parapet. The aged mortar crumbled beneath the strength of his grip. "Thank you, Doctor," he heard himself say, even adding on a rare note of grace. "For all you've done. I'll not forget it."

As the physician's despondent steps retreated, Morgan stared blindly over the merciless peaks.

You owe me that much.

He owed her everything. A lifetime of penance for a crime he could never atone for.

Somewhere in the forest below, a branch succumbed to the weight of the ice. Morgan flinched at the brittle crack, bracing himself against the inevitable sound of anguish that would follow in his mind. Sabrina's scream. His mother's scream as she surrendered her life for his own. It echoed a sound that would haunt him all the grim days and lonely nights to come—Sabrina's delicate bones snapping just like the stem of the Belmont Rose in his clumsy hands.

•

Chapter Twenty-one

On the third day after she regained consciousness, Sabrina deigned to grant her husband an audience.

Keeping his hope in ruthless rein, Morgan slipped silently into the chamber. Pugsley napped by the fire. Enid sat in a chair by the bed, reading aloud to Sabrina. Her pale face was drawn and her fat ringlets hung lank around her cheeks. She gave a guilty start at the sight of him and hastily excused herself, refusing to meet his eyes. Morgan knew that she, like himself, was shouldering part of the blame for Ranald's duplicity.

He remained by the door, clutching a wilted bouquet of gorse in one fist and drinking in the sight of Sabrina with a raw thirst that surprised even him.

She had never looked more like a princess—so regal, so unapproachable.

She sat propped among the pillows, a lavender ribbon binding her curls from her face. Her hands were folded in her lap. Hectic color brightened her cheeks. Morgan moved forward, feeling like a barefoot peasant approaching her throne. Anger surged through him, unexpected and unwelcome, an anger he had no right to feel.

He paused at the edge of the bed, unsure where to sit, where to look. The quilts humped over Sabrina's splinted legs filled his vision. She stared into her lap without acknowledging him. The haughty cast of her expression warned him he had not been invited to sit on her bed. He was no longer welcome there. He felt another flush of anger, dangerous and electric.

He thrust out his hand, offering her the flowers. He had scrabbled beneath a crust of ice for them, rooting them out with the desperation of a beggar. As Sabrina eyed them from beneath her lashes, they seemed to wither to what they were—a pathetic clump of weeds. A woman like Sabrina wasn't deserving of weeds, but of fat armfuls of fragrant roses.

Morgan wanted to jerk them back, to cast them in the fire, where they belonged. But it was too late. Her delicate fist closed around the crushed stems, taking care that their hands never touched.

"Thank you. They're lovely," she lied, laying them on the quilt.

Morgan jerked a chair around and straddled it. The awkward silence stretched.

Sabrina's soft voice broke it. "I'm sorry about Pookah."

Morgan sensed her words were sincere. A fresh flare of grief stabbed him. "He never suffered."

A small, bitter laugh escaped her. "That's what Eve said about your father. It must be a MacDonnell creed for a death well met."

She fixed her gaze on him; Morgan almost wished she hadn't. Her blue eyes held an arctic glitter that chilled him. Why the bloody hell didn't she cry? A troubled Dougal had confided that she had accepted the news that she would never walk again with imperturbable calm. It was as if all her tears had frozen on that icy ledge. A memory came unbidden to him in an agony of desire and regret—the salty warmth of her tears on his tongue mingled with the intoxicating taste of their passion.

His voice came out harsher than he intended. "Ranald told me all about Eve. About both plots to kill your da, one of which my own fa—" Morgan hesitated, unable to bring himself to say the word. The old man's crafty machinations had been the undoing of them all— "one of which Angus himself condoned. He also told me about Eve's poor aim in the hall at Cameron. After your father disarmed us all, Ranald went in search of her to try and stop her. But it was too late. She'd already found the dirk and hidden behind the tapestry. It seems I owe your clan and your father an apology."

"So it does, doesn't it," she said mildly.

Morgan stared. It was like conversing with a stranger who was vaguely bored but willing to tolerate one's company for the sake of politeness. His desperation flourished.

"There was one thing Ranald could not explain, lass. Your presence on the road that day. On Pookah."

She was calm now, almost heartlessly matter-of-fact. "Eve informed me that you were part of the plot to kill my papa. That you had failed the first time and had gone to finish the job. That when you were done massacring my unsuspecting family, you were coming back to the castle to strangle the life out of me."

Morgan was stunned. Her cool words confirmed his worst fears. "And you believed her?"

Sabrina lowered her lashes in a gesture that might have been coquettish in a less desperate moment. Morgan leaned forward, pretending that both his heart and his future didn't teeter on the brink of her reply. She was silent for a long time. Her hands were no longer still, but twisting, one against the other, in her lap.

"Answer me," he said, the quietness of the command belying its importance.

She threw back her head, dark passion erupting in her eyes. "Of course I believed her, you fool! Why shouldn't I? You've spent half your life teaching me of your contempt for my clan, your greed and jealousy because we have the common decency to live like human beings instead of animals. Have you ever given me cause to believe you'd choose honor when murder was at your disposal?"

Morgan gazed at her in stunned disbelief, unwilling to accept that his touch, his tenderness, his erotic possession, had taught her nothing about the kind of man he was. It was beyond him to conceive that the hatred between their clans was too strong to be mastered by what they had shared. He reached for her.

She recoiled violently, her repulsion too visible to be anything but genuine. A shrill, pathetic note caught in her voice. "Don't touch me! I can't abide it! It makes me ill! You're nothing but a crude barbarian and I never want your filthy hands on me again!"

Morgan's world went scarlet. His fingers splayed to cup her delicate jaw, bearing her back against the pillows. Her pulse fluttered madly beneath his thumbs. He exerted no pressure, but simply held her there while he searched her face for a truth he could tolerate. As he stared dead into the face of her callous betrayal, his hands flexed in a moment of near madness. Genuine fear flared in Sabrina's eyes.

Morgan loosened his fingers and backed away from the bed, paralyzed with self-contempt. The harsh rasp of his breathing echoed through the chamber.

Still she continued, as if sticking the knife in wasn't enough. She just had to give it a wicked twist. "Don't you understand?" she spat out between clenched teeth. With a cruelty he could never forgive, she struck her final blow, jerking the quilts away to expose the shapely calves that had once clung to his waist with such fervent passion, now pale and limp, strung together with nothing but wood and rope. "You did *this* to me! Your intentions toward my father are irrelevant now. I'll never forgive you for what you did to me! Never!"

Morgan straightened his plaid and threw back his shoulders. He strode to the hearth and drew the Cameron claymore down from its pegs. Sabrina paled but did not flinch.

He dropped the heavy blade across the foot of the

bed. "There's one lesson you failed to learn from Eve, lass. If you must cut out a man's heart, use a blade. 'Tis both cleaner and kinder." He gave her a stiff bow. "If you'll excuse me, I've no wish to do you continued harm by inflictin' my unwelcome presence upon your exalted person." He spun on his heel and marched out, leaving her alone.

After Morgan was gone, Sabrina reached blindly for the humble bouquet she had tossed so heartlessly on the bed. Crushing the brittle stems in her fist, she curled into a ball on her side and shoved the blooms against her mouth to muffle her rending sobs.

A week later Sabrina sat propped up in the bed, awaiting the carriage that would carry her home to Cameron.

Dougal had dressed her with the same tenderness and patience he had shown her as a child. She had been as passive as a broken doll as he eased her arms into her sleeves and arranged the skirts of her velvet pelisse in careful folds to hide the splints. Unable to bear her stillness, Dougal had retreated to keep watch at the window.

He sighed heavily as he turned from the window to study his daughter's profile. It was as pale as pearl and so brittle it looked as if it might shatter beneath a harsh breeze. Her full lips were pressed together in an embittered line. Her eyes were cool and distant, as if she had gone somewhere that none of them could follow.

His heart spasmed with helpless fury. He wanted to blame Morgan or God or callous fate for breaking his beautiful daughter, but each time he passed a mirror, he saw only his own guilty eyes. He might pity Morgan, forgive God, and someday make his peace with fate, but he could find no mercy in his heart for himself.

His worst fear was that he was making yet another terrible mistake by taking Sabrina away from this place. She had been the one to insist upon being removed from MacDonnell as soon as the road thawed and the doctor pronounced her fit for travel. At first Dougal had even thought to make her stay, to make her fight for the fierce man who had avoided her presence ever since the night Dougal had entered the chamber to find her asleep, damp petals of gorse clinging to her tear-streaked cheeks.

But her plaintive cry of "You must take me home! I want my mama!" had stirred his awesome love for her and overwhelmed his good intentions. He hadn't the heart to deny her anything. His own capricious whims had already cost her far too much. If only Beth were here! Beth would know what to do. She had always been the one with the moral fortitude to deny Sabrina the extra cross bun that might make her stomach ache, the one to insist Sabrina remount her pony after she'd taken a tumble and was clinging to her papa's legs, begging for a reprieve.

The patience of Sabrina's stance chilled him. She looked as if she would sit forever, even if the carriage never came.

No longer able to bear it, Dougal forced a jovial smile. "Come now, lass, you haven't been out of that bed for days. The sun's trying to peep out from behind a cloud. Let me carry you to the window and give you a look outside."

"No, Papa, I don't want to—"

This time Dougal ignored her querulous protest. With painstaking care he lifted her and carried her to the window. He sank down on the broad ledge, bundling her against his chest just as he had when she'd been a little girl and awakened screaming from a nightmare. But this was one nightmare neither of them could awaken from.

Secure in her father's embrace, Sabrina felt the lump in her throat melting. His was a compassion she could not bear. Choking back all the tears she'd swallowed since driving Morgan from this chamber, she buried her cheek against Dougal's chest, relishing the safety it represented even though they both knew it was only an illusion. There were some monsters against whom even her papa was helpless.

Dougal rubbed his beard against her curls. "I cannot help but blame myself. If I could only have foreseen it would come to this . . ."

Sabrina tried to speak, but couldn't.

His lilting voice pressed on. "I love my sons more than my life, but you, princess, were always my heart. I would have done anything for you. Perhaps I spoiled you, but I couldn't bear the thought of you going without anything you wanted." He chuckled softly. "You were so easy to spoil. Never greedy. Never grasping. Always saying, 'Thank you' and 'Please, sir,' rewarding your besotted papa with kisses and smiles." His grip tightened. "But when Morgan MacDonnell came to Cameron, I discovered there was something you wanted that it was not within my power to give you."

The Cameron carriage appeared in the distance, lumbering slowly around the dangerous curves.

"I saw the hunger in your eyes when you looked at him," Dougal whispered. "I heard you weeping in your chamber when he rebuffed you. God forgive me, but when he returned to Cameron as a man, I finally saw a way to give you your heart's desire."

Sabrina was crying silently now, the warm tears rolling down her cheeks, trickling off her chin to wet the fur of her muff. The carriage rumbled into the courtyard, rocking to a halt on the cobblestones below.

Dougal's words quickened. "I don't expect you to believe my motives were completely unselfish. I saw in your union the future of the Highlands, our clans united to live in peace, grandchildren to brighten my waning years . . . a mad scheme perhaps, but from the beginning I sensed something in the lad. It was almost as if the blood of the ancient MacDonnell kings still flowed through his veins. I truly believed God had given me a sacred charge to prove him worthy." He kissed the crown of her head. "But I never would have done so at your expense. I'm sorry I was so terribly wrong."

Swallowing a denial, Sabrina lifted her brimming

eyes. She did not dare give him absolution. If she did, he might force her to stay. But even in the condemnation of her silence, her father saw some glimmer of hope, of dangerous possibility.

He searched her face. "You don't have to go. It's not too late to change your mind."

Sabrina remembered Morgan's closed face, the crumpled gorse blooms now dried and pressed between the worn pages of her Bible. "Aye, but it is, Papa. Later than you know." She buried her face in his cravat, sighing wearily. "Take me home, Papa. Just take me home."

The courtyard was deserted as Dougal carried Sabrina into the chill winter air. Enid walked at his elbow, her round face blotchy but set in stern lines. Brian, Alex, and Dr. Montjoy trailed after them, their hands empty of all but the Cameron claymore wrapped in its sheath of wool. Sabrina had asked that everything except what she wore and her Bible be left behind for the good of Morgan's clan, including the Christmas gifts of salted meat, bolts of tartan, and carved wooden toys that had accompanied her papa's journey. Not even Dougal's halfhearted protests had stopped her from leaving her own gift for Morgan—something special to warm his cold winter nights until he found a new wife.

As Sabrina's desolate gaze swept the empty courtyard, a wave of fresh pain broke over her. She knew she deserved no better from him, but it still hurt that Morgan hadn't even troubled to give his wife a casual farewell. She turned her face into her papa's shoulder. He gently eased up her hood.

A Cameron footman flung open the carriage door. Assisted by Brian and Alex, Dougal settled Sabrina on the cushions and climbed in beside her. Enid and Dr. Montjoy took the opposite seat. The luxury of the carriage now seemed obscene to Sabrina. With its plush velvet cushions and fringed window hangings, it was more opulent than any single chamber in Castle MacDonnell. It had probably cost more gold to outfit than the MacDonnells would see in a lifetime.

She stared straight ahead, her fists clenched around the handkerchief hidden in her muff. Her papa reached to draw shut the window hangings, but Sabrina stayed his hand before he could bury them in the lavish gloom. He gave her a puzzled look but said nothing.

The carriage lurched into motion. Brian and Alex rode alongside the outriders as the graceful vehicle rumbled out of the courtyard.

"Why, I'll be damned," Dougal breathed.

Sabrina jerked her head up, knowing her papa rarely swore. She felt the coachhorses slow to a hesitant trot. Leaning forward, she peered out the window only to discover why the courtyard had been so deserted.

The MacDonnells had come to bid farewell to their mistress in the only way they knew how. They flanked the narrow road in two lines, standing at silent attention as the coach passed between them, all wearing the finery Sabrina had made for them.

Their familiar faces blurred before her eyes. Alwyn, forcing a brave smile even as she dabbed a tear from her cheek with the tail of her braid. The children, their faces scrubbed clean, their hair combed. Fergus staring straight ahead, his face ruddy, his expression fierce. The old woman from the kitchen, still sporting the incongruous pink ribbon in her lank tresses.

Saddest of all, Ranald, standing apart from his clansmen, his arm still bound in a grubby sling. His sheepish gaze searched the carriage window for Enid. She turned her unforgiving face away from him. The carriage found empty road again and gathered momentum, carrying Sabrina away from Castle MacDonnell for the last time.

Her hands slipped from her muff. She could not simply ignore a tribute she had fought so hard to win.

Surprising them all with her strength, she shoved open the window and leaned out. Her hood fell away from her hair. Drawing the crumpled handkerchief from her muff, she waved it in her own salute. A broken cheer went up from the road behind them.

It was then, looking back, that she saw him. Standing on the battlements, silhouetted against the pewter sky like a statue of one of those MacDonnell kings of old, utterly motionless except for his long hair blowing in the wind. Her eyes devoured him until they rounded a curve and he was lost from her sight.

She collapsed against the cushions, numb to the fierce squeeze of Enid's hand over hers, the whisper of her papa's palm across her disheveled hair. Numb to everything but the primal beauty of the pipes that came wailing over the mountains, excoriating her raw heart with their plaintive and mocking farewell.

Morgan thought he might stay on the battlements forever.

The cold did not trouble him. Whenever its irksome fingers began to pinch and prod him, he would simply draw another bottle of brandy from the fancy wooden crate and take a deep swill. What a thoughtful man his father-in-law was! Perhaps Dougal had intended the brandy to douse the Christmas pudding, but Morgan much preferred to douse himself. 'Twas fitting, he thought, chuckling. He had made quite a pudding of himself over Dougal's heartless daughter.

He hefted the bottle and roared, "To Sabrina Cameron, the fairest bitch of them all!"

The liquor's heat pulsed through him, warming him all the way to his numb toes. He gazed fondly at the bottle, admiring the swirl of the golden liquid. No wonder his own da had loved the stuff. 'Twas far more pleasant to drown in than self-pity. Toasting the newfound philosophical bent of his thoughts, he drained the bottle and tossed it over the ramparts before opening another.

In his time with Sabrina, he had allowed himself to forget the one inescapable reality of life. Nothing lasted forever. He had learned that lesson early and well by witnessing too many quick, violent deaths at the hands of others and at his own hands. Life, like hope, could be snuffed out in the blink of a ruthless eye. He flexed one hand in front of him, mildly amused to discover it now had ten fingers.

He should never have let himself forget. Should never have let Sabrina's beautiful, treacherous eyes trick him into daring to hope the future was possible. A future of Christmases shared before the fire and laughing, blue-eyed daughters and watching his wife's dark hair frost with white as the seasons passed.

The empty bottle rolled from his stiffening fingers. Aye, he would stay on the battlements forever. There was no longer any real reason to descend.

Yet when the shadows of winter twilight crept around him and the stars winked to life like brittle shards of ice, Morgan rose and angled toward the stairs, blindly seeking the place that had become his own private heaven in the hours between dawn and dusk. The narrow passageway twined into darkness. Morgan stumbled over a missing step and slammed into the wall.

Too bad God had such a vicious sense of humor, he thought. If not, he'd be lying dead at the foot of the stairs, his neck broken. He reeled through the empty corridors, tripping over piles of rubble that were no longer there, smacking his brow on a low-hanging portal when he forgot to duck, all the while humming under his breath a ballad Sabrina had taught him about a scornful lass and her constant suitor.

His hand was on the knob of her chamber door before he realized where his drunken foray had led him. The ballad's chorus faded to a mumble. His hand shook as he thrust open the door.

A woman sat at the dressing table, her cascade of hair gleaming in the candlelight.

For an instant, hope beat within Morgan, wild and unfettered. He dared once more to dream. He blinked. His fuzzy brain scrambled for clarity. Perhaps Sabrina had never left him at all. Perhaps it had been only a trick, petty revenge for the many pranks he had played upon her as a lad.

The woman pivoted on the stool, crushing his hopes with the single clumsy lurch. Not his ethereal bride, but a mocking apparition wearing one of Sabrina's gowns.

All semblance of sanity fled him. Before he realized it, he had her down on the floor, his hands fixed around her throat. But Eve was not willing to die a graceful death. She bucked against him, eyes blazing, lips moving in a choked stream of curses. Beneath the thick layer of powder, her face went scarlet, then dark.

Morgan stumbled to his feet, pressing his palms against his temples as if he could somehow silence the murderous fever roaring through his skull. A shaky laugh escaped him. "You're the third person I've almost strangled in the past few weeks. I really must guard my temper with more care."

She clambered to her feet, eyeing him cautiously, one hand massaging her mottled throat. "Ye've been drinkin', ain't ye? I can smell it on ye like a whore's perfume. The stuff is poison, lad. Ye saw what it did to yer da."

Morgan took a menacing step toward her. "No, Eve. I saw what *you* did to my da. And I always thought your worst crime was teachin' Ranald to play the bagpipes."

Eve held her ground. She crossed her arms over the puffed bodice of Sabrina's gown. " 'Twas an accident."

He continued to advance, biting off each word. "Like your ambush of Dougal Cameron? Like Pookah's death and Sabrina's plunge over the cliff?" He stared down at her, contempt mingling with every breath.

Unexpected tenderness softened her eyes to smoky green. She lifted her hand to correct a tousled strand of his hair. He caught her wrist before she could touch him.

"Ye must understand," she begged. "I did it all for ye, lad. For yer future and the future o' Clan MacDonnell. If ye only knew how much I'd sacrificed for yer precious clan. Now that the wee Cameron bitch is gone, I can tell ye. I've waited all me life to—"

"More lies!" he roared, thrusting her toward the door. "More of your twisted truths! Well, I've no desire to hear them!" A chilling calm came over him. His finger was steady as he leveled it at her. *"Outcast!"*

"No!" she screamed. Her hands flew up to cover her ears.

Morgan drew himself up, shaking off the protective mantle of drunkenness and allowing himself to feel the full agony of his mother's unwitting abandonment, Eve's betrayal, Sabrina's desertion. He spoke in Gaelic, the ancient words of kings and chieftains flowing like song from his lips. "Outcast. From this moment on, you are banished from this clan. If you set foot on MacDonnell lands again, I'll have you stoned." Switching to English, he caught Eve's wrists, wrenching her hands from her ears. "Do you understand, woman? I never want to lay eyes on your face again."

With a piteous cry, Eve tore herself away from him and stumbled out the door. The sound of her weeping lingered long after she had fled.

Morgan stood in the middle of the floor, breathing hard, his hands clenched into fists. Eve had lit every taper in the chamber. His desperate gaze searched the room, finding nothing but mocking reminders of what he sought. Sabrina's genteel touch was everywhere. Candlelight sparkled off the crystal stoppers of her perfume bottles, burnished the chess board to a mahogany gleam, caressed the leather spines of the books. The light's brutal clarity opened his eyes, forcing him to see the elegant trappings for what they were without their mistress to bring them to vibrant life.

Toys. Trinkets. Baubles. Empty illusion. Books with blank pages. Games that were eternally lost. Instruments with no songs.

Roaring like a wounded beast, Morgan snatched up the clarsach and smashed it on the edge of the table. He tore at the books, severing their spines, scattering their pages. He swept the dressing table clean with his fist, oblivious of the shards of glass that stung his flesh, then smashed the upended trunk against the wall. He snapped the chess board in two over his knee, hurling the chessmen into the fire, where their impassive faces melted in smoking wisps of flame. He tore the creamy linens off the bed, rending them with his bare hands.

Unbearable weariness overtook him. Stumbling

over the splintered stool, he fell heavily and lay surrounded by the carnage of his dying dreams.

A shy tongue lapped his cheek. Morgan pried open one eye. Bright button eyes surveyed him. A pug nose nudged his arm.

Shaking his head in exhausted bewilderment, Morgan curled his arm around the grizzled little dog and drew him close. Pugsley nestled gratefully into his warmth.

Gazing bleakly up into the shadowed rafters, Morgan whispered, "Aye and a fine pair we are. It seems the wee bitch abandoned us both, didn't she, lad?"

Pugsley's only reply was an enigmatic whimper.

PART THREE

You may break, you may shatter the vase, if you
    will,
But the scent of the roses will hang round it still.
                            —Sir Thomas Moore

But ne'er the rose without the thorn.
                            —Robert Herrick

Flowers of all hue, and without thorn the rose.
                            —John Milton

Chapter Twenty-two

The shiny black carriage lurched over narrow roads rutted by the melting snows. Dougal and Elizabeth rode in tense silence, deaf to the musical splash of a waterfall cascading through a deep gorge, blind to the profusion of wildflowers rioting over the stony hillsides and all the other dazzling charms of a balmy spring day in the Highlands.

Elizabeth's hands were clenched in her lap, so stiff they might have been gloved in steel instead of satin.

Dougal gave his beard a fretful rub. "What if he refuses to see us?"

"He has to see us," came his wife's unswerving reply. "He owes her that much. If not for him, she wouldn't be in this predicament."

If not for me, Dougal echoed silently, the weary refrain making his head ache. He forced back a shudder as the carriage lumbered around the treacherous curve that had cost his daughter everything but her life.

It had been agonizing for all of them to witness

the initial aftermath of Sabrina's accident—the constant tremor of her hands, her tears at the smallest frustrations and disappointments, her difficulty in performing simple tasks in which she had once excelled such as embroidery and playing the harpsichord. Christmas had been a strained affair at Cameron, replete with forced smiles and festive meals that had been picked at with little enthusiasm.

Dougal couldn't put his finger on the moment, but after Christmas everything had changed. The bewildered pain in Sabrina's eyes had sharpened to something dangerous like dry tinder just waiting for a spark.

He had carried her down to the drawing room one evening and settled her in a chair before the fire so they could all suffer through the ritual of pretending everything was normal.

"Thank you, Papa," she said dutifully as he tucked a quilt around her legs.

"My pleasure, princess."

"Would you like to sing a duet tonight, dear?" Elizabeth asked, looking up from her embroidery.

"I don't believe so. My throat was a bit raw when I woke from my nap." Sabrina cleared it as if to illustrate.

Brian straddled a stool and swept a chessboard between them. "The only singing the lass'll be doing tonight is singing for mercy when I best her at chess." He reached over and tweaked one of her curls.

"Take care, brother. She's been known to sneak your pawns off the board and hide them in her skirts." Alex's hearty laughter struck a false note, making Elizabeth wince.

Sabrina summoned up the ghost of a mischievous smile that tore at Dougal's heart. "Don't be silly, Alex. I never cheat unless I'm losing."

Dougal was unable to resist the urge to peer over his ledger as his two youngest children inclined their heads toward the game. Sabrina's profile, etched by firelight, was pensive. Her delicate brow furrowed as she reached up several times during the game to absently massage her temples.

"Aaaargh!" Brian's groan bespoke a mortal wound as he staggered back on the stool. "What foul villainy is this? The wench captured my king! Ah, defeat, thy taste is bitter!"

Alex rolled his eyes at his brother's theatrics. Sabrina was still staring intently at the board, the most peculiar expression on her face. Suddenly her arm shot out. The heavy chessboard crashed to the floor, scattering the pieces in all directions. Brian's mouth dropped open.

Sabrina's eyes blazed with fury as she snapped, "You let me win! I know you did. Do you think I'm stupid? Do you think I landed on my head when I fell?"

They all stared at her, astonished by the sight of their even-tempered angel turning into a virago before their eyes. Even as a child Sabrina had never been given to tantrums. Then Elizabeth might have rebuked her; now she could only wad her embroidery into a knot, her hands shaking.

Sabrina's gaze swept them all, granting none of them a reprieve from her bitter passion. "I feel like one of Mother's finches living in a cage. I feel your eyes on me all the time. I can't stand it! You tiptoe around me and make bad jokes and expect me to laugh! You let me win all the games as if it had never occurred to me that I could lose!" Her voice rose on a shrill note. "What are you all staring at? Haven't you ever seen a cripple before?"

Dougal could bear it no longer. He rose from his chair and knelt before her. For an instant her expression was so savage, he thought she might strike him and almost wished she would.

Then her head dropped and the lush silk of her lashes veiled the rage simmering in her eyes, leaving them all to wonder if they'd only imagined it. "Take me back to my chamber, Papa," she said plaintively. "My head is pounding so that I can hardly think."

Dougal was jolted back to the present when their carriage rolled to a halt in the courtyard of Castle MacDonnell. An air of bleak desertion hung over its ramparts. The looming walls blocked the sunlight, holding spring at bay. As Elizabeth descended from the carriage, she drew her shawl tight against the chill.

Skeletal fingers of ivy twined up the weathered blocks. The darkened windows peered down at them like gaping eyes. Gazing around nervously, the footmen and outriders drew their weapons.

"Put those away," Dougal snapped, startled by the harshness of his voice in the eerie silence. "What are you trying to do? Start a war?"

Exchanging sheepish glances, they obeyed, but the elderly coachman muttered something about the "dastardly MacDonnells" and kept his own musket propped defiantly across his knees.

Beneath the pressure of Dougal's hand, the door to the castle swung open with a rusty creak. Before he could protest, Elizabeth swept in ahead of him.

Dougal almost ran into her back when she froze in her steps, her gaze raking the hall with undisguised horror. "You allowed our daughter to live in this filth?"

Dismay and bewilderment mingled in Dougal as he surveyed the carnage of Castle MacDonnell. Splintered ruins were all that remained of the furniture—tables toppled and smashed, benches split in two as if by the mighty blow of a giant's fist. Cobwebs frosted the chandeliers, rippling like ghostly veils in a draft neither of them could feel. Sprouts of ivy had slithered through the arrow slits, choking out the meager light and forcing their greedy tendrils into the crumbling mortar as if to proclaim it was only a matter of time before their dominion over the hall was complete.

Dougal shivered. It was as if the entire castle had fallen under some dark enchantment, some eternal winter of the soul.

He shook his head. "No," he whispered, hesitant to profane the unholy silence. "Our daughter never lived in this place."

Grimacing in distaste, Elizabeth lifted the hem of her skirts high above a floor littered with sparrow droppings and the bleached bones of small, hapless creatures. From a darkened corridor came the scrabbling of a larger animal. Thrusting Elizabeth behind him, Dougal drew his pistol.

A quavering voice emerged from the shadows, followed by a white-faced man with arms raised. "Don't fire, me lord. I ain't armed."

Biting back an impotent surge of anger, Dougal slipped the pistol back into his jacket, knowing it was best out of sight should his wife inadvertently stumble upon Ranald's identity. "We've come to have words with your chieftain."

Morgan's cousin shuffled his feet and scratched at his dark thatch of hair. His swarthy complexion had paled as if it had been weeks since he had seen the sun. His other arm still hung at an awkward angle as if it had never quite healed.

"I canna say that would be wise, sir. He ain't been down in many a day. He'll see me only when I bring him food." His eyes avoided Dougal's. "Or drink."

Dougal summoned all the arrogance and authority of his rank. "We've risked ambush from your clansmen and ridden all the way from Cameron on those goat paths you call roads. We're not leaving until we see Morgan MacDonnell."

Once Ranald might have defied him. Now he only shrugged. "Suit yourself. But I'd suggest the lady stay below. Don't glower so. I'll come back and look after her."

Dougal cast his wife a dubious glance, but she dredged up a heartening smile. "Go, love. Do what you must. I'll be fine."

As Ranald led him up the crumbling stairs and left him standing alone before the chamber that had once belonged to his daughter, Dougal hoped he would fare as well as his wife.

His tentative knock garnered no reply. He eased open the door.

A snarling ball of fur exploded around his ankles. Dougal shook his leg, believing for a confused second that he'd been attacked by a rabid rat.

"Pugsley! Stand down!" The roar seemed to tremble the very rafters.

The little dog slunk behind an overturned table, a less than penitent smirk on his muzzle. Realizing he'd only been gummed, not bitten, Dougal swiped his brow with a handkerchief. "Sweet Christ! The pup's always been a bit ill tempered, prone to dyspepsia even, but I've never seen him . . ."

He trailed off as the chieftain of the MacDonnells emerged from the chaos of the chamber into the rays of the sun slanting through the western window. Dougal still found himself caught off guard by Morgan's massive stature. Somehow he always expected to find the slender, defiant lad he remembered. But all traces of boyhood had been vanquished from this man's barren, glittering eyes.

Morgan's chest was bare, his tattered plaid knotted at the waist. His stony jaw was unshaven. Beneath the tawny stubble, the planes of his face had been honed to dangerous perfection. His crystalline eyes were shot through with tiny veins of scarlet. Dougal shivered to imagine his sleepless specter haunting the castle by night.

With the sun haloing his tangled mane, he looked like a fallen angel scorched by the flames of hell, a creature of darkness untouched by the light that surrounded him. As he swaggered forward, the stench of whisky fumes rolled off him in stinging waves. He stopped a few feet away, legs splayed, arms folded over his chest.

Dougal dreaded throwing himself on this man's dubious mercy. But for Sabrina, he would do anything, even sell his soul to Morgan's new master. "I've come to speak to you about my daughter."

"What about her?" Morgan's voice was flat, as soulless as his eyes. "Has her condition worsened? Has she died? Or did you just bring the documents of divorce for me to mark?"

Morgan spoke as if all those possibilities bore equal weight, infuriating Dougal. "A divorce won't be necessary. I've arranged for an annulment."

Morgan cocked his head to the side. A spark of dark amusement flickered in his eyes. "How clever. You

Camerons always did have your ways around the law. What did you tell the magistrate? That I'd never laid my dirty MacDonnell hands on her?" He crooked one devilish eyebrow. "Well, I did. And she liked it too."

Dougal clenched his fists, remembering the many times he'd been forced to bear Angus MacDonnell's drunken taunts. He must not forget his mission. He would fall down on his knees before this man if need be.

His hands slowly unclenched. "My daughter needs you."

Dougal flinched as Morgan threw back his head and roared with laughter. He stumbled over and collapsed against the wall, wiping helpless tears from his eyes. "Christ, man! Was crippling her not enough? Do you want me to finish what I started? Shall I kill her now?"

Downstairs Elizabeth sat rigid in a straight-back chair Morgan's clansman had found for her, her polished fingernails clicking out a fitful rhythm on its arms. Ranald perched on the edge of the hearth like a chastised lapdog, shooting sly glances at her from beneath the sinful length of his lashes. A pity such a pretty creature had to have been born in such squalor, Elizabeth thought. Her gaze searched the massive rafters. The only sound from above was the eerie whisper of the cobwebs dancing in the drafts.

Ranald cracked his knuckles. Elizabeth jumped, the haunted atmosphere of the castle beginning to tell on her nerves. "Where are the others of your clan?" she blurted out, preferring the sound of her own voice to silence.

Ranald shrugged. "Scattered. Morgan sent them all away. Gave 'em the sheep, the cows, all but a few chickens and a pittance o' salted meat."

"And you? Why do you stay?"

He gave an undue amount of attention to rubbing a spot of soot into his trews. "He's me cousin. I canna verra well leave him here to die, can I?"

She leaned forward and peered into his angelic face, fascinated by a glimpse of a loyalty she would never have suspected in a MacDonnell. "You honestly believe he would die without you?"

He met her gaze squarely. "No, me lady. I believe he would die *alone* without me."

Elizabeth's wordless shock was interrupted by Dougal's disheartened step on the stairs. She gathered her skirts and rose, but her husband only shook his head. "I begged. I pleaded. I did everything but crawl. He will not relent."

At first Dougal believed the sheen in Elizabeth's eyes was unshed tears, but as he moved to comfort her, she shoved past him and marched up the stairs.

"Beth, you mustn't!" he cried, racing after her.

Ranald danced at their heels. "I wouldna if I were ye. 'Tis not a wise idea at all. I canna be accountable if—"

Elizabeth hesitated at a fork in the corridor, but Ranald gave away Morgan's whereabouts by sprinting ahead of them and throwing himself across the door.

"Stand aside, sir," she commanded.

Ducking his head in surrender, Ranald obeyed. Elizabeth splayed her hand on her husband's chest. Her steely eyes glinted with determination. "I want the both of you to return downstairs. I don't care what you hear or what you think you hear, do not come up here unless I call for you. Do you understand?"

For an absurd moment Dougal was tempted to laugh. He could not remember a time when he had loved his wife more. He stepped back, gave her a genteel bow, and proffered her the door. "The pleasure is yours, my lady."

Elizabeth threw open the door. Over her head Dougal caught a glimpse of Morgan's stunned face. Within his jaded eyes came the first flare of uncertainty, of raw vulnerability.

Elizabeth rested her hands on her hips. "Snap that stubborn jaw of yours shut, Morgan MacDonnell. You'll get no pity from me."

She swept into the chamber, slamming the door in Dougal's face.

Dougal clapped Ranald on the shoulder as they descended the stairs. "Say a prayer for your chieftain, lad. He's just met a harsher taskmaster than the devil ever thought to be."

Sharing a flagon of well-mellowed beer, Dougal and Ranald kept their own vigil below. As the hours passed, Ranald started at each new noise, but Dougal just swirled his beer around in his earthenware mug, hiding a small, secret smile.

Voices raised in anger were followed by a thunderous crash that sent Ranald's beer sloshing over the rim of his mug.

Dougal lifted his own in a toast. "To Beth," he whispered.

The cacophony worsened. A masculine bellow of rage was broken by the shattering of glass. More shouting followed, then came the unmistakable snap of an open palm meeting flesh. Ranald's eyes widened. Dougal bowed his head at the thick silence that followed. The ominous absence of noise lingered until even Dougal began to fidget in his chair. He drew a pendant watch from his jacket.

Elizabeth appeared at the top of the stairs. Her skirts were furred with dust and streaked with something that looked like huge handprints. As she descended, she smoothed her disheveled hair, her sharp features aglow with triumph and joy.

She held out her hands to Dougal. "He's vowed to help us. He says he'll do whatever he can for Sabrina. Whatever it takes."

Thumping down his mug, Ranald bounced up from the hearth. "Aye, I knew our Sabrina wouldna desert him. I never met a sweeter, more unselfish lass in all me life."

He began to dance an impromptu fling, missing the exaggerated arch of Dougal's eyebrows and the finger of warning Elizabeth laid to her husband's lips.

• • •

"You inept creature! I asked for the strawberry tarts, not the apple."

The flushed maid studied the silver tray laid across Sabrina's lap in open confusion. "No, miss. You asked for the apple. I swear you did."

Sabrina thrust the tray back at the servant. "Take them out of my sight this instant. I may be crippled, but I'm not daft. I clearly remember requesting the strawberry. And don't swear. It ill becomes you."

The tray tilted in the maid's shaking hands. A steaming tart plopped in Sabrina's lap. "Dammit all!" she shouted. "Must you be so infernally clumsy?"

Lower lip trembling, the maid plucked the tart from Sabrina's lap and dabbed at the fresh stain on her dressing gown. A long-suffering sigh escaped Sabrina. Her head fell back against the divan's bolster as if her neck no longer had the strength or will to support it.

She waved the maid away with a limp hand. "Oh, just leave me be. My digestion is ruined. I'm far too upset to eat now."

As the daunted servant crept from the salon, another maid abandoned her dusting to trail after her, casting Sabrina a reproachful glance. The woman's hushed voice carried clearly in the afternoon silence of the London town house.

"There now, girlie, don't you cry. There ain't no pleasing Her Highness when she's in a snit. Asked me to hand her a book this morning and it no more than an inch from her dainty little fingertips. Why, I'm just biding my time until she starts bellowing, 'off with their heads!' every time something don't suit her."

Hateful creatures, Sabrina thought, palming her brow to see if she could detect any hint of fever. She was well aware that the Belmont servants spent most of their time in the servants' kitchen discussing their master's invalid niece. But why should she care? She'd rather have their malice than their pity. And besides, it was human nature to gossip about freaks, was it not?

As if to prove her point, Enid waddled into the salon, waving a thin pamphlet. "Look what Stefan brought me from the street vendor!" She collapsed in a tiny Louis XIV chair, kicking her slippered feet in delight. "Just listen to this. 'Mrs. Mary Toft of Godalming recently gave birth to her fourteenth rabbit.' "

"How nice," Sabrina murmured. "Would you press my brow, Enid? I'm feeling rather feverish."

Enid absently obeyed, still scanning the pamphlet. "It says here that the king's physician was sent to investigate and arrived at Mrs. Toft's lodgings at the most propitious moment to deliver rabbit number fifteen! You're quite cool, dear. No fever at all."

"How would you know? You're not a doctor." Sabrina couldn't seem to stop the querulous note in her voice from rising. "You'd be interested in me only if I birthed a litter of hedgehogs right here in your mother's salon!"

Enid lowered the pamphlet. Her sweet smile couldn't quite hide the hurt in her eyes. Sabrina wanted to apologize, but couldn't find the words. They'd become like a foreign language to her in the past few months. She would open her mouth to ask for an extra pillow or comment on the weather only to have a whining demand or tart rebuke snap from her lips. How could she blame Enid for looking at her as if she were a stranger when she'd become a stranger to herself?

"You're right, of course," Enid said, tucking a cashmere shawl around Sabrina's shoulders, "How selfish of me. Here I am going on and on about such nonsense without even considering your feelings. Shall I read to you?" She picked up the volume resting at Sabrina's elbow. "Homer again?"

Sabrina nodded. Enid launched into Odysseus's journey to the kingdom of the dead, but Sabrina could derive no enjoyment from the familiar tale. She now thought Odysseus an insufferable bore and Penelope a passive idiot. What sort of romantic fool would while her life away, waiting for a man who might never come?

Sabrina turned her face to gaze out the window at the elegant environs of Hanover Square, remembering the winding road that had brought her to this place. A gentle breeze rife with the scent of hyacinths and newly warmed earth caressed her brow.

When Sabrina's condition had shown no sign of improving, her parents, on the advice of Dr. Montjoy, had brought her to London, hoping a change of scenery might lift her spirits. At least here in London she was no longer a constant reminder of her papa's misguided guilt.

Enid's voice droned on, robbing the Greek bard's majestic prose of all its drama. Sabrina plucked fretfully at the smothering softness of the shawl. She had spent those first dark days at Cameron crying herself to sleep each night. But even in her despair she'd nursed a tiny flame of hope in her heart. No more than a spark to brighten the darkness and give shape to the fervent prayer she whispered to God each night before sleeping and each morning upon awakening.

On Christmas Eve she discovered that God had denied her prayer. She was not to bear Morgan's child. She would not be allowed to carry even that much of him with her. She had cried that night, dry, wrenching sobs that tore at her very soul, but after that she had not shed another tear or so much as thought a prayer. Why should she pray to someone who obviously cared so little for her?

Shortly after that, fresh ailments began to plague her. An unbearable tightness of the chest. Stabbing pains in her temples. A feeble cough. Assorted aches throughout the rest of her body. The more she dwelled upon them, the worse they became until she awoke one morning quite convinced she must be dying. The Cameron carriage had been ordered to London posthaste.

The Belmonts had dutifully taken her in and propped her on their divan, where she ruled their household with the aplomb of a spoiled young queen.

Sabrina was sometimes beset by a strange sensation of distance, as if she were watching from the chandelier while another girl performed a part in some badly acted melodrama.

Enid's chair creaked as she shifted her weight. Sabrina still failed to understand the Belmonts' predilection for cramming the rooms of their massive town house with furniture better suited for wraiths. Every time one of them plopped down in one of the gilded and curlicued chairs, Sabrina held her breath, awaiting the imminent collapse of its spidery legs.

All the Belmonts were round, but in the past few months Enid had grown rounder yet. Sabrina stole a glance at her cousin, despising herself anew for her petty pang of jealousy. Not even a jeweled stomacher could hide the swelling mound of Enid's belly. A thin layer of ceruse muted but could not quench the radiant glow of her skin. While Sabrina withered to a bitter old woman in a young woman's skin, Enid bloomed with the child of the man she had loved.

It had tested even Uncle Willie's jovial good nature to send his daughter away to avoid scandal only to have her return pregnant. Even more galling was Enid's obvious lack of repentance and her poorly concealed delight at the prospect of bearing the nameless bastard of a reprobate Highlander.

Tugging at his sparse hair, the beleaguered duke had locked Sabrina's father in his library before he could escape, where they had labored around the clock to concoct a fictitious husband for Enid—an obscure Highland laird named Nathanael MacLeod who had both wooed and wed her in the wilds of Scotland, then had the misfortune to perish during their honeymoon in the same alleged carriage accident that had crippled Sabrina.

The romantic tale had made Enid something of a celebrity in London. The men clucked over her while the women offered their heartfelt condolences. Even her priggish ex-fiancé, Philip Markham, had appeared on her doorstep, obviously seeking to bolster his own reputation for noble sacrifice by graciously accepting the child of a deceased Highland lord as his own. Enid soaked up the unexpected attention, glowing and swelling so profusely that Sabrina half feared she might pop with pleasure. The two of them had entered into an unspoken agreement to never discuss their time in the Highlands, both finding the subject too painful.

Sabrina gazed over the neatly clipped lawns and clean-swept pavements. Sunlight crept across her lap rug, teasing her face with a promise of warmth. At least Enid had the comfort of being believed a widow. She had an excuse for the wistful expression that sometimes darkened her eyes. Sabrina had nothing. Nothing but pity.

To ease the annulment process, her father had decided that no one in London but the magistrate was to know she had ever been wed. It was as if her time with Morgan had been nothing more than an illusion, a tender erotic dream from some other woman's life. She would awaken in the night, confused by the darkness, the smothering curtains of the four-poster, the pathetic uselessness of her legs.

Trembling with the panic of doubting her own sanity, she would scramble for the Bible she kept tucked beneath the feather mattress. She would claw at the worn pages until the dried spray of gorse came tumbling out. Only then would her breathing ease. Only then would she remember the stricken expression on Morgan's face and find the courage to press the blooms between the pages, her hands no longer trembling, but resigned.

As Sabrina watched, a little boy with hair the color of sunshine went scampering across the street, chasing a rotund puppy. A man and woman strolled hand in hand, her laughing face turned to his adoring one. A hedge thrush warbled into song, piercing Sabrina's heart with the bittersweet vibrance of its melody.

She huddled deeper into her shawl. "Would you close the window, Enid? I do believe I'm taking a chill." As Enid laid the book aside and rose to obey, the sunlight struck Sabrina's face with full force. She flinched and pressed her eyes shut. "And draw the drapes, won't you? The light hurts my eyes."

She sighed with relief as the heavy drapes swept shut, bathing her in undemanding gloom.

Chapter Twenty-three

"*C'est magnifique!*" the Frenchman proclaimed, kissing his bunched fingers.

Morgan trembled and snorted like a prize stallion about to bolt as the tiny tailor minced around him, pausing only to prod the muscled planes of his abdomen. Pugsley roused himself from his contented stupor to growl low in his throat at the tailor's daring.

The little man leered at Morgan. "*Quelle bête jolie!*"

"What did he say," Morgan demanded, glowering at Dougal. "Should I kill him?"

"He said you were a pretty beast, and I'd rather you didn't," Dougal replied dryly from his seat by the window. "At least not until after he bills us for his services. I've heard they're dreadfully overpriced."

Ranald kissed his bunched fingers and blew Morgan a mocking kiss. "Don't be so hard on the wee feller, Morgan. I do believe he's taken a fancy to ye."

Within the space of a week, the Cameron solar

had been transformed into a tailor's shop. Bolts of broadcloth and silk covered every available surface. A tailor's dummy watched the proceedings with faceless amusement.

As the tailor tucked a paper of pins between his rouged lips and disappeared behind him, Morgan swiveled his neck, not trusting the bewigged man out of his sight. His worst suspicions were confirmed when he felt a stealthy pressure on his plaid. He jerked back, resulting in a fierce tug-of-war over the threadbare tartan.

"Why so shy, Morgan?" Ranald chided. "I've seen ye drop yer drawers with far less urgin' than that."

"Not for the likes of him!" Morgan gave the plaid such a tug that the tartan gave and the little man went spinning across the chamber. Dougal caught him before he could tumble out the open window.

The tailor spat out a mouthful of pins, followed by an outpouring of vituperative French. His face flushed to an alarming scarlet. He waved his clenched fists in the air and stamped his feet. Morgan stared with new respect, astonished that such a wee creature could work up such an impressive rage.

The diatribe ended in broken English. "I come far from Paris. He must allow me to measure him, *mais oui*?"

Obviously afraid the little tailor was working himself into an apoplexy, Dougal laid a diplomatic arm around his shoulders. Throwing a warning glance back at Morgan, he guided the man away from the object of his wrath and began to croon in soothing French.

Feeling both foolish and vulnerable, Morgan adjusted the tatters of his plaid with as much dignity as he could muster.

Ranald sobered. "Don't get discouraged, man. Remember what the Cameron's wife told ye. The poor lass is wastin' away without ye. She could die if ye don't help her."

Neither of them saw Dougal's eyes roll heavenward. The Cameron himself didn't know if he should be petitioning for forgiveness or for the heavenly aid he would require when his son-in-law learned the truth.

• • •

"No, Morgan. Not that fork, the other one."

Morgan snatched his hand back as if the gleaming silver had burned it.

"The one on the right, next to your napkin."

Elizabeth's voice chimed like bells inside his aching head. She never lifted her voice, never lost patience with him no matter how unfailingly stupid he appeared to be. He would have almost preferred that she scream at him and tear at her hair as she must have longed to do.

He fumbled with the myriad of silver, every clink echoing in the condemning silence. By the time he had located the proper fork for spearing the tiny oysters, a maid had appeared to whisk them away. A bowl of soup materialized in front of him, its meaty aroma making him feel desperate with hunger. He raised the bowl to his lips, already anticipating a long, thirsty gulp.

"Morgan! You must learn to use your spoon."

He lowered the bowl, sloshing soup down his ruffled stock. Brian and Alex were staring at him from the other end of the table. Dougal coughed sharply, and they devoted their attentions to their own soup. A buxom maid hid a giggle behind her apron. Winking at Morgan, Ranald picked up his bowl and drained it in one gurgling slurp.

To Morgan, a wee bowl with a handle seemed a ridiculous way to eat soup. Before he could ease two mouthfuls down his throat, the irksome maid had reappeared to take it away. His stomach rumbled its disapproval.

A plate appeared to appease it, layered with steaming mutton, fat white potatoes, and bread slathered with golden butter. Determined that this portion would not escape him, Morgan flipped his dirk out of the waistband of his tailored breeches and stabbed it toward the plate.

Elizabeth's hand came down over the bread. The

blade thudded to a halt between her fingers, missing her pinkie by half an inch.

She shook her head in sad reproach. "You must never use your dirk when eating, Morgan. How many times must I remind you?"

A betraying heat flooded his face. "I'm not hungry," he muttered, pushing away from the table.

As he turned to go, his mother-in-law cleared the delicate, swanlike throat that Morgan longed to wrap his fingers around. He swung back and gave all a crisp bow that earned her approving nod.

After he was gone, Ranald said, "I'm glad *he* ain't hungry 'cause I'm bloody famished." He scraped Morgan's mutton and potatoes on his heaped plate. "I don't know what ye're all lookin' so gloomy about. He's comin' along nicely. Why, I'll wager ye'll make a gentleman out o' him yet!"

It was a full fortnight before Morgan discovered a genteel skill at which he might excel. Oblivious of the pale, gangly music master seated before the harpsichord, he tilted his head, savoring the angelic strains of Bach pouring from the keys. His palm met Elizabeth's as they circled the space cleared in the middle of the solar.

Here his natural grace served him well, the elaborate steps of the minuet no different from those required for swordplay or dodging pistol balls.

As they came together, bodies brushing in the briefest of contacts, Morgan closed his eyes, stealing a breath of roses from her upswept hair. Remembered desire struck him low in the gut, but when he opened his eyes, it was not to ebony curls and sparkling sapphire eyes, but to auburn hair streaked with silver and green eyes softened with compassion. He stumbled, but Elizabeth's flawless rhythm corrected him easily.

They stepped apart. Morgan held her hand aloft as she twirled around him in a rustle of satin. "Dougal has arranged for you to have a secretary at your disposal in London," she said.

"Sabrina was goin' to teach me how to write. But

there always seemed to be somethin' better to do . . ." He trailed off, remembering who he was talking to. He cast Elizabeth a guilty glance.

A knowing half-smile curved her lips. "I dare say there was."

They met in the center of the floor again. A smile touched Morgan's own lips as his hand briefly encompassed the narrow curve of her corseted waist. He found it a subtle delight to touch a woman this way, a courtship ritual rendered all the more compelling for its delicacy and grace.

"I can't wait to dance this way with . . ." His words faded on a sharply indrawn breath as he remembered he would never dance this way with Sabrina. She would never know this alluring wedding of motion and music. Guilt and agony flooded him. His feet froze in place.

The harpsichord faltered. Elizabeth shot the music master a fierce look and he resumed playing, his gaze glued to the music stand.

Without missing a step, she came into Morgan's arms. "The last thing my daughter needs is your pity."

After a moment of hesitation, he nodded. As the final notes of the dance chimed, Elizabeth sank into a graceful curtsy at his feet. He bowed and lifted her hand to his lips.

Tilting her face to him, she said, "Had your mother lived, she would have been very proud of the man you've become."

Morgan pressed a kiss to the back of her hand. "I should like to think so, my lady. I should truly like to think so."

"Who'd've ever thought ye'd let a Cameron with a blade near yer throat? Yer poor da's probably turnin' in his grave." Ranald chortled and tossed a handful of dried raisins in his mouth.

"As well he should be," Morgan muttered. "Since the wretch is to blame for most of this."

The icy steel of the straight razor rounded his Adam's apple and swept upward, scraping the angle of his clenched jaw. He forced himself to remain utterly still beneath the cool competence of Elizabeth's hands. She would have made an able surgeon, he thought. Or an assassin.

Perhaps she and Eve shared more qualities than he had realized. But Elizabeth had lived her pampered life secure in the adoration of her husband and children, while Eve had fought a constant battle against his clan's contempt and his father's apathy. His eyes clouded at the thought of his banished clanswoman. She had always been part of his life, and her absence stung almost as deeply as her betrayal.

Elizabeth wiped away the scented soap, gestured for him to stand, and stepped back to admire her handiwork. Morgan felt the tension drain from his shoulders. A mistake, he quickly realized, for a brisk clap of her hands summoned forth a bevy of maids and menservants. They flooded the solar, swarming like gleeful ants around a pool of spilled honey.

Even Ranald was cowed by the invasion. Gulping, he grabbed the bowl of raisins and retreated behind the drapes.

Morgan would rather have faced a legion of bloodthirsty Chisholms than this plague of eager Lilliputians. They poked and prodded, tugged and measured, buttoned and tucked until he wanted to scream. The simian tailor crawled around his feet, muttering French obscenities around a mouthful of pins and seeming to take great pleasure in jabbing him at unpredictable intervals. Morgan swallowed a bellow as a pin pierced his calf.

"*Pardonnez-moi*," the wee tyrant muttered with a moue of feigned regret.

A dapper manservant whipped a foamy linen cravat around Morgan's throat. Morgan felt as if he were choking. Surely no hangman's noose could have been so binding. Yet he bore it all with a show of stoic indifference until he saw Elizabeth approaching through their ranks, a powdered and curled bagwig perched on one fist and a glass pot of ceruse in the other.

"Enough!" he roared.

The servants froze in a silent tableau of apprehension. The tailor's rouged cheeks paled.

Shaking off every humiliation he had endured in the past month for Sabrina's sake, Morgan drew himself up and pointed straight at Elizabeth. "I have never struck a woman, my lady, but if you are laboring under the delusion that you are going to put that—that—hideous *thing* on my head and paint my face, then you may very well be the first."

Dougal had slipped into the solar just in time to hear Morgan's speech. Seeing the first traces of a genuine sulk on his wife's face, he lifted his hands and slowly applauded, each clap falling like thunder in the shocked silence.

"Congratulations, my darling. I do believe you've created a gentleman." The servants stepped back in deference as Dougal circled Morgan, looking him up and down. "The precise speech, the arrogance, the regal bearing. Quite impressive, wouldn't you say?"

Morgan stood stiffly at attention as Elizabeth's pensive gaze swept him from the polished buckles on his shoes to the velvet queue taming his unruly hair at the nape. Her pout melted to an approving smile. "*Quite* impressive," she echoed.

"Very well, then," Dougal said crisply. "You're all dismissed. There will be no further need of your services."

As the servants obeyed, Morgan sank into a chair, relieved to no longer be the center of their avid attentions.

Dougal paced the solar. "All the arrangements have been completed. As you insisted, Ranald will act as your footman. You're to have lodgings, a secretary, and an allowance at your disposal."

"I've no need of charity," Morgan said.

Dougal peered into his face. "Have you ever tried living in London with no money in your purse? No, I can see you haven't." Stroking his beard, he resumed his pacing. "Beth and I have taken temporary lodgings in Bloomsbury. Sabrina is not to know we're in London. All you're lacking now is an entree into society."

"Perhaps a title," Elizabeth suggested, sitting on the edge of the settee. "No one in London can resist a title. MacDonnell is an ancient name. Surely your family was entitled before they took up thievery and depravity as a way of life."

Morgan shot her a dark look. "I never paid any mind to such nonsense. What good is a fancy scrap of paper from the king when you've no gold to go along with it?"

"Think, lad," Dougal commanded. "Search your mind. There must have been some mention of it somewhere."

Morgan frowned. "Halbert," he muttered half to himself. "Lord Halbert, Baron of . . ." Dougal and Elizabeth exchanged a hopeful glance. "No, no, that's not it at all. Sir Halbert—"

A cheerful singsong voice drifted out from the window:

He'll make soup o' yer bones,
And cloaks o' yer skin.
He'll lunch on yer liver
And dine on yer shins.
If he marches yer way, ye'd do well to flee . . .

Dougal marched to the window and snatched back the drapes. Ranald smirked up at him and sang softly, " '. . . Horrid Halbert, the dread Earl o' Montgarry.' "

Elizabeth cupped a hand over her mouth, muffling a giggle of mingled horror and delight at Morgan's stunned expression.

A jubilant smile broke over Dougal's face. He whirled to face Morgan. "Hell, man. You're a bloody earl. You outrank me. I'm but a lowly viscount."

Elizabeth rose and spread her skirts in a playful curtsy. "Well my lord, are you ready to claim your countess?"

Morgan's eyes glinted with raw determination,

making him look more pirate than nobleman. "Aye, my lady. And she'd best make ready to be claimed."

Sabrina smothered a bored yawn behind her fan.

The orchestra was tuning up, the discordant notes flaying her taut nerves. Simply another interminable Belmont ball to be endured, she reminded herself, no different from the private theatricals, the afternoon poetry readings, or her aunt Honora's beloved card parties, where Sabrina was displayed upon her upholstered divan for the sympathy and diversion of London society.

She snapped the fan shut, afraid to admit even to herself that she was beginning to take a perverse pleasure in their pity.

Uncle Willie and Aunt Honora appeared on the stairs. A light smattering of applause greeted their arrival. Her aunt's tiny ringlets danced like sausages popping in a fire. The entire Belmont family looked soft and unfinished around the edges, like unbaked bread dough. As her uncle approached, Sabrina marveled anew that her willowy mother had emerged from such bovine stock.

Uncle Willie chucked her under the chin. "How's my favorite niece tonight? Enjoying yourself, my dear?"

"I'm your only niece, and I might be enjoying myself more if it weren't for this tiresome headache. I've had simply the most horrid—"

"There, there, that's all very nice, pudding, but the Duke of Devonshire just arrived. I really must pay my respects." Giving her a fatherly wink, he hastened away.

Sabrina sighed at his desertion. Enid was standing by the tall casement windows, basking in the attentions of her dogged ex-fiancé. Her skin glowed peach against the dove-gray of her mourning gown. An enthusiastic footman began bawling the names of the new arrivals.

Enid's brother, Stefan, less portly and infinitely more graceful than his father, danced down the stairs. Sabrina's spirits brightened. "Hullo, coz." He leaned down to press a dutiful kiss to her cheek. "Holding the beaus at bay, are you?"

"Doing my best," she chimed, clasping his hand before he could escape. "I do believe I'm taking an ague though. It's dreadfully drafty in here. Would you mind trotting back upstairs to fetch my shawl?"

"Anything for you, princess," he murmured, poorly concealing the weary roll of his eyes.

"Not the wool, Stefan," she called after him. "The cashmere. Wool makes me sneeze." The very thought of sneezing made her sneeze, and she dabbed her nose with a lace handkerchief.

By the time Stefan returned with the shawl, the cavernous ballroom had half filled and Sabrina was surrounded by fawning well-wishers. She sent one attentive young gentleman to fetch her a glass of champagne while another was ordered to search out the source of the pesky draft. Wielding her wistful smiles and fluttering lashes like weapons, she exerted the only power left to her.

Two rather plain young women dwarfed by their upswept ringlets hovered by the wall, conversing behind their fans. Their thinly plucked brows drew together in obvious displeasure as they eyed the besotted men swarming around Sabrina. Beneath the clink of champagne glasses and murmur of conversation, their low, malevolent voices carried clearly to her ears.

"Pathetic little flirt, isn't she? Flaunting her infirmity is the only way she can get a man's attention."

Sabrina kept her smile pasted on, thankful for the heavy ceruse that hid her flush of anger.

"Given to tantrums, they say. One of the Belmont underfootmen told our cook that only last week she . . ." The woman dropped her voice to a whisper.

Her companion giggled. "She behaves like a child because she's only half a woman. Any man who would pay court to her would have to be less than half a man."

Their surreptitious glances raked her useless legs. Rage flooded Sabrina. She wished she could jerk back the lap rug and show them some hideous deformity that would send them all shrieking from the ballroom in horror.

An eager male smile drifted into focus. "Miss Cameron, your champagne?"

A glass was pressed into her trembling hand. Before she could thank her benefactor, the first strains of music soared out from the orchestra. One by one her admirers made their painfully polite apologies and drifted away to join the dance. One of the women who had discussed her with such malice could not resist tossing a triumphant sneer over her shoulder as she took the proffered arm of a pock-marked young gentleman in a poorly fitted frock coat.

Sabrina tapped her fingers on the divan. The rich notes of the music throbbed through her veins, echoing the pulse of her furious heartbeat. Even Enid was dancing, her hands stiffly locked with Philip Markham's.

Sabrina wanted to despise them all, even her loyal cousin, for their unappreciated ability to whirl and bow and sway to the graceful cadences of the music. Oddly enough, she had never before felt such compassion for Eve, such a strange sense of kinship. Morgan's clanswoman had spent her life drifting on the fringes, invited to the banquet, but never allowed to dine. Sabrina took a sip of the champagne. Its bitterness burned her raw throat.

Had the world turned differently and the Mac-Donnells never come to Cameron, she might be twirling among them now. She searched the painted faces of the men, wondering if she might have found them handsome, might have fallen in love with one of them. They seemed silly and callow to her now, vacuous creatures content to flit from ball to card party to theater. Their soft hands had never known a callus. Their perfumed skin had never smelled of sunshine and sweat earned from an honest day's labor.

Had any of them ever hunted to put food on their family's table? Had they ever risked everything, even their lives, for those of their own blood? Had they ever waded through calf-high snow to rescue a drowning sheep?

Had they ever made a woman cry out their name in a moment of cresting ecstasy? Surely their wigged and powdered hair had never curtained a face strained with passion. Had never tickled a woman's skin as they slid down on her in the seductive darkness of night.

Sabrina pressed her eyes shut, unable to bear the wild, yearning flutter of her heart.

The music drifted to a pause. She opened her eyes to find a bevy of gentlemen already abandoning their partners to stampede to her side as if beset with guilt for daring to enjoy themselves while she languished on the divan. A weary sigh escaped her. For once she wished they would all just go away.

On the stairs, the footman cleared his throat. His voice vibrating with a note of pure majesty, he threw back his head and announced, "The Earl of Montgarry!"

Just what the party needed, Sabrina thought, tossing back a cynical swallow of the champagne. Another simpering nobleman.

An odd beat of silence followed. The guests were all blinking raptly at the steps like a herd of vapid sheep. Curious as to what might be fascinating enough to capture even their jaded attentions, Sabrina craned her neck.

As she met the glacial green eyes of the man on the stairs, the champagne glass slipped through her numb fingers to shatter on the marble floor.

Chapter Twenty-four

Sabrina couldn't breathe. The familiar tightness swelled like a rock in her chest. The candle flames of the chandeliers wavered and dimmed beneath the hypnotic flare of her husband's eyes. Only when his gaze moved on with a dismissal so casual and blatant as to be insulting did she dare to suck in a wheezing breath.

Morgan.

Morgan, utterly magnificent, his coat a wine-colored justaucorps that hugged his waist and flared over his narrow hips to reveal matching knee breeches, cut to perfection against the tapered muscles of his thighs. The lace-edged purity of a snowy cravat framed his bronze jaw. His unpowdered hair was caught at his nape in a black velvet queue. It gleamed like spun gold beneath the kiss of the chandeliers.

Sabrina had thought the Morgan she had known to be a dangerous man, but as this elegant stranger surveyed the thunderstruck crowd, a faint smirk of amusement quirking his chiseled lips, she realized he was much more than that.

He was a killer, a thief and assassin of female hearts who would give no quarter and take no prisoners. His masculine beauty was irresistible. She dragged her eyes away before it could blind her.

The whispers were already beginning.

"Who on earth is he? The Earl of Montgarry? I've never heard of him. Might we have met his parents in Edinburgh, dear?"

A disapproving male murmur. "Damned barbarian, don't you think?"

An excited female thrill. "Oh, barbarous indeed!"

Sabrina discovered she had twisted her handkerchief into a hopeless knot. Her mind staggered, still unable to believe that Morgan MacDonnell was standing in the ballroom of her uncle's town house rather than ruling over his Highland castle and giving some strapping Scottish lass like Alwyn his golden-haired babes. Morgan the Earl of Montgarry? She must be going mad. Morgan wasn't an earl. If he was, then she would be a countess. Her eyes widened in fresh astonishment.

The faces of her aunt Honora and uncle Willie floated by like puzzled balloons as they hastened to greet their guest. Across the ballroom Sabrina saw that Enid, too, was transfixed by the sight of Morgan. She clutched the collarette at her throat, her face grayer than her gown. Sabrina feared her cousin was going to swoon. This time there would be no Ranald to catch her. Her priggish Philip appeared far too stiff, his face set in lines of perpetual disapproval. Enid's gaze flew to Sabrina, reading the helpless fear in her cousin's eyes.

Loyal as always, Enid pushed her way toward the divan with Philip dogging her heels.

Enid was not the first to reach Sabrina. As if awakening from a trance cast by the enigmatic stranger, several of the men rushed to her side. One knelt to pick up the shards of glass while another peered into her face and dabbed at the champagne spilled on the lap rug.

"I do say, Miss Cameron, are you all right?"

"You didn't cut yourself, did you?"

Another gentleman grabbed her fan from her lap and began to cool her wildly, blowing a cloud of his wig powder up her nose.

Finding their attentions a terrible distraction, she sneezed and snatched the fan back. "What are you trying to do? Kill me?" she snapped before remembering to soften her rebuke with a tremulous smile.

Enid reached her then, insinuating herself at Sabrina's side like a mother lioness protecting her pride.

Morgan stepped off the stairs, the breadth of his shoulders beneath the classic tailoring of his coat dwarfing every other man in the ballroom. The crowd was mesmerized by his wolfish grace. Her aunt and uncle led him toward the divan, their doughy features blurred with confusion. Enid squeezed Sabrina's hand so hard that her joints cracked in protest.

At Morgan's inescapable approach, terror flooded Sabrina, making her breath come fast and her fingertips tingle. Since the accident, she had often awakened screaming from nightmares of being trapped by fire—of writhing, her useless legs tangled in the sheets while flames licked at the curtains of her bed. But this man was more deadly, more consuming than any fire. All the emotions she'd sought to bury were rushing toward the surface like a fountain about to burst. Gulping back her panic, she stared into her lap, paralyzed by more than just her shattered legs.

Morgan came to a halt on the other side of the divan without even glancing down at her.

"Enid, my dear," Uncle Willie said, "the earl has requested an introduction." The guests were staring and Sabrina could hear the sharp note of warning in her uncle's voice. What sort of risky game was Morgan playing? "He says he was an acquaintance of your *poor deceased husband.*"

Aunt Honora ducked behind her fan until nothing was visible but her fluttering rabbit-eyes. Enid pried her hand out of Sabrina's.

Morgan reached across the divan and lifted it to

his lips, the gesture fraught with mocking grace. "Aye, my lady." Sabrina shivered at the caress of his husky burr. Not even its newly polished edges could completely hide its lilt. "As soon as I returned from my travels on the Continent, I heard of poor Nate's untimely demise. He was a fine and upstanding fellow. You've my deepest sympathies."

Sabrina had to admire Enid's aplomb at accepting condolences for a husband who'd never existed. "Why, thank you, my lord. His death was a great shock to all of us. It was so very kind of you to remember me."

Philip stepped forward, fairly bristling with self-importance. "Just how were you acquainted with Lady MacLeod's husband?"

Sabrina stole a glance at Morgan from beneath her lashes, then wished she hadn't. His smile was dazzling. "The usual ways. We grew up together in the Highlands, took the Grand Tour together, studied in Edinburgh. And who might you be . . . sir?"

Philip drew himself up to the height of Morgan's cravat and cast a protective arm over Enid's shoulder. "Mr. Philip Markham. Lady MacLeod's intended."

"My *ex*-intended," Enid corrected him sweetly, shrugging away his arm.

Sabrina knew how a child must feel. They were all talking over her as if she were invisible, leaving her at eye level with the sophisticated cut of Morgan's breeches. His tailor must have been an absolute master of his craft, a veritable *artiste*, a . . .

Morgan thrust his knee forward in a casual pose. Sabrina's mouth went dry. She swallowed hard and wished for her spilled champagne.

Enid struck just the right note of courtesy and challenge. "So tell me, my lord, how long will you be honoring us with your presence?"

Morgan's enigmatic smile reverberated through his voice. "Only as long as my business requires."

For the first time, his gaze dropped to Sabrina. She could feel the heat of it, searing the crown of her inclined head.

Enid was growing bolder yet, too bold for

Sabrina's tastes. "Please allow me to introduce you to my cousin, Miss Sabrina Cameron. Or, perhaps, both hailing from the Highlands, the two of you have already met?"

Without a trace of awkwardness, Morgan dropped to one knee beside the chaise. Sabrina stared into the ruffled folds of his cravat as his warm, blunt fingers cradled her icy hand, delivering it to the merciless perfection of his lips. Remembering the dark and exquisite sensations those lips were capable of giving, Sabrina felt a warning tendril of flame uncurl low in her belly.

His lips barely grazed the back of her hand. "I'm afraid I haven't had the pleasure."

Liar, she thought viciously. Her anger gave her the courage to tip her head back and meet his eyes.

"My lord," she murmured. "The pleasure is all mine."

Something flickered behind the shifting waters of green and gold in his eyes. Something angry and more than a little frightening. Then the taunting threat of recognition was gone, leaving their depths barren and flat.

He straightened, coolly dismissing her. "Perhaps, your grace," he said, addressing Uncle Willie, "you might introduce me to some of your guests. I hope to secure some invitations while in residence. I've always felt that no business, however demanding, should preclude a gentleman's pursuit of the more"—his voice caressed the word—"*satisfying* aspects of life."

"Oh, do allow me," Aunt Honora offered, emerging from behind her fan to take Morgan's arm. "I know a certain young lady hovering behind the potted palm who is positively drooling for an introduction."

Sabrina's aunt and uncle flanked him, leading him away. Uncle Willie dared to throw a baffled glance over his shoulder.

Philip snapped open a silver box and tucked a pinch of snuff up his nose. "Presumptuous fellow, don't you think? I've never cared for Scots myself. Arrogant savages, the lot of them, if you ask me."

Obviously shaken by her duel of wits with Morgan, Enid snapped, "Oh, shut up, Philip. Nobody asked you." Throwing Sabrina an apologetic glance, she rushed after her parents.

Before the miffed Philip could even take himself off in a huff, Sabrina was once again the center of attention.

"I've fetched you a fresh glass of champagne, Miss Cameron."

"Shall I fluff your pillows?"

"Would you care for some pâté?"

But her gaze was still locked on the broad back of the man who commanded the ballroom as if he owned it. Once again she was beset by the sensation of being trapped in a bizarre comedy of errors. The idea might not have been so jarring if she hadn't feared she was destined to be the butt of every joke. For the first time in months, a broken litany of prayer was spawned in her brain.

Please, God, oh, dear God, please . . . But even then she wasn't sure if she was praying for Morgan to go away or to never leave her sight again.

Morgan had never felt quite so given to murder. Since the true objects of his wrath were safely ensconced in their cozy parlor in Bloomsbury, doubtlessly toasting their son-in-law's immense folly, he contented himself with stealing murderous glares at their offspring, all the while forcing himself to turn in the dance and murmur polite replies to his various partners.

Poor, pathetic Sabrina! How desperately she needed him! A tiny whimper escaped the woman whose hand he had suddenly clenched.

"So sorry," he murmured before passing her on to the next man in the minuet.

Morgan now recognized the odd looks and warning glances exchanged between Dougal and Elizabeth in the past weeks for what they were—subterfuge, a skillful concealing of reality behind twisted truths and bald lies. Why, they had feared for their daughter's very survival if Morgan couldn't restore the bloom of health to her wan cheeks! Little did they know they now had far more reason to fear for her survival.

Against its will, his gaze was drawn back to the regal curve of Sabrina's divan. The provocative set of his jaw drew a timid flutter from his current partner's sparse lashes.

Morgan had steeled himself for weeks for his first sight of Sabrina. He had expected to find her languishing in a darkened room, her vibrant flesh melted against her delicate bones. He had not expected to find her painted like an absurd doll and holding court over a besotted bevy of fools like some invalid courtesan. An inadvertent growl escaped him as he watched her bestow a tender smile on one of the undeserving wretches.

"Did you say something, my lord?" His plump partner stepped heavily on his toe.

He forced his grimace into a genteel smile. "Just thinking how light you are on your feet, my lady." But not on his.

As his partner tittered her delight at the compliment, Sabrina lifted a languid hand only to have it caught and kissed by a simpering fellow in a powdered bagwig. Morgan's scathing gaze raked her. She looked absolutely ridiculous. Her rich, dark hair had been plastered close to her head and drawn into a topknot crowned by a tiny cap of lace. Her skin had been painted ivory, smothering the natural roses in her cheeks. As the shawl slipped from her shoulders, Morgan saw that the ethereal shade extended beyond her creamy throat to the swell of her breasts, most of which were revealed by the daring décolletage of her gown.

He noted cynically that none of her overattentive beaus rushed to correct the errant shawl. One bespectacled fellow even stood on tiptoe to admire the view.

As Sabrina pursed her lips in a rouged smirk, a rush of savage lust colored Morgan's temper. He wanted to charge to her side, to shake her until the silky black curls came tumbling around her face, to scrub the glaze from her skin with his palms, to jerk down the bodice of her gown and search for any hint of the rosy warmth that had haunted his dreams for so many long, lonely nights. His desire and fury blended in a wave so potent that he was seized with fresh despair. A pang of fresh rejection stabbed him.

He was a bloody fool to have come here. Sabrina did not need him. She had never needed him. She had sent him away, tossed his flowers aside, and pronounced him unfit to touch even the hem of her precious skirt.

He would simply make his apologies to his puzzled hosts and take his leave. Then he would ride back to that narrow town house in Bloomsbury Square, throw his allowance and his fancy clothes back into Dougal and Elizabeth's smug faces, and curse the day he had ever laid eyes on any Cameron.

Determined to escape this farce while he still had the will, he passed his partner on to the next man and pivoted to find himself palm to palm with Enid Belmont. Locking fingers, they circled each other like wary predators.

Happy to find a target for his withering sarcasm, he raked a gaze of mocking admiration down the swell of her abdomen. "I'm heartened to see your *husband* left you something to remember him by, *Lady MacLeod.*"

She lowered her lashes in demure agreement. "As am I, *Lord Montgarry.*"

Sabrina's cousin was cooler than Morgan remembered. Cooler and more worthy an opponent. They parted, dipped, and came together again. He stole another curious glance at her stomach.

Despising himself for the foolish leap of hope in his heart, he steeled his voice to deliberate nonchalance. "I don't suppose Miss Cameron has been similarly blessed."

Enid shook her head, but as she circled behind him, she whispered, "She was devastated."

A merry peal of girlish laughter floated out from the divan, clawing Morgan's lacerated heart. A sneer curled his lips. "It shows."

The black plunge of his spirits deepened. What right did he have to condemn Sabrina? If not for the ruthless ambitions of his clan, she might even now be twirling among these dancers, the brightest star in their vaulted firmament. Knowing he would never have another chance to sate his grim curiosity, he began to snap off questions each time the hapless Enid came within his grasp.

"How does she get about?"

"Her room is on ground level. Stefan or Father carries her. Or one of the footmen."

"And when she leaves the house?"

"She doesn't. She hasn't been outside since coming to London. She says fresh air makes her head ache."

Morgan frowned, unable to imagine his once-exuberant bride willingly surrendering the glories of spring. "What of her legs? Do they pain her? Were they as bad as the doctor feared? What happened when she tried to walk?"

Enid avoided his eyes. "She never tried."

Morgan gave up all pretense of the dance. Ignoring the annoyed guests forced to maneuver around them, he caught Enid's shoulders and searched her face. "She never tried to walk? Not even once?"

He had finally succeeded in throwing Enid off balance. She blinked back tears. "Dr. Montjoy encouraged her to in the beginning, but each time her feet touched the floor, she cried so at the pain that Uncle Dougal couldn't bear it."

An odd look had come over Morgan's face, a look of such speculative good cheer that it made Enid take a nervous step backward. She was even more astonished when he snatched her up and pressed a ferocious kiss to her mouth.

"That's my good girl. But you look a trifle pale. Why don't you go fetch yourself some warm milk before you swoon?"

Then he was striding through the crowd, leaving Enid to press her palms to her flaming cheeks and wonder what new devil she'd unleashed on her beloved cousin.

Sabrina hid her shaken state behind a mask of frenetic gaiety. Her hands batted the air like delicate birds, plucking the sleeve of one rapt gentleman while sending another scampering for a shawl that might do better service to her coloring.

All the charms she'd spent years perfecting on her father and brothers were unleashed on her uncle's unsuspecting guests. No one drifted away to join the dance. They lingered at her side, captivated by her winsome smile. Even the women were drawn into her spell. Her generosity of spirit was such that they decided among themselves that the rumors of her tantrums must be nothing more than jealous gossip.

But even as Sabrina kept her audience panting for her next clever word, Morgan was always there, his combination of polished elegance and raw virility threatening to explode at the edges of her vision. The men sized up his towering form, nostrils flaring as if a wild stallion had dared to storm their paddock. The women tripped over one another in the dance to position themselves in his path.

She feigned a coy giggle and ducked behind her fan to steal a glimpse of him, feeling like a lovesick six-year-old all over again. When she failed to find him, she felt even sicker. Had he gone? Left with one of the women throwing themselves at his buckled shoes? Would she ever see him again?

"Terrible accident," one of the men was informing a newcomer to her circle of admirers. "An icy road in the Highlands. The carriage took a tumble. Lady MacLeod lost her husband and Miss Cameron . . ."

Miss Cameron lost everything, Sabrina thought, smoothing the lap rug. The fictitious carriage accident was too close to the truth. She closed her eyes, hearing again the sharp report of a pistol and Pookah's agonized scream.

Her nostrils twitched as a new scent fought its

way through the stale cloud of perfume and rice powder. Pine, crisp and fragrant, blowing like a fresh wind through her lungs, bringing with it visions of wide blue skies and snowcapped mountain peaks. Pine mingled with the intoxicating maleness of sandalwood shaving soap.

Sabrina's eyes flew open as she realized that Morgan was leaning lazily on the back of the divan, drinking in every word. Dear God, she thought, how long had he been there? For once the others were oblivious of him. They were too busy staring at her legs. His breath—sweet, heated, untainted by champagne— stirred the lacy lappets on her cap. She eased her shawl up over her tingling breasts, only too aware of the view his casual stance afforded him.

The gentleman seemed intent on finishing his grim tale. "Miss Cameron was thrown from the carriage. Broke both her legs. Quite beyond repair, I fear."

Sabrina flinched, knowing only too well how the man's thoughtless words must be affecting Morgan.

A droll voice came from behind the divan. "I lost a mare that way once. Sad case. Had to shoot her."

Morgan's tactless remark caused all heads, including Sabrina's, to swivel toward him. He didn't look sad at all. His green eyes were positively twinkling with good cheer. Sabrina's admirers glared at him.

A timid hand touched hers. Thankful for the distraction, Sabrina turned back to find a young girl peering at her with genuine sympathy, her face framed by mousy ringlets. "Your legs, Miss Cameron? Do they pain you?"

Sabrina sighed with relief. Her health was always a safe topic. "At times. Right before a rain they tend to ache dreadfully."

The girls' voice sank to a fearful whisper. "Are they . . . *deformed*?"

Sabrina frowned, afraid to admit that she hadn't looked at them in months. She always kept her eyes carefully averted when the maids were bathing her, and at any other time they were smothered by a lap rug or dressing gown. She didn't even bother with stockings anymore, since her feet never touched the floor.

She parted her fingers to illustrate. "Perhaps only a tiny bit."

Without hesitation Morgan strode around the divan and snatched back the lap rug. Sabrina's gown had ridden up to her thighs. Cool air rushed over her bare legs. She gasped, mortified to be so exposed. The girl who had dared to ask collapsed in a pretty swoon only to be caught by the man behind her. The others recoiled in horror, then crept nearer to gape. Sabrina was frozen in place by her own humiliation.

Morgan studied the length of Sabrina's legs, his thoughtful gaze sweeping from her thighs to the tips of her toes. The crowd held their breath as if awaiting an opinion from the king's physician himself.

"They don't look deformed to me," he pronounced, dropping the lap rug. "A bit pale and scrawny perhaps, but serviceable."

Protected by the crowd's mute shock, he bent to bring Sabrina's hand to his lips. His eyes glinted with pure challenge as his warm lips brushed her knuckles "Miss Cameron. Till we meet again."

Sabrina felt her chest tightening, her breath coming in furious little pants. "Why—you—you wretched—"

Morgan was accepting his cloak from a bemused footman when Sabrina's sputters swelled to howls of outrage.

The footman's eyes twinkled. "I do hope you'll call again, my lord."

Tossing an edge of the cloak over his shoulder as he would have his plaid, Morgan gave the man a conspiratorial wink. "You can bloody well count on it."

As Morgan came striding down the front steps of the town house, Ranald whipped open the door of the waiting carriage with his strong arm.

He took one look at Morgan's thunderous expression and shook his head in sympathy. "Went poorly, did it? What did the wretches do? Toss ye out on yer ear?"

"On the contrary." Morgan threw himself against the leather seat and loosened his cravat with a savage jerk. "I'd say it went just as it was intended to go."

Slamming the carriage door, Ranald hopped up to ride on the steps like a proper footman, then spoiled the effect by poking his head in the carriage window. Unlike Morgan, Ranald took great delight in their new finery. He'd spent most of his time at their lodgings in front of the mirror, preening in his satin livery and dusting fresh powder on his wig.

"Where the hell are we goin'?" he asked, then grinned sheepishly. "I mean what address shall I give the driver, me lord?"

Morgan's jaw tightened. The single word shot from between his clenched teeth like an epithet. "Bloomsbury."

They reached Bloomsbury after only three wrong turns and Ranald's brief skirmish with a drunken sailor. By the time Morgan descended from the carriage, a light rain had began to fall, glazing the cobbled street and painting airy halos around the street lanterns.

Leaving Ranald to admire his reflection in a shop window. Morgan ducked inside the handsome town house, marched up the narrow steps to the second floor, and lifted his hand to knock. He heard the tinkle of crystal, the murmur of voices in gentle accord.

Fresh anger seized him. He slammed his fist against the door. It flew open beneath the force of the blow, crashing into the opposite wall.

The Camerons looked up from the cozy supper they'd laid before the hearth, both looking as guilty as if Morgan had caught Dougal with Elizabeth's skirts around her waist.

Morgan shook his head, disgusted by their domesticity, the steadfast affection that had sustained them through years of joys and hardships that he and Sabrina would never share. He wanted to overturn the table, wreck the simple room, drain the bottle of brandy sitting on the pristine tablecloth.

Dougal rose, tense and wary. "You saw her, I take it?"

"You lied to me."

Dougal's eyes shifted briefly to his wife's face. Morgan was sick of their sly glances. He grabbed the brandy bottle, but instead of draining it, hurled it to the hearth. Elizabeth flinched at its shatter.

She toyed with her napkin, arranged her silverware into a precise pattern. "We had no choice. If we had told you that our dear, sweet-tempered daughter had turned into a shrewish creature even we didn't recognize . . ." She trailed off, running out of silver.

"So you believed if I had known that, I wouldn't have helped her?" Morgan asked.

Elizabeth's silence condemned them all. Resting a hand on his wife's shoulder, Dougal drew himself up. "The only question now is will you still help her? Now that you've seen what she's become."

Morgan impaled Dougal with his unforgiving gaze, his voice husky with betrayal. "Even when I hated you, I always believed you were a good man, Dougal Cameron. But now I know you're no better than my own da. Jerking our strings, making us all dance like bloody puppets to your tune." His hands clenched on a chair back. He met Elizabeth's beseeching gaze. She was the only woman he could refuse nothing. "Aye, I'll do your dirty work for you. I'll push her hard until she remembers how to fight for herself. But we all know what the cost will be. When I'm done with her, she'll hate me and not you."

With those words Morgan left them to their cozy supper, to the soothing beat of rain against their windowpanes. Ranald had taken shelter inside the carriage. Drawing the collar of his cloak up against the chill, Morgan climbed in to join him. One look at Morgan's face and Ranald knew to keep his silence.

As the carriage clattered through a shallow puddle, splashing an arc of water into the air, neither of them saw the solitary figure on the corner left dripping in its wake.

Chapter Twenty-five

"I won't go back in there with her! His Grace can toss me out in the gutter if he likes. It just ain't worth it." The maid wiped her reddened eyes with her apron.

"Now, Bea, don't say such things. You know your mum depends on you to put meat on the table for your little brothers and sisters."

"But she's a monster!" the maid wailed, hurling herself into the comforting expanse of Cook's arms.

Cook patted her heaving back, exchanging a helpless look with the other servants who had sought shelter in the smoky haven of her kitchen. They had huddled in a nervous knot all morning, arguing and taking wagers on who would be the next hapless soul to be cast into the young lioness's den. Even the handsome bonuses offered by the duke were losing their allure.

Cook cringed at the demanding tinkle of the servant's bell. She glared at the ceiling, wishing with uncharacteristic malice that the duke's invalid niece had the gold cord of the bellpull knotted around her delicate little neck. Master Stefan had rigged the unfortunate device when Sabrina had arrived, not knowing that its tinkling melody would haunt them even when they fled the house.

The girl had been in rare form since the ball the previous night. She'd kept the household awake until dawn, ringing every five minutes for chest poultices, leg rubs, and cool cloths for her throbbing temples. Their good-natured employer had since locked himself in the library while Enid and Master Stefan retreated to the relative peace of the garden.

Cook shivered with dread as the bell rang again, its relentless jangle deafening them all to the firm knock on the front door.

The object of the servants' trepidation lay alone on the settee in the morning room, seething with ill temper.

Sabrina gave the bell rope another vicious tug only to have it come off in her hands. She stared dumbly at it, her panic growing. There was no rush of footsteps in the corridor, no whisper of satin livery. No one was coming, she thought. Perhaps no one was ever coming. Perhaps she was to be left alone with only her doubts and fears for company.

And her legs.

She averted her gaze. The gilt cupids emblazoned on the mantel simpered at her. Although the heat in the room was stifling, she had forced the servants to lay a fire in the marble hearth. The morning sunlight beat through the casement windows like a taunting fist. Sweat trickled between Sabrina's breasts. She plucked fretfully at the bodice of her dressing gown, then forced herself to lock her hands in her lap.

The stiff gesture might have fooled others, but it did not fool her. Her control was slipping. She had clung to it for months, manipulating herself and everyone around her as if she could somehow atone for that one near-fatal moment when she had lost control and gone plunging over a cliff. Without its armor to protect her, she feared she would break into a thousand fragile shards and scatter in the warm spring wind.

"Damn you, Morgan MacDonnell," she whispered.

Morgan was the one who had dared to stride back into her life and jerk her off balance just as he had always done. He was always there to shove her, but never around to catch her when she fell.

She looked at the blanket shielding her legs, then peeked at the door. As long as there were people rushing in and out to do her bidding, she had been safe from the temptation Morgan had dangled before her. Safe from the mocking challenge in his sunlit eyes.

The silence bore down on her, intensifying with each tick of the bronze table clock on the mantel. She could bear it no longer. Drawing in a breath for courage, she cast the blanket aside and parted the skirt of her dressing gown.

Sabrina studied her bared legs as if they belonged to someone else. She tilted her head first to one side, then the other, afraid to admit that Morgan was right. They looked paler and thinner than she remembered, but rather ordinary. She wiggled her toes, childishly fascinated by the simple motion.

"Here you are, darling. I brought the poultice for your poor chest."

Sabrina snatched the blanket back over her legs as Aunt Honora breezed in. A sullen servant trailed her at ten paces.

Sabrina hid her guilty relief at their interruption behind an imperious sniff. "I do hope it's wintergreen. Mint gives me hives."

Her aunt clucked soothingly. "The apothecary was fresh out of wintergreen, dear. We shall simply have to make do."

The tear-stained maid held her steaming burden a safe distance away as Sabrina snapped, "Have you seen my shawl? It's freezing in here."

Aunt Honora swiped her shiny brow. "But sweet-cakes, it's really quite warm."

"Not if you have bad circulation and are left lying in a draft all day."

Aunt Honora was rescued from the lash of Sabrina's tongue by the appearance of Enid and Stefan.

Enid beamed as Stefan thrust a bouquet of lavender blooms under Sabrina's nose. "Look, coz, see what sis picked for you. We thought some nice flowers might bring you cheer."

Pollen shot up Sabrina's nose. Waving the flowers away, she started to sneeze. "Take them away. You know I can't abide hyacinths."

Enid and her mother exchanged a dismayed glance. Stefan muttered something beneath his breath and jammed the blooms into a vase on the mantel. But even the maid's dour expression turned to alarm as Sabrina's sneezes deepened to gasps.

"Oh, dear Lord," she choked out between wheezes. "My throat is closing. I can feel it. Help me. Please help me!"

Aunt Honora's frightened cries brought the servants running. Stefan clapped Sabrina vigorously on the back while his mother sent a footman scampering to fetch the doctor. Before the man could reach the door, he collided with his master, knocking the duke's wig askew.

"Here now," Uncle Willie boomed. "What the devil is all this ruckus?"

No one noticed the butler and his towering companion standing before the gilt doors at the opposite end of the morning room. The butler intoned, "The Earl of Montgarry."

No one paid him any mind. The duke was bellowing, Enid and the duchess were sobbing, and the servants were rushing about in various states of panic.

Giving their guest an apologetic look, the butler cleared his throat politely and tried again. "The Earl of Montgarry!"

Sabrina wheezed harder, clutching her throat and turning a charming shade of lavender to match the hyacinths. The others gaped at her, frozen now in open horror.

After patting the rueful butler on the shoulders, the smiling earl marched down the length of the room, jerked the flowers from the mantel, and dashed the vase of cold water in Sabrina's face.

Chapter Twenty-six

A stunned silence fell over the morning room. Sabrina's gasps died to shocked little hiccups.

At her disgruntled expression, the onlookers' appalled faces began to change—a twitch here, a frantic blink there, a chewed-upon lip. Stefan balled his fists in his pockets and turned toward the window, his shoulders hunched. The butler, whose sole responsibility was maintaining dignity in the Belmont household, began to cough behind his hand. He hastily excused himself as if afraid the noble madman would dash the goldfish bowl in his face if he didn't gain control of his erratic breathing.

Sabrina blinked up at Morgan, water dripping from her dark lashes, pooling in her lap, plastering the satin of her dressing gown to her heaving breasts.

Morgan dismissed her without compunction, bringing Aunt Honora's plump hand to his lips. "Do forgive my impertinence, your grace. I have an elderly dog given to such fits."

"Fits?" Sabrina echoed, her voice as clear and biting as a bell.

He slanted her an unreadable glance over her aunt's hand. "Of wheezing. Fits of wheezing, of course."

"I'm surprised you don't just shoot him."

Aunt Honora's flustered gaze danced between them. Morgan took advantage of her confusion by seizing control of the moment.

"Do allow me."

Whipping a handkerchief from his frock coat with a flourish, he knelt beside the divan and began to mop Sabrina's brow, scrubbing away the thin glaze of ceruse. His fingers caught clumsily in her topknot, dragging free a soft spray of curls.

"Let's loosen this so you can breathe, shall we?" His big, nimble hands danced down the tiny buttons of her bodice, exposing the unpainted swell of her breasts.

Glaring at him, Sabrina shoved his hands away and clutched the dressing gown closed at the throat before he could strip her nude right under the unsuspecting eyes of her aunt and uncle.

His relentless cheer was undiminished as he marched to the window and flung it open. " 'Tis no wonder the lass can't breathe. Being shut up in this stuffy old house would make anyone asthmatic. The only tonic she needs is some fresh air."

"I hate fresh air," Sabrina said weakly, already sensing defeat. "It makes me ill." She felt very ill indeed as Morgan whipped a sinister-looking contraption fashioned of iron and wood into the room. "What on earth is that? A medieval instrument of torture?"

"This, my dear Miss Cameron, is a gift. The very latest invention. It's called a wheelchair. Now you'll no longer have to be carted about like a bundle of firewood."

As it rumbled across the Persian carpet, Sabrina saw that it was indeed a chair fitted with wheels. She became even more alarmed when Morgan pulled away her blanket and folded it neatly in the hard wooden seat.

"A pleasant turn about the garden will do you well," he announced.

She snatched the skirt of her dressing gown over her legs. "Excuse me, sir. I don't know who you think you are—"

Morgan swept her into his arms. The giddy throb of her heart at his effortless motion reminded her exactly who he was. Her husband. At least until the end of the month, when her father would arrive with their annulment document for her to sign.

She resisted the temptation to lay her cheek against his broad chest, to snuggle into his brawny arms—the only place where she might ever feel safe again. Instead, she held herself stiffly while he lowered her into the chair. Sliding his hands beneath her dressing gown, he arranged her legs with jarring familiarity and an even more surprising gentleness. Her breath quickened at the shock of his hands against her bare skin. Their calluses betrayed his gentleman's ruse. She refused to meet his eyes.

As Morgan arranged a pillow behind Sabrina's head, Aunt Honora tsked beneath her breath. "I do believe I should accompany you. It isn't proper to—"

All it took from Morgan was one pointed glance at Enid for the duke to realize that Morgan was the one kink in his plan to salvage his daughter's reputation. Until William could reach Dougal Cameron for advice, they were all no more than pawns in the earl's enigmatic game.

"Nonsense," he reassured his wife. "A breath of fresh air is just what our little buttercup needs."

"Uncle Willie!" Sabrina cried, stung by his betrayal.

Her protests were in vain, for Morgan was already whisking her down the waxed parquet corridor to the French doors that led to the garden.

Sabrina flinched as the dazzling brilliance of the sun struck her full in the face. She squeezed her eyes shut and held her breath, anticipating the pain that would stab through her temples.

A gentle breeze caressed her skin. The sun gilded her face with warmth. She eased her eyes open, blinking rapidly to sift the foreign brightness into patterns she could comprehend. A minty green haze had crept over the clipped arbors and terrace, transforming the tame city courtyard into a wonderland of possibilities. Tender new leaves unfurled on the yew hedges. A spray of baby-pink blossoms climbed an iron trellis. Birds hopped and twittered, plucking at the fallow earth while butterflies flitted in sultry languor from bloom to bloom, their wings a gossamer whir on the jasmine-scented air.

Sabrina took a tentative whiff, perplexed when no sneezes, wheezes, or even so much as a sniffle resulted. She wanted to hate the fresh beginnings spring represented, but she could not stop her gaze from darting after a bee, the lazy beauty of its flight etched with a clarity she'd forgotten in the chill, sleepless nights of winter.

Morgan guided the chair around a chortling fountain, his silence more palpable than the crunch of the chair wheels on the flagstones. It made Sabrina jumpy. It was futile to try to make any sane conversation with him, she thought. He was obviously a madman. He might be strong enough to abduct her, but he could not make her talk.

"You never told me you were an earl," she blurted out.

"You never asked."

"As forthcoming as always, I see. I never could abide your incessant chattering."

"Among other things," he replied.

Sabrina remembered shouting that she couldn't abide his touch, and relived every breath of his humiliation at her hands. Had he come here to return her cruelty? To take his revenge and humiliate her before all of London? A chill caressed her spine. She knew from past experience that Morgan MacDonnell was not an enemy to take lightly.

What more exacting punishment could there be than to be forced to watch as he chose a new wife from one of the simpering society beauties who would probably find it terribly romantic to wed a mysterious Highlander?

Her flippant tone sounded forced, even to her own ears. "So what did you do? Murder the real Earl of Montgarry? Steal his clothes? Ravish his wife?"

Sabrina realized too late that they were teetering on the edge of two shallow steps that led into a graveled terrace. Instead of hurling her down them as she deserved, Morgan caught the arms of the chair and tilted it back, bracing its weight against his hips. The corded muscles of his forearms imprisoned her. With her heart beating madly in her throat, Sabrina gazed upside down at him, held captive by the insolent threat sparkling in his eyes.

"I haven't ravished anyone"—he said softly—"lately."

The potent musk of sandalwood and pine wafted from him, drugging her starved senses. Not since her accident had Sabrina felt so powerless, so utterly at a man's mercy. His smooth-shaven jaw was mere inches from her lips; his heated breath mingled with her sigh.

Her eyes fluttered shut, too cowardly to witness another fall from which she might never recover.

The chair thumped down the two steps, jarring her. Her eyes flew open to discover the pastoral scenery streaming by at an alarming rate.

"I wasn't aware you'd taken up racing," she shouted over the rumble of the wheels. "It's a rather civilized sport, don't you think? Probably pales in comparison to rapine and mayhem."

Morgan's strides showed no sign of slowing. He took a cobbled corner on one wheel, forcing her to dig her whitened fingernails into the chair arms to keep her seat.

Her voice rose, querulous, demanding, laced with the bitterness she'd nursed for months. "If you don't slow down, I'm going to be ill all over those shiny new shoes of yours." She jerked the pillow out from behind her head and waved it at him. "If you've come to finish the job you started, why don't you just put this over my face? It will be much neater."

That did it for Morgan. He jerked to a halt and tilted the chair forward, dumping her into a soft bed of moss and dirt.

Sabrina landed on hands and knees. Her topknot tumbled over her face. She sucked in a breath of pure outrage.

Morgan came around to stand in front of her. "Sorry," he said, his voice silkily unrepentant. "I must have hit a rock."

Sabrina slowly lifted her head, infuriated anew by the arrogance of his splayed legs, the flawless cut of his breeches, the crisp, polished leather of his shoes. She felt trapped in a time lapse, right back where she had started with him, all the years between melting to minutes. How neatly they had fallen back into their childhood roles!

She glowered up at him through her tangled strands of hair and said softly, "You've always liked me on my knees, haven't you, Morgan MacDonnell?"

A mocking fire smoldered in his eyes, invoking the erotic visions she had fought so hard to exorcise. "As I recall, it showed off your talents to their best advantage."

"I hate you!" She struck blindly at his shin only to jam her fingers.

"Good," he replied calmly as she sank back on her knees to suck her throbbing knuckles. "That will make everything much easier."

Folding his arms over his chest, Morgan stared down at his wife, his impassive countenance hiding his roiling emotions. He wanted to hate her. He truly did. In those bleak, brandy-soaked dawns at Castle MacDonnell, when her shrill words of accusation still tore through his aching head, he'd almost convinced himself he did. Even now, if he could have found her pathetic—crouched in the moss, hair tumbled over her face like limp silk, dirt smudging her cheekbone—he might have been able to turn and walk away.

But the feral glitter of her eyes mesmerized him. Defiance was written in every delicate bump of a spine so stiff, he feared a touch might break it. Despite being toppled off her throne, she was still fighting so damned hard to be a princess. Instead of pity, another emotion knotted his gut, as intense and dangerous as a double-edged sword.

It galled him to admit that Dougal had been right. Sabrina needed him, and far more than she might ever know.

He knelt beside her in the dirt. "I didn't come to watch you crawl. I came to watch you walk."

Sabrina shied away from him, flinging her hair out of her face. "Don't be ridiculous. You heard Dr. Montjoy. You of all people should know that I'll never walk again."

Morgan wasted no time arguing with her. He caught her shoulders and dragged her to her feet. When she would have slid down his body like a limp rag, he wrapped an arm around her, braced his hips against a low stone wall, and splayed his legs to bear both their weights.

After spending so many months keeping people at a distance with her childish fits and sarcastic barbs, Sabrina found Morgan's nearness intolerable. The warmth of his big, unyielding male body threatened to melt the wall of ice she'd built around herself. Her hands bit into his forearms, clinging against their will, his irresistible combination of tenderness and strength making them tremble harder than her legs.

She and Morgan were pressed together so intimately that it was as if they were interlocking answers to a question neither of them dared to ask. His breath grazed her temple, stirred her tumbled curls.

She buried her cheek in his cravat. "Damn you," she said in a broken whisper. "What right do you have?"

His voice was as implacable as his grip. "Every right. I'm your husband."

"Not for much longer," she dared to say.

"That depends on you."

Her breath caught as she was flooded by a blinding mixture of fear and hope. "What do you mean?"

He captured her chin between his thumb and forefinger and tilted her face to his. "If you don't allow me to call on you in the next four weeks, I won't give you your precious annulment. I'll knock on the door of every magistrate between London and the Highlands and tell them all you willingly spread your pretty Cameron legs for a wretch like me. Then you'll be forced to divorce and your father's noble name will be in ruins."

The cold, merciless beauty of his face held her transfixed. "Why?" she breathed. "Why are you doing this to me? Is this your idea of revenge?"

For a brief instant a conflict raged in Morgan's eyes. Then his lids swept down, veiling them so effectively that Sabrina might have imagined it. He swung her around and set her neatly on the wall, dusting off his hands as if she had sullied them.

A brittle smile curved his lips. "Believe what you like. Perhaps I want revenge. Perhaps I just want you off my conscience."

"Don't be ridiculous," she said, curling her fingers around the smooth granite. "Everyone knows MacDonnells have no consciences."

He straightened his cravat and headed down the path toward the garden gate. "I shall call tomorrow at two. If you don't wish me to introduce myself as your long-lost husband, I suggest you smooth my way with your aunt and uncle. Good day, *Miss* Cameron."

"And if I help appease your guilty conscience, what do I have to gain?" she called after him.

"Freedom," he tossed over his shoulder. "The day you walk will be the day you'll be free to walk out of my life forever."

The garden gate slammed with a clang.

Sabrina exhaled sharply, realizing he'd left her perched on the stone wall as helpless as a garden worm. The terrace was hidden from the house by a narrow row of bay trees. The only sounds that drifted to her ears were the cheerful tinkle of a fountain and the sated drone of a bumblebee staggering drunkenly from bloom to bloom. The wheelchair sat a few steps away, sleek wood and polished iron, mocking and unattainable.

She wasted no time glaring at her feckless limbs. Using her hands to balance herself on the edge of the wall, she arched her legs, stretching until her toes sank into the cool earth. Instead of the agony she expected, she felt only a dull ache. Muttering an oath under her breath, she dared to shift a fraction of her weight.

Her legs sagged. She slid down the wall, landing on her rear with a jarring thump.

Her hands fisted in the dirt. Rage roared through her, glorious and cleansing, making her feel alive for the first time in months. Her mewling tempers were no longer enough to satisfy. She would find no more contentment in railing at fate. Now her fury had a target. A golden-haired, green-eyed smirking giant of a target.

Throwing back her head to the dazzling azure of the sky, she began to bellow for help in a voice the Belmont servants would later swear was heard halfway to Edinburgh.

Chapter Twenty-seven

The mantel clock chimed twice. Sabrina started violently, earning her a perplexed look from both Enid and her aunt. Neither of them could understand why she insisted on sitting in her new wheelchair when any one of the upholstered chairs in the salon would have been more comfortable.

Oblivious of their concern, Sabrina turned the page. She'd been reduced to reading one of Enid's lurid pamphlets and was less than fascinated to learn that Mrs. Mary Toft's prolific production of rabbits had ceased after being threatened with a gruesome female surgery by the most notorious male midwife in London. A prison sentence for Mrs. Toft was forthcoming.

The clock ticked away the minutes. Sabrina peeked at her reflection in the polished base of the candelabrum sitting on the venetian table at her elbow. Under pretext of scratching her ear, she eased a tendril loose from her stern topknot and unclenched her jaw, making a conscious effort to soften her expression.

A stranger stared back at her. A woman, shy, uncertain, lips parted in trembling awareness of her own vulnerability. She bore no resemblance to the brittle creature Sabrina had come to expect.

Discomfited by the realization, she smoothed the skirts of her pale jade dressing gown. It was one of her prettiest, but she hadn't worn it for Morgan, she assured herself. He probably wasn't even coming. He'd only been teasing her as he'd always done. He was as insufferable a man as he'd been a boy.

Enid interrupted the serene nip and tuck of her knitting. "Shall I read to you, cousin?"

"No, thank you," Sabrina replied absently. "Why should I be read to when I have two perfectly good eyes?"

Enid and the duchess exchanged another puzzled glance.

A maid tiptoed into the salon. She offered Sabrina afternoon chocolate from a silver tray, her chapped hands trembling as if she expected to have the steaming liquid dumped over her head. As soon as Sabrina took the porcelain cup, the servant crept toward the door.

"Beatrice."

The maid cringed to a halt. Two bright spots of color appeared on her dumpling cheeks. "Aye, miss?"

Sabrina smiled at her. "It's quite good. Thank you."

Bea gaped at the young miss, amazed at her transformation. Somehow she'd always thought of the master's niece as sallow and plain. But she was actually pretty without her lips puckered as if she'd been sucking lemons. Bobbing a hasty curtsy, Bea rushed out, eager to share her discovery with the other servants.

Laying the cup aside, Sabrina licked a chocolate mustache from her upper lip like a nervous cat. The hands of the clock swept away the precious minutes until she felt her heart must surely be beating to its rhythm. She feared the hollow chime that would signal the half hour might stop it altogether.

A masculine voice reverberated in the corridor, its

rich tones speeding Sabrina's heart anew. She dropped the pamphlet, then snatched it back up, studying its pages without realizing it was upside down. She peeped over the top of it as Uncle Willie escorted Morgan into the salon, slapping his broad back as if they'd been friends for years. Sabrina suppressed a shiver, fearing their amity did not bode well for her.

Morgan once again played the solicitous gentleman with flair. He fawned over Aunt Honora until her ringlets were dancing with delight and complimented Enid on the skill of her knitting. When he swung his smug charm toward her, Sabrina ducked behind the pamphlet, wishing herself invisible.

He bent to bring her hand to his lips. The pamphlet fluttered to the carpet.

He brushed his lips over her knuckles, maddening her with a taunting flick of his tongue invisible to the others. The disappointment that clouded his sunny expression would have wrung tears from a rock.

"Why, Miss Cameron, I'm afraid I've been remiss. I should have told you to dress. We're going out today."

Sabrina stiffened, beset by fresh images of disaster. Pointing fingers. Mocking glances. Sly whispers. *Why would a magnificent man like Montgarry dance attendance on a cripple?*

"Out," she echoed dumbly, as if he'd suggested they charter a carriage and fly to the moon. "I don't go out."

"You do now." His smile was so pleasant and his eyes so completely devoid of patience that Sabrina could already see her mangled body lying in a London ditch. "I shall wait while you dress." Bracing his hands on the arms of the chair, he leaned forward and whispered, "Unless, of course, you'd prefer I assist you."

His words invoked visions of blinding clarity: sunbrowned hands unlacing her corset to reveal the pale, tender skin of her back; petticoats collapsing in a deflated heap; heated lips brushing her thigh as deft fingers peeled away her lacy garters. Sabrina struggled to catch her breath, afraid to examine why they were all visions of disrobing, not dressing.

Aunt Honora's trill broke his spell. ". . . quite improper without a chaperone."

Morgan straightened, his smile as smooth as a swallow of fine brandy. "Nonsense. I'm sure Lady MacLeod would be more than happy to accompany us. As a matron and widow, her reputation should be beyond reproach."

Uncle Willie's cheek twitched with the nervous tic he was developing when faced with Morgan's skewed but irrefutable logic. "Yes, well, my man, I suppose if you say so . . ."

In an uncharacteristic fit of self-preservation, Enid took charge of the situation. Casting aside her knitting, she swept across the salon and began to roll Sabrina's chair toward the door. "If the earl will be kind enough to wait for us, I shall help my cousin dress."

They all ignored Sabrina's plaintive wail of "But I don't want to go with him. He's a lunatic!"

Sabrina endured Enid's fussing in sullen silence. Using every maternal skill at her disposal, Enid gowned, coiffed, and fluffed Sabrina, even daring to press a kiss to her taut cheek before delivering her into the hands of the enemy.

"Judas," Sabrina hissed as Morgan rolled the chair toward the side door being thrown open by a beaming footman.

Sabrina had her revenge when they emerged into the bright sunlight and Enid came face-to-face with a liveried and bewigged Ranald. It had obviously never occurred to Enid that Morgan would forgive a crime as heinous as Ranald's and actually allow the scoundrel to accompany him out of the Highlands.

She turned white, then bright pink. Ranald gaped at her rounded stomach in open astonishment.

Morgan's amused murmur underscored their shock. "I didn't tell him he was going to be a da. I thought he'd rather hear it from you."

Sabrina allowed herself a waspish grin, but her mean satisfaction was short-lived. Morgan snatched her out of the chair, holding her as tightly as if he feared she would bolt, all the while knowing she couldn't. Their noses brushed as he settled her on the leather seat.

"Bully," she muttered.

"Brat," he countered.

Enid tilted her own nose skyward and swept in after Sabrina while Morgan hooked the cumbersome chair on the back of the carriage. He climbed inside, folding his imposing form on the opposite seat with lazy grace.

"Why don't you just hang a placard on the door?" Sabrina suggested as the vehicle rolled into motion. "A HALFPENNY TO SEE THE FREAK. They might even publish a pamphlet on me."

"Don't be ridiculous." His insolent gaze raked her from the dangling lappets of her cap to the pointed toes of the slippers peeping out from beneath her flounced underskirt. "You're worth at least tuppence."

Sabrina folded her gloved hands in her lap, trapped into uneasy silence by the glittering challenge of his eyes. As they rounded a corner, Ranald's face popped up at the carriage window. Enid snapped down the embroidered shade.

All of their gazes shifted upward at the great noise overhead as if a giant spider were clambering over the roof. Ranald's face appeared at the opposite window, his nose pressed flat against the glass. Enid ducked behind her fan.

The carriage rolled to a stop. Even in the closed vehicle the air was permeated by the tangy smell of the river. The chatter and bustle of a crowded thoroughfare surrounded them. Sabrina craned her neck to find herself staring up at the forbidding edifice of the Tower of London.

"How fitting," she said dryly. "Puts one in mind of Castle MacDonnell, although I dare say it's a trifle cozier."

"Would you have preferred Bedlam?"

"I would have preferred *bed*. My *own* bed at my uncle's house."

He slanted her a wicked grin. "A pity you didn't tell me sooner. It could have been arranged."

Sabrina's fists clenched. The wretch was even more infuriating than she remembered.

She held herself rigid as Morgan climbed out of the carriage and lifted the chair down to the stone bridge built over the ancient moat. Disdaining Ranald's hand, Enid clambered down after him, her pretense of indifference wearing thin beneath Ranald's pleading gaze. She folded her plump hands over her stomach, looking acutely miserable.

But Morgan left Sabrina little time to brood on her cousin's unhappiness. As he lifted her gently to the chair, she gripped his forearms, her nerves strumming a discordant tune. People streamed around them. Laughing. Gawking. Whispering. Just as she had feared they would.

A red-haired little boy tugged his haggard mother to a halt and pointed. "Look, Ma, there's somethin' a matter wi' the pretty lady."

Sabrina bowed her head. At least children had the decency not to whisper.

Morgan saw the color breach Sabrina's cheekbones as the careless stares of the crowd pierced her armor of defensiveness.

He tucked the lap rug around her legs, his voice resonant enough to be heard even over the curious murmurs of the crowd. "Will that be to your liking, your highness?"

Sabrina's head flew up. A tendril of genuine hatred curled from her heart. How dare he mock her now! But as she searched his eyes for treachery, all she saw was their sunlit flame burning steady and bright. It was a sight she had long ago forgotten—kindness without pity, compassion without the cloying burden of sympathy. For the first time she felt the joke was not on her, but between them.

The crowd was now staring with open awe and respect, speculating aloud on whether she might be foreign royalty come to visit their beloved Tower. An elderly gentleman paused to explain that the odd wheeled conveyance was probably a variation of the more common sedan chair borne by two footmen.

Words of gratitude caught in Sabrina's throat. All she could manage was a regal smile for Morgan and an imperious wave toward the gate.

Ranald's face fell when Morgan skirted the armory, where they might have examined the sword that cleaved off Anne Boleyn's head. Enid looked crestfallen when he disdained the Jewel Office, where they could have beheld the shimmering glory of the imperial crown. But as he rolled the chair into a nearly deserted yard off the western entrance, where each stone archway was fitted with an iron lattice, Sabrina knew it had been his destination from the beginning.

Morgan hadn't brought her to see weapons or treasures. He'd brought her to the Tower menagerie to watch the white bear shambling around his den, to laugh at the monkeys scampering free over the courtyard, to marvel at the lion, whose haughty stare was ruined by a yawn of immense proportions. Morgan's delight at seeing such creatures for the first time was infectious. Sabrina caught herself watching his face more than the animals, starved for a glimpse of that rare genuine smile.

As Morgan fed a handful of nuts to a raccoon, Sabrina felt a prickle of unease at her nape. The scarlet-garbed keeper was dozing by the gate. Ranald and Enid stood a few feet away, casting shy glances at each other. The shadowed archways revealed nothing. She shrugged the feeling away. It had been so long since she'd been out among people that she was given to fancy. It was probably one of the onlookers from outside stealing a peek at the mysterious "royalty."

She felt a shy tug on her skirt and looked down to discover a tiny monkey. She was so captivated with the little fellow that she didn't see Morgan give Ranald a signal behind her back.

Ignoring her sputtered protests, Ranald captured Enid with one arm and the bored keeper with the other, leading them toward the far end of the yard. Enid's dismay turned to fascination as the keeper began to regale them with the tale of an unfortunate viscount who had wandered too close to the lion's cage.

"Two fingers?" she echoed in delighted horror. "Did the lion gobble them up or spit them out?"

Morgan waited until they were out of sight before dropping to one knee at Sabrina's feet.

Sabrina started violently as a pair of warm masculine hands slid beneath her skirt. "What do you think you're doing?"

"Your legs have just been sitting for months. We've got to get the blood stirring again."

Sabrina gazed at his inclined head as his powerful hands massaged her calves, his fingers firm and sinuous against the silk of her stockings. A stubborn strand of hair had escaped his queue. She resisted the urge to brush it back, to test its tensile strength between her fingertips. His deft ministrations were certainly effective. Blood was pounding in her heart, thrumming through her ears, melting through all the sly, greedy pathways of her body.

Everywhere but her legs.

"You're wasting your time," she snapped. "I cannot walk."

Morgan tipped his head back to meet her gaze. "Are you afraid of walking, lass? Or afraid of falling?"

As Sabrina stared into the quicksilver depths of his eyes, she feared she was already falling. There was still no trace of pity in them, nothing to feed the mewling monster that had lodged itself in her soul.

The pads of his fingers fanned in a hypnotic stroke against the back of her calf, glided over the racing pulse behind her knee, wandering up until they caught between the edge of her garter, brushed like feathers against the naked skin above. Morgan's breathing lost its rhythm. The knowing chatter of the monkeys broke their reverie.

He snatched his hands down and began to rub

her calves, chafing her flesh so briskly that a helpless "Oh!" escaped her.

He shot her a guilty look. "Did I hurt you?"

No, but you will. Biting her lower lip, she shook her head.

Without bothering to explain what he planned, he circled behind the chair, bracing his hands beneath her arms, and lifted her. She dangled in the air like an expensive doll. He eased the chair away with one foot, then lowered her until her slippers touched the stones.

Then he let her go.

Sabrina clenched her fists, standing but refusing to attempt so much as a step. "I shan't play your silly game."

Morgan gave her a little push. She listed forward like an unbalanced bowling pin. He caught her by the starched bow of her gown and set her upright again.

"There we go. That's a good lass. One step is all I ask for today. Let's try it again, shall we?"

She pinched her lips in a mutinous line and locked her knees. He gave her another gentle shove. This time he wasn't quite quick enough to catch her. She toppled forward, forced to break her fall with her gloved hands.

Morgan's smug silence echoed louder than the amused howls of the monkeys.

As Sabrina lay there, studying the stones beneath her hands, she said in a small, tight voice, "They really ought to sweep more often. The dirt is atrocious."

In the following week Sabrina was to become acquainted with every inch of flooring in London. The smooth, cool expanse of marble at Westminster Abbey, the luxuriant Persian rugs of the shops on Ludgate Hill, the mosaic tiles at the Academy of Music whose pattern she would later trace in expert detail on a stray scrap of her aunt's stationery. Only the thick grass of the newly restored pleasure garden at Vauxhall afforded her aching rump any relief.

And always above her, behind her, surrounding

her—Morgan, pine and sandalwood, persistent, yet distant, his manic good cheer in the face of her failed attempts to walk making her want to scream.

Morgan MacDonnell was twice the monster the first Earl of Montgarry had been. Halbert only took his victim's skin; Morgan wiggled beneath it with diabolical skill. He became her own green-eyed Satan wrapped in finely tailored knee breeches and lace-edged cravats. He taunted her, prodded her, rolled her through a genteel hell of his own devising.

This was the Morgan she remembered from childhood—stubborn, crafty, mischievous, his eyes never losing their amused glitter at her expense. His humor was brittle, his sarcastic ripostes leaving scratches so invisible, she never had the solace of crawling off to lick them. His mocking smile haunted her dreams.

She despised him.

She loathed him.

She lived for the moment when he would stroll through the door of her uncle's town house and start her heart thundering again.

She was no longer allowed to languish on the divan in her dressing gown. She was expected to sit, fully dressed, spine rigid and muscles throbbing, on the hard wooden seat of the wheelchair. No matter how horrid, surely not even Halbert could have devised such a torture for his hapless enemies.

Morgan called each afternoon at two without fail, courting her aunt's and uncle's goodwill, charming a smile from Enid, infuriating Philip Markham, whose own calls were thwarted when he arrived only to discover Lady MacLeod chaperoning her cousin and the enigmatic earl on some new adventure.

London society buzzed with gossip about Morgan's slavish attentions to her. He escorted her to card parties and afternoon theatricals. At the balls they attended, he remained steadfast at her side and was never caught stealing so much as a yearning glance at the dancers. His tender benevolence toward one as unfortunate as herself elicited adoration from the women, admiration from the men, and hissed retorts from Sabrina.

More than once when they were out, Sabrina felt again that wary prickle at the back of her neck. She would turn only to find nothing more than a fleeting shadow, an illusion of darkness in the bright spring sun.

One afternoon as Morgan's carriage rounded a curve, she saw a bearded man and a veiled woman standing on the teeming corner. A startled cry welled in her throat, but by the time she could turn around, they had been swallowed by the crowd. Morgan simply lifted an eyebrow as if to comment upon her sanity. She settled back in the seat, shaken, and wondered if she wasn't more homesick than she realized.

She still could not fathom why Morgan chose such public liaisons. By the end of the second week they'd visited every amusement in London save for a public hanging and Bedlam. Surely it couldn't be scandal that concerned him, she thought. Any man who had grown up under the cloud of notoriety cast by Clan MacDonnell probably didn't give a fig about what others thought of him. Besides, it was her reputation at stake, not his.

Between Morgan's visits, Sabrina fumed, too obsessed with her new tormentor to waste her malice on the servants. She began to massage her legs each morning upon arising, rubbing them until the blood rushed like spring sap through her veins. She attempted her own simple steps in the privacy of her bedroom. The servants soon learned to ignore the odd thumps, crashes, and oaths that came from behind her locked door at all hours of the night as she met with no success.

By the beginning of the third week, Sabrina was starting to panic.

Morgan simply wouldn't go away. No matter how nasty her temper, how acid her wit, he kept popping up on the doorstep. He shrugged away insults that would have sent the servants into tearful fits.

In the bleak months since the accident, she'd managed to drive a wedge between herself and everyone she had ever loved—Enid, her brothers, even her parents. But Morgan stood immovable in her path, six feet three inches of taunting male, giving off a flame so volatile, she feared it might thaw even her frozen heart.

She lay in her cold bed one night, heart pounding, body seized with trembling at the thought of him.

Her hands clenched into fists. She had failed once to drive him away, but now she'd had months to practice her art. All it would take was a few well-placed digs, a dagger between the ribs in a vulnerable spot.

Her plan should have given her some satisfaction. Instead, she pulled the quilts up over her head, burrowing like a small, frightened animal into a darkness of her own making.

"But, miss, her grace asked me to tell you—" The maid slammed the door just as the vase crashed into it and shattered.

Sabrina heard the slap-slap of fleeing footsteps. She had been terrorizing the servants all day, knowing word of it would reach Morgan before the night was done.

She swung back to the mirror, the first weapon in her rebellion against him. She had painted her skin stark white, emphasizing the hollows beneath her cheekbones and the rouged bow of her lips. Her hair was drawn up so tightly that it gave her eyes an exotic slant. A frivolous scrap of eyelet crowned her topknot. Frothy lappets trailed from it like gossamer cobwebs. She knew very well that her filmy white dressing gown edged in flounces of lace made her look frail and pitiable, as fragile as the Meissen vase she'd just destroyed.

She saw her future in the flat blue eyes of the woman in the mirror. A future without Morgan. A future without hope. A future spent wrapped in this shroud of girlish lace, her hands withered, her skin shriveled over sunken bones. The neighbors would speak of her in whispers. *That eccentric maiden niece of the old duke's. Came to spend the spring and never left.*

For she could never again return to the Highlands. Would never even dare to dream of the mist hanging low over the heathered hills, the cascade of a waterfall tumbling through a lush glen, the heady scent of wild roses clawing their way up a barren hill.

The door behind her inched open a crack. Stefan eased his head in, obviously prepared to snatch it back in the event of flying pottery. "Mama sent me to fetch you. Are you ready, coz?"

"Aye," she said softly to her reflection. "As ready as I'll ever be."

Sabrina reclined on the plush divan, propped up by a mountain of fluffy pillows. A champagne glass dangled from her pink-tipped fingers. She had charmed the champagne from one of the guests, since the petrified servants had taken to giving her a wide berth. She doubted if any of them would have offered her a glass of water had she plucked a candle from one of the standing candelabrum and set herself afire.

She scanned the milling crowd. Still no sign of Morgan. Aunt Honora was fluttering about, the dim light giving her the appearance of a frazzled angel. She clapped her plump hands for all to take their seats, as excited as a child over her private theatrical.

Sabrina suppressed a groan as a slender man garbed in alternating patches of white, red, and green took the stage. She had never cared for pantomime and was only too familiar with the oft-told comedy of Harlequin and his shrewish wife, Columbine. Brian and Alex had acted it out for her birthday last year. Her chief amusement had been derived from how ridiculous Alex's hairy knees had looked peeping out from under one of her mother's petticoats. She felt a pang of nostalgia at the memory.

A stir by the door caught her attention. Without realizing it, Sabrina abandoned her languishing position and craned her neck. A blade of raw yearning stabbed through her as Morgan worked his way through the crowd, flashing his devastating smile like a weapon. The guests whispered behind their fans and snuffboxes, more entranced by the imposing earl than by the story unfolding on the stage. Sabrina wondered if he realized how effective his late entrances were. Or how taxing on her poor heart.

As he nodded his greetings, his hair gleamed gold in the candlelight. Knowing she might never have another chance, Sabrina drank in the sight of him. When he had first arrived in London, she had believed the tailored clothes had given him his confidence. But now she realized he had always had the grace and bearing of a king. Not even a tattered plaid and bare feet had been able to hide it. She bowed her head, steeling herself against the emotions welling in her throat.

When she looked up, Morgan had been brought to a halt by a frowning footman. The man's nervous gaze darted toward the divan. Sabrina collapsed against the pillows, drawing the back of her hand across her brow in a gesture of abject frailty.

She was rewarded by the briefest slip of Morgan's mask of civility. His jaw clenched in the brooding scowl she remembered so well. But he recovered quickly, giving the footman an encouraging wink and winding his way toward the divan.

Ignoring the chair beside it, he sank down at the foot of the narrow couch, narrowly missing Sabrina's toes.

She jerked them out of harm's way and sneezed. Dabbing at her eyes with a lace handkerchief, she said, "I do believe your shaving soap is vexing me, sir."

"It could be the pillows. Perhaps you sucked a feather up your nose."

Morgan stared fixedly at the stage, fighting the urge to give Sabrina a blast of his temper that would scatter feathers from London to Glasgow. A woman seated in front of them swiveled her long neck and peered over her fan, reminding Morgan of why he had chosen a public forum for their battles. He did not trust himself alone with Sabrina. He was afraid of giving in to his guilt, of coddling her as all the rest had done.

He was even more afraid of giving in to his desire,

of surrendering to the dangerous temptation to still her shrewish tongue with a thrust and parry of his own.

That temptation was even stronger with her wrapped in a gauzy confection more suited for trysting with lovers in her bedchamber. The lush scent of lilacs drifted from her skin, making a mockery of the clean, sharp roses he remembered. He wanted to lay her back on that divan in front of them all, rake his fingers through that silly topknot, part her creamy thighs and bury himself deep . . .

The audience roared as a leering Harlequin tossed a shrieking Columbine over his shoulder. Morgan couldn't say he blamed the man. He was beginning to understand the terrible temptation of using brute strength to master a woman against her will. Shaken, he clenched his fists, blinded to the antics on the stage by a rush of new fury and old shame.

Sabrina's foot lashed out, striking his hip. "Scoot over! I can't see. You're blocking the stage."

A loud "shush!" came from the row where Aunt Honora was seated. Several more necks craned in their direction. Harlequin paused in his silent tirade to shoot them an annoyed look.

Morgan reached behind him and caught her foot. His thumb played over its sensitive contours with ruthless skill. "A bit stronger today, aren't we, dear?"

Her foot immediately went limp in his grasp. "It was probably just a spasm. They're quite painful, you know."

Instead of releasing her foot, Morgan pressed his thumb deeply into the valley between its pads, probing with a suggestive rhythm that quickened Sabrina's breathing. He was so attuned to her that he could feel it like a whisper against his back.

Her foot came to life again. She jerked it away from him.

"Your spasms seem to be worsening," he said. "Perhaps it's not too late to reconsider amputation."

Hoping to buy some time to compose herself, Sabrina said, "My throat is sore. Would you fetch me some champagne, please?"

But a lazy crook of one of Morgan's fingers brought a footman scurrying over. "The lady would like some champagne."

With obvious trepidation the footman proffered a glass to Sabrina, his hand shaking so hard that the golden liquid sloshed over the rim into her lap.

"You clumsy wretch!" She dabbed the stain with her handkerchief. "My uncle should fire the lot of you."

Still staring at the stage, Morgan shot out one laconic word. "Apologize."

"I'm sorry," the footman blurted out.

"Not you. Her."

"Her?"

"Me?" Sabrina said in unison. "I should think not!"

"You were insufferably rude to the man. Now, apologize."

"Pardon me, my lord," Sabrina said with scathing sarcasm. "I'd forgotten the MacDonnells were the last bastion of good manners in the Highlands. If he'd have spilled champagne on you, you'd have probably just whipped out a pistol and shot him."

As the confrontation on the divan showed signs of escalating into full-scale warfare, the terrified footman hastened away.

Morgan swung around to face her. Sabrina recoiled from his thunderous expression. Even Harlequin and Columbine paused to gape as Morgan's voice rose to a roar.

"I won't tolerate your bloody tantrums!" Fury broadened his accent, sending the r's rolling and the g's flying. "Puir wee lass! Puir pathetic princess! It was easy enough to play angel of the manor when everythin' you'd ever wanted was shoved into your greedy wee hands, wasn't it?"

"Not everything," she whispered, but he did not hear her.

"But one knock to your precious Cameron crown and you turn into a whinin', snivelin' brat. Showed your colors true enough, didn't you?" He leaned forward. She pressed herself into the pillows, but there was no escaping his righteous wrath. His voice softened, audible only to her. A smile of savage good humor lit his eyes. "If I'd have known you were goin' to be such a bitch about survivin', I'd have shot *you* instead of Pookah."

Sabrina's hand crossed his face with a solid crack. The crowd gasped, totally aghast. Morgan didn't even flinch. He was as immovable as a rock. Sabrina's desperation grew.

She slapped him again, hard enough to leave the mark of her hand on his cheek. He just stared down at her, this man who could crush her skull between his bare hands, the anger in his eyes replaced by a quiet pain that had nothing to do with her blow. His face was so beautiful, so resolute—like an angel hewn of marble.

Its chiseled planes swam before her. Warm tears swelled in her eyes. She was terrified they would spill down her cheeks and she would cry before them all.

The words tore from her raw throat, resounding shrilly through the silent room. "Why won't you just let me be? What's wrong with you? Aren't you man enough for a real woman?"

Morgan flinched then, almost imperceptibly, the sun-crinkled lines around his eyes betraying him. He straightened slowly, as if a great weight rested on his shoulders, and Sabrina knew she had finally succeeded in committing an unpardonable sin. She had humiliated him publicly, and to a MacDonnell there was no worse affront.

His eyes were as distant as the Highland mists she would never see again. He bowed from the waist, the restrained dignity of the gesture damning them both. "My apologies if I offended you. Good evening, Miss Cameron."

As he wound his way stiffly through the crowd, Sabrina knew he had not meant to say good evening, but good-bye.

Chapter Twenty-eight

Rain pattered on the flagstones outside Sabrina's window, its rhythm both melancholy and soothing. It struck the leaded glass of the terrace doors and ran down the panes in wavy rivulets, blurring the garden beyond to bearable shades.

A timid knock sounded on the door.

Without shifting in the wheelchair, Sabrina said, "Come in."

The door swung open behind her. "I brought you some tea, miss. Cook thought you might enjoy some fresh scones. Bought the apples from a street vendor with her own wages, she did."

Sabrina summoned up a smile as Bea's freckled visage bobbed into view. "Why, thank you, Beatrice. Tell Cook I'm sure they'll be wonderful."

Bea set the tray on the tea table at Sabrina's elbow, then stood, wringing her apron and shifting from foot to foot.

"Is there something else, Beatrice?"

Bea was staring at the worn Bible resting beneath Sabrina's folded hands. It had been sitting on her lap for three days, but no one had ever seen her open it. "I was just wondering if I might bring you another book to read. Or perhaps a bit of embroidery to lift your spirits."

Sabrina shook her head, resuming her dreamy perusal of the rain-drenched garden. "No, thank you. But it's very kind of you to ask."

Still Bea hovered behind her. "Shall I comb your hair for you, miss?" The touch of her fingers was feather-light in the thick mass that rippled past Sabrina's shoulders. "I never would have guessed there was so much of it." She snatched her hand back as if realizing she'd been too familiar.

But instead of a rebuke, Sabrina gave her another gentle smile. "I can comb it myself, but thank you for asking."

Bea sighed, forced to content herself with tucking the eiderdown quilt tighter around Sabrina's legs. "I'll send Teddy up with some wood for a fire. We don't want you catching a chill in the damp. Would you like me to move you away from the door? There might be drafts."

Sabrina shook her head, the motion as unfocused as a sleepwalker's. She heard Bea pause to pat a pillow and toss a stray stocking over a chair back. Sabrina could see the maid's reflection in the window; her homely face was screwed tight with concern.

"If there's anything you want, miss—anything at all—you'll ring for me, won't you?"

Sabrina nodded. The door had already closed behind the servant when Sabrina whispered, "Don't worry, Bea. I'm a Cameron. We always get what we want."

She leaned her head against the chair back and closed her eyes, even the dismal light beyond the window too bright to bear.

• • •

Bea entered the kitchen two hours later, carrying the untouched tea tray.

She shook her head sadly, dimming Cook's expectant expression. "Not a drop. Nor did she eat so much as a crumb."

Cook sank down heavily on a stool, poking her finger into one of the cold, gummy scones. "If someone had told me a week ago that I'd be trying to tempt the young miss's appetite with anything more than arsenic, I'd have thought them batty." Her face cheered. "What if I fix her up a nice poultice for her chest?"

Bea shook her head. "She hadn't any bodily complaints. She hadn't any complaints at all. I've never heard so many thank-yous and if you please, ma'ams in all my life. She'd have probably served me the tea if I had asked her to."

Cook rested her dimpled chin on her palm. The two women sat in glum silence, both surprised to realize they preferred the challenge of Sabrina's tantrums to her painful politeness. The last light had gone out of the young miss's eyes, leaving them as vacant as an extinguished candle. She had abandoned her elaborate dressing gowns and cashmere shawls for a plain lawn nightdress and a faded eiderdown quilt. She wore her hair loose around her shoulders or in two simple plaits like a child.

She refused to leave her bedroom, sitting in that uncomfortable wheelchair for hours on end, staring out the casement windows into the garden as if waiting for something that would never come. Or someone.

Thumps and curses no longer resounded from her room at night. There was nothing but that same empty silence.

Cook shook her head woefully. "If I didn't know better, I'd swear the young miss was suffering from a broken heart."

Bea took a sip of Sabrina's cold tea, then grimaced. "A week ago I'd have sworn she had no heart."

Cook topped off the tea with a splash of gin from a bottle marked *vanilla*. "Well, as my old ma used to say, God rest her dear soul, whatever don't kill you will probably cure you."

Bea lifted the cup. "I'll drink to that."

They clinked the bottle and cup together in a gesture that was as much prayer as toast.

Someone was tugging the sleeve of her nightdress.

Sabrina opened her eyes, moving from sleep to wakefulness with unnatural ease. There seemed to be very little difference between the two these days. Both were colored in comforting shades of gray. She gazed up at the wooden canopy without blinking, weighed down by a sense of loss so keen and overwhelming, it lingered in her mouth like a bitter aftertaste.

"Sabrina, oh, please wake up!"

She turned her head to find Enid crouched by the bed. Her cousin's nightdress was sodden with rain. She wore slippers encrusted with goo that looked suspiciously like garden mud. Lank ringlets tangled around her face. But her cheeks were rosy and her eyes sparkled with such life that Sabrina wanted to shield her face from their brightness.

"You'd best get out of those wet things," she said. "You don't want the baby taking a chill."

"Later. But right now I need your help. It's Ranald."

Sabrina ruthlessly quenched the hope that leapt in her throat. "Ranald? I would have thought he'd gone back to the Highlands by now."

"So would I." A dizzy laugh escaped her cousin. "But he hasn't. He refused to leave until he could see me one more time. He wants to discuss our future."

Sabrina frowned, the future a concept so foreign, it seemed beyond understanding. For her, there was only the passage of minutes that blended seamlessly into hours.

Enid clutched her arm, her words tumbling out in a frantic litany. "Philip has invited me to the masked ridotto at Vauxhall tomorrow night. But it's Ranald I plan to meet, since it's a masked ball and he can move freely among the guests. But Mama refuses to let me go unless you promise to accompany me. She seems to think I have a way of getting into scrapes when I go off by myself."

Sabrina's gaze slid down to Enid's rather prominent stomach. How much more of a scrape could Enid get into? She suspected her aunt's insistence that she accompany Enid had more to do with getting herself out of her bedroom. And out of the house. She was left with only one question.

"Will he be there?"

Enid bowed her head. Firelight sifted through her pale hair, painting it gold. "No. He's making ready for their journey home."

Home, Sabrina thought. Morgan's feet propped on the hearth. A verdant flush of green creeping over the glens. Melted snow sluicing down the mountainside in a silvery cascade. Home, where he would be free of her at last. It was only a pity she would never be free of him. Not even the documents her father was bringing for her signature at the end of the week would set her free.

Enid's expression was more expectant than her rounded belly. "Please say you'll come."

Sabrina remembered kneeling at Enid's bedside at Castle MacDonnell, begging her to leave the warm cocoon of Ranald's arms and brave the snowy night. She had been running from Morgan that night too. But he had been fool enough to come after her. He would not make the same mistake again.

Summoning up a smile, she stroked Enid's hair, remembering all the sacrifices her cousin had made for her. "Of course I'll come. Perhaps it will give me a chance to make amends for being such a selfish beast." She threw back the blankets in invitation. "Now, climb in here before that babe of yours starts to sneeze."

Kicking off her muddy slippers, Enid obeyed, bounding into the bed with a cheerful force that set the bed frame rocking.

• • •

The following evening, Sabrina was already regretting her decision as Philip rolled her chair to a deserted spot against the wall of the assembly room where the ridotto was being held. Curious stares pierced her skin like tiny darts. It was her first public appearance since her row with Morgan had scandalized society. Hoping to avoid notice, she had chosen a simple white gown and dressed her hair in a coronet of braids.

Perhaps she should have worn a mask as well, she thought, then smiled ruefully to realize that would have made her no less recognizable. None of the other guests were being wheeled in like tea services.

Outside, the gentle spring rain had ceased, but a low growl of thunder boded another storm. Lamps festooned along the walls punctured the gloom of the long, high-ceilinged room, giving the masked guests a mysterious air.

Philip parked the chair with a flourish. He thrust his face into hers, enunciating each word with painstaking care, as if her infirmity had rendered her both deaf and daft. "There now, Miss Cameron, are you quite comfortable? I can't help but feel responsible for you. After Enid and I are wed, I do hope you'll come to think of me as a brother."

Enid mercifully saved her from replying by appearing at his elbow with a crystal cup of punch and a napkin piled with sweetcakes. She was lifting a cake to her lips when Philip plucked it away.

He favored her with a patronizing smile. "I do believe that will be quite enough, dear. You do want to be able to fit into that beautiful wedding gown after the little one is born."

Enid's eyes blazed behind her mask, but at that moment the door at the far end of the room flew open, letting in a gust of wind and the piquant scent of approaching rain.

With a dismayed gasp Sabrina dropped her handkerchief. "Oh, dear! I'll never be able to reach it. Philip, if you would be so kind . . ."

Philip bent to retrieve the scrap of linen. By the time he straightened, Enid was gone, shooed by

Sabrina toward the dark-eyed, devilishly handsome masked stranger standing in the doorway.

"Well, I do say," Philip said, handing her the handkerchief. "Where the devil did she go?" He swiveled his thin neck to scan the milling crowd, his pinched features so crestfallen that Sabrina felt a moment's pity for him.

But that didn't stop her from pointing out an overweight girl in a feathered mask identical to Enid's. "Why, there she is! If you hurry, you might be able to catch her before the first dance."

He jerked his coat free of invisible wrinkles and darted after the girl. Sabrina sighed with relief when no one rushed over to take his place. She sensed a sly fear in the curious looks she was getting. Perhaps they had decided she was not only crippled, but dangerous. She was glad they were ignoring her. She found their pity repugnant to her now, just another shameful reminder of what pride had cost her.

The crowd was a young and lively one. The orchestra struck up a merry quadrille, the country dance a striking contrast to the sophisticated gowns and jeweled masks. Sabrina tapped her feet without realizing it, measuring out the rhythm of the Highland fling Fergus had taught her.

A fresh gust of wind rippled the flames of the lamps. Both her feet and her heart seemed to grind to a halt as she saw the golden giant silhouetted against the darkening sky.

Hope took wing in her heart. She had been wrong after all. Morgan had come back for her.

But the wings of hope folded, sending her crashing to earth when she saw the masked beauty clinging to her husband's arm.

Chapter Twenty-nine

Morgan's face might have been hewn of polished marble. It was utterly impassive, utterly beautiful, giving no sign that it might ever crack into something as human as a smile or even a scowl. Sabrina's heart contracted with longing.

She wanted to hate him, wanted to resent the tall, leggy beauty pressed so intimately to his side. But wasn't this what she had desired for him? A woman who could walk into a room on his arm, who could dance, who could give him everything she could not?

All Sabrina could do was stare, frozen by a hunger so keen, it stole her breath away. Their gazes met across the crowded room. Sabrina thought she saw the flicker of a scowl darken his brow. But it might have been only a trick of the unreliable light. Then the orchestra began to play and Morgan's companion tugged him into the genteel steps of a minuet.

• • • •

Morgan silently cursed his own folly, knowing he should have left London a week ago. He executed the intricate turns of the dance with flawless grace, his bland expression hiding the turmoil of his thoughts more effectively than a mask. He'd been a fool to let Ranald talk him into lingering one more night when even Elizabeth Cameron's pleas had fallen on deaf ears.

He was acutely aware of the stares passing between him and Sabrina. The crowd was positively drooling for a taste of fresh scandal.

He searched the crowd for Ranald, wanting nothing more than to strangle his cousin for this new betrayal. Ranald had begged Morgan for his assistance in his wild scheme, swearing on his MacDonnell honor that Sabrina would not be in attendance. Morgan snorted under his breath. MacDonnell honor, indeed! What a joke! Angus had taught him from boyhood that the two words were mutually exclusive.

Morgan had not expected to find Sabrina sitting among the frenzied gaiety, perched like a princess on a throne. He stole a glance at her. *His* princess, he thought, fighting a fierce rush of possessiveness. Demure in white, her folded hands and coronet of braids restoring the purity of the little girl who had so boldly and foolishly offered him her heart. But she was no longer a little girl. She was a woman now, her eyes darkened with vulnerability.

He was forced to turn in the dance, drawing his eyes away from her. Why in God's name hadn't he left sooner? he wondered. It had taken him a week to convince Dougal that he'd washed his hands of Sabrina for good. He was still stinging from the bitter rebuke in Elizabeth's eyes.

"You look so fierce, my lord," his partner exclaimed, her lashes fluttering beneath her jeweled mask. Her voice lowered to a suggestive murmur. "Perhaps we should have lingered at my lodgings for a more *private* celebration."

Morgan had come to the ridotto with every intention of spending his last night in London living up to the MacDonnell reputation for drunken debauchery.

Out of the many invitations he'd received, he'd deliberately chosen this young, widowed viscountess, hoping her statuesque blond elegance would be the perfect antidote to Sabrina's dark, elfin beauty.

He refused to think of it as committing adultery. Tomorrow morning Sabrina would sign her elegant signature to an official document and his marriage would be over, wiped away as if it had never been.

He brought the viscountess's gloved fingers to his lips. "I fear you're right, my lady. Coming here was a grave mistake."

He cupped her elbow, fully intending to guide her to the door, Ranald be damned, when the minuet ended and the lilting strains of an ancient Highland air filled the room.

Morgan closed his eyes, hearing not the civilized notes of violin and harp, but the bittersweet melding of bagpipe and clarsach. It cut through him like a blade. Eve and his other clansmen drifted through his memory, but this was another world, a world where they could never belong. He opened his eyes to see Ranald slinking away from the orchestra pit, and he knew who had prompted the unlikely melody.

Some of the dancers struggled to find a dance to fit it, but most wandered off the floor, seeking fresh punch and cake. Knowing it was a mistake even before he did it, Morgan allowed himself one last look at Sabrina.

Her eyes were fixed on the remaining dancers. In her face he saw none of the bitterness or jealousy he had expected, but only a wistful yearning like that of a child shown a treasure she could never have.

Murmuring an excuse to the puzzled viscountess, he crossed the nearly deserted dance floor. Every eye in the room followed him. A shocked hush fell over the crowd as he held out his hand to Sabrina.

"Would you care to dance, my lady?"

Sabrina gazed at the spot in the air just past his hips. She caught her trembling lower lip between her teeth, her every emotion written plainly on her unmasked face. Uncertainty of his expectations. Fear that this was just another of his cruel jests. And most fragile of all, hope that it was not.

Morgan held his breath, afraid to hope himself. Then, risking the laughter and censure of others and so much more than they would ever know, she laid her small hand trustingly in his.

The dark eyes she lifted to him were luminous. "I would be honored, sir."

The spectators held their own breath as he leaned down and swept her into his arms, holding her as gently as a child against his chest.

Sabrina hooked an arm around his neck, unable to resist rubbing her cheek against the warm, familiar texture of his throat. She hadn't felt this exquisitely alive since the accident.

The other dancers stood like statues as he twirled with her, eyes shut, cheek resting on her crown of braids. Theirs was a new dance, yet older even than the poignant ballad that sang wordlessly of love and loss. Older than the thunder rumbling its majestic hymn against the domed roof.

The music lilted to a halt. Sabrina opened her eyes to find Morgan's mouth a hairbreadth away from hers. She parted her lips in silent invitation. Before he could accept, a clipped voice rang out.

"Unhand that woman! Have you no scruples, sir? Perhaps that's the way you uncouth Scots treat a lady, but we English are a civilized people. We don't tolerate such shocking displays!"

Sabrina didn't know whether to laugh or groan as Philip Markham planted himself firmly in their path. Morgan was saved the trouble of swatting him like a fly when Ranald came charging to his defense.

"Uncouth?" Ranald bellowed. "*Uncouth?* What the bloody hell do ye mean callin' the chieftain o' Clan MacDonnell uncouth? Why, he's worked his fingers to the bone becomin' the most couth man in London. If ye want uncouth, I'll give it to ye, ye prancin' prig!"

Philip blinked, his righteous indignation quailing before the unexpected attack of this masked dervish.

"Who allowed you in here?" he said weakly. "Does anyone know if this man has an invitation?"

Philip's query met with only shrugs and averted glances. No one offered to search Ranald for it.

Ranald tore off his mask and wig and lifted his fists, ready to brawl. "These here are the only invitation I need to smash yer uppity face."

The crowd gasped anew as the pure Gypsy beauty of Ranald's face was revealed. Several of the women tittered behind their fans.

Sabrina's own mouth fell open when Morgan's roar of surprise drowned them all out. "Why, I'll be damned! Nathanael MacLeod, as I live and breathe! Nate, you canny rascal. They told me you were dead!"

Ranald lowered his fists and puffed out his chest. "Aye, but it takes more than a wee tumble from a carriage to kill an *uncouth* Scot."

Enid burst from the crowd with a theatrical sob that would have put Columbine to shame. "Oh, my darling husband! You're alive!"

Unable to bear this fresh excitement, two of the women swooned into their partners' arms. All Sabrina could do was stare stupidly from Ranald to Enid to Morgan, realizing the scoundrels had planned this from the beginning.

"But *you* can't be her husband," Philip whined. "I've already bought the wedding gown. I'm going to marry her."

"Like hell ye are." Ranald threw the first punch. Chaos erupted as Philip's friends came rushing to his aid.

Sabrina ducked as a crystal cup went sailing past her head. Morgan pressed her face into his chest and plunged through the fracas, his grace serving them well.

"Shouldn't you help Ranald?" she screamed above the din, spitting out a mouthful of his cravat.

"Help him do what?" he yelled back.

Over Morgan's shoulder she saw two satin-garbed gentlemen reel into a limp heap as Ranald cracked their heads together. Sabrina was forced to concede Morgan's point.

A squat young man hurled himself at Morgan, obviously intent upon her rescue. Sabrina snatched up a champagne bottle and smashed it over his head.

"Livin' up to your MacDonnell name, aren't you, lass?" Morgan said, crooking an eyebrow. He stumbled to a halt in the relative calm before the wide double doors and lowered her until her toes touched the floor. His boyish grin was irresistible. "Not much different from dodging Grants and Chisholms on the battlefield, is it?"

Two women rolled past, powdered faces contorted in fury, fingers curled into claws. "Oh, I don't know," Sabrina said, still dazed by his proximity and the bizarre events of the night. "I think the Grants might be more a tad more couth."

His eyes sobered as he gazed down at her. His hands still rested beneath her arms, gently cradling the sides of her breasts. She drew in an unsteady breath as his thumbs stole out to caress their peaks. An angry cry went up behind them. They turned to find Ranald and Enid barreling breathlessly toward the door, hand in hand.

"Damn!" Morgan swore. "I thought we'd have more time."

Time was definitely in short supply as the crowd stampeded toward them. Morgan propped Sabrina on a table out of harm's way before whirling to throw open the doors.

Thunder clapped with vengeful fury. A cool blast of wind rushed through the open door, extinguishing the lamps and throwing the room into chaotic darkness. A cacophony of screams and bellows rang out.

Sabrina trembled in the shadows, wondering if Morgan had abandoned her. She didn't have long to wonder.

With the wind and darkness came a rush of pine and sandalwood to intoxicate her reeling senses. Strong, familiar arms encircled her, drawing her into an embrace as wild and defiant as the approaching storm.

Morgan's lips seized hers in a kiss as darkly intimate as the mating of their bodies had once been. His tongue plunged into her mouth over and over again, branding her with a possessive rhythm that sent liquid heat melting from all the secret crevices of her body.

Every erotic thing he'd ever done to her was in that kiss. Every possession. Every stroke of his hand, every flick of his tongue, all wrapped in one soul-stealing kiss that left her utterly breathless and whimpering for more.

But he drew away from her, no more than a faceless shadow in the darkness. She thought she felt his hand touch her hair. Then the damp air struck her skin, empty of his presence.

A shuddering sigh tore through her. It was only then that she realized Morgan had left her standing on her own two feet.

She slid down the wall into the cushioned pool of her skirts. Touching two fingers to her trembling lips, she wondered if his kiss had been a kiss of promise or of farewell.

Late that night Sabrina sat on the terrace outside her bedroom in her wheelchair. The Belmont town house was dark and silent. Uncle Willie had locked himself in the library with a bottle of port while Aunt Honora had fled to her bedroom with a severe case of the vapors.

Sabrina didn't think she would ever forget their flabbergasted expressions as a bloodied and disheveled Philip Markham explained that their daughter had fled the ridotto with her dead husband. Sabrina had to admire their composure. They had simply thanked the stunned young man and retreated to their separate strongholds, leaving Sabrina to the care of the servants.

She tipped her head back to study the sky. Clouds scudded in from the west, their charcoal underbellies absorbing the moonlight. Lightning danced between them, scenting the air with an acrid tang. The sculpted tops of the bay trees whipped in a frenzied dance.

Before Morgan had come to London, Sabrina

would have cowered in her bed at the approach of such a storm. Now she welcomed the threat of its primal fury, yearned for a taste of it with a wild, sweet hunger she'd repressed for too long.

She got her wish when a fat raindrop pelted her in the mouth. A surprised start of laughter escaped her. The rain began in earnest, striking hard and sharp like pebbles against the thin skin of her nightdress. Instead of rolling herself inside to seek shelter, she threw back her head, letting the water cascade down her cheeks and throat, cleansing her with its crisp zeal.

In the next flash of lightning she saw him, illuminated against the darkness like a golden wildcat. He had abandoned his frock coat. His ivory shirt was open at the throat. The wind whipped his unbound hair around his shoulders. His newfound civility had been stripped away, leaving him raw and dangerous, a predator in a world of prey.

The air between them crackled with challenge. Exhilaration rushed through Sabrina, sharp and electric.

Morgan didn't bother with the chair. He simply scooped her up and carried her inside, laying her among the pillows on the rumpled bed.

"But the chair," she protested. "It might rust."

"Let it," he said, striding back to latch the terrace doors, muting the fury of the approaching storm. Wind drove the rain against the leaded panes, enclosing them in a watery haven.

Sabrina watched him stir the ebbing fire to life, suddenly shy. The damp shirt clung to his broad back.

Her words held a half-teasing note. "Surely you've been in London long enough to know it's not proper for a young lady to entertain a gentleman in her bedroom."

He faced her, all humor vanquished from his eyes. "Not even if she's his wife?"

His wife. Morgan's proprietary tone sent a thrill through Sabrina.

Morgan knew coming here had been another mistake in a long line that had started when he had agreed to make Dougal Cameron's daughter his bride. The distance between them was fracturing with each of her shy smiles, each nervous dart of her tongue to moisten her lips.

His wife. The words should have been as holy and irrevocable as God intended them to be. As holy as the Bible peeking out from under the edge of her mattress. As holy as the rumpled linens and soft feathers she reclined upon.

Sabrina pressed herself into the pillows as Morgan's shadow fell over the bed, afraid not of him, but of herself.

"I can't," she whispered, averting her eyes.

He sank down on the bed and cupped her chin in his hand, tilting her face to his. "Whatever may happen upon the morrow," he said gently, "you're still my wife tonight."

Sabrina was struck by a wave of shyness. The tears she'd held back for so long spilled from her eyes. "You don't understand! I'm not worthy of you. I'm not a whole woman anymore. I don't know what to do. I can't pleasure you as you deserve."

Morgan kissed one tear away, then another, his tongue smearing the salty wetness. A deep chuckle rumbled from his throat. "Ah, lass, you're more than woman enough for me. And you can pleasure me in ways you've never dreamed."

The unbearably sweet heat of his mouth traveled lower, tracing the arched curve of her throat, the hollow beneath her collarbone, finally flowering on the pebbled bud of her nipple beneath the damp lawn of the nightdress. A moan escaped her as he gently flicked it with his tongue, then sucked her with a raging hunger that sent tendrils of raw pleasure cascading through her womb.

Her fingers twined in the rough silk of his hair. He lifted his head, meeting her pleasure-dazed gaze with one of his own. "Let's get this thing off. It's all wet and I don't want you takin' a chill."

Sabrina knew there was little danger of that. Her skin tingled as he peeled the nightdress away, leaving her shivering and naked beneath him. She had never been quite so aware of her own helplessness. This man could do anything to her. Anything at all. He was her husband, she reminded herself desperately. But she still couldn't shake the tantalizing sensation that what he would do to her in the quiet, dark heart of her aunt and uncle's house was somehow wicked. Forbidden.

But for now all he was doing was kissing her. Softly. Tenderly. Slanting his mouth over hers. Deepening its possessive angle with each warm, sweet stroke of his tongue against her own until she was lost in his rhythm and begging for more with the arch of her naked body against his clothed one.

His teeth nipped her neck. "Lord, lass," he muttered against her skin, "I always knew the Camerons would be the death of me."

He slid down her, lavishing kisses on her breasts, her concave belly, the tiny mole at the arch of her hipbone. Firelight shimmered through the skein of his hair as it swept across her thighs.

"Don't!" she whispered fiercely.

Morgan lifted his head, battered by dark bewilderment. Surely the lass wasn't so cruel as to deny him now. If she was, it was all over. He might play at the role of bully, but if it came to actually forcing her, he might as well get up and walk out of this room with both his clothes and his pride still intact.

"Don't," Sabrina said more gently, drawing him up the length of the bed.

Her hands curled over his shoulders, easing him back on the pillows. Morgan stiffened, reluctant to give up that much control.

"Please," she whispered.

Sabrina wouldn't meet his eyes, but he could sense from the faint tremble in her hands that whatever she wanted from him was vital. Perhaps the greatest gift he would ever give her. He sank back among the pillows, surrendering to the gentle ministering of her hands.

Morgan had never allowed himself the delicious sensation of being undressed by a woman, not even as a child. He leaned up as Sabrina unlaced his shirt and drew it over his head. His breath caught as she framed his face in the soft wings of her hands and kissed him. She stroked his hair away from his face, the hypnotic motion almost making him drowsy.

But that drowsiness faded instantly as her lips glided down the column of his throat and sleeked down his chest like a touch of flame.

Sabrina felt the rigid muscles of Morgan's abdomen quiver beneath her lips, heard his grunt of half pleasure, half pain as her tongue teased the line of gilded hair that ran from his navel to the top button of his low-slung breeches. His grunt deepened to a groan as her teeth caught the brass button and dragged it loose from its mooring.

His hips arched off the bed. "Have you any idea what you're doin' to me, lass?" he gritted out between clenched teeth.

"Some," she replied, freeing the second button in like manner. The broadcloth of Morgan's breeches was stretched taut over the swell of his flesh, its flawless seams strained to bursting.

"Damned tailor," he muttered. "I wish I had my hands around his scrawny wee neck . . ." His voice broke on a hoarse groan as the last button gave, freeing his burning flesh to the tantalizing whisper of Sabrina's breath.

He tangled his hands in her hair, forcing her to meet his smoldering gaze across the golden expanse of his skin. Her eyes sparkled with a light he'd thought never to see again.

Sabrina was captivated by him; it was as if God had created a creature of flawless masculinity just for her delight. "Please? May I?"

Those were the last words Morgan had expected to hear from her. He collapsed on the pillows with a dazed shake of his head. "How can I refuse when you ask so prettily?"

"Just close your eyes and pretend I'm Circe," she commanded primly. "If you don't succumb to my wiles, I shall turn you into a swine."

He folded his hands behind his head in a deceptive posture of lazy abandonment. His heated gaze promised sweet revenge. "Never let it be said that Morgan MacDonnell doesn't know how to go gracefully to his fate."

Morgan was to learn more of grace beneath Sabrina's tender dominion than he'd ever believed existed. When her soft lips enfolded him, he thought he would come apart right then, right there. He clenched his teeth and arched his throat in a guttural groan. Ecstasy spilled through him in a blinding torrent, Sabrina's generous mouth granting him a glimpse of heaven itself.

Sabrina moaned deep in her throat, freed at last to lavish on Morgan all the love she'd hoarded in her heart for years. She savored him, glorying in her power to pleasure him. It was her first taste of power since she'd tumbled over that cliff, and she loved Morgan anew for surrendering it to her. He was her magnificent golden beast, and she realized then that she had never wanted to tame him, but only to drive him even wilder than he was.

His hands caught in her hair, enslaving her even as she held him in thrall with nothing more than the honeyed promise of deliverance from her sweet torture.

Biting off a reverent oath, Morgan reached the limits of his endurance. In a switch that left her breathless, Sabrina found herself lying beneath him. His fingertips traced her lips in wonder, as if to memorize their shape and softness around his flesh.

The sculpted planes of his face were taut with helpless need. "I cannot wait, lass. 'Tis been too long."

He threaded his fingers through the soft, dusky curls between her legs, groaning in delight to find her already melting into his hand. Sabrina's eyes darkened with both apprehension and passion. But even in his urgency, Morgan took the time to arrange her pliant legs, gently parting them to accommodate his girth.

His lips descended on hers, laving them, soothing their swollen contours even as his heavy manhood thrust deep within her, cleaving her body and heart with one majestic stroke. Sabrina had forgotten such raw pleasure was possible. Morgan's mouth consumed her wild, soft cry.

"Princess," he whispered against her ear. "My beautiful, beautiful princess. I want to spoil you. Pamper you. Indulge you."

He proceeded to do just that. Spoil her for any other man's touch. Pamper her with pleasure. Indulge her with the throbbing length of him until she could do nothing but cling to his shoulders, her broken cries one unending hymn of gratitude. But even that wasn't enough for Morgan. He reached between them and gently raked his thumb over the tingling bud nestled in her silky curls.

Mindless in her ecstasy, Sabrina arched against him. Her limp legs came to glorious life, wrapping around his waist, her heels digging into his lower back to urge him even deeper into her.

Morgan had only an instant to savor his triumph before the rippling pulsations of her silky sheath shot him into rapture. He bucked hard against her, his hoarse roar indistinguishable from the voice of the thunder.

Morgan sat on the edge of the bed, fully dressed, and watched Sabrina sleep. He stroked the bare curve of her back, fascinated by the near translucence of her skin. It glowed in the thin dawn light, giving off a radiance that coaxed his hand lower to trace the hollows and dips of her spine. With a disgruntled murmur she burrowed deeper into the pillow.

Morgan smiled. With her hair tangled and the sheet covering only the gently rounded orbs of her buttocks, she looked less a princess than a harem girl after a rough night with the sultan.

His hand wandered to her silky calf, squeezing the tensile strength of her muscle. He would never forget that glorious moment when her beautiful legs had tightened around his waist.

Aye, the lass would walk again, he thought. He'd

see to it. His smile spread to a devilish grin. He'd simply been going about it the wrong way. He should have known there was a more effective and far more pleasurable way of getting her blood flowing again.

Somewhere deep in the recesses of the house, a clock sounded five times. Morgan knew he'd best leave before the servants arose. It wouldn't do for the poor Belmonts to find another disreputable Scot preying on their womanfolk. He also needed to send word to Dougal and Elizabeth, to tell them he'd decided to stay in London and fight for his bride.

Stroking Sabrina's hair, he struggled against a wave of doubt. She'd trusted her body to him once before and then had only him to blame him when it had been broken. It might be a long time before she was ready to entrust her heart to his care.

Sighing, he covered her with the quilt, then rose, tucking his rumpled shirt into his breeches. An object thumped to the floor at his feet.

Morgan looked down to discover the Bible he had seen sticking out from beneath the mattress the previous night. He bent to pick it up, knowing instinctively that out of all books, this was the one to be revered the most. The fragile pages flipped open, spilling out a barren spray of twigs and leaves.

His heart started to pound in his ears.

His hands trembled as he caressed the paper-thin petals between thumb and forefinger, recognizing the gorse native to his Highland slopes. He gazed at Sabrina in fresh wonder. She had thrown him away, but hadn't been able to bring herself to throw away this ugly clump of weeds. Instead, she had saved them, pressing them between the pages of this book like her dormant heart.

Morgan gently tucked them into the pocket next to his own heart and slid the Bible back into its nook. Excitement raced through him. He had much to do before he could return to this house.

As Morgan eased himself out of the garden gate, a thin wafer of sun was already rising in the east. Steam from the night's rain hissed from the pavement to form a morning fog.

So intent was he on his plans that he almost stumbled when a cloaked figure lurched into his path.

"Have ye a halfpenny to spare, me lord?"

Morgan frowned, thinking it a bit early for beggars. But the beggar's threadbare cloak was soaked through, as if he had slept outside in the storm. Remembering all the times he'd been hungry and wet, Morgan drew out his purse. He started to dig into it for a handful of silver, then plopped the entire bag into the beggar's extended hand, wanting to share some of his own happiness and hope with someone less fortunate.

"Spend it in good health, my friend."

"Thank ye, my lord," the beggar called after him. "I'll not forget ye, I swear it."

But Morgan had already forgotten the beggar as he strode whistling down the pavement, his step jaunty, his thoughts for once not on the past, but on the future.

Sabrina awoke with a smile on her lips for the first time in months. Early morning sunlight slanted through the terrace doors. She stretched, exulting in the lazy ache of her muscles. She felt like a child again, waking to a sunny day that was filled with possibilities.

She arched her feet beneath the sheet without realizing it, then stared at them, entranced by the fluid motion. What if she were to behave as if it *were* one of those days? What if she simply sat up, swung her legs over the side of the bed, and put her feet on the floor?

After slipping into her discarded nightdress, she threw back the sheet and inched her legs toward the edge of the mattress until they dangled above the floor. A trickle of sweat eased down her temple. Catching her tongue between her teeth, she pushed herself forward, using her hands, and flexed her toes until they touched the cool floor. She slid her bottom over the edge of the mattress. Her feet flattened against the polished hardwood.

Sucking in a deep breath, she slowly transferred

her weight from the mattress to her feet until she was standing. Standing, but not walking. She had done as much many times before.

Ignoring the trembling weakness of her calf muscles, she inched one foot forward, then the other, digging her toes into the wood in a desperate search for balance.

Exhilaration raced through her veins. She might not be more than a few inches from the bed, but she had gotten there all by herself. She had walked. Wouldn't Morgan be shocked when she was able to run into his arms? The thought made her giddy. She swayed. Her hand shot out to grasp the knotted end of the bellpull as she crashed to the floor.

She tugged the rope with both hands, setting up a jingling carillion of joy. "Beatrice!" she yelled. "Bea, come quick!"

The young maid burst into the room, hair braided and still wearing her nightdress. Her dumpling cheeks were flushed. "Oh, miss, what is it? Are you hurt? Did you fall?"

Sabrina was already using the bedpost to drag herself back up. "Of course I fell. Isn't it wonderful? I can't wait to fall again!"

She didn't have long to wait. She let go of the bedpost, listing first to one side, then to the other. Bea rushed to catch her and they both crashed to the floor in a sprawl of tangled limbs. Sabrina's laughter was infectious, melting Bea's own alarm to poorly stifled giggles.

"Shall I wake the master and mistress?" Bea asked breathlessly. "I know they'd want to see this."

Sabrina was shamed at the thought of all her dear aunt and uncle had endured for her in the past few months. "Later perhaps. But I've an errand to run first. Have Teddy bring the carriage around to the garden gate."

Bea hastened to the door to do her bidding.

"Oh, and, Bea?"

"Aye, miss?"

Sabrina grinned. "Bring me some breakfast first. I'm famished."

Sabrina poked her head out the carriage window. "Hurry, Teddy! Are you sure you have the right address? Can't the horses trot any faster?"

"We have the earl's address and we're going as fast as we can, miss," said the beleaguered footman. "We almost trampled that nice gentleman at the last intersection."

The nice gentleman had shook his fist at the back of the carriage and loudly questioned the driver's parentage. Sabrina bounced up and down on the carriage seat as if she could somehow urge the horses to trot faster by example. The warm morning breeze stole tendrils from her loosely done topknot. The storm had washed the narrow London streets clean and laced the air with sparkling purity.

To Sabrina's eyes, the entire world looked fresh and full of hope, even the cloaked beggar hunched on the corner of Morgan's street.

The carriage rolled to a halt on the opposite side of the street from a humble wooden house. She threw open the carriage door in Teddy's shocked face. "The chair, Teddy. I'll get the door. You get the chair."

As Teddy went around to unhook her wheelchair from its moorings, Sabrina hoped fervently that she wouldn't require the use of it much longer.

Smiling at the thought, she tapped her feet impatiently. But before Teddy could reappear, the door of the house swung open. A man and woman appeared on the stoop. Chattering voices and a burst of male laughter drifted to the carriage. As the woman tipped her head back to smile at the bearded man, her veil slipped, revealing thick auburn hair swept up in elegant simplicity. The sun glinted off the silver threaded through it.

Sabrina sank back into the shadows of the carriage, her smile fading.

Another man appeared behind them. A rumpled

giant of a man, rakishly handsome with his unshaven jaw and stocking feet. His white teeth flashed in a devastating smile. The bearded man slapped him on the back, then paused on the stairs to toss him a fat purse.

Sabrina watched her parents walk arm in arm down the street, their steps lighter than even the iridescent air. Morgan stood on the stoop a minute longer, grinning and tossing the heavy purse in his palm as if to measure its worth. Then he turned and went back into the house.

Thirty pieces of silver.

The thought came to Sabrina fully formed, ugly, and fraught with betrayal along with the memory of Morgan's passionate words in her father's dungeon. A passion that had nothing to do with her.

They're all I have. All I am. I'd do anything for them.

Even line the MacDonnell coffers with ill-gotten gold by romancing Dougal Cameron's daughter for a price.

Sabrina remembered the man and woman she'd seen on the corner, her eerie sensation of being followed. Had her parents witnessed it all? Every fall, every tantrum, every scathing exchange? Her gloved hand flew to her mouth, choking back a hysterical sob.

Had her papa paid Morgan in one lump sum or given him an allowance for each daily call? Did his pretty smiles cost extra? His kisses? And what of last night? The three of them had obviously been celebrating. Had Morgan regaled them with the details of their liaison? Sabrina closed her eyes at the memory of her mouth on his sleek flesh, the taste of him fading to ashes on her tongue.

Humiliation burned like a live coal in her stomach, sickening her with its heat.

Her papa would do anything for her.

Morgan would do anything for his clan.

Even Eve would have approved of the terrible cunning of their scheme, its irrefutable logic.

Teddy appeared at the carriage door, flushed with exertion from wrestling with the chair. Sabrina stared at the iron and wood monstrosity, hating it, hating them all. She knew now that her father's money had paid for it.

"Take it away," she demanded.

A baffled frown crinkled the footman's brow. "But, miss, you said—"

"I don't care what I said. Take it away. I never want to see it again."

She slammed the carriage door while waiting for him to return. He reappeared at the window, his expression as miserable as she felt. "Where to now, miss?"

"Home," she said, staring straight ahead at nothing. "I'm going home."

Chapter Thirty

Sabrina's parents appeared at the house on Hanover Square barely an hour later, their expressions fairly bursting with secret delight. A subdued Bea ushered them into the morning room, where Sabrina was sitting behind the delicate shield of her aunt's writing desk. They rushed across the room to her, even her mother's graceful gait marred by an exuberant bounce.

"Darling!"

"Ah, there's my wee princess! We've missed you so!"

Sabrina turned her cheek to their kisses with cool aplomb as if it had been only hours since they'd parted instead of weeks. They exchanged knowing smiles, convinced her composure was a ruse.

After exchanging pleasantries about Alex and Brian and the spring planting at Cameron, her father cleared his throat and affected a stern expression.

He drew a folded document from his pocket. "I

don't have to tell you why we've come, lass. I've finally obtained your annulment papers."

"Does it always take such a dreadfully long time to secure an annulment?" she asked him.

Her parents exchanged another guilty look, both mumbling something about, "constraints" and "extenuating circumstances."

"At any rate," her papa said heartily, snapping open the paper with a flourish. "All you have to do is sign above the magistrate's seal and you'll be rid of that nasty MacDonnell lad forever."

He dangled it in front of her nose, obviously expecting her to refuse.

Sabrina snatched the paper from his hand and smoothed it on the desk. Her mother's mouth fell open. An odd sound escaped Dougal, and Sabrina knew he was one syllable away from betraying himself. Without even bothering to read the document, she dipped a quill into the ink bottle and signed her name below the official seal with none of its usual embellishments. She sprinkled sand across her signature, shook the paper clean with a brisk motion, and handed it back.

"There. It's done. May we leave now?"

"Leave," her father repeated stupidly. His hand clenched around the paper as if he were resisting the urge to wad it into a ball. "Leave for where?"

Elizabeth plucked at her handkerchief, her expression bereft.

"Home," Sabrina said. "Cameron. My bags are packed and in the corridor."

"Aye, lass, whatever you say," her father said vaguely. "We shall go now if that's what you wish." He turned away from the desk as if he could not bear to look at her, his steps weighted as if he'd aged ten years in ten minutes.

"Papa?" Sabrina held out her arms. "You'll have to carry me. Don't you remember? I can't walk."

At precisely two o'clock that afternoon, Morgan strode up the steps to the Belmont town house, forced to peer over the towering bouquet of hothouse roses in his hand. It had taken every ounce of his control to keep from coming earlier, but he felt such a momentous occasion required a touch of ceremony.

His eager knock was answered not by the butler, but by a freckled maid with red-rimmed eyes. She was too preoccupied to even comment upon the flowers.

"I'll fetch His Grace right away, sir." She dabbed at her nose with her apron as she led him into the entranceway. "I'm sorry. I must be a frightful mess. I once would have done anything to be rid of her. But now that she's gone . . ." She dissolved into fresh sniffles.

Morgan didn't want anyone to suffer today. "There now, lass. There's no need to carry on so. I'm sure Miss Enid will come home for Christmas and the like. You should be happy for her now that her husband has returned from the dead. That baby of hers needs a father."

"Oh, I am happy for Miss Enid, sir. I was referring to the young miss."

"The young miss?" A chill of foreboding seized Morgan. He stopped in his tracks.

The maid kept walking. "Miss Sabrina, sir."

Morgan dropped the roses. He strode after the maid, catching her by the shoulders and spinning her around. He searched her tear-stained face for a truth he was afraid to learn. "Sabrina? Sabrina's gone? Where? When? How long?"

The maid trembled in his implacable grip. "Since her mum and dad came to take her back to Scotland."

Morgan gave her a shake without meaning to. "When? *How long?*"

"A few hours. Since about ten this morning."

Conflicting emotions buffeted Morgan. Bewilderment. Fury. Despair. Was this yet another Cameron betrayal? But whose betrayal? Dougal's or Sabrina's?

The maid quailed before his fierce expression. He released her and stormed for the door, crushing the fallen roses beneath his heels.

Chapter Thirty-one

Morgan's mount flew over the heathered turf, its iron-shod hooves barely skimming the earth. If he wanted, he could close his eyes and pretend for an instant that he was back on Pookah, the wind whipping through his hair, the scent of freedom flaring his nostrils.

But Pookah was dead and Morgan had learned that there were some things more precious than freedom. More precious even than pride. Pride would have dictated that he return to Castle MacDonnell and mass his clan for an attack on the treacherous Camerons.

Instead, he was thundering toward Cameron alone to lay final siege to a woman's stubborn heart, his only concession to pride the bright new tartan that enveloped him.

Violet clouds tinged the horizon. The sky slowly darkened to the sapphire blue of Sabrina's eyes. A fat moon hung above the mountain peaks like a frosted pearl. Morgan aimed the horse for that guiding beacon,